888 Love

*** *and the* ***

Divine Burden

of Numbers

888 Love

*** *and the* ***

Divine Burden

of Numbers

ABRAHAM CHANG

FLATIRON
BOOKS
NEW YORK

888 LOVE AND THE DIVINE BURDEN OF NUMBERS. Copyright © 2024 by Abraham Chang. All rights reserved. Printed in the United States of America. For information, address Flatiron Books, 120 Broadway, New York, NY 10271.

www.flatironbooks.com

Library of Congress Cataloging-in-Publication Data

Names: Chang, Abraham, author.
Title: 888 love and the divine burden of numbers / Abraham Chang.
Other titles: Eight hundred eighty-eight love and the divine burden of numbers
Description: First edition. | New York : Flatiron Books, 2024.
Identifiers: LCCN 2023040990 | ISBN 9781250910783 (hardcover) | ISBN 9781250910790 (ebook)
Subjects: LCGFT: Romance fiction. | Novels.
Classification: LCC PS3603.H35727 A15 2024 | DDC 813/.6—dc23/eng/20231208
LC record available at https://lccn.loc.gov/2023040990

ISBN 978-1-250-91079-0 (ebook)

Our books may be purchased in bulk for promotional, educational, or business use. Please contact your local bookseller or the Macmillan Corporate and Premium Sales Department at 1-800-221-7945, extension 5442, or by email at MacmillanSpecialMarkets@macmillan.com.

First Edition: 2024

10 9 8 7 6 5 4 3 2 1

To all the girls I've loved before—
and for all the women who have loved me.

And to the two who count the most—
whom I count on the most:
Erica and Ma.

Prologue

FEBRUARY 24, 1994

Soundtrack highlights:
- "New York Minute"—Don Henley
- "The Last Worthless Evening"—Don Henley
- "Desperado"—Eagles (w/ vox by Don Henley /
karaoke cover version vox by Su Su)

Young was startled awake by the screeching squawk of the back-door gate opening—that distinct, familiar sound it made when Su Su was sneaking out of the house for his latest funtime foray into the wilds of female friendship. If he heard more of a rickety creak, the gate was being closed, meaning Su Su was stumbling back home, stale Marlboro and Tsingtao stink clinging to him like his latest pink-lipped *lah mei*.

It was mostly the day (Thursday) and time (4:47 a.m.) that Young was struggling with. He had fallen asleep studying AP History at the dinner table. Drooled on his binder, his neck hurt. He thought: *Why is Su Su up so early? It's his day off.*

"You taking the Harley into the garage now? You finally got her to start?" Young, now out the back door, *whispershouting* at his uncle so as not to wake his parents, his kid sister.

"Holy shit! *Xia shi wo le!* What the hell are you doing up already? I thought I was being super quiet. It's freezing out!" Su Su pulling Young farther away from the house, toward the back of the yard.

The squeak and squelch of worn leather—the jingle-jangle of buckles, clasps, metal studs—it was coming from Su Su and his outfit. He looked ready to ride, and not just to Uncle Tang's garage.

"Su Su, what's going on? Where are you going?"

Young's uncle took his face in his hands, kissed him hard on the forehead and cheeks, hugged him tight. It made Young feel like he was a boy again. He loved this.

"Oh, Young Gun! My *tian cai*! My little genius! I'll never make fun of you again! You were right all along! Ever since you were a sweet baby—lining up and counting your Hot Wheels over and over again. Lucky boy! Our brilliant *shuai guh*! Growing up so smart and handsome!"

Young smiled broadly. He couldn't remember the last time he saw this joy (*manic as it was*) spread across his uncle's (*sober*) face. He couldn't remember when he'd embraced him so hard (*while sober*) and Su Su wasn't draped over his shoulders for support.

"What do you mean, Su Su? Where are you headed? And why so early, and—"

"My Young-and-the-Breastless, my Cream-of-Some-Young-Guy, I've got all the time in the world—and yet I don't have the time to explain! If I hit the road soon, I can make it out to see Alexis. Remember I told you about her—the one with the Van Halen tattoos and the big *nay-nays*?"

"Wait—isn't she down in Georgia? But don't you have to help Ma set up for the charity banquet this weekend?"

"That's all taken care of. Nothing extra cash can't solve. Remember—you can always earn more money, but not more *time*. Of course, you know! You know all about time—and numbers."

"You're just leaving? Now? Where? When are you coming back?"

"*Dong, nan, xi, bei*—anywhere! Whichever direction my compass points me to that looks good! But west first! Cowboys, cactus, dusty happy trails, girls in short shorts! DEFINITELY WEST!"

"Ma, Bah know about this? And what about Mei? Are you in trouble? Is something wrong? This is crazy!"

"Nothing's wrong! It's all going right for once! And I need some crazy, *guai*. I need it. It's about damn time." Young hears the words catch in his uncle's throat.

Su Su turns away, walks over to the fence separating the Wang household from the neighbors who they rarely see—the ones they've only met twice, in all these years. He looks over at the buzzing streetlamp at the corner—half-broken, but sturdy and constant, it's still humming the theme song of Flushing, Queens. Su Su lights a cigarette.

"Here, here—*lai bah*. Come on. I know you've been sneaking smokes after school. You can split one with your uncle. I won't tell your ma, but I'm sure she knows."

Young takes a deep drag and coughs. His uncle slaps him on the back.

"*Aiya*. Bad habit. Maybe don't pick it up. Another thing you don't want to learn from your *wang ba dan* of an uncle, right?" Su Su takes a last sharp inhale, mashes the rest deep in the dirt, buries the butt with the toe of his black boot. "What time is it, Young?"

"It's 5:12."

"Is that a good time? I'm still not entirely sure."

"What do you mean?"

"You know? Your numbers—your system? Is it auspicious? *Lucky? Safe? Blessed?* Good numbers?"

"5:12 is 5 plus 1 plus 2—it adds up to 8—*the best*. But it's 5:13 now, and 13 is bad luck. Even if all the digits add up to 9, which is another good one. The 13, though—I hate it."

"OK, OK. Help me get her through the driveway and down the block first. And we'll aim to be on the road at exactly 5:30. Adds up to 8. That's lucky, right?"

"Yeah—yeah. That's a great time. But you still haven't explained anything."

"Ah—so much talking, Young! Chit, chat, chit, chat—all those movies you like! I like the *boomboompewpew* Star Wars ones we used to watch together. Not the black-and-white *blahblahblah* ones you rent now. Young-Not-Old, sometimes you don't need all these words—just the feeling, the doing, the motion, *the action*. Listen to your Su Su: you need to get the balance right. *Yin/yang.* Stereotypically Asian—but true, too! There's a time and place for all of it. But I know how you are, and I love you and indulge you. You'll get your words and explanation soon.

"Ah, more of my *hu shuo ba dao*, right? I contradict myself all the time! Who loves to talk more than me? I just usually need a few beers first! But there's something I left for you in the basement. And it's not more action figures from Taiwan. OK, come on—it's almost time."

Young helped his uncle roll his motorcycle to the end of the block. It was heavy, but it looked good, renewed. Su Su must have been working on it for a while. Lost in his world of school and friends, Young hadn't realized that his uncle had polished the chrome, oiled the parts, had it ready to blaze again.

Once they had the Harley parked by the beat-up stop sign, Su Su straddled it, kicked, revved, and pulled Young close. He brushed the hair from his nephew's eyes, held his cheek in his rough hand, and patted him hard on the chest.

"Protect this. *Your heart, your heart.* You've got time for the other important bits—your brain and balls are still growing. I know you'll get strong. But this—*this*—is still far too tender." Su Su, tapping Young's chest with the back of his fist.

Young could feel his breathing quicken. He wanted to clutch his uncle's hand and take it off the handlebar, demand more reason and rationale. But Su Su had donned his helmet, flicked down the visor, his eyes obscured by the curvature of the lens. Young could see his own distraught reflection there, but his uncle looked like a badass hero (*or villain*), and he was leaving.

"I love you, *guai*. I promise I'll write! I'll tell you about my adventures! You'll be proud of your Su Su—or at least be really fucking jealous!" Su Su, sounding muffled and distant, but still right here.

"I—I don't know what to say." Young, struggling to find the words.

"How about '*Jiayou, Su Su*'? Some encouragement before I put the pedal to the metal?"

"*Jiayou, Su Su.*"

"Damn straight, *guai*."

The engine roared, and the bike was in motion around the corner—slow at first but picking up speed. Young was rooted to his spot, leaning against the familiar rusted post of the sign.

Su Su lifted his right hand: the index finger, the pointer finger, the thumb raised. That imaginary gun that used to shoot at aliens, the weapon of choice for the bandit who told him to "stick 'em up"—the robber to his cop.

This was the number 8, when you count on one hand, "the Chinese way." (Su Su had taught him: *Like this for 6—and this for 7. But 8 is the best one—it's like THIS.*) The number 8 was the most supernatural, lucky, fortuitous number—with the perfect expression, in the most powerful way. Young's magical motion: casting spells of protection, defending against the invisible waves of evil and misfortune that threatened to crash down upon him and those he loved. The silent sidearm that eased his fears, shooting through all the dark and doubt.

888, bangbangbang, 888

Young said a prayer for his Su Su, raised his hand in the air, pulled the trigger. *Action, reaction.* He could only hope that God, the universe, heard the silent mystical sound, exploding louder than that hot motor growling in the growing distance.

Onward to the unknown—for infinity or just a little while? Young felt like this was the end of something, the beginning of something else. It could exist as both, for now. Was it going to be good? *Blessed?* Best to be sure from the start—

bangbangbang.

Good and Bad Numbers

(UPDATED VERSION: MAY 1997)

1: The first, the best. GOOD.

2: Pairs. GOOD.

3: The Trinity. Father, Son, Holy Spirit. SO GOOD!

4: *Si*. Death. BAD. AVOID.

5: High five. GOOD!

6: The beginning of the worst. BAD. AVOID.

7: LUCKY. SO GOOD!

8: In Chinese, *ba* sounds like *fa*. Get rich! Good fortune! SO GOOD!

9: One of my favorites. Ephesians 2:8–9. SO GOOD!

10: A nice, even number of completion. But *shi* sounds like *si*. UNDECIDED.

11: Two #1s. *Make a wish.* GOOD.

12: Dozen. GOOD.

13: Unlucky. BAD. AVOID. *(But, 1 Corinthians 13:4–8. Always GOOD.)*

14: Double 7s but also *shi-si*—UNDECIDED.

15: Triple 5s. GOOD. *(Number 5 is alive!)*

16: Sweet Sixteen. GOOD. *(As in, John Hughes good.)*

17: #1 with a lucky 7. GOOD? *(Also that Winger song?)*

18: Adulthood. *Chai* = Life. GOOD.

19: Stephen King's number. GOOD. *Thankee-sai!*

20: Number of completion *(same for most multiples of 10, except the ones with 4s).* GOOD.

21: Drinking age. Blackjack. Triple 7. Birthday. GOOD!

22: Double deuces. GOOD. *(And* Catch-22.*)*

23: Historical TV specials say this is worse than 13! SO BAD. AVOID.

24: Triple 8s, but also has a 4 and adds up to 6. UNDECIDED. GOOD?

25: 5 times 5 and adds up to 7. GOOD.

26: Adds up to 8? UNDECIDED.

27: Triple 9s. The inverse of triple 6? Lots of famous people died at this age. Has a 7. UNDECIDED.

28: Has an 8. Adds up to a number of completion. GOOD.

29: Has a 9. Adds up to 11. But looks weird? UNDECIDED.

30–32: MOSTLY UNDECIDED.

33: Age when Jesus died. Double 3 = Double Trinity. UNDE-CIDED. GOOD?

34–41: MOSTLY UNDECIDED.

42: The answer to the universe! GOOD. *(Don't forget your towel!)*

43: Sum of 7, but don't like the look of it. UNDECIDED.

44: SO BAD. ALWAYS AVOID.

45–50: MOSTLY UNDECIDED.

69: FUNNY. GOOD.

77: YES. GOOD!

88: SO, SO GOOD!

101: The basics. GOOD. *(And Depeche Mode.)*

121: Elementary school. GOOD.

143: Erena, Erena, Erena. *SO GOOD.*

215: Junior high school. GOOD.

217 / 237: Never stay in a hotel room with either of these. *(Stephen King, again. And Stanley Kubrick.)*

311: In the grand scheme of things, ultimately GOOD—*for her. (Though it's down, down.)*

333: Trinity × 3? UNDECIDED. GOOD?

4_4: SO BAD. ALWAYS AVOID.

451: Fahrenheit. GOOD.

555: YES. GOOD.

6_6: THE WORST! SO BAD. AVOID.

777: SO, SO GOOD!

888: THE BEST. *BANGBANGBANG.*

∞: *(Basically an 8 in recline.)*

CHAPTER ONE

"Pleased to Meet Me"

NOVEMBER 1995

Soundtrack highlights:
- "Cherub Rock"—The Smashing Pumpkins
- "World in My Eyes"—Depeche Mode
- "High and Dry"—Radiohead

Young worked at Jim's Undertow twice a week. He would have picked up another two shifts if he wasn't spending most of his time in Bobst Library reading up on cytochrome c and balancing valence equations. Jim barely paid minimum wage, but he was fun to be around. He had great back-in-the-day stories of the East Village (friends with Joey and Marky) and would treat Young to some Gray's Papaya hot dogs (with sauced onions) every now and then.

Working at Jim's was more than a means for pocket cash—it was what Young looked forward to every week. It was access to all the movies and music Young could consume. The Undertow (*Get Caught in the Undertow!*) was primarily a secondhand media store with a small video rental section upstairs. Much of the unending stockpile of DVD screeners and CD samplers that came across the "pre-enjoyed inventory acquisitions desk" originated from a bevy of interns (those lucky enough to score entry-level marketing jobs at BMG or Warner in Midtown). A third of the merchandise was stickered with "Property of Universal Music Group. For review purposes only." The merch had razor slashes across its bar codes, holes punched in Hootie's face or through Alanis's hair, Sharpie-coded lot numbers on disc rims that someone, somewhere, thought would deter grubby hands from liberating the goods from the latest press-mailing pile.

The dust in the back room was unbearable at times, and the variety of unidentified, questionable substances splattered across the stock (cocaine residue? Apple cider vinegar? Lighter fluid?) made gloves and Lysol required precautions. But the endless rows, stacks, shelves, spinners, and crates filled with DVDs, CDs, videotapes, fanzines, and ratty old concert T-shirts made Young salivate.

Young was responsible for coordinating, cleaning, collating, clearing, and coding: sorting by genre, by artist, by director, by format. All this wonderful disorganized organization calmed the chattering clack that tumbled through Young's head, the unscratchable itch that came from behind his left ear, pulsed out of his eyelids, then settled in at the base of his skull.

The hardest decision Young had to make that day was if Yaz (aka Yazoo) should be filed under Synthpop, Dance Divas, or simply under Y. (Then again, maybe he could create a special promo sign—"New Wave for Neophytes" or "Vince Clarke Keyboard Collabs"—and feature it alongside Depeche Mode, Erasure, and Alison Moyet's solo work.)

Every smooth plastic slipcase sliding into its tight shelf slot was therapeutic. Every hard square locked into a plastic guardrail was a serotonin trigger. Everything in its place—and its place was never static. Change, nonpermanence, always moving and shifting, deviant disorder replaced by soothing symmetry. Patterns that he could latch on to for a while, then pivot, replace, reset, and repeat. Young loved this.

NYU was expensive, but grants and financial aid had taken care of most of the bursar's bill. However, waking up and pulling back curtains to see the rising arch in Washington Square remained a dream. The practical fact: Queens was a forty-five-minute subway ride plus a fifteen-minute bus ride away. He was relegated to the life of a commuter. Not quite a derided "townie," but the closest you could get as a middle-class resident of the outer boroughs.

With his ACT (32) and SAT (1420) scores, Young had secured a spot at UC Berkeley, but the earthy-crunchy lifestyle would never work for him. He wore black. He listened to Nine Inch Nails, the Sisters of Mercy, and Iron Maiden. He read *The Sandman*, *Watchmen*, *The Invisibles*. And Vonnegut. And Simić. He snuck menthol cigarettes. He liked walking in the rain. He was a moody black-is-the-color-of-everything New Yorker. He didn't mind perpetuating the cliché. No one would ever describe him as "cheery."

CalArts, USC—that sunny vision of the unattainable Hollywood elite. NYU Tisch was right here and more realistic, street-level genuine. Scorsese over Spielberg any day (though he still loved *E.T.* and Indiana Jones).

Young figured he could at least audit some film classes, maybe sit in on lectures. He could find a group like Coppola, Lucas, Milius, and Schrader did back in the '70s. Didn't need to be "official." He could learn through osmosis—make friends, absorb by living on the edges. *Guilt by association.* He could just—sneak in and observe. He had an NYU ID. He'd find a way to be among the future directors and screenwriters who would be showing at Cannes in ten years' time.

Or: he could focus on humanities, maybe even apply for grad school—*film school!* Do it for real, out in the open. He'd make a lousy doctor, research assistant, pharmacist. Pre-med courses were just so that Ma wouldn't blink when she cut a tuition check, asked to see his grades—her doctor in training (psychiatrist, biochem expert, *MD somethingsomething*). He would find honorable, respectable, gainful employment after graduation. There was time, and he'd work hard.

Or: he could manage the biochem and lab sections and take Intro to French Cinema or Writing for the Screen. He could do it all: pre-med track, warrior-poet cineast. *No sweat. (And no sleep, no sanity.)*

Young had survived the rigors of the top-tier Stuyvesant High School. He'd done well—not the best, but he was smart enough and willing to put in the work. He was *nen gan*: the textbook definition of the Chinese can-do ideal.

But Young also had many daily excuses. He counted them in shame and disgust. He had to take care of his *mei mei*. He had to help Ma at her functions. Bah needed him to shuttle rounds of fresh samples to the Botanical Garden. He had to keep an eye on Gina while Paris was up in Michigan. He had to make sure Su Su didn't forget him. And he still had to mend the shredded organ in his chest, anesthetize the persistent buzz in his head.

Young believed that the best art came from a place of quiet retrospection, introspection. One needed to look back from a place of serenity and cull the most gruesome, soul-atrophying *(yet cinematic)* details as fodder. He wasn't quite there yet. In no way was he ready to collect, create, contribute.

Young was still living it. He was mired in the haze of insecurities and petty pain, treading muck in his own miasma of stagnancy. He couldn't get out, couldn't move forward. *Stuck.* He wasn't ready to say much of anything. For now, it was enough to just exist. *Do what you should, do what you are told. Observe and report, path of least resistance, head down, hopes and dreams on hold.*

* * *

Su Su had sent Young another photo that he tossed in the front pocket of his JanSport. Little written this time except *"Hot sun, hot fun—party time in Spain!"* No return address, no clue where he was headed to next.

At least he knew his uncle enjoyed getting acquainted with the locals in Ibiza. Sweaty, shirtless, and tan—Su Su was wearing a comically large Cat in the Hat–style hat, a chartreuse feather boa draped across his broad shoulders, and circular mirrored sunglasses (no doubt covering his bloodshot, rave-rolling eyes). His arm around a bleached-blond beauty's brown waist, fingers splayed across her taut stomach—her belly button ring peeking through between the angle of middle and ring finger, his other hand pointing, as if to say, *Check out this bodacious bauble!*

Young loved these periodic updates sent from some alternate world, where his sullen uncle was transformed into this grinning goofball. He was ashamed that he was jealous, even angry that he couldn't see any clear path to happiness opening for himself. Why should he be living vicariously through his thirtysomething uncle, when it was supposed to be the other way around?

* * *

Jim liked to showcase "Staff Picks" and made sure the films on the end caps of the tight aisles played into the seasonal push ("Christmas Carnage with TROMA!") or with current events ("GRUNGE IS DEAD! *REALITY BITES* and *SLACKER* available now!"). The rental section on the second floor was never as busy as downstairs. Young squeaked markers across the poster board: "Young recommends— *LÉON: THE PROFESSIONAL!* Luc Besson's brilliant thriller filled with action, humor, and heart! Jean Reno is a revelation, Gary Oldman is a fiery force, and Natalie Portman is a star on the rise! For lovers of *HARD BOILED* and *THE KILLER!*" In the corner: a caricature of himself—evidenced by the signature wild coif of black hair—holding up a peace sign / V for Victory.

Young barely salvaged his masterpiece from his shaky red Sharpie, startled by the Undertow housephone clattering loud: *"Hey, got a nice young lady coming your way! Needs help with Asian cinema. Figure you could manage that, Egg Foo Young!"*

"Ha, ha, Jimmy. Send her up." Young strolled over to Kurosawa, paid his respects to Ozu, propped up *Game of Death* under the "Kung Fu for Fools" promo table, and waited for his promised patron.

He could hear the bludgeoning speed metal (Megadeth? Overkill?) cranking out of her headphones. He could smell her shampoo (Pert Plus?) and the cherry smell of her gum (Hubba Bubba?).

"Hi, hi! Jimmy downstairs said you could help me with anime. You the guy?" she said, overly cheery. Her eyes were blinking, slowly widening, waking up to the realization that they were alone among the monolithic shelves of multimedia.

"Yes, I'm the guy. The only guy here. Upstairs, that is," Young stammered, wincing. A snatch of the Pixies floated into his brain—the earworm countdown, something measured and steady to help him calm his nerves: *and God is 7 and God is 7—*

Young found it hard to place her ethnicity. Having grown up in Queens, surrounded by immigrants—in three syllables he could easily identify the different Chinese dialects, could spot a Mainlander, a Canto, a Taiwanese. He could tell Japanese apart from Vietnamese, Filipino, Hawaiian, Singaporean, Korean, etc. It was all in the shade of brown and the dip of vowels. If any average Caucasian American could tell the difference between Italian, Irish, and French, any "mellow yellow fellow" should have equal expertise in Asian-spotting.

But he needed more time with this girl. This girl made him *uncomfortable*—the slouchy hooded sweatshirt, the tight black jeans, the scuffed Doc Martens, the army-issue rucksack—

"Listening to some Exodus or Testament?" Young, motioning to her headphones. "I definitely went through a metal phase when I was younger."

"Huh? No, this isn't Christian music—*no way*! Are you kidding?" Her voice was as sweet and clear as that of any of his musical theater friends, but she had the kind of back-throated rasp that made him sweat.

"Not what I meant. Exodus and Testament, thrash metal bands? Not Christian metal at all. You're thinking of Stryper or Whiteheart—completely different."

"OK, I'm confused. I wanted to get some anime. I'm not interested in Christian rock or whatever you are proselytizing about. Just some Asian cartoons everyone keeps bugging me to check out." Pulling back her hood and slipping the blaring headset buns down. Young thought he might fall through to the basement, *poof, splat*. Or he might just float away heavenward. She had *brownamberhazel* almond eyes, a two-shades-off-true-black bob, and a perfect Tinker Bell nose. She was gorgeous.

"No, no," he stammered. In his head rolled *888, get it straight, bangbangbang,* his own self-soothing rhyme. "I apologize, completely wrong observation. I was commenting on your choice of soundtrack." Young motioned to her gigantic headphones again.

"No shit, Sherlock. You should have just asked what I was pumping through my cans instead of assuming. The whole 'ASS-U-ME' thing—like a third grader? Loads of avoidable misunderstandings! Ask the right questions, and you'll surprisingly get some straight-up answers. Let's start over, from the top." She took a deep breath and clicked off her Walkman. "Sinawe."

"Excuse me?" Young wondered if that meant "sorry"—maybe that was Malay?

"Sinawe. It's Korean heavy metal. And it's *fucking awful*! I promised my cousin Min Jee I was going to give it a go—her favorite tunes when she used to tool around NYC. It's either 'definitely decent' or 'ca-ca cacophony' with her. This totally sucks. Hella sucks. Sucks balls. Nuts. Testes."

Korean. And goodness, such a filthy mouth, Dear Lord!

"Erena, by the way," she said, adjusting the strap of her bag across her slender shoulder. "Pronounced: *ER-in-uh. ERRRR-uh-nuuh.* Spelled E-R-E-N-A."

"Is that another band?"

"*I'm Erena.* Erena Ji-Yoon Renee Valentina Yasuda. It's a mouthful—and one day, when I'm a badass lawyer, you bet I'm adding the 'Esquire' to the end. It's a lot, but it accurately conveys the lineage of this petite package of pulchritude—*little bit of this, little bit of that.* It's like the whole Axis ran riot over my entire family tree! Hello? *Humor?* I made a funny? Come on! Just shake my hand already! It's a normal social convention!" She had a firm grip and pumped his hand hard, once.

"That's a beautiful name: Korean, Japanese, and bonus extra European! I'm unfortunately not blessed with the same. I'm Young Wang. The 'Wang' is actually pronounced *WOHHNNG*—but everyone just says it like *WAAAHNNG*. And yes, I've heard all the jokes." Young smirked. "It's Chinese. Young Zheng Wang. Young as in 'ocean' and Wang as in 'king.' Zheng as in 'noble.' I'm either Aquaman's best friend or worst enemy! Joke there. *Humor?* Made a funny?" He felt better. Dorky, but better.

"Aw, kinda shy and cute—and you try to be funny! I like it! And in case you haven't caught on, I'm very clever. I'm known for my humor, Chick-King of the Sea." She winked at him. It was devastating.

Young felt the inevitable slide. The thrumming in his head alternating for attention, but losing out to the sweet timbre of her voice (breathy soprano with that caramel echo). Her words split through all the other noise—nothing from outside on St. Mark's, no buzzing from inside his scrambled coconut of a skull.

"*Akira* or *Grave of the Fireflies* or whatever this is, with the big ol' titties on the cover. Or this one with the cyborg!" Erena pulled the videotapes from Young's carefully curated "ANIME! Ani-Way You Want It! That's the Way You See It!" section.

"Maybe stick to the first two. Both classics of the genre, but on opposite ends of the spectrum. Are you in the mood for dystopian cyberpunk body horror? Or would you prefer a gut-wrenching emotional journey about the impact of warfare on the innocent?" Young settled into an easy patter, confident introducing his old friends to someone new.

"Neither! Don't you have some Sailor Moon or something happy? Not pervy, more fun-filled? Uplifting party time versus bleak nihilism, ya know?"

"If you don't mind that it's basically a movie for kids, you can't go wrong with *My Neighbor Totoro*. Studio Ghibli is known for top-tier whimsy and magic—better than Disney, by far. But I always thought Totoro had a creepy smile, though ultimately cute and cuddly. And the Catbus is pretty fun! The English dub is all we have—not many options there, no fan-subbed Japanese language versions. You'd have to go to Elizabeth Street in Chinatown for those. So, you've only got that one vocal track choice. And Totoro—he's fat and he flies." Young shrugged. He couldn't read Erena's face. Confusion? Fascination?

"I'll take it! You had me at 'Catbus.' What the fuck is that? I must see this bewildering creature for myself!" She took the videotape and shook it to hear the reels rattle inside. "While I'm here, might as well get some new tunes. Do you have some clearance stuff I can pop in now? I've got to purge these puppies of that nasty *hangook* noise."

"Three bucks or under impulse bin up front. What kind of music do you like? Favorite band? Particular genre?"

"Crash Test Dummies."

"More like a favorite of 'all time'? Do you like synthpop or alternative guitar rock?"

"I love Crash Test Dummies. That 'Mmm Mmm' song was on repeat like you wouldn't believe! That guy's voice is so deep—and the lyrics were just as deep (but that other meaning of deep). Like it was about a kid in a car accident and the girl with the birthmark, and then the kids in the church. Wow, right? Just wow." Erena, beaming bright at her memory of the one-hit wonder.

"Uh, anything else you like?"

"I dunno. I'm kinda into the Dead and Janis and Phish. (My folks played hippie music exclusively. ALL. THE. TIME.) But that gets self-indulgent quick with those wanky guitars. I like Ani DiFranco, but she can be absolutely aggro sometimes—and I'm mostly about being chill lately. Too much school stress. Why exacerbate it? I guess Spin Doctors, then? Or sometimes Snoop Dogg? But I guess it's really Crash Test Dummies in the end." She smiled earnestly and picked up a copy of 4 Non Blondes. "Bingo!"

Young was befuddled. She seemed to represent the antithesis of all he held dear. Her taste in music was *atrocious*. But her energy, her life force—she made him feel *something*. He promised himself (and his nagging best friends, one Miss Gina Villanueva and one Mr. Paris Choudhary) that he would be open-minded this year—do new things, meet new people, have new experiences, and start moving forward again. *The brave city mouse forgets the freshman failures, swears off the sophomore slump.*

"How about I give you this mixtape I've been listening to? It's got a few favorites, some new stuff—it's pretty eclectic. This place is basically my free-use archive, so I take advantage. And no Christian metal on this one! I swear!" Young, looking to spread the secular gospel of the Afghan Whigs, Pulp, Suede—

"That's really sweet. I'd love some new music!" Erena twisted the headphone cord around her palm. "This old yellow Sony SPORTS Walkman, I mostly use it when I run in the park—my go-to device when I blast shitty rock tunes. My fucked-up Discman, the antiskip never works. I only use it when I'm studying in the library and not in a hurry."

"Well, here. I'd love to know what you think. My shifts are usually on Tuesdays and Thursdays. I may tack on a Wednesday or a Saturday, if Jim needs the extra help. I commute from Queens to NYU, so I'm in the area all the time, regardless."

Erena took the cassette tape and shook it to hear the reels rattle inside: "Same here! Well, I'm a dorm-er at NYU. A few years of hardcore learning in the Big Apple before I head back to the Golden State—or wherever's next on my agenda for complete domination! I'm a global citizen! I belong to the world! London, Paris, Sydney— you're next! I thought you might have been a Cooper Union dude, but awesome we're both on team purple and white! Rad school colors, right? Yeah, I'll for sure swing by when you're around." She opened her wallet. "I've actually got a study group session in twenty minutes. Jim hooked me up with a membership card downstairs. Ring me up, good sir! I'll be sure to look out for that pussywagon thing! *Catbus, Catbus!* Just making sure you were paying attention!" Her finger guns went *powpowpow-bangbangbang.*

She shifted her dead-shot aim—one eye closed, finger gun at the ready—to the middle shelf, just behind Young's shoulder. "Are those for sale? The Animaniacs you got lined up behind the counter?"

"Oh, those! They're Happy Meal toys. I've been doing double duty: getting a cheap meal and collecting these for my baby sister. Well, more like kid sister. She's almost a dozen years younger than me, so I'll always think of her as a baby. Janine—well, everyone calls her Mei—is seven going on eight, but she's tiny, and everyone thinks she's younger than she actually is. We pamper her, but she's not spoiled. But I feel awful that I'm not around as much, so I try to bring her a little surprise every now and then. So I've got like three Yakkos, three Wakkos, and just got those two Dots in this week! (It was a lot of cheeseburgers.) I've got a full set for her, a full set for me, couple of extras. I'm figuring out which ones should be kept 'mint-in-bag' for future collector-slash-potential-resale purposes, and which ones are suitable for playtime fun. You've obviously seen the cartoon! The show is actually really clever—jam-packed with pop culture references that are clearly not for kids. I mean, what seven-year-old is going to get a Siskel and Ebert parody? Mei's the main reason I don't mind commuting back and forth so much."

"Take a breath, dude! You had me at 'collecting these for my baby sister'—that's super thoughtful of you. Are these Animaniacs human/dog hybrids? Cat people? Monkeys? I'm not sure what they are, but they're funny and super cute. Wakko is my favorite! How much you want for the extra? Too soon for your geeky 'resale purposes'?"

"Consider it a gift with purchase! 5 dollars and 50 cents even for *Totoro*, with tax included—that's why all the rental prices are in weird numbers." Young's face felt hot as he stared at Erena's hands. She unzipped her bag and pulled forth her cash. That's when he saw it: the Magic 8-Ball, embroidered on her wallet. *Bang.* He couldn't deny it anymore.

He had felt something from the moment they started speaking, the hairs on his arms spiking through his thin long-sleeved black T-shirt. And now the opening beats of Erasure's "Oh L'Amour" floated up from the speakers downstairs. He couldn't have chosen a better music cue for this moment, even if John Hughes himself were directing. (Though John Hughes may have argued for something less on-the-nose romance—maybe "Bad" by U2? What says "Surrender, let go, take action" better than that one?)

Young took the crumpled bill and noticed her easy smile. Her fingers grazed his palm as she dropped the two quarters. He swallowed hard and committed to action: volition versus fear (*the mind-killer*); Green Lantern igniting his ring; Frodo tossing the One Ring; Johnny Cash giving the Ring of Fire an extended middle finger—*go, go, go.*

Everyone is on email now, he thought. *It's no big deal, it's a normal social convention. Be brave. Go for it. ACTION.*

"Hey, are you on AOL? What's your email address? I'm online sometimes when I can't sleep or if I'm working on a paper at home. Internet is slow and expensive and my mom hates it when I tie up the phone line. But here's my handle, in case you want suggestions about what to watch next."

Young wrote on the back of an Undertow business card. He spelled out his online identity in the best scrawl his trembling hand could manage. "It's a nerdy joke. It's a reference to one of my favorite—"

"Ha! 'Indepalmamyhands76'! I get it! Such a nerd! *Scarface* is entirely overrated, but *Dressed to Kill*—I mean, *wowza*." Erena got on her tiptoes, looked Young straight in the eyes, and tapped the card playfully on his nose. "I know my movies, just don't know much about anime. But word to the wise, you may want to rethink that name. To the uninitiated it may sound like you"—she made the obscene hand motion for "jerk off," scowled, and stuck out her tongue—"like, *a lot.*"

Young felt his mind start racing and calculating the panoply of possibilities. *He could help her with her taste in music—that would be easy! She was open-minded, that was a given! Potential otaku material in the making, the Ghibli films were a gateway to any number of anime gems! And how she referenced* Dressed to Kill *like it was nothing? That was a deep cut! Why not* Carlito's Way? *A much easier, more recent reference! Not to mention books! She seemed eloquent, well read! Maybe she was poetic with profanity like Tarantino and Kevin Smith? What about comic books or literary graphic novels? Start off with some Neil Gaiman, Frank Miller, Grant Morrison. Then ease into some Uncle Stevie with* The Dark Tower! *And then—*

"'Fartprincess1,'" said Erena, writing the screen name on the back of another card.

Young's heart sank. He paused. Gulped down hard on the stone forming again in his chest.

"Hey, I get it. If you weren't serious about getting in touch—I understand if you were letting me down easy. I just thought we had a nice conversation." He felt the hot flush of embarrassment flood his face and grabbed a copy of *The 36th Chamber of Shaolin* to have something to shrink behind—all the better, should he suddenly come into a cache of Pym Particles.

"I'm being 100 percent real! That's my email address—*honest*! It keeps away the perverts . . . well, not all of them. And my friends think it's hilarious, because *it's true*! Mel and Janey are 'doucheydiva007' and 'itchyass911,' respectively and respectfully—we are a brilliant trio! Come on! *I do humor*, remember? I promise. It's really me. Do you want my NYU email address? I never use it, but if it makes you feel better and you'll stop acting like such a weenie, I can give that to you. I've got a phone number, too! My roommate Helen might pick up, but I do reside there. *Promise.* Here's my dorm line." Erena was laughing, but Young could tell she was trying her best to keep it light and genuine.

"Seriously, Young," she said, "I'd like to talk more. I didn't have the best experience last year, and my head's stuck in California mode. I want to give NYC a real chance this year and make the most of it! I don't know many quality people here. A little kindness goes a long way. You're the nicest non-creep-o guy I've met in the past six weeks, ever since this semester started." She fidgeted with her hoodie drawstrings. "You speak in coherent sentences. I thought that wasn't going to be such an issue in New York, but you'd be surprised. And you looked me in the eye most of the time—only checked out my ass, like, twice."

Young felt his confidence rise. "Give me some time, and I'm sure you'll find increasingly awful things about me. But I'll email you, and we can make plans to meet up at the vertigo-inducing library sometime?"

"M. C. Escher design that death trap or what, right? Whoever was the architect must be a straight-up dick! All right, fellow NYU-er, let's see how this goes. Oh, and would you look at that, you've got a *maneki-neko* waving behind you."

Young turned around: the familiar bobbing paw, the glittering gold, the red-collared lucky cat on the counter.

"It's an embarrassing story. My mom gave this to Jim as a gift. Wanted to thank him for saving me from scooping ice cream and for this gig being the source of my spare cash, free access to all of this—THIS stuff—that I love. These lucky cat figures are all over Flushing—Chinese, Korean, Vietnamese, most Asian stores and restaurants have them in Queens—but you know it's really associated with Japanese culture."

Erena unzipped her sweatshirt—the glimpse of her bare neck, the tiny mole by her collarbone, a charged jolt, unexpected and welcome. She pulled out a thin metal chain, a similar beckoning cat pendant hanging from the end. "Nicky Neko, meet Mr. Big Wang! It's his lucky day, isn't it? Catbus, cat people, cat jewelry—looks like there's a pattern developing! Maybe it's a good sign? But truth be told, I'm mostly a dog person. *WOOF! WOOF! AWOOOO!*"

The volume and verve of Erena's joyous barking ignited the startled electricity ripping through Young, raising the hackles on his arms, his neck, his—

"Haha! You totally jumped! Scaredy cat! See! Another fortuitous feline! Better go buy a lottery ticket, Hello Kitty! You might hit the jackpot, tiger! See ya around campus, Young Gun! Go, NYU Bobcats, or whatever!" The wink was devastating.

She gave a little wave with her rolled-up copy of *The Village Voice* and clomped down the stairs. Before he tucked the card in his pocket, under her gaseous pseudonym Young scribbled down her name (*Erena Yasuda*), the time (*7:17*), and the date (*11/2/95*).

February 23, 1994

Dear Young,

I'm writing this to say that I might not see you again until the next millennium. Honestly, I'm not sure when I'll be back—or if I'll be back. I always loved visiting New York, but it was never truly home for me. The thing is, I've come into some money, enough that I can hop on this beat-up Harley and finally get out of your basement!

My only regret: I won't get to see you in these next formative years—finishing high school and becoming the BIG MAN ON CAMPUS at some lucky university! You're a tough kid and I know you'll finally sack up. You'll figure this shit out for yourself, by yourself. And please, don't do this premed thing you are set on—it's not meant for you, my Young Squire. Look where all those years of law school ultimately got me: working for Uncle Tang, changing oil! But, hey—I've never been happier!

I guess I have to explain the money, Young-at-Heart: you won't believe it, but I won the lottery! All those extra singles spent at the corner store finally paid out! *DA YING!*— THE BIG WIN! In the grand scheme, it's not *that* much—but enough that I don't have to work for a good decade! So I'm hauling my ass out of here to finally see the world!

You'll have to come find me when you have a break from

school. In the meantime, you'll be fine without your dumbass hippie uncle. Your Su Su is in the wind. Like they say: *I'll see ya, when I see ya. Hasta la vista, baby! In a while, I'll be in a different domicile!*

Before I go, I wanted to tell you that the numbers might really work, might actually mean something. I teased you ever since you were small, how you obsess over those digits. But maybe you were right all along, my *tian cai*, my little genius. I only needed the patience to see the patterns in the fabric of the universe: God's private code, His divine rhyme, open to those who pay attention.

I played some good ones—numbers that meant something to me. Auntie Yi Shen was my "38," because her pet name for me was *"San Bah"*—"3–8," *a dummy-dum-dum*. Auntie Corrina was my "24"—always my *"24-Hour Party Babe."* I'm sorry I made you call all those teasing temptresses Auntie or *ai yi*. But hey, look where it got me! *Screw that noise, boys! I got blotto and won the lotto!*

Young Buns, like I told you—I believe we only get seven great loves in life: man, woman, thing, whoever and whatever gets your motor running, not only in your head and heart but right in the balls. You'll know it when you *feel it*—the tingling in your aching *dan-dans*.

When you find that light and warmth—from whoever, whatever—don't waste that feeling. It may end in tears, but choke it down, pick yourself up—*go with it*. Life is just a series of undignified boners, but they lead us to our own patch of happiness.

It hasn't been all bad these past years, mostly because of you two kids. And I'll miss your dad's garden. I'll miss the *xiao long bao* at Shanghai Johnny's. I'll miss *oolong cha* with Pastor Chen. He was always patient with me.

I'll even miss my sister—despite all the self-centered,

self-serving bourgeoisie shit lately! She did invite me to live here with you when I needed distance from the Best Coast. Still fun when she's had a couple, I guess. I see her old self the most when she's tied on a few. Unfortunately, she can only let go once she's finished her duties, at the close of those formal Flushing functions. I'll always love her, but I don't think I like her very much right now. And I'll never figure out how she pushed you two good nuggets out of her stinky bits!

My Young One, I'm really sorry that I have to sneak out in the middle of the night like this. Decided to rip off the bandage and disappear like the no-good *wang ba dan* that we all know I am.

But I'm tired of being such a strange, sad, mutated version of the badass I used to be. I miss my punk rock aesthetic—my peace, love, and harmonics—my metal mania.

My lucky number seven—she's still out there. I've burned up my previous six, and I've got to chew up some asphalt to see what's ahead over that hill. I've got to feel like myself again first, tune back to the celestial frequency.

I'll miss that Forest Park trail we used to bike along. I'll miss cold brews on the rooftop. I'll miss Mei Mei's morning songs. I'll miss you the most, Young Gun.

I'll write you along the way, send you some souvenirs, maybe an occasional pic or two. Envision me soaking up some sun with a crew of brown-skinned hotties! (I'll try to figure out that electronic mail thing—but no promises.)

But Queens can't hold me! NYC can blow me! I'm hopping on my hog—getting a nice leather cut, blasting Zeppelin— and I'm storming through the Midwest to scare every racist motherfucker I see! Wait until they check out this giant *liu mang* roaring down Main Street, USA!

Peace and grease!

Your ever-loving, one and only,

Su Su

P.S. I've set aside some money for you. I left your bah in-structions to give you a fat wad when you graduate Stuy and enroll in whichever great university. Do something fun with it! Do NOT waste it on comic books and that fancy movie shit you collect. Do NOT spend it on textbooks.

And be sure to see Uncle Tang after you graduate. I left something with him for safekeeping. It is yours to do with what you wish, when you wish. I'm not going to need it—at least not in this lifetime. Do NOT give it to your mom for safekeeping—you'll never see it again! Save it for someone special or sell it—it's yours. *Yours.*

P.P.S. The basement is under your control now. I left my *Playboy*s under the bathroom sink, and there's also some pocket cash. Take a nice girl out and treat her well. (But not *too* well—remember what happened with me and "Auntie" Becca! She still has my Camaro! She's *literally* a bitch on wheels.) You're welcome, you perv-Cream-of-Some-Young-Guy! Ohh la la, *shuai guh*! A-1, cool dude!

P.P.P.S. When you explain this all to your ma, give her a hug for me and tell her I'm sorry. I'll call her later when she's cooled off. But don't show her this letter. Or do—I don't care. I'm motorin', I'm rich—and I'm gone!

First Love: "Born to Run"

1982–1983

Soundtrack highlights:
- "New Song"—Howard Jones
- "American Girl"—Tom Petty and the Heartbreakers
- "Goody Two Shoes"—Adam Ant

You do not eat paste. You behave yourself. You color in the lines. You love reading and pore through all the details of the animals in Richard Scarry books. You hate math. Your favorite toy is the Snoopy Stunt Cycle that you got for Christmas last year. Your least favorite toy is the Frieda the Frog puppet that stopped squeaking—the ribbon tongue no longer capable of ribbiting. You cannot dribble a basketball, but you can sink a few buckets (*underhand*). You sing quietly during chorus—your favorite time of the week—but you belt out the same songs when you are alone on the toilet at home. You think Mrs. Rose is a very nice teacher.

There seems to be some confusion among your classmates about how you say your name versus how it's spelled. You tell them, "It's actually pronounced *WOHHNNG*—like 'Wong.'" They ask, "Why don't your parents just spell it that way then? Don't they know how to spell? *Don't they speak American?"*

You try to explain that when you translate names and words from a foreign language into English, things don't always—

"Guess they're WONG—NOT RIGHT!"

The cruelty of children is learned on the playground. You can bear the teasing (*YOUNG-NOT-OLD! DANG WANG! WANG'S TANGY THANG!*)—but even at the tender age of six-going-on-seven you realize it could be so much worse than mildly offensive name-calling.

For the Chinese-speaking friends and family, you will hear your name as such: *WONG ZHENG YOUNG*. But for everyone else, it's just *YOUNG* (rhymes with "dung"), which you hate; *WANG* (rhymes with "bang"), which you love, love, love.

* * *

Your parents have been in the States for close to a decade—long enough to feel comfortable in the Chinese community in Flushing, but still unsure if their English is as good as they think it is. When they go to the city (Manhattan is "THE CITY"—Queens is just "Queens") for steaks at Mumbles, you notice that they speak slower to the waitstaff, each word measured. They whisper to each other in Chinese.

Your dad ("Bah" in Mandarin) is a botanist and splits his time between the Queens Botanical Garden and Queens College, where he teaches environmental science lab sections. He's tall, strong, tan, and quiet. (And every Christmas you make him repeat "BAH, HUM-BUG!" ad nauseam—much to your delight.) Your mother ("Ma" in every language, it seems), a former pageant queen from near Shang-hai, sells beauty products in Chinatown (Brooklyn and Manhattan) and Flushing. Her skin is so fair, it's almost translucent. She stays out of the sun, wears bright-red lipstick, slim and tiny like an exotic bird. She's a bit of a local celebrity—everyone (Chinese, at least) seems to know her.

Your parents encourage you in everything. They ask you to draw them pictures: bugs, robots, cartoon characters. You sign your art with a big "Y." Sometimes you draw a circle in between the two outstretched arms of the letter—your round globe of a head. *This is me!* Your parents take great pride in your cleverness. They scrawl lengthy notes in spindly Chinese characters on the back of your masterpieces and send these off to Yeh Yeh, Nai Nai in Toronto and Gong Gong, Po Po in Taiwan. They make you draw more pictures and send these to who-knows-who-else: Friends and family across the ocean? Chinese kids who dream of America? Who are these faceless masses getting your best Papa Smurf doodles, your best Optimus Prime sketches?

One day you receive a picture of a cat with no mouth. You learn that this is Hello Kitty. Ma explains that the Chinese characters below read "NI HAO." She tells you that her best friend from high school ("Xia Ai Yi" to you) has a little girl about your age: Wen Ding, or "Wendy." She is going to be your new pen pal. She can teach you some Chinese. You can help her with English and teach her about life in *Meiguo*. You groan and draw the Pac-Man family for Wen Ding / Wendy, and write H-E-L-L-O interspersed between power pellets. You doubt "Wendy" will know who Pac-Man is (much less Ms. Pac-Man, Baby Pac-Man, Inky, Blinky, and crew), but she would appreciate your cleverness. But you think: *This feels like homework.*

* * *

You are fortunate that your elementary school, PS 121, is full of children of immigrants like you, from Honduras to Hungary, Ireland to Iran. Your annual class pictures depict the American Dream come to fruition. Nearly everyone has an accent and/or brings a smelly lunch. You want cheeseburgers and pizza. Bah pays for your "regular food" during the day and makes you home-cooked Asian—not just Chinese cuisine (*I can make sushi for you myself! Easy!*)—for dinner at home.

Your best friend is Paris Choudhary. Paris's parents are both doctors and speak with lovely British accents. They even lived in Hong Kong for a while, doing medical missionary work before moving to Queens. They are devoted Catholics and resent the bratty White kids who pantomime racist gestures (*dots, not feathers*) when they walk by their stoop. Your parents get along amazingly. Paris has more Transformers (*even Jetfire!*) than anyone you've ever met. He gives you half his cucumber and butter sandwich, and you share a piece of your *char sao bao*. You become friends for life.

You spend hours lining up your robots and military forces in rows. You take great pleasure in seeing them in their squads and subdivisions: *lion robots always travel in teams of 2, unless all 5 go out together; super-soldiers can be grouped in manageable teams of 3 or 5; super-buff mystical warriors go out in 3s (but their enchanted animal companions don't count); transforming robot convoys can stretch as long as 8 vehicles.* You are a little lord of habit, you dwell in predictable routine. Above all, you want order in your fiefdom.

Your uncle visits. He is your mother's only brother. You insist on calling him "*Su Su,*" even though your parents tell you he's really your *xiao jiu jiu*. (You call all those "not really real uncles" from Flushing "*Su Su.*" Why make things different and difficult when it's your *actual* uncle?) Su Su brings you the best toys from overseas—the special *original* versions. They have Chinese and Japanese characters on the boxes (*where they were originally born*) and none of the American names: Cliffjumper? Jazz? Ratchet? *Those are the made-up ones, the fakes*—not the other way around.

You think Su Su is the best, even though he laughs and makes fun of your "special system." Deliberately and unceremoniously moving He-Man around, G.I. Joes scrambled haphazardly out of battalion order, Voltron lions lackadaisically out of sequence. He thinks you won't notice, but you always do. You huff and stomp your feet.

He laughs like a giant and picks you up and onto his shoulders. You grasp his hair, hang on to his ears. You love this.

Su Su indulges your fascination with organization and numbers. He teaches you to count to 10 on one hand—"the Chinese way": *1 through 5—you can do it the regular American style—but 6 is "hang loose," 7 is a duck bill, 8 is a finger gun, 9 is crooked pointer, 10 is crossing your fingers.*

This is magic. You practice with both hands. It becomes your kung fu, your uncanny mystical arts. Finger gun 8s for good luck (when no one is looking, or from inside your pockets). *Bang, bang, bang—bangbangbang.*

"Don't do that during Sunday school, or Pastor Chen will yell at you! Why did you have to teach him that! Now he won't stop!" your mother hollers at her brother, swats him with the rolled-up A&P weekly circular. He snatches it out of her hand and whacks her across her behind. She yelps and runs into the living room. You laugh. He waves the newspaper like a laser sword and tosses it over to you. He calls you *Obi-WANG Kenobi.*

He points at himself and says: "Han CHINESE Solo!" You shrug, not sure what he means. "You'll get it when you are older, when you learn some history." He blasts you with his finger guns and a rebellious wink. You love this.

* * *

Star Wars is your favorite movie. You're not sure why George Lucas didn't go with "Dark Vader" and "lifesavers"—these names would make much more sense (*names don't have to be so complicated*). *The Empire Strikes Back* puzzles you and makes you sad (Han trapped in carbonite! Luke with a junky cybernetic hand! Leia forlorn and in braids, not buns!).

It's not until you see *Return of the Jedi* in the spring of 1983 that everything is right with the world again (much of this you credit to Princess Leia in a gold bikini). A happy ending, capped with a celebratory song by the Ewoks. You try to sing along (phonetically) to "Yub Nub."

Princess Leia is the epitome of loveliness. You vow to marry her when you are old enough, but your heart disintegrates when you hear she is, mistakenly and egregiously, going to marry Paul Simon. *That annoying little guy with the guitar! The one that your parents listen to, the one with the partner with the burnt cotton-candy clown hair!* He won the hand of your beautiful space princess.

You know you shouldn't, but you pray that she changes her mind—breaks up with him—or, or—*divorce!* You hear the kids at school talk about divorce all the time. This should happen for Carrie Fisher. You are fine with handsome Han Solo (Harrison Ford: definitely a *shuai guh*) kissing her, but someone so shrimpy, undignified, and unheroic is not worthy. *Hop on the bus, Gus—forever.*

* * *

You dream of George Lucas. In the dream, he has salt-and-pepper curls with a matching beard, thick black-framed glasses, a blue-and-yellow plaid shirt with a puffy navy sweater-vest, dusty jeans, and low-top white Adidas. You recognize him because his face is inescapable. He's in all of the Star Wars books, newspaper clippings, and TV specials you've seen.

He's standing over a replica of the surface of the Death Star and fiddling with some foam pieces surrounding the trench where Luke speeds through in his X-Wing. He notices you creeping up behind him, peeking over his shoulder, and turns to you to say:

Oh, hello. I didn't see you standing there. I'm George Lucas. Creator of your favorite thing in the entire world: Star Wars! I know it makes you so happy, but also a little sad. It's OK, Princess Leia was never meant to kiss and hug little Chinese boys like you! In fact, do you remember ever seeing a Chinese person in any of the Star Wars movies? Well, maybe there is one under a Stormtrooper uniform? Maybe not! Maybe there is an alien one in the bar scene in the first movie? Maybe not! Sorry, your parents are a different kind of "alien"! Wait, what—they have blue passports and not green cards? Well, congratulations there!

The Jawas don't count either. They may be small and speak in a funny language, but it's definitely not Chinese! (It might be a language from an island or desert nation though—I'll never tell!) But I promise you, if I ever make any more Star Wars movies—we'll try to get in more Brown and Black folks. You'll always have Billy Dee! And that green alien that you think has nice boobies—we'll count her, OK? Our secret!

I know Princess Leia makes your heart soar, but she's meant to be with a prince (or a scoundrel). And princes (and scoundrels) don't look like you. They are usually of a "paler species" and come from Corellia—not Queens. They don't look like Paul Simon, either, but that's a whole other problem there! TIME TO WAKE UP! DON'T WET THE BED AGAIN, YOUNG (CINNA-MON) BUNS!

* * *

You accept the cold fact that you will never get to kiss Carrie Fisher. You'll never feel the white silk of her hooded robe. But Denise Scolerio in your class has a Leia-likeness: it's in the eyes, the brown hair, the immaculate skin, freckles like stars. To you she looks like regal Rebel scum, especially when she isn't picking her nose.

You want to get closer to Denise to see if she could handle a blaster, swing fearlessly across fathomless chasms, or survive the bitter frost on Hoth. But mostly to ask if she'd play kickball with you at recess, and maybe let you call her your girlfriend.

She likes Strawberry Shortcake and lets everyone smell her fruity-scented plastic cat companion, Custard. She even lets Alexa Fernandez keep her Grimace Happy Meal toy. You decide: Denise is a jewel of a humanoid, worthy of the legacy of Alderaan, in a galaxy of scurrilous bounty hunters. *Help me Obi-WANG, you're my only hope?*

At snack time, Denise tells Mrs. Miner that she is allergic to chocolate milk. Rachel Gold can only drink skim milk. They walk up to the desk together and wait to be sent to the cafeteria to pick up their "special choices." You claim that you too are allergic to that stinky chocolate milk, that you too should only have plain milk. "Fine," Mrs. Miner huffs. "You can go to the lunchroom together."

Paris looks at you like you are insane and shakes his head as if to say, *I've seen you drink chocolate milk like a maniac at my house! What in the name of* bantha poodoo *do you think you're doing?*

(This is something that you will regret for the rest of your life. All those years of chocolate milk lost, so that you could perpetuate this lie—a lie that you maintain well through 1986, when you finally realize that your secretive habit of chugging Yoo-hoos behind the bodega was not the best use of your precious allowance and was likely the root of your intestinal distress.)

The three of you hold hands and walk to the cafeteria together. The ninety seconds it takes to get there are bliss—ninety seconds of feeling these plump, warm hands. Sometimes the girls would skip and giggle. You skipped and giggled, too, like the best of them.

You would get to repeat this dairy ritual more times than you could count that year. For a moment you thought maybe Rachel liked you, when she slapped you in the butt to hurry you up that one time. But it was always Denise for you. Her galaxy of freckles and princessly pigtails trumped Rachel's bland curls and lisp.

* * *

The field trip to Old Bethpage is a tradition at PS 121. Permission slips are signed. Tessa Fenner's mom and Peter Melman's mom will chaperone. Ma packs you a ham sandwich, carrot sticks, apple wedges, and some Haw chips (pink discs of exotic dried fruit), Chinese candy that no one ever wants to trade for their Oreos.

The Old Bethpage actors reenact how *Lawng Aislandahs* made clothes back then; how they made *buttah* and had fun playing with sad corn-husk dolls by candlelight. You amuse yourself and pretend to be Captain Kirk (you can like *Star Trek*, too), traveling back in time to fire your phaser at all these mind-controlled humanoids. *Pewpewpew, bangbangbang.*

The only good part is at the close of the tour, when everyone gets tickets to spend at the Olde Trading Post. Five tickets each to use at the "shoppes" and stations around Old Bethpage. You can get birch beer, pretzel rods, penny stick candy in a dozen flavors—but you can't get everything.

You find Denise at the rack of shiny candy sticks with tears in her eyes. She didn't calculate the number of tickets she would need for all the treats she wanted—two pretzel rods too many, already in her belly.

You spend your last ticket on a cherry stick and offer it to her, like a miniature lightsaber (*lifesaver*). She lights up and takes it shyly. She thanks you, and you feel like you might fall into the dust of the wooden floorboards—*poof, splat, fade to black.* (You think George Lucas would agree—and he would likely use a wipe transition for this moment.)

"Want a lick?" She presents the candy, gleaming with her spit. You comply. It's almost like kissing.

* * *

You snuck glances at Denise when you could and cherished all the milky hand-holding. The year went on as you daydreamed and mastered how to add, subtract, spell. You don't remember much else, but what happened, you wish you could forget.

* * *

It surprises you when you hear the chanting on the playground. Susan Lee and June Park are screaming "*Uh-oh, Spaghetti-os! You got boogers up your nose!*" They make faces and chase Denise and Mary Montisanti around the playground.

Denise and Mary *singshout* back, *"Me Chinese, me make joke, me make pee pee in your Coke!"*

This melody does not impress you. You do not like this reject of a commercial jingle, not one bit.

They pull down on their eyes. Fists fly, feet fling, screams reverberate off the concrete walls: *"HIIIIIIIII YAAAAAAAH!"*

These theatrics do not impress you. You do not like this display of mismatched amateur martial arts, not at all.

At first everyone thinks this is funny—until Susan starts to cry. Then June starts to cry. The boys on the playground join in on the chanting (even Edward Chan—which makes no sense).

Mary scatters and races for the slide, distancing herself from the entire scene. This escalation is not what these girls had expected: the playground whipped into an impromptu hand-to-hand combat, rhyming rumble, frenzied tournament.

Denise, however, still thinks this is the height of hilarity. She playfully chops and punches you in the arm. (You call this "Fist of the Freckled Fury.") She runs circles around you, kicks at the air. You aren't sure what to feel.

Dear God, please help me be patient and kind. Help me not to say bad words or trip the cute girl I think I love. Jesus, help me. I pray, I pray. Amen, amen.

Mrs. Rose strides over, red in the face. She blows a flurry of sharp whistles and starts yelling at everyone: *"SIGNAL, SIGNAL!"*

The kids in the yard mutter and put two fingers in the air in compliance: peace signs / Vs for Victory. As everyone freezes in their tracks, silence travels in ripples—the entire schoolyard now being affected by this momentary madness.

Mrs. Rose is saying that this is unacceptable, that she is disappointed in everyone. *EVERYONE.* She singles out Denise, pulls her over with one arm and you with the other. She makes her apologize to you. Denise is inconsolable. She can't speak, can't breathe, can't look up.

"So-so-sorry. I was just playing. I didn't mean to hurt you." Denise exhales through a moist cloud of spittle and sweat.

Mrs. Rose releases the two of you. In minutes everything is forgotten. Kids are snickering and already onto the jungle gym and swings.

The rest of the afternoon is spent cutting multicolored felt flowers and tacking them up on the corkboard, a communal art project: "Harmony in Our Neighborhood."

But you remember.

I'll make pee pee anywhere I want—in your Coke, in your skim milk, on your shoes, on your dress. Stupidstupidstupid. Pewpewpew. Bangbangbang.

For the rest of first grade, you favor holding Rachel's hand. More often than not, your palms are clammy and squirmy. Denise still drinks her skim milk and chomps her graham crackers. She is cute as ever, but lacking anything remotely intergalactic or majestic anymore.

* * *

You look at your reflection in the mirror and meet your gaze. You avert your eyes—stare at the potbelly that's been growing since you've been chugging sugary soft drinks and crunching candy in secret. You swear this round taut balloon will recede once you master *1,000 tiger punches* and hit your growth spurt (*any day now*). You'll be tall, strong, handsome—like your uncle, like your father.

Maybe your eyes will even grow bigger. You raise your eyebrows and open your mouth, stretch your jaw, wiggle your ears. You exercise your body, your face—though deep down you know some things won't ever change. No matter what you do, some girls you were never meant to kiss.

But right now—maybe she was sneaking sips of Nestlé Quik and tossing back her wavy brown hair, wiping the sweetness off her freckled upper lip? Maybe she thought of the nice, funny Chinese boy that she really liked that one field-trip day. That dumb boy, who didn't realize her clumsy karate chops were just an excuse to touch him.

She lived just five blocks away, but it may as well have been five parsecs in a galaxy far, far away. The real distance between you seems infinite.

This love was what it was, but it was never meant to last. But you'll remember.

She was your first. She will always be your first.

Su Su Special Delivery and Road Trip Revelations: Daytona Beach

MARCH 1994

On the breakfast table, an opened cardboard box: a neon-pink teddy bear with googly eyes; a fluorescent yellow sun visor with a matching muscle shirt with "Spring Break '94" printed on it in graffiti bubble font; a bottle of dark rum with a mermaid on the label; and finally, a photo with a letter paper-clipped to the back.

The photo:

Su Su is getting acquainted with the locals at Daytona Beach. Muscular, shirtless, and tan, wearing neon-green board shorts paired with neon-orange sunglasses slid to the tip of his nose. Peering over his shades, a forefinger pointing at the buxom blonde perched on his lap, as if to say, *Check out these killer nay-nays!*

The letter:

Dear Young,

Greetings from the Sunshine State! Had a fun time with Alexis in Georgia, but now on to Florida with Francine! She's smoking hot (and she's a grad student—so she's age-appropriate)!

I have a thing for blondes—and brunettes and redheads. Winning them over, it takes extra effort! My English is pretty good. I know enough to be *dangerous*—in multiple languages! (Especially body language, you know?)

Young One, with charm you need confidence and passion! Su Su is the master! Charming number-one *shuai guh*! You can be number two! But your bah, when he was younger and going after your ma—WOW—he was really the *sifu*! So many girls after him then! He's "quiet" now—but they thought he was "mysterious." (So maybe you can be number three.)

These attractive qualities are universal. But when you are a *dongfang ren*, to the Western girls, any non-Chinese, non-Asian girls (actually, maybe Asian ones, too), they may think we are all weak nerds, have small *ji-ji*, and are lousy lovers. Then how do you explain the billions of us all over the world? *Over a billion served—right?* I haven't heard any complaints! Your *ji-ji* may not be huge—but what do they say in those high school funny films you like? *I'm a grow-er, not a show-er?*

Confidence and passion will overcome many shortcomings! But you have to be brave. I know you are scared. Scared of girls, scared of a lot of these things, but you aren't going to break anything.

When you were little, your Transformers—you just lined up your cars, all sitting pretty on the rug. They were not moving—not TRANSFORMING. You admired them from afar or you just left them in the box. They were meant to be touched, played with, handled, *enjoyed*. Time to stop observing and be part of the action, Young Stud. (I don't want you getting robots and girls confused—but you know what I mean.)

You have the extra benefit of being tall—and handsome! (Born blessed with those elusive double eyelids!) Just be patient, you will grow into your large frame—like Bah, like Su Su. We can trace our strength to our ancestors: hearty farmers, proud warriors, and even the nerdy scholars in our bloodline were big and powerful. What we all share: *being brave and moving onward*. We can face anything—even cute brunettes! When Miss American Pie meets the Red Bean Cake Rebel, it's all sticky sweet anyway!

Peace and grease!

Your ever-loving, one and only,
Su Su

P.S. *If bigger is better, brighter is mightier!* Go buy some clothes with color! Wardrobe can't always be black or white—life isn't that way. Why dress like it?

CHAPTER TWO

"Signals"

NOVEMBER 1995

Soundtrack highlights:
- "Get the Message"—Electronic
- "Is There Something I Should Know?"—Duran Duran
- "Girls & Boys"—Blur

SUBJECT: Hello, new friend!
DATE: 11/11/95 11:11:11 Eastern Standard Time
FROM: indepalmamyhands76
TO: fartprincess1

Hey Erena (AKA "fartprincess1"),

Sorry, might have missed you at the Undertow! I had to cancel some of my shifts to help out a friend. She's been having a hard time lately.

Anyways, was curious what you thought of *Totoro*? Did you enjoy the whimsical magic? I hope it wasn't too childish for you!

If you're still interested in animation, *Toy Story* got some great reviews. I haven't seen it yet, but I'm planning to soon. The cutting-edge 3D animation will change the landscape of filmmaking. *Exciting!*

Sincerely yours,
Young

SUBJECT: Took a ride on the Catbus, now my pussy hurts!
DATE: 11/15/95 17:05:24 Eastern Standard Time
FROM: fartprincess1
TO: indepalmamyhands76

Yo, Young Tongue! (AKA "indepalmamyhands76—until it makes me go blind from doing it too much!" HAHA! BURN!)

Dude! *Totoro* was fucking AMAZING! Trippy, fat, fuzzy thing with that massive shit-eating grin! Absolutely creepy! You were right! LOVED the Catbus and the other little creatures! FUCKIN' CLASS-A! Helen laughed her ass off, too! (But I think she had some "extra help" to get into the mood.)

Thanks for that mixtape! I LOVED—half of it! The other half sucked my balls! My nuts! Based purely on your sad music selection—I think you have some serious problems. SO DARK, MAN! You need fun, light, groovy jams feeding your ears! All that doom and gloom creates an angry, flaccid man. Give the Trent Reznor stuff a break. Listen to some NO DOUBT, baby!

And please, look into "testicular fortitude." If you want me to see your cartoon movie with you—*I am down.*

Goodness gracious! I was waiting for you to ask me out like a normal human. You did so well when we first met! Signals over the air were apparently not clear enough! Just get to it, loverboy.

Buy the tickets. I'll be free. (I'm sticking around NYC for Friends-giving with some dorm buds. Not flying home until Christmas.) I'll take you out for pizza after. Fair warning, I may be mildly "lactose intolerant"—hence, my email address.

Cash rules everything around me, dolla dolla bill ya'll,
MC E-ZA, the Sweetface Thrillah

P.S. Sorry about your friend. Hope she's feeling better.

P.P.S. Still working on my Wu-Tang Clan rap name, but you get the easy layup of "Young Dirty Bastard"—because, *duh.*

SUBJECT: Films and future fun!
DATE: 11/16/95 8:08:08 Eastern Standard Time
FROM: indepalmamyhands76
TO: fartprincess1

Hey Erena,

Your email made me laugh out loud! Yes, I was asking you out! You saw through my ruse and lame attempts at charm!

How about the Friday after Thanksgiving? We can meet in Union Square? I'll get tickets for the 8:00 show. Sound good?

In the interest of getting to know each other better (and having some topics of conversation to mull over pizza), how about we start with some of our favorite movies? They don't have to be all-time favorites or anything (*Haha!* Remember our conversation about music?) Just some films that have particularly resonated with you?

I'll start with three of my favorite trilogies:

1. Star Wars—obviously!
2. The Godfather—I and II are pure genius. I reluctantly have to include III.
3. Kieslowski's Three Colours trilogy (*Blue, White, Red*)

Looking forward to making plans! Would love to see your list! We'll have something fun to talk about!

Sincerely yours,
Young

SUBJECT: Cheeseballs and ball-balls!
DATE: 11/18/95 15:10:12 Eastern Standard Time
FROM: fartprincess1
TO: indepalmamyhands76

Young Hung-Like-a-Donkey (*YOU WISH!*)—

Such a nerd! I like killing-time games though, so I'll play.

TRILOGIES:

1. Lethal Weapon
B. Rambo
'▪ Indiana Jones

And a bonus one! I WISH they would make more of *THE THING*. John Carpenter is the maestro! And Kurt Fuckin' Russell is *pure hotness*! The manly facial hair! The special effects and all that tasty tension—*I eat that shit up!* That movie makes me cackle and scream in delight! MY FAVORITE!

They better make a damn sequel. Gimme two more! *THINGS* followed by *MORE THINGS*. That's a top-tier trilogy, right there!

Extra credit: what do the above selections have in common?

I'm Audi 5000,
Ms. E (*if you're nasty*)

P.S. Answer: *All examples of the male psyche running rampant over the constraints and repercussions of a patriarchy that has forgotten its very constituents.*

Acceptable alternate answer: *Shit gets blown up by hot, buff old dudes.*

SUBJECT: Popcorn is on me.
DATE: 11/20/95 10:10:10 Eastern Standard Time
FROM: indepalmamyhands76
TO: fartprincess1

Hey Erena,

You must stop making me laugh so hard! You are the epitome of wit and delight! *You do the humor!* Points for you!

I'm very excited for Friday night! *Toy Story* has been getting rave reviews. It's going to be great!

A slice or two afterward would be perfect. How about Joe's or Patsy's? I'll be so bold as to forgo any garlic. And I hope you will, too.

> Can't wait to see you.
> Silver screen, our moonlit scene.
> Start of something new?

Until then! Have a nice Friends-giving!

Sincerely yours,
Young

SUBJECT: Drinks are on me. I'll be all "wet." :P
DATE: 11/21/95 11:11:11 Eastern Standard Time
FROM: fartprincess1
TO: indepalmamyhands76

Young Lungs-Screamin'-My-Name—

Not sure if it was kind of racist or kind of sweet—but I will see your haiku and raise you my own:

> Feed me pizza, please.
> If we have some fun, more soon?
> C U Next Tuesday?

Bottoms up, tits down—*gobblegobble,*
Erena-chan

P.S. No promises for a second date. I just didn't want to miss an opportunity to spell out "CUNT" in a poem. It's still 5–7–5, baby! *Dou itashimashite, iie iee*—you're so, so welcome!

* * *

Soundtrack highlights:
- "Don't Give Up"—Peter Gabriel and Kate Bush
- "Interlude"—Morrissey and Siouxsie Sioux
- "Stop Draggin' My Heart Around"—Stevie Nicks and Tom Petty

* * *

SUBJECT: Misunderstanding?
DATE: 11/25/95 20:08:08 Eastern Standard Time
FROM: indepalmamyhands76
TO: fartprincess1

Hey Erena,

Wow. I'm not sure what happened, but I'm so sorry if I offended you in any way. I really, really like you. I just wasn't comfortable with how fast things were moving.

I'm glad you let down your guard and felt like you could open up to me. I'm always here to listen to whatever you have to say—and you have some amazing things to say.

It was hard to keep up with everything (your eloquence is only matched by your speed!). I know you didn't want to go into specifics, but *wow*—the way you see the world! I wish I was that brave and free! I've only been out of the country a few times, and my past travels come with mixed emotions. I'm envious that you had the means and determination to pick up and go. Everyone fights their way to New York, but I may never want to leave.

I'm glad you shared your thoughts on being a *hafu*—how you are learning to embrace your Japanese and Korean heritage, need to sort out the rest of your ancestry. I'm so sorry that you and your family had to go through such messed-up situations in California. I can't imagine how your dad, your grandfather, and your relatives could have endured that—*for generations*. My family are new here. I'm the first to be born in the US, and we are stumbling along, learning as we go.

We all have versions of these kinds of stories, but I was lucky to have been born when I was born, where I was born. I'm grateful to live in such a diverse place as Queens.

So, the hard part:

I could listen to your voice all night long. I didn't mean to leave so suddenly after we kissed and—you know. It was an epic night— seven different locations, in the span of nearly as many hours!

At the risk of sounding cliché: I wanted to be a gentleman.

I saw a glimpse of the real you behind the veneer of your bravado and profanity-laced tirades—and I liked what I saw. I want to see more of that. I didn't want to sully that moment of clarity and truth with something merely physical and lustful.

Erena, I think you are hilarious. I think you are beautiful. I think you are brilliant.

Let's make plans to see each other soon?

Sincerely yours,
Young

SUBJECT: Let's talk?
DATE: 11/27/95 19:07:07 Eastern Standard Time
FROM: indepalmamyhands76
TO: fartprincess1

Hi Erena,

I tried calling you a few times. I spoke to Helen, and she seemed really nice. She promised she would let you know I called.

I don't want to seem too pushy. Just let me know that you are doing OK?

Again, I'm sorry for taking off the other night (morning, really).

I'll be completely honest, I mentioned this a little the other night, the relationship I was in before—I'm still not 100% myself yet.

You're the first person I've connected with in a long time. You completely surprised me in the very best way. I promised myself that I was going to do the unexpected this year. If you can believe it, this is not like me.

I'm feeling like the anti–Kurt Russell right now. Does that make me Pee-wee Herman? (Trying the humor angle—best to leave that to you from now on?)

I think you are worth the risk of humiliation here. I would love to hear from you.

Sincerely yours,
Young

SUBJECT: Trying you again.
DATE: 11/28/95 21:09:09 Eastern Standard Time
FROM: indepalmamyhands76
TO: fartprincess1

Hi Erena,

Third time's the charm? Fourth time, I'll get labeled a stalker. Consider this my last-ditch effort.

I know we had an amazing night, and I'd love a chance to repeat that.

If you knew me better, you would realize how very hard this is for me. I'm trying to be brave. I think you are worth fighting for.

Can we talk or meet up soon?

Sincerely yours,
Young

* * *

SUBJECT: YOU.
DATE: 11/29/95 00:12:42 Eastern Standard Time
FROM: fartprincess1
TO: indepalmamyhands76

OK, fine, Young. You got me.

First: The way you were looking at me that night? You have no poker face *whatsoever*. I am a hot piece of ass, but no one has eyeballed me that way—with a combination of puppy dog eyes and scientific study. Somehow you made that creep-o stare *endearing.*

Second: How the fuck do you get off on this pseudo Psych 101 bullshit? And I quote: "seeing behind the veneer of all your bravado and profanity-laced tirades"?!?!?! Do you come up with this shit by yourself, or do you have a Pinocchio–Steve Martin feeding you lines somewhere? *For serious?*

Third: Just because I tell you ONE sad story about my dad's side of the family—the whole Japanese internment thing—and I get quiet for a second and not my usual chatty self, you think that's the "real me"?

Look, buddy—I am all of these things and none of these things. I have a potty mouth because I like to amuse myself and those around me—my verbal dexterity is not for the fainthearted! I like to sprint my face off because I miss running with my track friends. I like my stupid stuffed koalas because they remind me of my mom.

I was homeschooled before middle school, had a unique upbringing with my beatnik parents, read a lot, got to watch all the VHS tapes I wanted, and was generally a curious, well-adjusted baby girl. That's it. Nothing more to it! *STOP DIGGING FOR HIDDEN MEANING.*

You say you are hurt—*fine.* We all get hurt. You say you aren't over some bitch. *WHATEVER.* You have problems with intimacy and chastity. *WORK IT OUT.* We've all got a past that messed with our heads and our hearts and our genitals.

The thing that got to me, the thing that bothered me the most— was that you looked *so scared.* Like a switch flipped, and you were suddenly terrified of living in the moment—being present with me, in the present.

And we were having such a good time! The movie, the pizza, the ice cream, the funny dude selling hats on the street, then playing cards, listening to Counting Crows at my place—and wow—surprisingly, you are not the worst kisser! I really, really liked your stupid fucking face! (You doll up nice. Clean-shaven is the best—and only—look for you.)

I would have been fine with you spending the night, and it didn't mean we would have done anything—except *maybemaybe-maybe* letting you get to second base. I'm not that easy. I'm actually super hard to get. *Consider that a fucking compliment, dickweed.*

But I was sorry the moment I put my hand up your shirt. *Shit, kid!* I rubbed your back a teensy bit and you freaked out. Practically leapt like a feral cat!

Before you took off, that look on your face—your mind racing in a million directions! I kind of wanted to laugh. And then I wanted to cry. And then I wanted to laugh again. And then, I just felt sorry for you—and sorry for me.

I get it, I get it. I'm a sexy little monster and you couldn't stand the heat! I frighten myself sometimes, I do! If you are some sort of scaredy-cat virgin baby, I will respect your boundaries. We could have talked it out, but you got stuck in your head, split, and ruined a good thing.

What girl doesn't like a good apology, compliments, and sweet talk? That shit works on me, but you are ruining it by being fake and "emotional," and it's not ringing true. At least not yet. Stop trying to be the "good guy" and "a gentleman in this predica-ment." *Say what you mean, mean what you say.*

You wanted me. I wanted you. You got scared. You left in a rush and hurt my feelings a little. NO SWEAT. DONE.

I'm tired of thinking THIS MUCH and explaining things thusly. Meet me in front of Bobst tomorrow at 5:00, OK? I'm not going to assault you or anything. You made me second-guess myself for a sec. My momentary lapse of reason is now over.

Less talk, more *rock*. Let's just *be*. Pretense on pause, Romeo. Buy me a hot dog and we'll call it even. (Or better yet, McDonald's—so we can get some Happy Meal toys for you and "your baby sister"—if she even exists.)

And *fuck you, asshole*. It needed to be said.

Second chances are for suckers.

PEACE OUT!
Erena

P.S. You seriously need to chill out with this "Sincerely yours" bullshit. All I hear is *The Breakfast Club*.

Give it a break, Young Duk Dong. Fresh start.

(And yes, *you suck*.)

Second Love: "Louder Than Bombs"

1986–1988

Soundtrack highlights:
- "Space Oddity"—David Bowie
- "Change of Heart"—Cyndi Lauper
- "Kiss on My List"—Hall & Oates

You get fitted for glasses over the summer. You suspect that they may be too strong and find it hard to wear them consistently. Nothing in your body feels right: you get headaches often, nosebleeds every few weeks, and you seem to be itchy all the time. You've finally mastered cursive. You can throw a Frisbee, but can't get a football to spiral for the life of you. You think Jamaican beef patties are the greatest food ever, especially nestled in coco bread (50 cents extra). Fortune cookies taste like cardboard, and the sayings inside make no sense ("Love is the only adventure for the brave." *Pffft.*), but you stash away the paper slips for the lucky numbers (7, 8, 27, 42, 99). You finally get a Nintendo Entertainment System for Christmas—and blisters on your thumbs from too many hours of Mario madness.

You aren't sure what you want to be when you grow up. You

never took the fireman, policeman, astronaut possibilities seriously. You want to be something that makes your family proud (and honors your ancestors' ancestors)—something that makes your lives easier. Someone respectable, under the radar, where you can hide (most of) your weird—and succeed with gainful employment (to afford the best toys and comic books). Doctor, lawyer, something like that? You hear that accountants make a decent living, but your special relationship with numbers may rule out this path for you. Too much temptation to nudge and fudge those fiddly digits. You still hate math anyway.

You root for the 1986 World Champion Mets. Keith Hernandez, Darryl Strawberry, Mookie Wilson, Rafael Santana, Lenny Dykstra, Howard Johnson—real hometown heroes that reflect the same shade of faces you'd see in Queens. Ron Darling is even part Chinese! A fastball-throwing *shuai guh*! But truth be told, you like baseball cards more than actual baseball. Real athletic prowess is not in your future. You decide to avoid throwing, kicking, catching, whenever possible. You give up on karate and martial arts. You are fine with being a "mellow yellow fellow." Brains over brawn (and coordinated skill) any day.

But you are thrilled to meet Gary Carter at a Macy's fan event. He is the tallest man you've ever seen in person. You are disappointed when they close the line for autographs. Ma sticks her dainty arm in the door to prevent the elevator from closing. She scoots you inside and corners him, tells a white lie: her baby boy is traveling to Taiwan and desperately needs his favorite player to sign his baseball card—*for good luck on the flight*. He does so graciously—and you feel guilty. "Aiya!" Ma whispers. "You'll fly to Taiwan one day! Mr. Gary forgives you. Jesus forgives Ma."

Your parents are comfortable in their roles. Bah has the same alternating Queens loop of Botanical Garden, College. He still holds your hand when you cross the street, kisses you good night like you are still a baby.

Ma has been on TV lately! She's a "pillar of the Chinese American community." The local news asks her to speak about Chinese New Year and the events at the community center. She wishes the viewers *gong xi fa cai, gong xi fa cai* in her sweet Mandarin. She's always beautifully groomed, and her English is lilting and lovely (*for an immigrant*). She's poised and graceful in front of the cameras and microphones. You are proud of her.

Ma paces the living room and reads her speeches over and over again. She constantly dusts and rearranges the furniture, though no one seems to be coming over to visit. Sometimes she cries over the sink and yells at herself. You're not sure why.

Bah likes to sweep her up in his arms, throw her over his shoulder, and spin around. You'd think your mother would hate this, but when she lands on the couch and he bends down to kiss her, you hear her squeal and call him playful names: *da xiong*, "big bear," *liu mang*, "hoodlum." (He stops doing this to her in the fall of '87 when you find out that you are going to be a big brother. Their only daughter arrives in April '88 and changes all your lives.)

You still write to your pen pal Wendy. She is living in Shanghai proper now. Xia Ai Yi calls Ma every now and then, but Wendy is too shy to say hello to you on the phone. She writes half her letter to you in Chinese, the other half in pristine English. She's putting you to shame. Your ma encourages your correspondence: "A good way to learn about the changing world and your culture. And maybe you can pick up her good study habits!" You're resigned to the fact that you'll probably never learn to read and write in the spidery-looking characters that are second nature to her. You ask Ma to at least show you how to draw your name in Chinese, the right way. You could at least sign your name in both languages, just like that try-hard Wendy. Ma teaches you the correct stroke order—"like this, then down, then the slashes at the end"—and writes the characters for *ni hao, peng you*. She asks you to try this in your next letter. You scowl and practice on scrap paper. You decide to simply stick with "Hello, friend." Your handwriting is ugly and misshapen in English, and you already have enough homework. Why complicate things? Who are you going to impress?

You'll have to order dishes in Chinese restaurants using the pictures, the English descriptions, the numbers—like any other *wai guo ren*. Or you'll try to order in Chinese and risk looking foolish when they correct your pronunciation, thinking: *Another ABC—American Born Chinese—at least he tries to speak Zhongwen.*

You ask Su Su to translate Wendy's letters for you. He says it's mostly about her goldfish and how she likes dumplings. You write that you aren't allowed pets, since you have jungles of unpruned plants to take care of instead. You tell her about pizza: "It's cheese, tomato sauce, on flat bread—what we eat in Meiguo." You wonder if they have things like this in China. Su Su explains that they *absolutely* have these things, but maybe not the same, urges you to suggest that you meet up and share some *real* pizza one day, or that she feed you dumplings instead—*romantic, a date*. He elbows you in the ribs and makes kissy faces. You feel bad for Wendy anyway.

* * *

Deng Li Jun (aka Teresa Teng) is the epitome of loveliness. She is your father's favorite popstar. Over the summer, he collects a dozen of her albums from Chinatown to play on the new stereo. He makes you listen to them the whole car ride over to Toronto to visit your extended family—ten hours of Chinese ballads and her sweet voice. You've memorized the gauzy cassette cover art, elegant and cherubic—different from the cold, taut beauty of your mother.

Kitty Pryde holds a close second, but only when John Byrne draws her. You watch *Weird Science* on VHS five times with your cousin Jake. Kelly LeBrock is a temporary summer goddess. But it's really the dueling bubblegum American titans of Tiffany and Debbie Gibson who are enshrined on your bedroom walls. (You hide the sexy Samantha Fox pictures under your bed.) Ma tolerates you buying *Teen Beat* and lets you spend your red envelope money on magazines and posters of the "red hair one and the blond hair one." She sighs in relief that at least her only son isn't gay.

Dear God, I hope you have a nice girl picked out for me—if only in my dreams. I pray that I meet her soon and that she will sing me songs and hold my hand and protect me—and not punch or kick me. Amen, amen.

* * *

Paris Choudhary is still your best friend. You spend most of fourth grade obsessing over video games and comic books. He likes Spider-Man and Batman. You firmly side with Doctor Fate, a Lord of Order—and avoid, avoid the Chaos Magic of the sexy, scary Scarlet Witch. You prefer Wolverine and his uncanny friends. You feel bad when Paris trades you his *X-Men* #95 (Death of Thunderbird issue) for a stack of Garbage Pail Kids (your doubles).

When you are tired of controlling Luigi and Mario, you watch MTV together after school. Paris rolls around on the floor with a "boner" whenever Tiffany's video comes on. It's in heavy rotation. The joke never gets old. You pool your money to buy snacks for your "Junkfood Jamborees" and generally act like sugar-high boys.

Denise Scolerio is in Mrs. Branson's class now. You see her in the halls, but you may as well be strangers. Rachel Gold slaps you on the tush once in gym, and that's the extent of your interaction all year. You're in Mrs. Vitelli's class. It's the best one: T-A-G, *Talented AND Gifted*.

You take pride in your exponentially growing vocabulary. You throw in a *spacibo* or *Fräulein* in casual conversation (*Thanks Colossus and Nightcrawler!*) and pride yourself on using big words in school essays (*grandiose, viability*).

You use the word *chaos* in the title of your oral report, but you are disappointed that it's not pronounced the way it looks on the page. You know what it means—context clues. The word accurately describes the Chinese New Year party last year. But "Chaos at the

Chows on Bowne Street" loses a bit of its clever luster with the hard *k* pronunciation: *KAY-oss*. (But it makes sense now: *Scarlet* and *chaos* sounds great—and *scary*.)

In the upper right corner of the written report: "Fantastic job! Almost perfect! Slow down and enunciate! Your handwriting needs improvement. Neatness counts!" You still get an A–, though. Yes, it's an A—but *minus*.

* * *

Natalie Chang's penmanship is masterful—the envy of all fifth graders. She isn't getting *minus-ed* for sloppy handwriting. ("Neat Natalie" isn't the worst nickname one could have, light-years better than "Young Dung.") Your classmates figure it's due to the unfair advantage provided by the imported tools at her disposal. Her relatives in Hong Kong send her assorted stationery products: the latest My Melody, Little Twin Stars, Hello Kitty (still without a mouth) erasers, puffy stickers, mechanical pencils.

Her pencil cases are famous. The latest in innovation, a testament to Asian ingenuity, a vision of the future: buttons that fling forth secret compartments, eject a drawer to the right, swing open a secret square to the left, pop free the padded top cover with a calculated click. You covet that high-tech housing for the tools at your disposal—order and organization for your Donkey Kong pencils, Gundam erasers, Mega Man markers.

You ask Natalie if her dad can bring one back for you—if they make any for boys. (You are sure Su Su could easily ship you a carton of awesome stuff, but Natalie doesn't need to know that.) You tell her it would be worth at least fifty Garbage Pail Kids (naturally, from your doubles). She blushes and nods. You think she's cute, even if she doesn't say much to you, doesn't say much of anything.

Two weeks later she makes her bid: at least a "POTTY SCOTTY" and an "APRIL SHOWERS" (she already has a "NAILED NATALIE"). The rest, up to you. *Deal*. She hands you the rectangular box, still wrapped in crinkly cellophane. On the main cover panel: a picture of a space shuttle stacked on top of a jumbo airplane. You gleefully push the buttons, and the compartments spring open with vigor and verve. You become the envy of all the fifth-grade boys. You think this is *so boss*. You love this.

* * *

Sixth grade: you barely recognize half the kids in your class anymore. Your classmates are a gaggle of the floppy-limbed—driven by the unpredictable whims of uncontrollable genitalia. The cracking voices, pimples, and budding bosoms make every interaction awkward—*all the time, every day.*

This collective pubescent horror show is punctuated with moments of pure transcendence. You get a glimpse down the blouse of Ms. Schneider—the new teacher, fresh out of grad school. You decide that now and forevermore you are a heterosexual.

Health class is divided into boys' and girls' sessions. Your school tries to manage with coed, but the laughter and tears generated from the collective hormonal conflagration is too much for any of your teachers to navigate.

Paris runs over after school with a videotape. He assures you it will blow your mind. You think it may be the new Van Halen ("Van Hagar," really) video. You know you are wrong the minute he hits PLAY. The illicit moaning and copious pink flesh on display (with additional green aliens joining in the fray) frightens and fascinates you. (Mostly, *and moistly*, frightens.)

When Pastor Chen preaches about purity and virginity to the preteens and teens on Fellowship Friday, you promise to do your best, *for Jesus's sake.* You'd hate to make Jesus cry any more tears than he has already shed for you.

Dear Jesus—forgive me for staring at Sondra's boobies. I promise to only glance and look away. I might still peek at boobies when Paris finds ripped-up Playboy *pages in the park trash. I'm sorry. Amen, amen.*

* * *

Natalie shows up on the first day of sixth grade with her new feathered hair and denim jacket. Her peachy cheeks are Teresa-Teng-terrific, her shy smile is Tiffany-teasing, her cute little tush, in black biker shorts, Debbie-Gibson-delightful. Her floral headband completes the look; she's an international idol popstar. You want to shake your love for her—in time to the little Cantonese you know: *yat, yi, sam.*

The summer months have been kind to few. Natalie, however, is blessed with superior genetics. Her skin is tan and spotless. She spent break in Hong Kong; the sweltering 36-degree humidity (97 degrees Fahrenheit, to you, "Young-kee Doodle Dandy") must have flushed out her pores.

Though her family is Chinese (from Macau, Guangzhou) and you are Chinese (by way of Taiwan, Shanghai), you have no ability to conspire with her in covert conversation. Her deep, long Cantonese vowels are fathoms from your shallow, clipped Mandarin diphthongs. Your ancestors separated by seas of understanding, their offspring communicating now in the tongue of colonizers. After all these centuries, their progeny end up as *wai guo ren, outsiders, others.*

You're an ABC—American Born Chinese—but it's your Queens, New York, accent that's most noticeable when you say *"wAAAHHH-durr"* (water) or *"hAAARRRuuuhhrr"* (horror) or *"aaahRRReehNNJJ-eeh"* (orange). Natalie is cruelly considered as a FOB—one who came here Fresh Off the Boat—even though she arrived on a 747 in 1981. Her slight accent is mostly noticeable, most of the time.

The other Asian kids probably understand it—the nuances and marked differences of the tawny mélange of the Orient. Someone is always poorer; someone's grandparents raped someone else's grandparents; someone's food smells more like a cadaver than the other's.

But for all the Western-leaning in the class, all they see are a Chinese boy and a Chinese girl, who would make *such a cute couple!*

Maybe one just a drop darker than the other, but nonetheless a natural matching set made in heaven—*tian tang (or tin tong).*

* * *

You dream of Steven Spielberg. In the dream, he is wearing a beige *Jaws* baseball cap, Ray-Ban sunglasses, and a tweed sport coat over a blue button-down shirt. You admire his choice in Reebok high-tops and dark-blue jeans.

He's got a monocle on a chain that drops from his eye. He's playing with some sort of light-level-measuring device that looks director-y. He's writing on a clapboard in chalk: "GOONIES 2: GOOD ENOUGH 4 U," as he turns around and says:

Oh, hello. I'm Steven Spielberg. I'm the mastermind behind Close Encounters of the Third Kind, *the Indiana Jones movies, E.T., and of course, I helped on a little film called* The Goonies—*your current favorite movie!*

You love my films and memorable characters, especially that rascally Short Round and Data—both played by the same actor—Jonathan Ke Quan! But what's this? You speak in nearly perfect English! And your friend Paris doesn't sound like any of the Indian children in Temple of Doom, does he? (And he sure doesn't enjoy any chilled monkey brains, right? RIGHT? I asked my buddy George—and he has no idea. I'm asking you if you know for sure.)

Neither of you has any hint of an accent! If anything, you've got a Queens / "Lawng Ais-land" thing going on. Yes, you might mispronounce some words and you might mix up your grammar—but what kid doesn't? You guys are different. Born and bred Americans! Real New York melting-pot kids! You can have real pizza for lunch—not pi dan shou rou zhou! *(And definitely no pregnant snakes, right? RIGHT? Lucas has no clue! I'm asking you if you know for sure. I don't want to yuck anyone's yum!)*

I wanted to remind you that in my movies, the characters come in all shapes and sizes—you sure love that Chunk! And they come in all colors!

E.T. is mostly brown and looks like Mr. Maldonado from down the street! Well, until he gets sick and ashy—then he looks more like Mr. Liederman.

You especially admire the ladies: that blonde Miss Willie and that brunette Andie—such cuties, huh? And that adorable Drew Barrymore! She did send you an autograph when you wrote to her back in '83!

What I'm saying is: the world is a big place, and you don't have to put "like and like" together. We all travel in tribes of mismatched misfits—like those goony Goonies! It makes it a more interesting place. Options, opposites, opportunities!

Let's say, if I were to continue the adventures of Short Round or Data—good ol' Shorty may never leave India, and he'd marry a sweet Hindu girl from the village! Data would move to the city after college, get an apartment in Portland, and end up with a rascally tattooed Irish girl who likes to make her own artisanal soap!

But hey, if Short Round and/or Data ever had the chance to meet a nice Cantonese girl and wanted to settle down near Tsim Sha Tsui—nothing wrong with that either! The heart wants what the heart wants! *And it's TIME TO WAKE UP! THAT'S NO BABY RUTH—YOU NEED TO POOP.*

* * *

Finally, it's time for the sixth-grade spring dance, marking the end of elementary school. Many of the kids you've grown up with will go to different junior high schools. They'll be replaced by other gawky adolescents from around a five-mile radius—a new cohort to be tormented by. It's the end of a lot of things, but the beginning of the things that count.

Ma buys you a dark suit from Marshalls. This is the closest you'll ever get to wearing real shoulder pads. Ma would never let you play football: "Doctors, lawyers, have to protect their hands!" You still can't throw a spiral anyway.

You wear your best assembly clothes underneath, a bolo tie with silver-tipped tassels and your black Nikes complete the ensemble.

Bah laughs proudly, and Ma beams at her firstborn. They take pictures. You don't smile.

This dance: your first real big social gathering (outside of Ma and Bah's boring adult events). Everyone bops and sways in circles. One at a time, a kid gets shoved into the middle to highlight their best Running Man, Roger Rabbit, or other *herkyjerkyshimmyshake* dance move. The B-boy techniques are reckless. Inevitably someone tries some ambitious floor work, and some kid gets swiped in the shins.

The teachers drink punch, munch Cheetos, and seem halfway like real people. They barely pay attention to your classmates—just another herd of pimpled masses—corralled out the door to be someone else's problem.

You think the girls look cute and seem so grown-up with makeup and hair done, in nice dresses. In comparison, the boys are playacting baboons: dirty jeans and Ocean Pacific T-shirts—all wiggling offbeat and whooping wild. You aren't surprised the girls don't show much interest.

You get red in the face when the opening synths, guitars, and horns start up for "Everybody Have Fun Tonight"—the anthem by the lilywhite dudes who somehow christened their band after your namesake. You get nervous, want to moonwalk to the water fountain, and flee down the hallway. But you feel a wave of euphoria when your classmates holler and point at you—in celebration—when the *"EVERYBODY WANG CHUNG TONIGHT!"* part comes on. You realize they are laughing with you, not at you—and you think: *This is fun.* You love this.

Natalie gets bumped into the center of the circle when "your song" gives way to Whitney Houston. *Yes, she wants to dance with somebody. Yes, she wants to feel the heat with somebody.* She blushes and yelps, sways and spins. She looks over to you—and you think your heart may rocket out of your chest.

* * *

Natalie's face is warm and ravishingly ruddy. You gulp hard, bolster yourself to be bold, and ask her if she wants to cool down outside.

Paris sees you heading out to the yard, his mouth agape and pointing—thinking you are a madman, shaking his head as if to say, *You can't sneak out in the middle of "It Takes Two"—that's the jam! You wanted to be inconspicuous, and here you are blowing up your own spot! Houston—we have a problem!*

He's on the verge of screeching something that may stoke infernal, riotous flames in the other boys to *Lord of the Flies* proportions. You give him your best Clint Eastwood squint and mouth *I WILL KILL YOU*. Paris shifts to silent smiles, thumbs-up. He does his best Worm to pull focus. He remains your best friend.

You and Natalie are alone now; there doesn't seem to be anyone around. No one else along the outlined baseball diamond, by the dimly lit first-base corner, where the two of you perch on the concrete ledge. The streetlights, the moon representing, reflecting what might be in your young hearts.

"You know, everyone is talking about how we would make the best couple."

Whoa, out of the blue! She's not pulling any punches! you think.

"But why do *we* have to be together? Why does everyone think *we* are a match? Because we are both Chinese? My family is the Hong Kong–British kind of Chinese—the Bruce Lee and Jackie Chan kind. They call me a FOB because I wasn't born here and I have a small accent sometimes. My family came over on a plane—not any boat! You were born in Queens? No accent, just Queens-type of talking. But is your family the Communist kind? The Peking duck, mainland, Mao kind? I don't have to marry a Chinese, you know. My parents said I can marry anyone I love. Maybe not a Black person, but a Jewish or Italian is OK."

"Ma says I can marry anyone I love, too—but she must be a Christian. Catholic is OK, but she would rather I marry a 'real Christian.' No saints, no crucifixes. If she's from Shanghai or Taiwan, that would be nice, but not necessary. She said White or Black or Brown is OK, too. Italians are great, since they are like Chinese families—loud, into fighting, eating lots of noodles. Jewish is always good, because they are God's chosen people. She laughed when she said that, so I'm not entirely sure."

"My family is Buddhist. I don't know what to believe, except I'm scared of the statues. I hate the stinky incense. All that repeated chanting, the smoke rising and filling the room—it makes me want to throw up."

"I know some people use incense to carry prayers up to heaven. I like that idea, but it still smells grody. Sometimes I get scared at Sunday school when Pastor Chen preaches about the Book of Revelation. I don't think we are tough enough to handle it, but it's important for us to be ready for the end—*THE END*—you know? It mostly sounds like stuff from Hellraiser movies." You roll your eyes back and open them wide. Blinking rapidly, curling your lips back, you chomp and gnash at her like a pincushion Cenobite.

Natalie giggles and tells you to stop messing around. You love the way she half snorts and covers her mouth (*like Hello Kitty might*). You hear Bon Jovi over the speakers from the lunchroom and ask her to go back in to slow dance. It's the perfect soundtrack cut. (You think Steven Spielberg would approve—though he might opt for a snatch of John Williams's score to carry the emotion instead of a pop song.)

Natalie takes your hand, and you walk to the edge of the dance floor. Surprisingly, the space is now packed with awkward, temporary pairs—the girls have taken the initiative, the boys at their disposal.

You barely touch Natalie's waist. She barely places her hands on your shoulders. "Never Say Goodbye" crescendos, and Jon Bon Jovi wails mournfully. He must know how it feels to go to JHS 215, while your true love goes to IS 27.

If the Changs lived a few blocks over, they'd be on your side of the zone border, and you'd still see Natalie every day. You curse the

Board of Education and your local legislators for keeping your budding love apart. At least you'll have the summer?

As Jon hits his signature ethereal, longing high notes, all the tropes in cinematic history urge you to *do something* at this very profound moment.

You build up the courage to close your eyes and move in. Natalie mashes her lips against yours. Out of the clear blue, just standing there—a millisecond and it's done. *She's your first kiss.* It could've been awful and awkward, but it's pleasant and perfect. You'll remember it feeling like cold butter melting on a soft, warm roll (a freshly steamed *mantou*, to be exact).

The tension of the slow dance is released, as the freestyle dance beats of Stacey Q thump loud. Natalie squeals and runs to her gaggle of girls. Her eyes are shut tight, and she's shaking her head joyfully.

Sarah Ruiz hugs her, and they jump in tandem. Then Julie Garten grabs Alan Sikorsky and smooches him. Jayna Nelson revolves Derek Harrison around and lays one on him. An impromptu session of spin the bottle erupts, but without any glassware, without the element of rotational chance, getting straight to the good parts.

None of the sixth-grade girls wanted to leave elementary school without their first lip-locks checked off their lists. Armed with this bit of experience, they would have a slim advantage over the other junior high girls.

The teachers have caught on to this sudden proliferation of mass kiss-assassinations, and whistles are blown furiously: "*SIGNAL, SIGNAL!*"

The autonomic response is immediate. You pause. You freeze. You put two fingers in the air in compliance: peace signs / Vs for Victory—like you were taught, ever since the days you started peeling crayons.

Paris freezes. Natalie freezes. Julie Garten freezes—but not before she manages to kiss Alan one more time for good measure. *She must really like him,* you think.

"What the hell has gotten into all of you? This is a shameful display of irrational behavior! Is this how the *graduating class of 1988 behaves?"* Principal Karsey screeches on the mic. The feedback is murder on the DJ's teetering speakers.

"This party is over! *Pack it up!* I hope your parents are waiting outside—otherwise, you'll be in the yard for the next half hour!"

Everyone shuffles out the doors, kicking streamers and plastic cups along the way. The teachers eagle-eye all the would-be pairs, shepherd these randy rascals to their waiting station wagons. *There will be no more of this haphazard kissing tomfoolery, no attempts at getting last licks on this field.*

Paris is glowing. Nina Simpson practically lifted him up by the armpits and let him have one. You knew she always liked him— ever since third grade, when she'd trade for his butter and cucumber sandwiches.

Natalie keeps her distance, but you catch her looking to you and giggling. She climbs in Sarah's mom's car, off to a legendary sleepover, no doubt. She rolls down the back seat window and mimes the universal sign for "call me": the "hang loose," brought to the ear (just like a number 6 on one hand, "the Chinese way").

The Choudharys drive you home. Paris slaps you with a flat palm, a hard high-five. He whispers, "Now, we are men."

You've had more than enough for one night. You trudge upstairs, exhausted. Ma is up, and you hear Mei Mei's cooing as she gurgles her bottle. Bah asks why you are you back so early.

Before you go to bed, you pull out your sixth-grade class directory—for one last look, for old times' sake. You sleep soundly and repeat the seven digits of Natalie's phone number to yourself like a lullaby.

* * *

When you call the next day, neither of you has much to say. She tells you she is going to Chicago for the summer, then seeing her grandparents in Guangzhou. You bet that she'll get the latest Sanrio character stationery when she's there. *That stuff is for babies*, she tells you.

You don't speak to Natalie again that summer. In October, you hear she is dating Lee Kwok at IS 27. Your heart sinks at the news, but you don't feel sad for long. He's a good guy. You remember trading Garbage Pail Kids with "BRUISED LEE" at the comic store. He throws a wicked spiral and speaks Cantonese. You can't compete.

* * *

You look at your reflection in the mirror and meet your gaze. You avert your eyes—small, but not tiny. You squint and see your father's mouth, your mom's nose—and the same shiny black hair as a billion others from the Middle Kingdom.

You think her hair looks like yours, same skin tone: not too dark, not too pale. The future would have been her *gung hay fat choy* to your *gong xi fa cai*, her *pei dan sau yok jook* to your *pi dan shou rou zhou*. To anyone else it was: "Enjoy your hot rice porridge! Happy Chinese New Year, you cute couple!" It would be warm, comforting, familiar for you two—drawn from the same pot, but somehow a different flavor.

One foot in the East and one in the West—you both found an equilibrium. But if the fault line was to expand, the calling abyss underneath—you knew which direction you'd leap. For her, you knew, too—and that chasm would only grow. You'd shout goodbye, sing your farewells from opposite shores: your *zai jian* to her *zoi gin*, each under a different heaven.

IS 27 might as well have been Hong Kong. She would always be somewhere unreachable, in between here and there. And you, too much or not enough of anything for her either. This divide could not have been crossed, even if you both traveled by plane or boat.

This love was what it was, but it was never meant to last. But you'll remember.

She was your second. She will always be your second.

Su Su Special Delivery and
Road Trip Revelations: Houston

APRIL 1994

On the breakfast table, an opened cardboard box: a plush bull with a tiny red bandanna; a bootleg NASA T-shirt, "HOUS-TON, WE HAVE A (drinking) PROBLEM!" with an astronaut holding some space booze; two bottles of Lone Star beer; and finally, a photo with a letter paper-clipped to the back.

The photo:

Su Su is getting acquainted with the locals in Houston. Ruggedly handsome, wearing a dusty brown cowboy hat, a lush mustache now over his curled, smirking lips. Half hidden behind a thick cloud of steam rising from an immense bowl of beef noodles, his chopsticks are pointing at the slim waitress in a silky red *ao dai*, as if to say, *Pho a good time, check out this hot mama!*

The letter:

Dearest Young,

Had a great time in Texas! *Yee-haw!* I'm heading farther west for more adventures!

It amazes me that I can find a Chinatown or at least some Asian food in almost any city along the way! (Even in those "bumblefuck" towns, you can at least get some noodles!) But the best Vietnamese food outside Saigon—here in Texas! Some of the best Korean and Chinese food, too!

But sometimes the most racist people against Asians—are other Asians. The haves and have-nots—somewhere, some-when, someone got over someone else! Always comparing the past, the present, the future—who is the top dog, who winds up as dog food, who ends in a pile of dog shit. *(And NO—we don't eat the dog!)*

We *dongfang ren* and *hua qiao*, we all have our stories of how we made it over to Meiguo—and some are not so happy and fun. Many of us escaping war, persecution, poverty—doing whatever we could to find a better life here. I used to joke that getting to the States in the '70s and '80s took *blood, sweat, and tears*—and we had to move *earth, wind, and fire.* (If you don't get my joke, someone needs to school you on some funk.)

Being born here, you understand the culture in a way that I never will—in a way that the rest of us immigrants, "aliens," "visitors," never will. You know exactly who you root for at the Olympics, you don't hesitate to put your hand over your heart and pledge to the flag. Even though I have been in the US longer than I ever was in China, even though I can curse like a *fuckin' American*, I'll never feel like a real one. My American Dreams and actual dreams are different. I love exploring this amazing country—but when I go to sleep, I always dream in Mandarin.

My wish for your future is that you will travel—here and overseas. I want you to see the real world outside New York.

Wherever you go, whoever you meet—when they ask, "Where are you from," you tell them proudly that you were born in the USA (*Bruuuuce!*), raised in Queens, New York, by way of a loving family, with roots in China. Chinese, Asian, American. This is your unique truth. You just need to find the best way to tell it, to live it.

For years, I used to just smile and say: *"Ni hao,* I'm Chinese." But when people ask me where I'm from now—I tell them it's more important where I'm going.

Peace and grease!

Your ever-loving, one and only,
Su Su

P.S. I just called and missed you. But your ma said you got into NYU! Congratulations, Young Scholar!

CHAPTER THREE

"The Kick Inside"

DECEMBER 1995–JANUARY 1996

Soundtrack highlights:
- "The First Part"—Superchunk
- "In Circles"—Sunny Day Real Estate
- "I Wanna Be Adored"—The Stone Roses

W hat's this?" Young asked as Erena gave him a little black box. "My birthday isn't for weeks."

"Not your birthday present. Just open it, *shuai guh*. It's gonna be *good*." Erena, poking Young in the arm with her chopsticks.

"Is this what I think it is? Wait—does this have anything to do with how you always have money?" Young hissed through gritted teeth. He made a cursory, forced-casual once-over of Midoria Sushi.

"Come on, *21 Jump Street*! Everyone has a pager now! I have one—and now you have one. These aren't just for shady weed dealers and emergency room doctors! Unless you were inferring that I was an incognito-ganja-genius Asian-girl Doogie Howser. This is meant to be used for us—for *play-play*," Erena teased as she shoved an entire piece of *inari* sushi in Young's mouth. "Eat. Never liked these sweet tofu football things. Isn't this so much better than going to some strip-club buffet?"

"I suggested a *tapas* bar, not *topless*. Why would I—"

"Excuse me, sir—*sir*? Let me stop you right there. You may not realize, but you've got a bit of an accent—*ACCKS-SEND-EH*—and you mumble half your words. I feel like I need a translator to understand half of your garbled Queens English—and I mean the Flushing, Queens, kind, not the proper British-royalty kind. But I get what I get from Mush Mouth here. Another reason why our new pager system is going to be *le tits*."

Young turned on the beeper and looked at the dull gray display light up orange. Erena explained the two basic options: 1) voice messages and 2) numeric messages.

Voice messages: If someone called your pager number and left a voice message, your own pager number would flash on your device. Then you would have to call your own number and punch in a pin code to retrieve the voice message. No microcassette tapes to record and rewind. It was all done "over the remote central mainframe"—high-tech cool.

Numeric messages: A callback number could be displayed, or just a string of numbers. First, dial the pager number. Wait for the tone. Then enter your numbers and hit # to send. Typically, it was a phone number that would flash on the receiving pager, so the recipient could return the call, or it could just be a line of numbers displayed on the recipient's brick. This was where the flexibility of the technology could really shine.

The numbers could be used as code.

Young's eyebrows elevated, and his posture changed from interested hunch to erect epiphany: "What do you mean, 'code'?"

"You are a nerd. And *I KNOW* you used to play with your calculator and type 80085 to spell BOOBS. Same basic idea here! You can use the numbers on the keypad like letters, and be creative. Some numbers are obvious, like 0 would be an O—and then you have the funky ones like 17 for N or 177 for M—*get it?* Squint a little, flip the box upside down, turn it sideways, and you'll see it." Erena smiled, picturing the gears engaging and whirring in Young's brain. The look of satisfaction on his face made her want to bite his arm, his neck.

"There's all sorts of shortcuts. Obviously you can use 911 as code for 'Emergency / call me right back,' or we can come up with code for something like 'Meet me at my room at 4:00'—it would be 120017*400. Do you see it? My gushy, squishy geekboy—I knew you would love this! You can share the number with your friends and family, but mainly I thought you'd use this with me. For us."

"I can't accept this. It's too much," Young said, flustered. "You must have some monthly bill to pay for the service."

"Don't worry. I got a deal on two pagers. *I know a guy.* Actually, you know a guy. You really should explore the downstairs at the Undertow more often." Erena shrugged and munched on some ginger.

"It's not my section. I keep to the movies and music. So, Terry knows this is for me, and he gave you a deal? I don't know him all that well—he's really into psychedelic '60s rock. Not a genre I am familiar with, so we never bonded over anything other than standard Black Sabbath and Argento's *giallo* films."

"It's always a whole saga with you! *Yadda, yadda, yadda.* So much fuckin' yapping. Look, I promised my folks that I would be easier to get a hold of—plus all of your back and forth to Queens, and your thing with numbers, it made sense to get you one, too. So, *voilà, bingobango.* DONE. Less squawkin', more rockin'! Now you've got a cool thingamajig and you can go *beepboopbeep.* You're welcome! Buy me this dinner. We'll call it even."

* * *

Young and Erena had only been dating a few weeks, but it felt—*exponential.* Time moves differently when sleep is optional and caffeine, nicotine, coerce the days into stretching wide.

Taking into account a quick break for Christmas and New Year's, it had been less than eight weeks together. Lengthy phone calls, emails, and the fact that neither of them had kissed anyone to welcome in 1996 made their exclusivity inevitable. When they reunited after Erena's brief trip home, boyfriend and girlfriend christened the new year together on January 5th with some bowling at the Pin Bin and a few chaste kisses. Inseparable ever since.

But Young felt like everything in his sphere was moving too fast. First-semester finals were tough yet manageable, but the new year meant a new set of intense classes—all pre-med track except for a required English course (the only fun one). Hours studying at Bobst, at local cafés, and at the campus center were a given. He would have to cut back hours at the Undertow—less pocket money for his passions and, now, for taking Erena out.

Home was going to be difficult without Su Su around to help with Mei. Young was disappointed that he didn't even call for Christmas or New Year's. The only recompense: another picture sent without a return address:

His uncle was getting acquainted with the locals near Santorini over the holidays: Su Su, wide-eyed and open-mouthed with a glamorous brunette hanging around his neck. Su Su was decked out in half of a Santa suit, jacket unbuttoned, tanned belly exposed, blue-and-white shorts underneath, his back to the open expanse of sea, double-fisting flaming shots of ouzo.

"*JINGLE BALLS, BABY! HERE'S TO 1996! Love you and miss you! Peace—and Greece! OPA!*"

* * *

Without Su Su and Young around, Ma and Bah had to entrust Mei to a parade of babysitters. Mostly older Chinese women who spoke little English but who had hearts full of faith.

Mei hadn't been sleeping well either. She would make the rounds in the middle of the night, creaking open her door and shuffling first into Ma and Bah's bed, then rolling out like a pint-size ninja before dawn to slip in next to Young. He'd often wake to find her cold butt pressed firmly to his face, her arms contorted and slick with spittle.

Sometimes when he'd come home after a marathon study session or a late shift at the Undertow, he'd find Mei sitting on the stairs, silently staring as he locked the door behind him. "Mei, why are you awake? What are you doing?" he'd ask. She'd shrug and smooth down Barbie's ponytail and wait to be scooped up and taken back to her room. With Bah's snoring reverberating and steady, Ma with her silk eye mask and earplugs in, Young's late-night returns usually went unnoticed except by this nocturnal creature. He'd sit with her in bed and sing her Chinese lullabies, the one about the disfigured (*why?*) tigers, "Liang Zhi Lao Hu." She'd usually be asleep before the fourth or fifth repetition—sometimes mumbling "Su Su, again."

* * *

Young tried his best to maintain his patterns and routines, but college had unmoored the balance of his ship. His best friends and longtime crewmates, Paris and Gina, were thriving on separate shores—out of state, but never out of mind. They tried to call or write, but time and tide made things difficult.

Young had only been able to see Paris and Gina twice over the short winter break, once when the Villanuevas and Choudharys sponsored tables at Ma's Taiwan Center Christmas fundraiser, and again when the three went to the movies and had coffee afterward.

Heat was life-changing for Young. Michael Mann's exquisite direction, Pacino and De Niro (not to mention a virulent Val Kilmer), the guns, the airport scene: it was cinematic rapture. Young wanted to dissect the movie with his friends, but Paris seemed unnerved the rest of the night. Young thought it was residual adrenaline from witnessing a near perfectly crafted film (*the gall, the balls, of not having the two leads together on-screen for more than a few moments!*), but it was more personal and real than the performances of SAG-AFTRA cops and designer-wear, professionally costumed robbers.

"Paris, yo, earth to Paris?" Gina prodded. "You OK there? Dreaming about holding up a bank and *brrapbrrrapbrrap*? What's up?"

Paris waved her off and asked her to pass the sugar. Young followed Gina's lead. "You haven't really said much. Is it school, or—"

"Just thinking. Look around—we have it easy. We can sit here together and drink our cocoa, shoot the shit. Goof off, and no one bats an eye. Living in Queens, where every shade of brown, gobbledygook language, and stinky cuisine is represented, and around every corner, someone who looks like you, sounds like you. The rest of the world at large—these people hail from lilywhite boonies! Here I am, at the University of Michigan, one of the biggest and best schools in the country, and I'm meeting actual people who have never had a meaningful interaction with a person remotely close to my level of melanin in their entire lives. Only seeing them in the movies or TV—never anyone real," Paris says intensely, almost spitting out the Swiss Miss from his hot cocoa. "I try to explain that I am *South Asian*, of Indian descent, and I get all sorts of 'You're not *Asian* Asian,' and the usual racist bullshit about curry and cabdrivers or convenience store clerks, like Apu from *The Simpsons*. And then I meet all these brothers and they're like, 'Cool, cool, you should hang with us.' And maybe I should. I was born and raised in motherfuckin' Queens, NYC. Home of Run-DMC, LL Cool J, Nas. Maybe I should identify as Black, since everyone wants to call me a ni—"

"*Whoa, whoa, whoa—dude!* The hell are you talking about?" Gina, in his face, coffee about to tip over. "Both your parents are *doctors*. You grew up with a *literal* white picket fence. You've never had a run-in with the police—other than the scared-straight field trip in seventh grade! You don't know shit about shit! And you better not claim something that you have no right to claim!"

"See, there you go. All fire and sass! You think other people see *you* as Asian? Give me a motherfuckin' break! You are a spicy Latina *MariaSelenaChitaRiveraRitaMoreno* to every other person in this here Dunkin' Donuts! You've got a perpetual tan, a curvaceous body, and your last name sure doesn't sound like no *ching-chong* to me. 'Villanueva!' Yup, when you meet 'Todd' or 'Brad' fresh from the Harvard 'Fuck Truck,' I'm sure they're gonna think, *She must be Filipina/Pinay*, and want to get to know the 'real you.' Eh, whatever. I'm sure they all have Asian *and* Latina fetishes anyway." Paris kicked back and crossed his arms.

Gina looked ready to knock the chair out from underneath Paris, throw her hot drink in his hot face, but Young placed a hand on her arm. He turned to Paris and placed his other shaking hand on his best friend's shoulder: "It can't be all that bad. Where is this coming from?"

"Look, bro, I love you—but the truth is, you don't have it nearly half as hard," Paris said defiantly, lips pursed tight. "The world is a fucked-up place for people who have dark skin. *You* get the smiles and nods when you walk into Macy's, see a policeman walking past, nice lady with a stroller—you haven't felt the pressure in the air just *change* when you make eye contact with a stranger. I had to be away from home and see the rest of the country to realize this. It's not everyone, but it's enough. No, no, I get that you've had some fucked-up interactions—we all have. But you might have a bit of an advantage, might be the 'right kind of Asian'—*close enough to White and being all right, BruceLeeDoctorLeeLeeKumKee*. I know you've seen some shit. But not like this."

Young took a breath and waited for Paris to lift the cup to his lips. "Other than my China trip and Toronto, I haven't really been outside New York much, or anywhere outside of the East or West Coast urban areas. I'm lucky we're from this pulsing city full of everybody—and I'm honestly too scared to leave. I feel invisible sometimes—but that's not all bad. I can hide and not be noticed, but I don't want to be perceived as *neutered, powerless*, either. Is that better than being seen as *dangerous* or *frightening*? Probably. Maybe. But it sure isn't doing my self-esteem any good."

The three friends sat in silence and sipped.

"It's good for me," Paris cracked wise, cutting the tension. "If you want some tasty wonton soup and 'pork flied lice,' have 'laundry-pick-up-at-end-of-day-special' for you!"

Young pounded him hard on the knee. Three sharp strikes. Gina pinched the thin skin of his elbow.

"*Ow-ow-ow!* OK, OK. I'm sorry! I just got worked up. Being away from home and traveling with the debate team through all these bumblefuck hick towns, I just ran into some fuckin' ill situations. If it were a slasher movie, I'd never make it out alive! The minorities and nonvirgins are always the first ones to go—two things stacked against me!"

"Do you hear your ridiculousness now? 'Debate team'—yeah, real street of you, 'MC Bombay B-Boy'! Or is 'French-Money' better? We'll never get a good nickname for this stupid-ass punk." Gina pinches again.

"*Stop it!* Did Wellesley bring out the tough lesbian you were always hiding inside? I knew all that girly pink stuff was a front! Young's gettin' *somethin' somethin'* with that new girl of his, but is Gina gettin' *some 'gina*?" Paris laughed as Gina tried to kiss/punch her two favorite guys—and she still loved/hated their entire misbegotten gender.

Young tried to convince himself that it had always been like this, would always be this way. They'd part, change, converge, and still be safe in the comfort of their trinity.

"So, babyboy, this hot California love we keep hearing about—tell us more. When do we get to meet the sexy little bitch?"

"She's back in town on January 5th."

"Ah, shit! I'll be long gone and back in frostbite territory: Ann Arbor, USA."

"I'm still around, and I don't hop on the Peter Pan until that Sunday night. What do you say to a night out with two smoking hot divas?"

"Maybe one diva. Once you meet Erena, I think you'll be using another name to describe her."

"Is she that bad? Or is she that good? I'm intrigued! I can't wait to meet this hooker you hired!"

* * *

"Happy New Year, bitches! And when I say 'bitches,' I do mean the both of you!" Gina yelled, running up to hug Young and to meet Erena.

"Hi, hi! So nice to meet you, Gina! Young warned me that you were hot and snarky! I like, I like! And this coat, this is so fucking killer! Vintage leather? You look so fuckin' hot in this! Oh my tits— can you please turn around and let me check out your ass? It's like a full-on smuggled panettone, a luscious holiday cake surprise hiding under those jeans! *Crikey!* Look at those pert pasties!"

"Young, I swear you must be practicing some arcane magic or you inherited a load of dough. How did this delightful young lady ever agree to go out with you?"

"I'm—charming?"

Both girls laugh and laugh until they need to hold each other up—fast friends, camaraderie forged by mutual affection for their inadvertent comedian.

* * *

Gina had suggested a night at Corners Billiards, a few short blocks from Erena's dorm and by the N/R station. The pool hall was cavernous and half full this time of year—the NYU kids trickling back to campus, the city still emerging from the saccharine overdose of holiday cheer.

Young was terrible at pool. He could never will his body to stroke the cue at the angles his mind could easily envision. But he loved the hefty colored spheres, the bold numbers in solids and stripes, the hypnotic cadence of click and clack and tumble.

Gina racked the balls and suggested that they play fast and loose with the rules—a friendly three-way game of sinking the balls sequentially, saving the 8 ball for last, for luck. Low pressure, and it would give them a chance to chat and bond. *Teamwork makes the dream work.*

"Erena, why don't you break. Young, you get how this game works? Try to sink the next ball, closest one in numerical order. I figured you would like that."

Erena chalked the tip of the cue with blue, easily sliding the slim pole between her knuckles, then hit the white globe with enough force to scatter the balls across the table. "Young—be a good dude, mate, and grab us a few Cokes first?"

Young was content to remain on the sidelines and cheer on his ladies. He suspected that Gina would test Erena's boundaries, and Erena—well, Erena would react. Getting drinks was an easy excuse to *avoid, avoid. (Triple 8, get it straight. Bangbangbang.)*

Gina lined up her shot. "I take it that I don't have to give you the if-you-hurt-him-I-will-kill-you speech?" The yellow 1 ball slipped neatly into a corner pocket, but she missed the blue 2 ball on her next turn.

Erena paced around the table, eyeing her move. "Totally, let's consider that chat over and done with!" She deftly knocked the 2 and 3 balls into the pocket below where Gina stood. "Had I known he would be such a handful, I might not have acquiesced to that second or third or fourth date. But here we are. Kind of stuck with the guy now."

"So, what was it at first? Did he start babbling on about the Fantastic Four or Green Lantern? Was it *The Evil Dead* or *Time Bandits*?"

"It was actually anime and heavy metal."

"His latest and most intense obsessions! Did he say something about 'taking a deep dive on oeuvre, canon, discography'? If you can keep up, you got him right in the nads and eating out of the palm of your hand!" Gina joked. "You know, he wasn't necessarily off the mark when he said he was charming."

Erena whiffed the purple 4 ball: "Nah, charming isn't it. *Fuck.* You might be right about that wizardry theory. It's more that he draws you in with his passion about the weirdest inconsequential things."

"Yes! He pays so much attention to the trivial—gets so worked up, you assume he cares that much for all the big stuff." Gina sank the 4 and then the 5, leaving the 6 ball on the edge of dropping.

"Well, does he?" Erena nudged green 6 in, that underlined digit spinning its goodbye.

"His friends, family, school, God—*ONE HUNDRED PERCENT, YES*. But the big real-life stuff competes with all the noisy nuggets ricocheting around in his head. He gets so lost in the details sometimes. You have to snap him back to reality. But also, that's kind of his most lovable quality."

"The macro and the micro—not sure he can separate or let go of the right things, or even compartmentalize in a healthy way. He doesn't realize he's being melodramatic, but—*come on*! Such a wanker, sometimes! It's just *Gremlins*, for fuck's sake, not a 'treatise on the horrors of pubescence,' am I right?" Erena shoved the cue, the maroon 7 ball in her sights.

"He's got his quirks. But once in a while he gets confident and switches into I-know-what-I'm-doing-follow-my-lead mode."

"Fuck. Yeah, that's hot. And he is actually really handsome under that motherfuckin' pelt."

"*Oh, the hair.* He's got a history with the hair. Not my story to tell. Leave that one for another day—a rainy-day tale of babyboy past. You'll love it." Gina paused, containing her chuckle. "We are some deadeye assassins, sis! Let's have a seat for a sec."

Gina motioned for Erena to take the high-top stool next to her. They leaned back and surveyed the smoky room, soaking in the East Village attitude and ambience.

"OK, girl-to-girl and we just met and you don't owe me *diddlyshit*. Just curious if you two ever had a *thing*? I am absolutely not the jealous type! Just fishing for some advice."

"To be honest, yes and no. We've known each other since we were twelve! We shared all the awesome and awkward together. We made a few mistakes in our time, and I emphasize—*MIS-TAKES-UH*, legit growing-up, innocent-kid mistakes. He's my best friend. He's my brother. I love him to pieces—but not like that. He's my Twee-dledum, and Paris—you'll meet him soon enough—is Tweedledee. Not to say that I'm Alice! I'm more the Red Queen. Head bitch in charge of beheading other bitches." Gina paused to see if Erena thought this funny—a friendly little *"Aaaaayy"* and elbow bump.

"As for advice: he wants someone to listen to him, but he *needs* someone to challenge him. Oh, and he will never admit this, but he really likes to dance. (And you can thank yours truly for teaching him some moves!) Something about the volume of the music, the beats-per-minute (who knows what he's calculating in that noggin), and the 'long legacy of tribal, communal experiences—expressed artistically in all media.' He's not the best dancer, but he tries. Bless his heart, he tries."

"I respect that. I appreciate that. And I could totally tell you were a dancer. So graceful, how you handle that pole." Erena, with a wink.

"Back at you, samurai! You take some kempo, judo? Your mastery of that stick is evident!" Gina, matching without a beat.

"Sorry I took so long, ladies. I ran into Jerry Jin from my stats class. We were talking about Alan Moore's *Swamp Thing* run and got caught up. Here's your Cokes. The ice melted, but it's still nice and cold. What did I miss?"

* * *

"We'll have Friday and Saturday to get into all sorts of birthday trouble. Helen will be at her boyfriend's, and we'll have the room to ourselves. It's going to be fuckin' epic, b-day boy! I've got ideas, but I don't want to be a complete douche and not respect your wishes. Lay out your boundaries because, believe me—I will push you! I'll make you have the time of your fuckin' life!" This last bit: Erena made sure to raise her voice an uncomfortable octave higher and stick her tongue out obscenely, channeling Gene Simmons.

"I'm happy having a quiet dinner, maybe something French—

nice conversation, over to the Angelika for a flick. That would absolutely be a dream for me! 'Happy twentieth b-day, Young. Here's birthday cake and candles.' *Yaaay. Smooch, smooch.* Ideal," Young whispered as he packed up his books, carried their trays to the trash.

Erena slipped both hands around Young's face. Young puckered his lips, expecting the usual kiss, but yowled in pain as Erena twisted his earlobes. She pulled his face to hers, blinked slowly.

Speaking calmly and assuredly, with surprising sweetness—and a touch of menace: "We are not doing some *substandard, artiste, bullshit birthday.* No boring-ass night, for a boring-ass couple of forty-year-olds. If we are equal parties in our exclusivity agreement, you are going to have to relent and actually *party* with me. Learn to *let go.* Your 'dream' vision of a good time? It's pathetic, it's fucking *matronly.* It's not even Pollyannaish—it's what Pollyanna's boring-ass aunt would do. We're young and alive in New York fuckin' City! We're going to do *something else.* You heard me when I asked you about boundaries? Yes? So, tell me what I *cannot do*—with you and *to you*—and leave the rest to me. *Capisce?*" She kissed him and bit his lower lip—equally exciting and scary.

"Fine! I'll have a drink, maybe something stronger. I've experimented a little before—*surprise.* No stealing. No violent acts. I'll do anything else. I swear. And, I'm serious—I don't want to have sex." Young, now sweaty and ruddy-faced.

"Sure! That's it? I can color inside those lines! Besides, getting lucky on your birthday would be so cliché. We're going to tear shit up downtown! You'll be guaranteed to be so tired, you'll have a limp dick anyway, but a huge smile on your face! I did score us some fake IDs. Necessary evil—OK, Poindexter? We'll rehash the whole night—watch the sunrise and scarf down corned beef hash at some greasy-spoon diner." Erena, grabbing Young's backpack and walking backwards through the doors. The crackle of winter, the dark streets of Greenwich Village, the thrumming breath of huddled youth, all just outside.

* * *

Friday, January 19th: Young arrived at Erena's dorm, as called at 7:00 p.m. sharp. She was late. When she finally came down to the security desk at 7:33, Erena was in sweatpants, with streaks of fresh tears down her face. Her hoodie was pulled taut around her head, her face poking out of the tight aperture, like a newborn stuck along its journey to meet the world.

Before she could give an answer to any of Young's questions, she pulled him into her room and unveiled. Young's tongue clung to the roof of his mouth. The air escaped him.

He pulled her close as she explained in a rush: "You know, I'm not vain or anything, but I'm pretty fucking cute most of the time. I'm just crying 'cause it burns like the *dickends*—Dickens—whatever. I didn't read the motherfucking instructions correctly! Got distracted getting everything else ready. Plain stupid—lost track of time and left something in too long." Erena applied ointment to the red splotches along her hairline.

She sucked in through clenched teeth—*ayayayyyyy.*

Her head was a stringy mane of shocking platinum blonde, her scalp a nasty inflamed magenta. As she moved her hand gently around the curve of her head, a few wisps of overly processed hair drifted away. The jar of purple Manic Panic sat on the dresser, unopened.

"I don't know if I can salvage our plans for tonight." Erena sniffled and held up her hand-stitched outfits: an impressive array of spandex, leather, chrome, and plastic pieces—purple piping along the sides—and some well-placed glow sticks gleaming through transparent pockets. Bright-orange toy laser guns in a sling bag completed the costumes.

"I wanted to have sci-fi/anime fun night with you: play dress-up, slurp lucky birthday noodles at Yokohama, and pretend that we were from the future—but I suck and screwed things up." She winced and sat down on the bed. "Do you mind if we just order pizza and give my flaming turnip head a couple of hours to rest? I can rally if we let the Tylenol kick in. I've got Cup Noodles also, so those can fulfill your 'Chinese birthday long-life meal' requirement. We'll eat and snuggle—*carefully*—and then hit the town?"

A lump in Young's throat—he gingerly kissed Erena, making sure he didn't touch her head as he stroked the sides of her face. "You are so incredibly amazing—and yet so stupid. I know how much it stings, all those chemicals on your scalp. Poor thing, *what were you thinking?*"

"Always wanted to bleach and dye my hair a funky color—figured college away from home was the best time to try it. Your birthday was the perfect excuse. It would have been so fuckin' rad if you had shown up and I had this millennial-sex-robot purple hair and greeted you in my lustrous, horny outfit. You would have passed out because your massive *nerdboner* pulled all the blood into your pants! But now you get all of this instead—*this*." She pointed to her inflamed iridescent scalp. "At least I went out and got this backup wig. In hindsight, probably should have made this 'Plan A' from the start. Pink, not purple, but still fucking sexy, right?"

She pulled out a small black bag with bright-purple tissue paper. "You are still going to love your birthday present. Happy birthday, big boy! T-shirt with your angry comic guy—Wolverine, *grrrr*—so you can dress the part when you buy your funny books! It might be a little tight—I wanted you to show off your man boobs! *Honk, honk*," Erena yawped as Young chased her around the room.

Painkillers masking the ache, endorphins releasing amid the flirtatious nips and slaps, Erena howled and tackled Young onto the bed, straddled him, sat on his belly. Young stared up into her face, the orange streetlamp glow framing her shock of wild blond hair, backlit like a fiery halo.

* * *

They left Erena's dorm room around 11:00 and strolled over to the Twilight Club in Chelsea. Erena had already been there once with

Helen at the close of the last semester and was raring to revisit the strobe-lit, liquid-fogged press of hot young bodies.

Young had a passing knowledge of DJ culture and the electronica / drum-n-bass / trance music bumping through the speakers. He liked it enough to not be annoyed and analytical—enough to move his body into some semblance of dance. It tickled his synapses, reminding him of bits and bytes of the music he already adored (so much owed to Vince Clarke, New Order, Kraftwerk).

Erena's avant-garde costume—electric-pink wig and bare midriff—was getting plenty of attention. She took in the twirling glow-stick dervishes, the shiny platform-booted angels, the colorful collegiate clowns, tracked the young women in pigtails and glittery tops and the pumped-up, spiky-haired studs, all of them grinding away on pacifiers. All of them passing their hands in front of their own faces, mesmerized by the light trails and stuttering drumbeats.

"Helen said half would be enough for us newbies," Erena shouted into Young's ear as the bass throbbed in waves through their clothes, the sweaty bodies jostling them closer, pushing them into the throng of dazed dancers. "Let's do this together, OK?"

Erena had a bit of Ecstasy, kept in a tiny plastic sleeve hidden in her bra, a yellow tab split in two. She cupped it in her palm and flashed Young.

Young paused—breathed deep, nodded his consent. He brought his forehead gently against hers: *Here's to new experiences. Will ask for forgiveness later. Amen, amen. Bangbangbang.*

Erena dry-swallowed half and put the other portion on her tongue. She kissed Young, slipping the rest of the E to him—a lustful, tender flick.

* * *

"Can you please tell me—why you like me?" Young whispered in Erena's ear. He was starting to feel twinkly and gelatinous, with no fear of the black hole above that was draining the stars.

"*What?* Kiss my neck again. Felt good." Erena responded, sloe-eyed and in slow motion, becoming the cosmic sloth of comeliness.

"*WHY DO YOU LIKE ME?*" Young hollered. He planted his feet and stood motionless in the middle of the wriggling mass of limbs and torsos, pulling her close, his hands tracing the shape of her small, soft shoulders.

"*Because you try. Because you care. Because you listen to me. Because you are so sure—and totally clueless. Because you are a little boy—and yet strong. Because you love my brain, and I'm not just a physical distraction. Because you make me study and want me to do well and succeed. Because you think about the future, and that excites and scares me. Because you don't realize you are handsome and smart—and you wouldn't care, even if you had a clue. Because you are in the world, but not of the world. You soak it in and want to share the joy you find, even if you are snobby and particular about it. And you are so adorably dorky—that it hurts me in here—andhereandhere. And I've lost track of time and of life and of the galaxy, of the cosmos. I don't know if this is what love is supposed to feel like, but I can't deny that I feel something. And I'm scared that this could be love. And I'm scared that this isn't love. And the way you look at me makes me think you might love me already—but you feel we might not make sense together. But don't we fit so strangely right—like a key and lock? And I want you to hug me and put your chin on my head and let me nuzzle into you, because that's my favorite.*"

All Young could understand: *Because. Totally clueless. Snobby. Dorky. Scared. Because.*

* * *

Hours later, when the effects of the MDMA wore off and two extra-large blue Gatorades were sloshing around in their queasy, empty bellies, Young and Erena made their way to the Moonlight Diner.

Waffles and greasy sausages, clinking bottomless mugs of black coffee—Erena beatific, a permanent grin of self-satisfaction: "Everything I guaranteed and more, *yeahhuh?*"

"You did it, girl. Best birthday ever," Young agreed, popping a bite of maple link into Erena's mouth.

"Fuckin'-A right, babycakes! More, more," Erena barked, pointed to her mouth.

Arm slung over Young's shoulder, Erena kissed his neck, nipped at his slow pulse—breathing in the smell of sweat, cigarettes, the last hints of his shaving cream.

She closed her eyes and let him lead her by the small of her back down the familiar route to the residence hall. He paused to take in her drowsy-lidded beauty, the sun barely edging its way behind gray stone and crumbling brick, the grunt and bluster of the M8 bus creeping beside them.

He studied the long fake eyelashes, smudged violet mascara, alluringly askew pink wig, those lovely chapped lips, and made a wish: *This is the year I grow braver, the year I get to be better. This is the one I should be better for.*

* * *

A half tub of Vaseline and a few days later, Erena embraced her new look.

"This is legitimately goth, right? Dark, dark jet black—hint of purple. It will wash out and I can try something else later, but I wanted to give you a thrill first. You like it? Got you all hot and bothered? What if I push my boobs together like Elvira? Horny for me? Want me to pretend I'm a vampire and give you a hickey?"

"It's more punk rock than anything. It does look really good, it frames your face well. Does it still itch though?"

"I talk about my sweet tits, and you ask about my scalp condition. Way to kill the mood, Dr. Dingus."

"You are a rare beauty, and I am blessed to be in your presence. I am concerned about your well-being and comfort level. What I consider really attractive is when a young lady doesn't have to rub her cranium constantly and peel off layers of dead skin."

"And that's why you are the 'official boyfriend.' I am not regretting this recent upgrade."

"I am very lucky to have a gorgeous girlfriend. And given time, it appears she has healing powers comparable to those of Wolverine, *grrrr*—capable of regenerating a healthy, luxurious head of hair!"

"*Wait, wait.* Gina said you had a thing about hair. Is this it? Some weird hair fetish? I don't know if I'm into it—"

"*The hair thing.* Gina and her big mouth—*ugh*! Not the same, but let's say, I can relate to what you've been through."

"Do I want to know? A tale for a rainy day?"

"It's going to have to rain sometime."

Third Love: "Hysteria"

1988–1989

Soundtrack highlights:
- "I Can't Wait"—Nu Shooz
- "What's on Your Mind (Pure Energy)"—
  Information Society
- "Forever Young"—Rod Stewart (and also the other
  one by Alphaville)

Everything seems more, *more*. Maybe it's the hormones or the few extra inches, the exponential sprout of fuzz on the ever-growing expanse of your body? Maybe it's just time that you were becoming a *person*? You are constantly in some form of pain: physical, emotional, spiritual—it manifests itself in your entire person-hood. You worry, you fret—most of the time, all of the time.

Worst of all is your adherence to your "system of good times" (as in actual hour-and-minute times, not a reference to that fun sitcom or general happy occasions).

Your Sony DREAM MACHINE digital clock and Casio calcula-tor watch are extreme sources of anxiety. You can't pinpoint when or where it began, but you cannot make any forward motion un-less the time adds up to an approved integer or otherwise displays a nonthreatening sign. Henceforth the mantra of the moment, the prime directive: you must receive the "sum of a good num."

7:11 is a great time to get out of bed. 7 and 1 and 11 are all GOOD. $7 + 1 + 1 = 9$, one of your favorite numbers (*duck bill, index, index, crooked index—"the Chinese way"*). Hence, up you rise to face the day with confidence that you will survive and thrive.

If you happen to wake at 7:06, you panic and shut your eyes until it passes. Your personal methodology dictates that 7:06 (a.m. and p.m.) is the worst time of day: digits that add up to the dreaded 13—but even worse, it equates to the *"Number of the Beast."* Based on your rationale: 7:06 is really six o'clock and sixty-six minutes, the triple six: what Iron Maiden warned you about, why you are glad you've never met a kid named Damien, why you hate black cats, goats, and snakes (even if, after all, they are also God's creatures).

On the other end, 8:08 is the best time ever (*finger gun, zero, finger gun—"the Chinese way"*). Since you were little, you knew the number 8 had special significance. Chinese people wanted everything in 8s. The explanation was that *ba*, the word for "eight" (also, a tone away from the word for "dad") sounds close to *fa*, the Chinese word for "rich"—or, technically, "grow." Superstitious and completely irrational, yes. But the more 8s you see around you, the more you welcome them into your subliminal and liminal patterns.

The smooth curves of the number 8, the infinite track looping perpetually, the portly belly shape of the digit—it is wholly satisfying, in a purely aesthetic sense. And 8 sounds like "ate"—and what are you but fearful of being hungry? (Bah and Ma used to scour the couch to find change for slices of pizza to feed their hungry, picky three-year-old. This is murder on your soul—gratitude in how things have improved.)

8:08 and everything's great! Bang, OH, bang! The unmatched joy of catching the very moment when those digits light up: clock or watch—digital, not analog. (Analog watch hands mean next to nothing, but might have eased your "timefears" if you had spent the actual effort looking for relief, rather than doing all the combat math in your head.) You savor those sixty seconds of the symmetrical sigil—declaring, consecrating that all is *safeandpureandgoodandholyandwell*.

8:08 is God's pristine minute of sanctuary. A moment for the good boy you try to be, that you hope He sees in you, despite your faithless little heart. You strain to hear Him speak in the pauses between heartbeats, in the flutter of wings knocking against the window. You ask for some silent reassurance through the divine math of the world, living in your head. You pray that this burden is something you don't have to carry by yourself—the one you struggle to hide, the one you fight to soothe.

Bang on, oh, bang on.

* * *

The morning of April 29, 1988, you wake to the news that you are officially a big brother—*guh guh*. Su Su, bleary-eyed but cheerful, says he'll pick you up from school later to head over to the hospital.

"First: breakfast sandwiches and hot chocolate—and then we can have a chat," he says. You run into Bagels n' Dream, fist clutching a ten-spot. (He always lets you keep the change—except that one time he gave you a hundo for gum. You said he was going back on his deal. He laughed and took a piece of Hubba Bubba, let you keep a twenty.) He parks across from the schoolyard. You have thirty minutes to scarf down a sesame and cream cheese before homeroom.

"It's a big day, Young. Everything is going to change for all of us. She's going to be *it*. Your one and only *mei mei*. No matter who else comes into your life, you will love her more than anything and anyone. You'll have a bond that no one can ever sever. Fights and disagreements, for sure. She may kick you in the balls, and you'll try to pull out her hair—or maybe not, since you're so much older. You might say you hate each other and argue, but it's all love in the end." Su Su slurps his deli coffee. You nod in agreement, even if you have your doubts—at least about the fighting. (*That's what Paris is good for.*)

"This is probably the last one. Unless your parents continue to *do sex* and make another one. Gross, right? *Eh xin?* So lucky to have two! Such a great boy, and I'm sure she's going to be the best girl. That's the dream: *yi ge nan, yi ge nu*—one of each." Su Su rolls down the window and lights up a cigarette. He's quiet for a minute—inhales, blows out thick streams of smoke. "Off to class! We'll roll out to Mount Sinai at 3:00 sharp—have to avoid the traffic! Big day, Young Gun! Love you!"

* * *

You'll always remember this visit: the chilly room with gauzy white curtains, the plastic cup of peaches that Ma saved for you, the un-eaten meat loaf on the slide-away tray. Bah, slouching and sleeping soundly in the lounge chair. He's been so tired for months—all that extra gardening work, all the nurture and care for the small frame of your mother, helping her grow their seed to fruition. Ma, in a white hospital gown with blue and green dots—her dark-black hair up in a messy bun, no makeup on but ever so beautiful. She sounds exhausted when she lifts an arm and beckons you over, calling you her *guai, bao bei.* You've never seen her smile so weak and yet so warm. She pulls you close. You hug and kiss her like you haven't since you were small.

Bah lifts your baby sister up from the bassinet and offers her to Su Su to hold. Su Su waves him off and motions to you—*Young first. Guh guh, xian.*

You sit down in the large chair, and Bah brings her over. You hold your breath. "Ten fingers, ten toes—perfect. No need to count, *guh,*" Su Su says and gives your ma a shoulder squeeze and kiss. "*Hao chou, do shi yan wei!*" Ma complains that her brother smells like smoke but tolerates his affection, welcomes it with a wry smile.

You're nervous and uneasy, on the verge of self-comforting

counting, but Bah is there to reassure you. He slips a pillow under your arm, lays your sister down gingerly, and she meets her big brother. You cradle her carefully, your right arm locked at the elbow, hand supporting her neck. She makes smacking noises and coos. She opens her brown eyes, and you feel like your heart can't take it—can't take this rushing warmth.

You're hers. She's yours. A forever bond. This love would never fade and would only get stronger.

Bah and Su Su recline on Ma's bed—make her the filling in their human sandwich. She leans her head on your father, then switches over to her brother. They watch as you fawn over this pint-size parcel and rejoice in their collective glowing pride. Their two *bao bei*— two precious treasures—doubling, multiplying their happiness.

"Is her English name really going to be Janine, like I suggested? Like Annie Potts's character from *Ghostbusters*?"

"Yes. We like the sound of the name—don't care about the movie. And we are calling her *Mei*—as in 'beautiful'—as in '*Meiguo*,' the 'beautiful country' that we Chinese call the USA. Also as in 'the month of May'—but she came a few days early! *Aiya!* April! And of course, she is your *mei mei*. We are always too complicated with names in our family. Never straightforward or simple—right, 'Su Su'? Can this one properly call you 'Xiao Jiu Jiu'?" Ma says, giving her brother a poke in the gut.

"Hell, no. We're sticking with Su Su!" You sputter and get shushed—stern looks from Ma for language and volume. Mei looks up at you, almost smiling. You love this.

* * *

Ma's metabolism is incredible. She's thinner now than before her pregnancy, constantly on the move. She has become the face of small business interests in Flushing. People look up to her, and she must keep up appearances: *If I can have one piece of chocolate a day, I will be happy!*

She powerwalks laps around the park every morning, clad in Lycra, talking to herself, cycling through her cavalcade of facial expressions, practicing her speeches in syncopation with her madwoman waddle. The attention she gets (*your mother!*) from the gawking sanitation crew and retirees makes you squirm in your skin.

Bah is doing well. He's even increased your allowance significantly, *fifty dollars a month!* You're grateful for this extra windfall, but you're puzzled at how he can afford it, especially with the added expense of your new baby sister. Bah tells you not to worry: *You are a good son—so* nen gan *and smart. You've been studying hard, starting junior high—praise God and have some fun.*

Bah's real pride is his tomatoes (backyard), his herbs (fresh basil, rosemary), and his potted flowers on the rooftop terrace (begonias, geraniums). He relishes every sunset he can spend with his hands in the dirt, his daughter napping sweetly beside him in the orange-and-red light of dusk.

You are getting used to having your uncle around all the time. When you were growing up, Su Su would visit a few times a year with armloads of presents from his business trips (*Ultraman from Japan! Monkey King figures from Beijing! Bootleg He-Man toys from Vietnam!*). He was always dressed in a suit and tie, shiny shoes, shinier hair. He spent most of his time on airplanes, but when he had to call someplace home, it was somewhere in California. But now he's here.

While Ma is getting ready for her events and shuffling from room to room in a tight *qipao*, Su Su takes the colicky baby from her with the ease of a magician's assistant. He handles your sister like a football or a raw chicken. He's dexterous and can read her emotions and needs like an empath (*just like Raven from the Teen Titans*). Bottles are always at the ready, at the perfect temp. Diapers and wipes—Mei is systematically poopy to clean in forty-five seconds. She is naturally smitten with your uncle.

Su Su sings Mei power ballads ("Open Arms," your favorite) and runs the faucet: the sound of running water helps calm her down.

Bah (on light percussion) shakes the jasmine tea in its golden canister. Your two male role models duet in the kitchen to tame the savage beastling.

Su Su mixes in with the righteous and the wicked. He often has coffee on the porch with Pastor Chen, and you hear them laughing loudly, catching up, thinking on their youth together. Your uncle has a steady procession of people (mostly from church) looking for help. He spends hours talking to them in the backyard, pacing, and writing notes for them in Chinese with English translations. You see young and old blessing him in Mandarin and thanking him in every other dialect they can muster.

You also catch a few ladies hustling out of the backyard—often while you are brushing your teeth in the morning. The squeak and whine of hinges are unmistakably from Su Su's basement bachelor pad entrance. You catch Ma smacking him hard in the arm and yelling at him for having another *lah mei*, another hot chick, over. He laughs heartily like a Mongolian invader and blows fart sounds on her cheeks. (He also does this to you and your sister. You love this.)

Your uncle is very good with his hands. You find him often without "proper clothes" on and more and more in ratty old concert T-shirts (KISS, Fleetwood Mac, the Eagles). Half the week, he's working at Uncle Tang's garage over in College Point. He comes home slathered in grease, smelling of Marlboros. He's cheerful for the most part, but you often see him from your window—sitting in a lawn chair and staring at the tomatoes, Bud Light gripped tightly, wiping the tears from his eyes with what clean real estate he has left on the back of his hands.

* * *

Paris is still your best friend, even if your interests are starting to take divergent paths. You both give Dungeons & Dragons a go, but the horrifying demons and the scary slew of possible number combinations from twenty-sided dice makes you queasy. He really gets into hip-hop (Public Enemy, N.W.A.) and newfangled Rollerblading instead. You try once and fall on your ass, teeth reverberating with the impact to your spine. You never put on blades again. Paris rolls infinite circles around you. He makes fun of the "White boy, sad boy" music and the "boring art-snob movies" you love. Your middle ground: you both love Ozzy Osbourne and *Xanadu*.

At the close of September, Gina Villanueva arrives and changes everything. She went to PS 109 and is one of the "new kids." Though really, you are all new at JHS 215, but your loyalties lie with the recognizable PS 121 faces. These "not-us-es"—well, you still don't know if they picked their noses, shat themselves, or vomited. You have no previous collateral/intel on these peripheral punks. You don't know if they are *actually* better than you or just *think* they are.

Gina, however, seems like a good egg. She helps Paris with his science labs and is headed for honors in all her Regents. Not only is she smart, she's got the lock for the lead in the fall play. No one is going to outdance her Janet Jackson moves or outsing her Sade vocals. You are jealous. *Ugh. She's a star.*

Paris suspects that Gina might have a touch of Indian in her. But she brings you *pan de sal* from a bakery in Corona and invites you both over to meet her cousins from Manila. She's Filipina. (It comes up that her parents speak a little Chinese because Gina's grandparents were houseworkers in Shanghai back in the '40s. When they talk with you in perfect Mandarin, you feel ashamed.)

Your growing bodies are insatiable. You are always eating, snacking, munching. Paris can't get enough pork—marinated, fried, grilled, roasted. He's over at the Villanuevas', gorging himself. The three of you gather to study, and it's pork rinds and Orange Crush at the House of Wang. Paris, though from a nice Catholic family (and who never turned down a cheeseburger), rarely dines on swine. Between your beloved *ti pang* and Gina's *adobo* pork, Paris is in piggy paradise.

Sometimes you think Gina is making kissy faces at you—you find her puckering and moving her lips. She hits you, snarls, and sticks her hand out for Jolly Ranchers instead. You soon learn that Filipinos often point with their lips, raise their eyebrows to say yes—all this silent, confusingly amorous communication. You think there is too much potential for misunderstanding. Yet you love this.

Veck Park is the center of the isosceles triangle between your three houses. On weekends, you play handball and watch Gina practice her dance moves by the courts. Inevitably, the older boys (much, much older) try to "kick it" to G. Harassment hazards for your ma and now for your new best friend—this place is a physical and emotional obstacle course for the women in your life. (Years later, you will realize that women deal with this *everywhereeverydayeverywhen*.)

Ma is oblivious to the lecherous men who salivate over her, but for Gina, it is more direct. Watching her deal out withering glances and fire off snarky remarks is a master class in emasculating these overly confident glandular misfits: *I don't talk to anyone who can't control their own bowels—and you smell like shit.* You never worry about her. She is a star.

* * *

You are obsessed with Robert Smith and company, Morrissey and Marr, and Gahan and Gore. You spend hours ruminating on their obtuse Anglo references and overanalyzing their overly clever lyrics— how these pasty British men sing of a life through jangly guitars with jutted-jaw irony, and somehow manage to reflect your preferred, parallel worldview: *repressed, depressed, well-dressed.* The chimes in "Pictures of You" give you chills. You fantasize of sneaking a kiss under an iron bridge. The spark of the engine and the windshield-wiper metronome of "Stripped" conjure up a petrol wasteland far too romantic compared to your semi-suburban Queens quotidian. You are intrigued but feel stupidly sheltered. You wish you were cooler. You wish you had more black clothing. You wish you had better things to observe and report on.

You entertain the idea of sending a mixtape to Wendy in Shanghai. Ma is delighted that you've continued your youthful cultural exchange, but she doesn't think it's worth the postage to even attempt it: *She won't like that crycry music you listen to! They have Michael Jackson over there and that's enough! Why don't you tell her you appreciate Beijing opera? You like it when I play the old tapes? Yes? Yes? Ask Wendy to tell you about some nice Chinese pop music, some Chinese history. Yes? Yes?*

You stick to the standard letters and tell her about church camp (*ticks everywhere and they had an archery range*). You ask if they were allowed to worship God in China (*you had heard things*). You describe live baseball games at Shea and how an enormous apple pops out of a giant top hat when the Mets hit a home run. You mention the new Vietnamese restaurant in Elmhurst and how you could eat pho every day of your life. You tell her that maybe one day, she could visit Meiguo and see all of this herself. You don't inquire about any Chinese stuff. You figure that if she (or the PRC) wants to push any propaganda, you'll get it without asking.

You send her a picture of you with Paris at Great Adventure: you are tan, wearing neon-green sunglasses and a *Yo, Joe!* T-shirt. Your arm is around your best bud: both flashing peace signs / Vs for Victory, posing in front of Lightnin' Loops.

Wendy sends you a short letter in reply. The gist of it: her dad got a big promotion, and she had a nice summer traveling. She includes a few pictures: from Tokyo, when they went to see the Yomiuri Giants play; from a Malaysian jungle resort, where she got to handle reptiles and eat some spiny exotic fruit.

You wonder if Communist Red China is reading your private exchanges sent from the *land of the free, home of the brave—good ol' Meiguo*. You keep things light and describe noncontroversial (but American) things: the weather in New York (*predictable*), the food (*hamburgers, hot dogs, apple pie*), the latest fashion (*Vision Street Wear, Champion*)—just enough without seeming like you are overtly chanting "USA! USA!"

She writes back in perfect English and describes her trip to Marseille and London in great detail: cloudy skies (*never full downpours*), freshly baked baguettes and scones (*merci, cheers*), her cool Beatles T-shirt from Camden Town. She includes a picture of herself in front of the Houses of Parliament: pink-rimmed glasses, big puff of hairspray-styled hair, red plaid pants, an oversize shirt with Paul, John, George, and Ringo ambling through a crosswalk on it. You can't help but be filled with envy. She is in such close proximity to your heroes. She could model *depeche mode* for Depeche Mode, could be maudlin for Morrissey, sorrowful for Robert Smith. You ask Ma how they can afford such amazing trips, be allowed such freedom— "Oh, Xia Su Su does computers." You wonder if maybe he's a spy.

You notice that Wendy has gotten tall. Not a spot of red or oil on her smooth face. Her poise and pose in these pictures flaunts the fact that she *just does this all the time*. This one is from Rome in front of the Coliseum—the actual arena where gladiators fought and died. Gelato melting in her hand, her lithe figure in the foreground of the ancient structure—you feel a sharp twinge of jealousy, but mostly you just want to watch the Mets at Giorgio's with some *real New York pizza* and a lemon ice.

* * *

You decide to stop buying comic books. *It's time to grow up.* You need to save your pocket money to hang out with the other kids at Starshine Diner, get matinee tickets at Cineplex Odeon. Your red envelope money is for Z Cavaricci pants, Fido Dido T-shirts, the latest Nikes or Reebok Pumps. You need to use your allowance wisely. Maybe meet a special girl and buy her some flowers, a stuffed bear. *Action figures are for children. Comic books are for babies.* You will yourself to believe this, however long it lasts. A pause on the things that delight you, in the pursuit of new pleasure.

* * *

Cross Bay Video is your Friday-night fix of choice. You don't mind biking down Union Turnpike by yourself. *The Princess Bride* becomes one of your favorite movies. (You've rented it so many times that the clerk asks if you just want to buy a used copy. You consider it but keep your options open.) You love the alternate universe where Columbo tells Kevin Arnold a bedtime story and André the Giant is a gentle hero (*but you still want him to chokeslam someone*). You think Billy Crystal and Carol Kane are national treasures. You repeat the Inigo Montoya line to yourself ad nauseam but never dare say it aloud, for fear something might happen to your father. You are a little disconcerted when you realize that Westley is slightly more beguiling than Princess Buttercup, though you are firm in your heterosexuality—*for the most part? Could it be? Inconceivable!*

Sometimes you go without Paris or Gina; it's nice to get a break from them overriding your selections. You rent *The Elephant Man* and are shocked that this is the same director who made *Dune*. You pick up movies with subtitles (in black-and-white) and without any machine guns or ladies with big boobies on the cover. People speak in foreign accents, and not everyone gets a happy ending, not everything makes sense. You see the world outside of Queens, outside of "THE CITY"—monsters and mayhem everywhere and everywhen. The humans are worse than the aliens, both the intergalactic and intercontinental kinds. Things are scary enough in New York—why ever leave? Maybe it's enough to *observe, rewind, return, repeat.*

* * *

Winona Ryder is the epitome of loveliness. She's been occupying your thoughts, ever since the one-two punch of *Beetlejuice* and *Heathers*. Her dark, dark hair and pale, pale skin—so alabaster perfect in her dewy-eyed winsomeness, so nonchalantly sexy but tough, so perky yet goth (you bet she likes Erasure *and* Joy Division, too), the antiestablishment punk girl of your dreams. And so close to looking Japanese but still definitely Caucasian.

(Years later, you discover in fanzines that you weren't the only Asian boy who fell hard for Winona Ryder. Her real-life anime features were crushworthy throughout the Far East and beyond. When she gets engaged to Johnny Depp, you realize that you wish him no harm. You think: *Makes sense. You've matured.*)

But for every Phoebe Cates, every Meredith Salenger, every Jennifer Connelly—for every new future cinematic ingenue crush in the big-eyed-brunette, pallid-complexioned vein—it's still Winona forever (née Winona Laura Horowitz). And she isn't the only cute Jewish brunette who will win your heart in '88–'90. (Other than Kitty Pryde, who will always have a place.)

* * *

You dream of David Lynch, Rob Reiner, and Tim Burton. In the dream, the three of them are in a diner, having coffee and doughnuts and playing some sort of game. You recognize them by their hairstyles: Lynch with his rockabilly fist of a coif, Burton with his dark wizard's mane, and Reiner with his delightful dad-ish cueball.

They alternate rolling fistfuls of dice and hollering gleefully. They are playing a board game, but you can't make out which one, and none of the rules make sense. You can't tell who is winning or who is losing. You approach the table, and they turn to you:

RR: *Oh, hello. I didn't see you standing there. I'm Rob Reiner. You know me from* This Is Spinal Tap, Stand by Me, *and your current favorite,* The Princess Bride. *You never did like* All in the Family *(not really the target demographic), but it's me—Meathead! I done good, yeah? Hey, let me introduce you to my friends—*

DL: *David Lynch, here!* The Elephant Man AND Dune! *(No* Blue Velvet *for you, not yet!) Nice to meet you, young man! What a firm handshake! Would you care for a nice hot cup of joe, or perhaps a fresh glazed old-fashioned? It's not exactly the highest quality stuff, but Tim here sure seems to like it.*

TB: *Actually, the coffee is pretty good. It's black. It's hot. But more importantly, it's dark and it has a wry sense of humor, like my films—* Beetlejuice, Pee-wee's Big Adventure, *and you are already about* to wet yourself over my Batman film. Trust me, Michael Keaton IS Bruce Wayne. And you know about Kim Basinger. So, you've got a thing for blondes as well. What do you think about Winona as a blonde in my next film? That will give you the best of both worlds—Betty AND Veronica. By the way—YAHTZEE.

RR: Yes, we know about all of it! You with the blondes and brunettes, the Leia one, then the Chinese one, and—just so many choices! So many lovely ladies to steal away your heart! And, uh, sorry about that Cary Elwes curveball. He is undeniably a very pretty man. It's a confusing time for you now! Who are you attracted to? ASIAN LADIES? LADIES THAT LOOK KIND OF ASIAN BUT ARE NOT? GAY? STRAIGHT? IF, AND, OR, BUT! You could have it all—or a combination, permutation! There's all sorts of peculiar goings-on in your mind and body that you'll just have to figure out. Here, you know who knows strange—David, you tell the boy. And by the way, DO NOT PASS GO, YOU GO STRAIGHT TO JAIL!

DL: Oh, darn it! You got me there, Robbie! Next time I'll sink your battleship! So, Young—may I call you Young? I understand that you've been feeling things that may excite and frighten you. Remember how scared you were of John Merrick, the "Elephant Man"? How he was terrifying to look at, like a monster—but was such a gentle, intelligent man who believed in God? And then all the horrors in Dune? How the Baron's pus and the alien creatures made you feel all slimy inside? How Sting was so cool and how you love the Police—but he was the villain in the film, and you were glad he got his throat slit? And seeing him with his shirt off also made you feel weird? And remember that sliver of bare thigh from the Queen-lady when she was captured? All the feelings you feel—from head to toe! The contradictions, juxtapositions, and complexities! Disgust and attraction! Faith and sin! All at the same time!

TB: Yes. All that David said. No limits to what you could be open to right now. It's time to experiment, explore, experience. And there you go, down the chutes and up those ladders again.

DL: Exact-a-mundo!

RR: *What my good buddies are trying to say, Young, is that junior high school and these early teenage years—it's going to be perplexing and not what you expect. You are not in control of all of 'THIS,' which is 'your body,' along with 'THAT,' the rest of you—your mind, your heart, your soul. Everything's in a perpetual state of chaos (pronounced: KAY-oss). You may not have the high drama of finding a dead body on the side of the railroad tracks, but your bumps in the road are going to feel like the end of the world anyway. So, chin up. Roll the dice—and it's OK to sometimes get a "scary 6" or a "frightening 4." Relax—you'll get another turn soon enough. Roll with the punches.*

DL: *And another thing, my Young Friend (or Fiend, if you prefer)—you can flip through the* Playboys *when you go to the barber with Paris. I know, I know—you love your* Movieline, Entertainment Weekly, *and* Rolling Stone. *But when you are among men in the sanctity of the scissor-and-straight-razor ceremony—you can take a peek at those boobies. And they come in all shapes and colors and sizes! The globe is filled with glorious, gorgeous gals—and their globes! It's OK to look and like. It's normal! Here, see this is the latest Playmate of the Month! Kelly something-or-other! Look at those cans! Look at those gams! It's natural! It's all a part of LIFE!*

RR: *Yes, the game of LIFE! Huzzah!*

TB: *Pink and blue—adding those little rods in that boxy white car—that's starting to look like your general strategy in the game of LIFE. (Unless you go the "blue / blue—Sting / Cary Elwes" route—but you may need to amend your rule book then.) And when LIFE gives you lemons, you make lemonade, and it's yellow like pee. And here you go with that "morning salute" again and—*

ALL: *TIME TO WAKE UP! YOU RUINED ANOTHER PAIR OF UNDERWEAR THAT YOU'LL HAVE TO SNEAK INTO THE LAUNDRY AGAIN—BECAUSE THAT'S NOT PEE OR POO OR PUS—IT'S SOMETHING ELSE, IT'S SOMETHING WORSE! HOLY CANNOLI, BATMAN! LOOKS LIKE YOU TAKE YOUR COFFEE WITH CREAM-OF-SOME-YOUNG-GUY!*

* * *

Jennifer Coscarelli and Melinda Giannopoulos do everything together. Both the same height (5'3"), same body type (skinny with flat
butts), and they both like the same things: New Kids on the Block
(Joey), *Dirty Dancing* (Swayze), Kipling backpacks (brown), assorted
hair metal bands (too many), and lanyard crafts (bracelets).

Melinda is a 100% Greek beauty with sky-blue eyes and a frizzy
flow of brunette locks. She is a mediocre gymnast and an above-
average volleyball player.

Jennifer is a self-professed "pizza bagel": an Italian father, Jewish
mother. (*Does that make you a boring "egg roll"?*) She is stunning—
smooth jet-black hair and large, almond-shaped jade-green eyes. She
could give Winona Ryder a run for her *otaku* adoration.

But her mouth is full of gleaming braces. Her penchant for high,
whooping laughs and snorts is just unattractive enough to disqualify
her from the "Top Hottest Girls List of JHS 215." (That elite tier is
unequivocally comprised of: Krystal Henson, Shannon Gould, and
Raylene Vigneron. Blondes who like the same things: New Kids on
the Block [Jordan]; *Dirty Dancing* [Baby]; Manhattan Portage [mes-
senger bags only—no backpacks]; assorted hair metal bands; and
absolutely no crafts.)

You stare at the back of Jenny's head and admire her straight,
silken tresses—more Asian-looking than Dana Shum's red-and-
purple-streaked headbanging nest. She smells like Pert Plus, baby
powder, and mint.

Jenny asks you for Tic Tacs (Wintergreen) every day. *Constantly.*
You think she has a fear of bad breath due to all the riot gear in her
mouth, but she's likely just a sugar fiend. But if she wants to maintain an aura of freshness around her, you will contribute to it gladly.
Palm open and eyes blinking at you—kooky grin and then that devastating wink. *Pop, clack.*

Jenny lets you borrow her new Aerosmith tape. You record *Good
Morning, Miss Bliss* (aka *Saved by the Bell*) for her on Saturday mornings

when she has cello lessons. She helps you with math problems. You help her with social studies. You bring her a moon cake to try, she brings you rugelach—and you both spit out the analogous sweets and laugh. You are friends.

Jenny's bat mitzvah will be the party of the year. It's in March, but she's been outlining all the details since the previous summer. She claims to have learned her haftorah by osmosis—listening to the reading on her Walkman while she whittled wood and painted in gouache at Shalom Yeladim Camp, the premiere Jewish summer camp for the arts, in the heart of the Poconos.

Not everyone in the class is going to be invited. She's got friends in the other homerooms, from out of state (*as far as Maryland*). It's going to be *selective*. And not every Jewish kid at JHS 215 is going to go either (the intricate politics of scheduling: venues, rabbis, caterers, competing weekends).

"You simply can't go to every bar/bat mitzvah—there would be too many! You've got to pick and choose and commit. Mine is going to be the best. It's going to be a rock and roll theme! A night full of surprises! Save the date, *Angus Young*! You swear?"

She can't wait to turn thirteen. She'll be a *woman*.

* * *

You turn thirteen in January 1989. You are nowhere near as excited. In fact, you are terrified for so many reasons. The dreaded thirteen—one of the worst numbers in all of history. Unlucky "1–3," the year when you officially morph into a frightened and frightening teenager.

The morning of January 21st, you feel no different. It's a chilly Saturday morning, and Ma and Bah kiss their big boy awake. Mei Mei snuggles up to you and licks your cheek. Su Su slips you a hundo before he takes off for Uncle Tang's garage.

Ma wants to spend the entire day with you—just her and her sweet boy—but she also needs to get her hair blown out. Bah and

Mei Mei enjoy a lazy day at home, while Ma takes you for *xiao long bao* and *so mein* in Flushing. *(You must have long-life noodles, every birthday. Never, ever forget. Some type of noodle during the day. Any noodle.)*

After your favorite meal, you stop by Monster City Collectibles for a fat stack of comics (X-Men, Spidey, Batman) and, because it's a special day, even some baseball cards (Topps, never Donruss). No one needs to know about your secret superhero shopping spree. You'll be all grown up come Monday. *Promise.*

You haven't even opened the salon door fully before the nauseating chemical smell drags the ginger soy back up your throat. The ladies welcome Ma to sit under a clear plastic dome while Auntie Corrina paints her nails lucky red. The other Ai Yis, in fluorescent pink smocks, clap their hands and shout *sheng ri kuai le* to the birthday boy.

Auntie Corrina puts her cold, slender hands around your rosy cheeks. She pats them gently, solidly. She's pretty and smells nice. (And she'll end up wrecking Su Su's heart within the year.)

Ma excitedly tells you that the salon has a new process, something that all the *ming xing* in Taipei and Hong Kong are doing—*all the biggest stars!* Auntie Corrina has offered "the process" for free, a birthday treat. The other women in their tight floral leggings *ooh* and *ahh* and cheer you on. Even Mrs. Shu with the pink tints agrees. You'll be a *shuai guh*—a handsome devil, a cool dude—guaranteed to turn heads. What teenage Chinese boy doesn't want to be a *shuai guh*, the envy of Flushing, Queens?

The "process" is called a "body wave." It will make your hair curl gently, make it softer—*wavy*—like all the top Caucasian male celebrities' hair. You're used to stiff, prickly black hair (when it's buzzed short) or shiny, slick, and greasy straight (your baby bowl cuts). Your follicle foundation should get mellowed out, and you'll look like Richard Grieco and that suave sly dog, Winona-wooer Johnny Depp. You'll be proud to sport "White guy black hair": a swish of movement, some sexy softness—*just so*. You'll be surfing the *shuai guh* tide in no time.

Auntie Corrina takes you over to the porcelain sink. She has you recline back and guides your neck to the padded cutaway. She starts gently massaging at the temples, then gets rougher as the lather thickens around the lumpy crown of your head. (You try very hard not to look down her shirt, but you can't help it. *They're right there.*)

The pungent chemicals get worked into your scalp next—a stinging tingle. You start to worry when dozens of pink foam curlers and foil squares begin multiplying across the geography of your skull. Your glasses are on the counter: all you see in the mirror is a beady-eyed, blurry alien doppelgänger from Venus, the plastic and metal antennae poised to transform you into "irresistible human mating" mode—or so you hope.

An hour passes, and Auntie Corrina is beaming: time for the big reveal. She gives you the soapy scrub-down once more and wraps a towel turban-style around your head. She fluffs your damp hair, pats your ears, dries the back of your neck. The sensation is delightful.

The salon is silent. And then a tense chuckle, followed by hesitant bursts of *Aiya! Hao shuai!* You've been around your mother long enough to recognize this patronizing, friendly, deflecting Chinese tone. You know it's bad.

Auntie Corrina hands you your glasses. You look up at your reflection in the mirror, you hope against hope to meet a new and improved, handsome gaze, but you are puzzled instead. You look like Eddie Murphy in *Coming to America*—not when he is handsome Prince Akeem, but more like Randy Watson, lead singer of Sexual Chocolate. *You are letting your Soul Glo.*

You appear to have moist, tight dark ringlets—*it's a Number 8 special, a stir-fried, soy-sauced Jheri curl.*

Ma already sees that you are on the verge of tears or a screaming, shampoo-bottle-clearing tirade. No chance she'll let that happen in the heart of her kingdom, where this flock of squawking birds would scatter gossip from Sanderson Avenue to Bowne Street before the tinkling bell of the salon door even stopped chiming.

Ma shoves some bills over to a deflecting Auntie Corrina, invites her to stop by for tea. Auntie Corrina wants to hug you before you go, but you're already standing impatiently by the door, coat on and hood drawn tight. Not even one last glance at her cleavage could entice you from flying out a second later.

* * *

You storm into the house. Bah is snoring open-mouthed with Mei on his chest. You try not to wake them as you lock yourself in the bathroom.

You meet the red-tinged stare of this monstrous, otherworldly visage—your very own. (If anyone could bear the sight and understand your inner workings, they would find a gentle soul—well-read and God-fearing. *"I AM A HUMAN BEING! AND I NEED TO BE LOVED!"*)

You have at least fourteen, "1–4," "10 + 4" (!) months left to go on your leaden braces and gummy rubber bands. Your chunky, scuffed bottle-thick glasses are the most stylish Bah's health insurance will allow, and Clearasil can only do so much—and now these tense, wet black curls.

You crawl into the shower and pull your knees to your chest, let the water cascade over you. You crank on the radio—permanently tuned to 92.7 WDRE. You let Robert Smith's copacetic caterwauling drown out your sobs. Just you and the forgiving rain, washing away the sadness and despair. *Was this the cure or was it making it worse?*

Ma is used to hearing you weep in the shower after "getting to know yourself" and feeling especially sinful for thinking about your choir partner, Sondra Tseng, *while doing it.* You'd sniffle and pray for God's forgiveness for being so, so dirty. *Rain, rain, wash this sin away. Amen, amen.* Ma would bang on the door and yell, "God doesn't care about what you are doing to your *ji-ji!* Hurry up and get out of the bathroom! Ma needs her blow-dryer for the fundraiser tonight!"

You soak under the showerhead for an hour, hoping to at least loosen the resilient coils. Bah knocks, and you hear Mei patting the door with her pudgy hand. You towel off, exit. Bah hugs you through the steam. He tries hard not to laugh, and you try hard not to bawl on his shoulder.

Su Su has no such decorum. He bounds up the stairs to get a closer look, chortling the whole way. He says that with some hair grease you'll look like Danny Zuko getting ready for his date with Sandy. You huff and ignore him. Grease is *not* the word, and you feel no peace.

* * *

Pizza for dinner (sausage), presents (from Ma and Bah: *Mega Man II*, more comics, a fancy Texas Instruments calculator. From Su Su: Guns N' Roses' *Lies*, Tiffany's *Hold an Old Friend's Hand*, R.E.M.'s *Green*), and cake (chocolate from Vinnie's, not Chinese fruit cocktail from Yi Mei).

Ma lies down next to you and speaks softly. It's rare for her to do this now, and you reluctantly oblige. She apologizes, calls you her *guai guai, xin gan bao, nen gan de bao bei*. You beg her to take you back tomorrow after church and let Auntie Corrina shave your head. She laughs: "Do you want to be a monk from Shaolin Temple? Do you want to make Auntie Corrina cry after she spent her own money for all the chemicals?" You respond: *YES and YES*.

She strokes your cheek, whispers that it will be fine: "Trust your ma, she only wants what is best. Once it gets a touch longer, you'll like it—just give it more time. Let it change and grow—you'll see. You'll look just like John Cruise."

Your eyes feel heavy as you think about how *TOM* Cruise embodies all that is *shuai guh*—that dark hair, only a swift brush different from yours. *So cool flying those jets, fighting demon Tim Curry, sliding across the floor in underwear and socks.* But Tom Cruise never had your heinous complexion, never had your protruding paunch. Tom Cruise never had to worry about what the kids in Homeroom 733 thought of his "body wave."

Screw it. Let's just call a perm a perm.

* * *

Paris high-fives you the way a best friend should. "Happy birthday, bud. What's up with the hat, dude? You think you can break the rules now that you're officially a teenager?"

Gina saunters up behind you and perches her chin on your shoulder. She gives you a dance mixtape she made: mostly hip-hop (A Tribe Called Quest) and freestyle (George Lamond), because you'd never buy any for yourself. The Maxell tape cover is inscribed with her bubbly script, tagged in graffiti hearts in assorted Sharpie colors. She asks about the sudden display of baseball love. You lie and say it was a present from Su Su. She gives you a birthday hug and slaps your butt as you head to homeroom.

* * *

You will always remember this walk into homeroom on Monday, January 23, 1989, a royal-blue Mets cap snug on your head. "No headgear is allowed indoors, Mr. Wang," Mrs. Tobias reminds you. You reluctantly unveil.

The collective gasp of twenty-three seventh graders is a thing to behold. The sight of twenty-three hormone-filled bodies doing anything in unison is nigh impossible (the harnessed energy of that collective willpower over all those gangly limbs and pitch-shifting voices—*it could bridge divides, unite the world*). Twenty-three, "2–3" independently sleep-addled brains sharing the same electrical impulse of thought: *What the hell have you done to your head, Young?*

No one dares to laugh. It's a bona fide stunned, pregnant pause. It's obvious that you are uncomfortable. If anyone were to lift your chin up and look at your downturned face, they'd see the tears glistening in those small brown eyes. They would find you incoherently mumbling and chanting: *888, bangbangbang, 888, bangbangbang. Triple 8—wish my hair was straight.*

Jenny swats at your arm lightly and asks for some Tic Tacs.

She repeats it, and you pay attention. You shake them out into her hand, and she pops them in her mouth, as always. She smiles and does the unthinkable: she runs her hand through your hair—*slowly*.

A huge metallic grin spreads across her face. Her eyes widen into shiny, animated discs of delight. She hollers and whoops. She giggles like a maniac and plays with your ringlets, like a favorite black poodle. She *loves it*.

"So cute! It's fluffy! *So soft!*" she yells. Melinda looks at her, perplexed, as if she's finally agreed to disagree. But when Janet Wreath joins in, and Gina gives your curls a tug, and Teresa Lane takes a swipe through your mop top—Melinda succumbs and pets the classroom favorite. You witness her *"Seven Stages of Exploring Young's Hair"*: from initial disgust to tentative curiosity, inevitable resignation, brave discovery, surprised enlightenment, bewildered amusement, and finally—simple joy.

Jenny single-handedly helps win over the girls of Homeroom 733 to your side. *The circle is complete.* You, the human alpaca, are a thing of beauty (at least temporarily). And in this act of kindness, you fall hard for her that day.

* * *

It's mid-February, and the latest class scandal is that Jason Steinberg's bar mitzvah is on the same day as Jenny's bat mitzvah. Jenny and Jason didn't even go to the same elementary school—didn't even have the same friends. They never thought it would be an issue—*but it is now*. Just as battle lines and alliances are drawn for the last Saturday in March, the Steinbergs relent and bump out Jason's celebration to mid-April. It's unheard of, *unprecedented*. Jenny and Jason exchange invitations at the peace accords held in the lunchroom—dry burgers, soggy macaroni salad, and chocolate milk, the victory feast for all. (And yes, you can have chocolate milk in public now. *Junior high is a fresh start for everyone!*)

Though the opportunity has opened up for accepting multiple invites now, the respective guest lists don't change all that much. You and Gina are requested to attend both events. Paris, however, will be going only to the Windsor Club to enjoy Jason's mixed candy bar. (Apparently Jenny's not a fan of "your perverted pal.")

* * *

Mrs. Villanueva drives the three of you to Roosevelt Field for a Saturday of shopping and messing around. Paris gets Jason a Sam Goody gift card, and you do the same. Gina buys herself some white canvas Keds and gets Jenny a "super cute purse."

You walk into Spencer Gifts and find the perfect Bon Jovi T-shirt for Jenny. You also grab a wacky birthday card ("Time to Rock Out with Your Socks Out!") to house your parents' gift of a check for $90. (For Jews: 18 = Chai = Life. 18 × 5 = 90.) It gives you great pleasure how your parents know to engage in this culturally appropriate gesture (thanks to their Interfaith Coffee Club), and in such a generous, heavenly number of completion.

You spend the rest of the time in the food court with your friends: dabbing the oil off Nathan's fries (*doesn't do squat*, and the three of you still get pimples) and slurping down an extra-large chocolate peanut butter Oreo Häagen-Dazs milkshake, split three ways. You toss pennies into the stale indoor pool fixture. You yell "What's up" across the open atrium to Jared Garbowski by the Benetton. You stroll past the B. Dalton twice to get an extra glimpse of the cute cashier. You put Paris in a headlock just because he's your best friend (and *deserves it for being annoying*). You take G's hand and rush past some sketchy-looking high school guys. You window-shop and covet the promotional Batman movie posters at Suncoast Motion Picture Company. You start a rousing rendition of "Pour Some Sugar on Me" when you walk past the echoey closed-for-renovation Macy's Furniture Center. Gina sings harmony, and Paris stomps his feet to the beat. It's a perfect night. You love this.

* * *

You meet at 4:30 to board the chartered school bus (*ooh, fancy*) at Hilltop Jewish Center. Your classmates and some other kids from Jenny's Hebrew school and camp, all decked out in their very best. The hair spray alone could punch a hole in the ozone layer above Utopia Parkway. The girls: in overly poufy and glittery dresses. The guys: in ill-fitting suits, much too big for their unpredictable bodies. And you, much the same, but with your coif carefully combed and blow-dried out.

The ride out to *Lawng Aisland* is a fun precursor to the actual party: the bus has been outfitted with a boom box, and Jenny supplied a mixtape as the opening act to the festivities. When "You Got It (The Right Stuff)" comes on, all the girls sing the verses and the boys are obliged to do the *oh-Oh-oh-OhhhhhOhhhhs*. Gina elbows you in the ribs to make sure you are not complacent—*Do your dang duty and hang tough.*

The crisp, fresh air of Patchogue clears away the funk of Aqua Net, Drakkar Noir, and a bus teeming with hormones. You are thoroughly impressed with the venue, Giancarlo's by the Waterfront— marble floors, giant windows, dark wood fixtures, *right by the water,* like they say. You've only been to one wedding (Ma's cousin—*all the way in Maryland*) that would even remotely compare. *This must have cost a fortune.*

Jenny excitedly greets you bus kids at the door. You all jump in the line, ready for some big fun. She takes each of her friends in with a quick hug or handshake and shows them to the main hall, explaining that her haftorah was a breeze. Rabbi Levine thought her *dvar Torah* was the best he had heard in years. Her cheeks and lips are an adorable peachy-pink, and her eyelashes have been done up with mascara. She's a vision in her light-blue dress and black shoes, her dark hair pressed to an obsidian shimmer. When she smiles, you notice that all her solid-metal mouthgear is gone. Her teeth are perfectly aligned now and finally unencumbered—gleaming, in all their glory. She's a winning beauty.

It's your turn on the receiving line, and you are offered a quick hug. She smells like Pert Plus, Ivory soap—*heavenly*. Jenny whispers, "I hope you brought mints. I'm going to need them! I'm so nervous!" She smiles at you, and you feel like your feet might give out under the plush maroon carpet—*poof, splat*. (You think Tim Burton would use stop-motion animation to depict you getting swallowed up by the floor—bolo tie, shoulder pads, body wave, and all.)

Gina saves you from assured embarrassment. She swoops in and steadies you by the arm. You head over to the buffet tables for the hors d'oeuvres (pronounced: *ORR-durrverz*) and some crudités (pronounced: *CROO-dee-tays*) and other fancy nibbles. You witness the amazing ice sculptures: a Les Paul, a Stratocaster, a Rickenbacker, a full Pearl drum set. *This must have cost a fortune.* The shrimp cocktail and raw oysters encircle these frosty paeans to rock 'n' roll. You hear Sherri Weitz tell Hannah Stern, *This is definitely not going to be a kosher kind of night.*

* * *

The smoke machines pump clouds of liquid fog onto the checkered dance floor, and the colored spotlights start to spin. A buff dude in a rainbow-speckled bow tie with matching suspenders gets on the mic: "*Good evening, friends and family of the Coscarellis and Silvers! We are the Patchogue Party Patrol and I am your host, Jimmy Jay! That's Anthony and Ricky, there's Sasha and TJ! Are you ready to paaaaaaaarty with us? Get on your feet! Yes, especially you, Nana Davis at Table 2! Now, let's give a big hand and welcome the woman of the evening, the bat mitzvah beauty—Miss Jennifer Rebecca Danielle Silver Coscarelli!*"

Jenny struts out through the plume of smoke in a sequined black dress, her hair up in a side ponytail—like she's entering the ring for the main event. She's throwing up metal horns—*outfit change, attitude adjustment.* "Rock and Roll All Nite" plays, and the dance floor fills with young and old clapping along.

"We are going to need some strong men for this next part! Come gather around and we are going to hoist the lady of the hour up in the air to celebrate her big day!"

You watch as Jenny bounces around atop a chair overhead and gets paraded across the dance floor. You've never seen her so happy and jubilant. She's always fun and bright in class, but seeing her like this, you appreciate her beauty, her ease and grace—her confidence.

As you link arms and dance the hora, everyone's eyes are drawn to Jenny. She tosses her head back and laughs as she gets jostled around. She's whisked away clockwise and then counterclockwise: *WHOOOOOoOoooOO!* Her eyes sparkle nearly as much as her dress, as much as her freshly freed teeth.

The music changes into party-time dance mode. The expected circles form for the uncoordinated wiggling around. You join the 215 kids (the campers keep to themselves) to bop along to Salt-N-Pepa, Paula Abdul, and the obligatory "Celebrate" from Kool & the Gang. Jared tries to dance up on Melinda, and she shoves him away into Jason. Terence rips his pants, and Rita breaks a heel. Gina shows the Party Patrol her advanced moves. It makes you uncomfortable how the *boogiebuffmuscleboys* eye her undulations approvingly.

"It's that time of night. Are you ready for some COKE AND PEPSI?" You shrug and look around. The kids in the room divide into two groups. The adults hustle to their seats, afraid of the coming chaos (pronounced: *KAY-oss*).

COKE! Half the room runs to the other side as the remaining half takes a knee; the runners sit on their respective partners.

PEPSI! The reverse happens. The last ones get eliminated. You see Jason proudly present his knee to Jenny. She graciously sits while everyone else scrambles.

Jason tries to play it cool, but his face is turning reddish purple. You think he might have trouble standing—not for any discernible joint pain, but perhaps some other issue in the general vicinity of his pants.

* * *

You are trying your best two-step-and-slide dance moves with Gina when "Sweet Child O' Mine" comes on. Jenny snags you by the hand and pulls you to the center of the dance floor. You are speechless.

Jenny maneuvers your hands to her thin hips and places both arms around your neck. You inhale deep—no perfume, just the scent of her soap and shampoo, clean and lovely. You look into her eyes. She smiles shyly at you and whispers, "I've been looking for you all night."

"I've been right here—dancing poorly!" you joke, sheepishly. You sweat, profusely.

"Young, I need some mints, *pronto*. Just toss some in my mouth! I shouldn't have eaten those garlic mashed potatoes, but they were so good!" She blows hot air in your face—*hooh hooh*—and laughs. You approve of this. You welcome this. You love this.

You reach in your jacket pocket for the ubiquitous transparent box. You take her hand, turn over her thin white wrist, and pour out a dozen frosty green pellets, your fingers lingering on her pulse.

She looks you in the eye, as if to say something—then suddenly smacks her palm against her mouth. *Pop, clack.* You're the only one close enough to hear the tic-ing and tac-ing of the sugary freshness, but everyone can hear Jenny holler WHOOOOOoOoooOO! as Slash and company crescendo on the bridge of the #1 Billboard hit song.

Jenny flips your tie up into your face playfully. She spins around and puts an arm across your shoulder. She's hopping up and down in time to Axl Rose's yelps when you feel another arm around you. You look up to see a large ring start to form—expanding as the loop breaks and welcomes another thrashing seventh grader into this mosh-pit remix of the hora. You are disappointed that you don't get more alone time with Jenny, but this communal sing-along and gleeful huddle is something you'll remember forever.

The song fades, and Jenny's camp friends whisk her away. Before she disappears for another outfit change, she turns to you and winks. It's devastating. She takes aim and points her finger at you: "Thanks, dude! Best head of hair in 733!" *Bang, bang, bang.*

A puff exhaled across the tip of her finger, and Jenny blows you a wintergreen kiss. You blush rose-red. You want to shoot back, but keep your fingers tucked in your pleated pants. *Bangbangbang*, indeed.

* * *

The night concludes with slices of strawberry cake and personalized party favors: ceramic piggy banks in the shape of jukeboxes, with your names on them. Ties are loosened, shirts untucked, and shouts of *You don't have to go home, but you can't stay here!*

The bus driver stomps out his cigarette: "Your chariot awaits, ladies and gentledudes," he growls as you file in for the long ride back to Queens.

You settle into your seat next to Gina as the bus eases out of the parking lot. Most of the kids are still buzzed from the sugar and coed activity, but others have started snoozing. The boom box is quiet, the windows fogging up with the warmth of the collective soft snoring, bodies radiating postparty heat. The highway lights of the Long Island Expressway cast rolling shadows across the bus seats. You drift off in thought, with the low hum of adolescent whispers and snickers as your soundtrack.

We've been such good friends this year! She likes me for more than my candy supply! And her parents were so nice tonight. I'm sure they would like me if they got to know me! Ma always said that the closest people to the Chinese were Italians and Jews! Kitty Pryde and Zatanna! Jenny is both! Food and family—we'd have lots to talk about! We both love rock 'n' roll! We could go see Warrant or Poison this summer! We could double-date with Melinda and whoever she ends up with—maybe Paris has a shot! It's going to be great!

"I think I'm in love with Jenny," you force out in a barely audible monotone to Gina, and hope she doesn't hear your pummeling heartbeat.

"You and every other boy in here!" she hisses at you. "Did you see how those fake eyelashes made her eyes pop? Must have taken hours with a flat iron for that hair! She was gorgeous tonight— *GOR-GE-OUS*—I will give you that. *Whooo.* I think *I* might be in love, too! If it wasn't for Sean, I might seriously consider it. And her braces! You knew she was waiting to get those off after school on Friday! Talk about *D-R-A-M-A.*"

You sneer at G as she pokes you in the gut. *Whatever.* You look at your customized ceramic jukebox coin collector, emblazoned "'Angus' Young." You compare it to Gina's lame "Gina 'Van Halen-ueva.'"

You have a real shot at this. *Shot through the heart—and Jenny is to blame. Bangbangbang.*

* * *

Monday rolls around, and the class is buzzing about Jenny's party, but the real news is her bump up in status. The kick-ass celebration— along with the removal of her braces—equates to the unshackling of her true social potential. She gets invited to sit with Krystal, Shannon, and Rachel for lunch.

You try to play it cool through homeroom. When you tell Jenny you had a great time, she gives you a perfunctory "Heh-heh, thanks." She doesn't ask for Tic Tacs. Must be too busy soaking in compliments to be worried about her breath, riding high on the cresting wave of adolescent adoration. The sugar boost would be overkill at this point.

At lunch, you see Shannon and Krystal compliment Jenny on her hair: *So shiny and pretty.* Rachel asks her how it feels to no longer be

a *braceface*. You expect Jenny to snort and chuckle at all this attention, but she holds her cool: *No big whoop. They were bound to come
off sooner or later.*

You are proud of her—and yet you feel sad, feeling that things
are about to change.

Jenny approaches the snack counter, and you hop in the line
behind her. Before you can offer to buy her some welcome-to-
womanhood-butter crunch cookies, Jason slides next to her and
brandishes a dollar bill: *Two packs, please.*

Jenny seems unfazed by this sudden act of chivalry, as if Jason
does this kind of thing all the time. But you, your mind is spinning.

"What'll it be, hon?" Mrs. Lidell asks you. You get your cookies
and *two* cartons of chocolate milk—*all for yourself.*

Paris snatches your chocolate chippers and helps himself to one.
Stuffing the entire treat in his mouth, crumbs escaping, he says:
"Guess the cat's out of the bag." He motions over toward Jason—
Jason, who is now holding Jenny's hand. Melinda is leaning against
her new beau, Dylan, and is nodding her head in approval at what-
ever the other happy couple is saying to her.

Your heart drops to the pit of your stomach, and you feel the
sweat bead around your warm crown of black wool. You see Jenny
laughing, attractive and confident in the cafeteria, but not as ethereal
as she was in that dress nights ago. Still as approachable and friendly
in her favorite red Champion sweatshirt, matching red scrunchie,
and acid-washed jeans, but today she seems so far from you.

You walk over to Gina and her potato salad: "Turns out they've
been dating for almost a month! She wanted to keep it quiet until her bat mitzvah stuff was over. He didn't really care, but now
it's officially *on.* Barbwire-free making-out time, here we go!" She
mouths: *SORRY, BABYBOY.*

For a moment you want to chug some drain cleaner, wake up in
the afterlife. But you pause. And you feel—you feel *surprisingly OK?*
Next year, everyone will split up into different high schools anyway. This will be a memory. Just like 215 expanded your world with

other kids from the surrounding school district, in high school there will be lots of new cute girls coming from all over—*maybe even from Brooklyn, maybe as far as the Bronx.*

Later, it will hurt. It will take over a year for the Price Club bulk pack of candies to dissolve in your solitary onion mouth. You'll feel a stinging thorn of loss every time your friend crosses the room to talk to her boyfriend, instead of turning around to gossip about Jonathan Knight and Tiffany (*it will never last*), asking if Skid Row will go on tour (*definitely, if they finish the new album*). You'll think of her every time you look in the mirror at the tight black tendrils, slowly loosening and easing their grip on your self-esteem.

You conveniently catch the flu in April and don't go to Jason's bar mitzvah. Paris has the time of his life (*I got in half a fast dance with Rachel!*). He shows off his personalized sunglasses—*P. C.*—initials etched on the side in a macho font, *in flames*. You think: *Kids' stuff, for children and babies.*

* * *

You look at your reflection in the mirror and meet your gaze. You avert your eyes—examine the relaxing, rippled texture growing out of your scalp, the blemishes across your cheeks fading.

Was she in her bathroom combing her beautiful black hair, putting on eyeliner, checking to make sure there wasn't any lip gloss on her pearly whites? She must be excited to meet him at the Cineplex. They would hold hands and pretend they were mature, but neither close to feeling like a real man or a woman—even if the rabbi told them so. Did her heart skip a beat when she forgot to check her breath? Did she think of you when she put a stick of gum in her mouth, just before she gave him a minty kiss?

Jenny still jokes around with you, on occasion. You still make her mixtapes every now and then. You'll sign each other's yearbooks at the close of eighth grade and part ways—as friends.

It's her perfect smile that will remind you of these childhood memories: sweet children on the cusp of growing up and breaking free—ready to stop playing games but still wanting one more turn, one more loop around just the same.

She protected you when the truth was hard to face. She covered your head, anointed it with kindness. And it was a breath of fresh air—a blessing, *a mitzvah* when you needed it most. But you'll never get a chance to kiss her jewel of a mouth or press your tufted dome to her frail forehead and whisper, "Thank you."

This love was what it was, but it was never meant to last. But you'll remember.

She was your third. She will always be your third.

Su Su Special Delivery and Road Trip Revelations: Las Vegas

MAY 1994

On the breakfast table, an opened cardboard box: a pair of pink fuzzy dice; a plush Siegfried and Roy white tiger cub, a deck of Harrah's playing cards, and a bootleg VIVA LAS VEGAS! T-shirt with a cartoon Elvis in a karate pose; a bottle of red wine with "Tanya's (second) Bachelorette" on the label; and finally a photo with a letter paper-clipped to the back.

The photo:

Su Su is getting acquainted with the locals in Las Vegas. Drunkenly debonair in a tux, unbuttoned at the collar—bow tie hanging by its last, lost-weekend-weary thread, mirrored shades reflecting the bright barrage of lights all around. His hand is in a fist, either mimicking tossing dice or making an obscene gesture, his head cocked toward the leggy, sequin-shiny showgirl beside him, as if to say, *Check out these priceless gams!*

The letter:

Dear Young,

Salutations from Sin City! I didn't get into too much trouble, and I actually won a LOT of money! It's funny when you don't need something and God provides an abundance! (Can't escape God wherever you are! Go ask Sodom and Gomorrah! You know your Su Su doesn't ask for permission but always asks for forgiveness!)

I've been meeting all sorts of people here—at the slots, at the craps table, at the buffets. Everyone loves to swap stories—where you're from, how you got here. You can tell who is genuine, and who the racists are: they may say "bless your heart," but you know they don't mean it.

One long night at the blackjack table (Young Buns, stay away—those numbers will drive you crazy!) I got to commiserate with some new friends over our gains and deficits. *A Jewish guy, an Italian guy, a Chinese guy walk into the Luxor—the new Egyptian-themed casino—ha ha!*

All of us, filled with pride, sadness, superstition—praying for our luck to change. Champs to chumps, throughout history: from God's chosen people, the glorious Roman Empire, the celestial Chinese Kingdom—to the Holocaust, Fascism, Communism.

"Caesar—pagan slave trader! Marco Polo—lying plunderer!"

"Who sheltered and protected the Jews—Shanghai! Who fought the Nazis and Japanese—China!"

"Mussolini, Hitler, Hirohito! Bastards!"

"Anthony and Cleopatra! How'd that turn out? I'm praying for Pharaoh to let my people go—and make some dough!"

"Fu Manchu!"

"Shylock!"

"Super Mario!"

"Maybe we all should have a grudge against the Japanese?"

Faith, family, culture, cuisine—prophets to fools, persecutors to persecuted. On top for a while and then down to the bottom of the deck—we understood how it felt, how our forefathers must have felt. We were Bugsy Siegel, Lucky Luciano, Chinese triad guy, just trying to beat the house. (We couldn't think of a famous gangster, so they just called me Bruce Lee.)

A little kindness goes a long way! We shared some food, drinks, laughs, and wished each other good fortune. We promised to get together in Brooklyn one day—maybe have some noodle kugel, linguini, or chow mein. (*L'chaim, salute, gan bei!*)

In the light of day, we had more in common than when we started. We all loved our families, our comfort foods, prayed to our God to smile down on us. We all appreciated our lineage but weren't constrained by where we came from—on our own paths, making our own luck. *All winners.*

Peace and grease!

Your ever-loving, one and only,

Su Su

P.S. Speaking of winners—I called, and Bah said you were going to prom with Gina—*winner!* But Ma said you were going just as friends—*loser!*

CHAPTER FOUR

"Some Great Reward"

JANUARY–MARCH 1996

Soundtrack highlights:
- "Where Is My Mind?"—Pixies
- "Seal My Fate"—Belly
- "Girlfriend"—Matthew Sweet

Young had started spending the night at Erena's, under the guise that he was studying too late to make it home on the train safely. The truth was his parents were too tired to notice that Young wasn't sleeping most nights under their roof anyway. Only Mei had really felt his absence, when she went midnight meandering and ended up spread-eagled alone in his empty bed.

Erena's roommate, Helen, had taken a leave of absence due to anxiety and the toll of too much partying. *(New York is so different from Minnesota!)* Erena was left with the entire dorm room to herself for the rest of the year. Helen's half of the concrete cube was now bare, a Pearl Jam poster the only reminder that someone else had once shared this space, lived their New York City dreams too hard, too fast.

Young had no issues staying overnight at Erena's and behaving.

They both were overachievers in their own right and had overly busy schedules that taxed their young bodies into submission. At most, they'd make out for a little bit and slumber, exhausted—ending up butt-to-butt, Erena snoring loudly into the pockmarked wall.

Erena claimed that she was generally motivated by "diarrhea and adrenaline" a good 90% of the time. She bragged that she had a perfect SAT score (*I test well, what can I say?*), could hold her breath for over three minutes (*Get me in a pool and witness my underwater handstands!*), and had an infallible sense of direction (*You head north, then northeast, and then go north again. Why is that so hard? Aren't you a real New Yorker?*). Young was thoroughly impressed by Erena's ease and erudition as she practiced her presentations. Her confidence and wit were mesmerizing.

Erena was reticent about her previous school life—how she had learned what she had learned, and how she did what she could do. It made sense that she had an extraordinary nontraditional education, as she had been homeschooled for a while.

She ran miles around the streets of the city: countless laps around the track at the NYU gym, along the FDR, around Washington Square Park. Eating in mass quantities, always hungry. Her furnace was being stoked constantly. The consequence: her mechanisms had to expel out as forcefully as they took in.

Young would take a book and laze about on a bench with a Walkman and an iced coffee. He did it not so much to watch her run, but to be near her—to witness the soft machine of her body in motion, a kinetic force, fluid perpetual motion. He'd see her rounding the curve, approaching with a huge smile on her face. He'd angle the headphones off his ear to hear her occasional bon mots: *Yooo hooo, loverboy! You're getting fat just sitting there!*

Young was no runner. Running was for sunny people who cared about their bodies. He was accustomed to his life of indirect exposure—basking in this radiance was glorious enough. He was happy to sit on the sidelines and cheer. *Observe and report on this stilted and stifled joy.*

"*GANBATTE!!!*"—a phrase Young had heard thousands of times in anime and film. It roughly meant: "GO FOR IT!!!" or "YOU CAN DO IT!!!" or "DO YOUR BEST!!!" The equivalent in Mandarin, "*JIAYOU!!!*"—literally, "add oil"—was also included in the pep rally rotation.

Young wasn't sure where the Chinese phrase originated, but it must have been mostly modern. When he was younger, Su Su explained to him that it was analogous to "put the pedal to the metal." Filling up the car was, after all, *jiayou*. "There ya go—keep on motorin'! *JIAYOU*, Optimus Prime!"

* * *

"You smell like onions, stinkboy."

"Well, I blame all the yakitori we just had. But you may as well be a literal onion."

"Because I have so many layers? Because I am bitter and sweet? And I make people cry? Especially you?"

"I concur. You are extremely complex. But how many grilled onions did you actually eat? I see the potential *root* of the problem—"

"*Ugh*, leave the humor to me, OK? And I eat until I'm full! I can pack it in! Onions happen to be a favorite!

"Well, it's a good thing I'm getting the gist of your system now. It dovetails nicely into my particularities."

"It's these shortcuts that will save us a lot of time in the future and help us avoid serious heartache—and save me from buying new pants."

"Well, 'worst feeling number one' and 'worst feeling number two' makes sense to me."

"Yes, yes. 1–1: *thirsty and must pee*; 2–2: *must poop and yet I am also weirdly hungry.*"

"How often do these situations actually come up for you?"

"More fucking often than not! This hot rod has its own idiosyncrasies! You have to pay close attention to the fuel consumption and waste remediation. I will react and convey the current operational status. During midterms and finals, this system is going into maximum overdrive! I am relying on my main man to support me through these vexing endeavors and trying times. *Fuel, waste. Consume, expel. Devour, evacuate.* It's simple, dude."

"I will do my best to attend to your needs."

"Thank you. Good pit crew! Absolute must! OK, test run. I give you the good ol' 1–1 signal—"

"And I go find you a beverage and the nearest bathroom. Snapple Peach iced tea is preferred. Or in a pinch, a can of Arizona, whatever flavor. Women's bathroom: preference is that it isn't a 'one-r' and has multiple stall options."

"Attaboy. And 'worst feeling number three'?"

"That one is gross."

"Men are assholes. *You are an asshole.* When I give you the '3–3,' get me a tampon and prepare to make out with me—maybe some above-the-waist action. I thought you would be looking forward to the 3–3."

"Not my preference, but I'm already duty-bound to this protocol. *All in.* So, what about me? What are my system shortcuts?"

"I've developed the aforementioned numerical shorthand to harness your reflexive lizard brain and maximize the benefit to myself! When it comes to something for you—well, I need to give that some more thought. Academics—you are fine. You've got your own methodology with paper grids and color-coded notes. I'm not getting in the way of that. *Good for you, Rain Man.* However, when you go all tunnel-vision mode and start glitching out—when you think how you sort your laundry has a butterfly effect on the integrity of the cosmos—*that's* cause for concern. I have to come up with something to reintegrate you into proper human society and reboot your software then."

"I've been really stable this year. I don't know if that's true—"

"No, no. This is still a work in progress. I don't have any empirical evidence verifying my suspicions just yet. But you and I, we both fucking know you might go off into la-la land come test and essay time! If you start getting spacey, I'll get you back to normal again. We'll work out something to kick-start you. But have you ever thought about getting checked out? Professionally?"

"*Have you?* Are your internal organs—specifically your gastrointestinal tract—in the range of normal? I don't know if I've ever met anyone that 'intakes and expels' at the rate I have witnessed. I'm fine as I am."

"I make it work, OK. My diet, my guts—all good. You and your nerves and your numbers and your peculiarities—it's part of your charm! We are both OK as we are. We can deal with these issues—and I'm not saying they are 'issues' per se—but once this semester is in the record books, we can revisit. *Deal?* Onward and upward? Do your best! *GANBATTE!!!*"

"*Deal.* Above and beyond reproach. We need to absolutely annihilate these grades. We can do it! Go for it! *JIAYOU!!!*"

"Hell yeah. I'm rocking a 4.0 this semester and enjoying the most jam-packed NYC life with my boytoy! Living the dream, mate! LIVING. THE. DREAM!"

"Do we high-five now?"

"YES. WE. FUCKING. HIGH. FIVE!"

* * *

Bah needed to travel upstate for a soil study, and surprisingly, Ma wanted to go with him. Young couldn't remember when his parents last had time alone. Did they ever do anything romantic anymore? Young suspected that Ma was burned out from hosting events and needed to get away from Queens, away from people. The fresh air would do her some good.

Young would babysit Mei for the entire weekend. He took the opportunity to tell his parents that he might invite a friend over to help him. "Paris and Gina still at school, so who is this friend?" Bah smirked. Ma looked concerned.

* * *

Erena was nowhere near ready to meet Young's parents. She arrived at the Wang house after they had left, overnight bag slung over her shoulder, head to toe in comfy gray sweats, in time for Friday-night-dinner-and-a-movie with Mei.

"Wow. I'm finally crossing the threshold! I feel like I should bow or some shit. *Honorable House of Wang.*" Erena stepped in to be greeted in the foyer by a dozen hanging pictures and as many pairs of shoes.

"Sneakers off, please." Young pointed to the house slippers waiting for her.

"*Duh,* I come from an Asian household, too. *I'm not an animal.* And yes, best behavior. Impressionable young mind on the premises! Watching my mouth, from now on. So, where's Mei? I can call her your *mei mei* or Mei, right?"

Mei was coloring in Charlie Brown and singing the Tevin Campbell theme song from *A Goofy Movie* (lyrics were nowhere near correct). She looked up when Erena sat next to her, placing the pine-green crayon neatly beside the black.

"Hi, Mei. Nice to meet you! I'm Erena. And look, a little Hot Wheels surprise! From me (and Ronald McDonald) to you! Your *guh guh* told you that we were going to watch movies and have some fun tonight—right?"

Mei looked up at Erena with her wide dark-brown eyes and thanked her shyly, then went back to coloring in Woodstock with canary yellow. Mei whispered, "I like cars and I like movies." She took Erena's hand and guided her. "Green for Patty's shirt. *Here.* And can you please help me read this part? 'Patty is *stoo-PEN-duss* at soccer.' Is that right, *jie jie*?"

Erena mouthed the words SO. CUTE. Young covered the phone receiver to mouth his reply—OF. COURSE.—as he ordered a pie with sausage and mushrooms.

* * *

After their pizza party dinner, Mei insisted on watching the VHS tape of *Beauty and the Beast* again instead of *Babe*, the new film Young had borrowed from the Undertow.

"Mei, didn't you beg me to bring this for you to watch tonight?"

Mei whispered in Young's ear. He laughed, kissed her repeatedly, and popped the tape in. Mei squeezed herself on the couch between her brother and Erena.

"What did she say?" Erena whispered over the swelling strains of the opening number about provincial life.

"She said she wants to watch this one instead, because she thinks you are like Belle—*smart and pretty*. And maybe if you watch the movie you will fall for her beast of a brother."

"Little does she know, right?" Erena picked up Mei and put her in her lap. "*Oh, oh*—what's she doing to me?"

"We call this *mo erduo*—feeling and rubbing earlobes. I used to do it to my mom when I was a toddler. It must run in the family. Not sure how or when Mei picked it up. She does it to all of us—it makes her sleepy. It wasn't so long ago that she had one hand around a bottle and the other hand on an earlobe. She must feel safe with you. It's soothing and feels nice."

"Maybe to the *feel-er*, not the *feel-ee*! *Ooooh!* It's giving me goose bumps!" Erena stuck her tongue out at Young. "And now she's twirling my hair. Not sure if that's any better."

"*Jie, jie*, what's this on your necklace?" Mei said, the melody of sleep in her words.

Erena pulled out the chain with a small figure at the end. Her *maneki-neko*—lucky cat, one paw raised, beckoning and greeting. "Min Jee, my favorite cousin (and one of my favorite people in the whole world) gave this to me on my sweet sixteen—my sixteenth birthday. I always put it on when I need a little extra good luck. Nicky Neko hasn't failed me yet! Isn't that right, puss-puss? *Meow-meow.* He agrees."

"You're funny, *jie jie*! *Guh*, can you get one for me, too? I want it sooner, not when I'm sixteen. As a surprise? Or for my birthday this year? I see the same kitties in the stores all the time. I love them. They wave and wave and wave—"

Before Gaston had finished singing about expectorating, Mei was asleep with Erena's hair—and cat pendant—nestled in her fist. Erena didn't mind.

* * *

"Confirmed: the plastic-tofu-container-as-dish-sponge-receptacle is a universal centerpiece in every Asian American kitchen! I thought it was just my boho, eco-conscious family who did that." Erena, drying the last of the dishes.

"Well, I thought it was just a Chinese thing, but guess it isn't." Young wiped his hands, planted a kiss on Erena's forehead. "Want a piece of chocolate?"

"Sure! What's with the stockpile of these 'Ferrari Rocker' candies?" Erena unwrapped the gold foil and popped the chocolate ball into the pink purse of her mouth.

"Ferrero Rocher. And these are Almond Roca. As long as we shall live, we'll never run out. *Behold*." Young opened the cabinet above the rice cooker, revealing the clear plastic trays, the large metal tins, the bow-tied boxes—stacks of chocolate-coated hazelnut, wafer, toffee, in heavenly perpetuity, *in excelsis Deo*.

"Who is the supplier of all this sugary scrumptiousness?" Erena marveled and examined the permutations of packaging: 8-packs, 24-packs, 36-packs.

"The Chinese American community at large. Anytime my folks do anything for anyone, we're bound to get some of these. My mom's only weakness: chocolate. She'll never run out. Take some back to the dorm with you. It won't be missed."

"But why only these? Why not like low-end Russell Stover or high-end Godiva? I mean, these are fucking awesome, no doubt—"

"It's the gold foil. It's considered lucky—ingots and bite-size bricks. I wonder if this company looks at their yearly earnings and wonders why these dang Chinese consume so much chocolate." Young crunched down.

"Contributing to the diabetes epidemic of the yellow persuasion. It's a genius ploy." Erena patted Young on the soft part of his belly and asked for the tour, in search of other treasure hidden in the House of Wang.

* * *

"How are the two of you even related? She is the most beautiful little girl in all fucking existence!" Erena, closing the door to Mei's room. "An exquisite human baby doll."

"Have you seen the pictures of my mother?" Young guided Erena to the hallway, motioning to Ma's photo gallery.

Ma, in her youth in Shanghai, sitting on a park bench. Ma, on a beach in Vancouver, radiant in sunglasses and a wide-brimmed hat. Ma, in Flushing, slim and stunning, next to Mayor Dinkins.

"My God. I am intimidated. When you said your mother was a model, I thought you meant like in the *Penny Saver*, and she's holding up a packet of instant noodles on sale at the Hong Kong Superstore. She is a genuine, Chinese-Michelle-Pfeiffer-circa-*Fabulous-Baker-Boys* hot mama! So I assume you got most of your looks from—"

Bah, standing in front of a government building in Taipei with Yeh Yeh and Nai Nai. Bah, suntanned and bare-chested at Ontario Place. Bah, looking ecstatic, rubbing a giant pumpkin at the world-famous Pete's Punkin' Patch in Ridgewood, New Jersey.

"Ah! Look at this handsome guy! Kinda goofy, though? Definitely a different energy than your mom. He seems so chill compared to her intensity. It's in the eyes. On the surface, I don't get this pairing, but I bet it's some yin-yang thing—or your dad has a giant monster schlo—"

Su Su, at the karaoke contest where he won, that first year he moved in, his hair slicked back, stubbly George Michael *Faith*-era five o'clock shadow and dark shades. Su Su, holding a giddy Mei, his lips puckered under a full tickly mustache, kissing a plump apple cheek. Su Su and Ma when they were teenagers, sprawled on the floor listening to records, with Po Po in the background, drinking tea.

"This guy? He looks so familiar! Where have I seen him before?"

"My uncle—we call him 'Su Su'—it's actually a funny story. In Chinese, Mei and I should really call him 'Xiao Jiu Jiu.' That's the proper name for your uncle if he is your mother's younger brother—*da jiu jiu* or *xiao jiu jiu* would indicate age in relation to your mother. 'Su Su' is actually the correct name for your uncle if he is your *dad's* younger brother—*bo bo* would indicate older brother. And I showed you my Yeh Yeh and Nai Nai, my dad's parents, and my Gong Gong and Po Po, my mom's parents."

"Good gracious—the Asian honorifics and necessity to know one's place! All part and parcel of filial piety. I am acquainted with this convoluted patriarchal framework of bullshitery."

"Seriously—but sometimes it's helpful."

"Yeah, yeah, *ojisan*—I get it. Continue."

"So, my uncle apparently takes more after my dad. They've been good friends ever since my parents started dating, when they were young. They are both darker-skinned—mostly from being in the sun so much—and nowhere near as fair as my mom. They both have the same build and height. Bah's is mostly from all the garden work, not genetics, like Su Su. My uncle's personality—when he's good, he's laid-back, like my dad, but he's got the extrovert charm of my mom. Su Su and Ma both have—uh—*short fuses* around each other. Bah can somehow tame those two beasts. He can whisper and get them both to calm down. Most of the time, Su Su just seems more like my dad's brother than my mom's. Plus, when I was a baby, I could never get the handle of the vowel sound of *jiu jiu*—*su su* was much easier to say. I think they thought it was cute, the way I'd spit and lisp. Hence, the name stuck, the joke stuck, and he's our

'Su Su' now. I'll have to explain it all to Mei when she grows up. That's going to be a pain."

"I swear he looks super familiar, though."

"A lot of people think he looks like a Chinese movie star. Have you heard of Chow Yun Fat?"

"No, no—that's not it. But I can see the resemblance. And yeah, I *absolutely* know Chow Yun Fat. Who the fuck do you think I am? *Asshole.* John Woo and all the double guns and doves! Min Jee dated this guy from Hong Kong who was all about it. We watched these poorly dubbed videotapes, but we never watched those for the dialogue anyway. I've seen my share of—OH MY GOODNESS—please tell me this is *you*—you had a perm? *A PERM!*"

"*Body wave.*"

"Whatever. It's a *perm!* That explains why your hair is so wild now—the lasting damage! *Oh, you sweet, sweet boy.* And is *this* you trying to look cool in all black? Goth phase! You never really outgrew that! And *what the fuck?* Is this supposed to be a MULLET? A *MULLET? YES!* Such a sorry excuse for hair metal glam! It's not supposed to fuzz out *aaaaallll* the way front to back! How did you even grow that? And the *GLASSES!* Did they keep getting thicker and thicker until the optometrist finally let you in on the thin lens options and contacts? *You poor, poor child.* Let me kiss you and take away all the adolescent pain and anguish marinating in the deep depths of your undescended testicles! *Seventh Grade Young Buns— look at the smokin' hot babe you manage to nab in the future! Don't worry! It gets better for you! It gets better!*"

Young shushed and dodged Erena as she approached him with fingers extended and wriggling, mischief emanating from each creak of the floorboards, tiptoeing over to *monsterkiss* her boy. Mei appeared behind Young, blinking back interrupted sleep, tugging at his shirt.

"*Guh.* We forgot to pray. Come say my prayers with me. *Jie Jie,* you come, too?" Mei's pudgy fingers tucked away in Young's palm.

Mei slid under her blanket, pointed to the floor, and then at her brother. Then, patting the open warm length of mattress beside her, she motioned for Erena to lie down.

"You ready?" Young stroked Mei's hair back, kissed the top of her sweaty head. "Dear God—," Young began.

"Dear God, thank you for this day. Thank you for Mama, Bah Bah, Su Su, Guh. Please be with Gong Gong, Po Po, Yeh Yeh, and Nai Nai in Heaven," Mei sped through, hands clasped in little fleshy rocks, eyes shut tight in concentration.

OH. MY. GOODNESS. SO. CUTE. Erena mouthed and looked at Young.

"Thank you for Mrs. Rosenbeck and Ms. Turner. Thank you for the nice weather and the apples. Thank you for bringing Erena *jie jie* to come visit me and play with me tonight. Please bless her and help her to not curse so much. Help me to have nice dreams tonight and to not wet the bed. Amen." Mei finished and snuggled her warm cheeks into the nape of Erena's neck.

Erena bit her lower lip, trying not to laugh. Young snickered and kissed Mei's forehead as he got up.

"Where are you going?" Erena, looking panicked.

"Just to pee. Stay with her until she's out. It won't take long." Young backed out of the room and heard Mei perk up and demand a Disney song, or she couldn't fall back to sleep.

Young pressed his ear to the door to hear Erena start and stutter—clearing her throat and then fully committing to an off-key soft warble. Her rendition of "A Whole New World" was completely half-remembered, with substituted lyrics, Mei giggling and Erena *whispershouting*: "Shhh! You are going to get me in trouble with your *guh!*" Mei started singing softly, with Erena joining in: the two voices blending sweetly together, sharp and flat, but harmonious at the same time.

Young slid down the wall and sat beside the door, listening to the satisfying snort and chortle growing steady and rhythmic. He closed his eyes and heard the clock ticking away the seconds in the dining room, the soothing sounds of rubber friction from the cars passing

by in the distance, the slow bend and tick of springs as Erena edged
her way off the bed.

She opened the door and closed it slowly, her eyes adjusting to
the dim light, bright in relation to the dark room she had emerged
from. She looked over at Young with a smirk. *"Hey,"* she croaked.

"You did good." Young took her hand and stood to meet her lips.
He kissed her softly. This felt like home.

* * *

Young and Erena spent the rest of the night on the couch, binge-
watching movies—*Big Trouble in Little China, Xanadu, Seven Samurai.*
Kissing and over-the-bra action. A mostly PG-rated evening, on-
screen and in the flesh.

* * *

"Morning! I have done my daily ablutions and I am ready to be fed
or to be responsible for the feeding." Erena pecked Young repeatedly
all over his face until he was fully awake.

"How are you so up right now? It's barely eight on a Saturday
morning."

"I wanted max quality time with you and *babycutie*. Then head
back to get a run in and really hit the books. *Ooh, your breath!* Please
brush that sewer pit so I can give you some sugar—as in these sweet,
luscious lips—and maybe some chocolate chip pancakes. What does
Mei eat?"

"Eggs. Waffles. We can go to the Starshine Diner. It's not too far
from here."

Mei was more than happy to hold hands with her new *jie jie* the
few blocks over to the diner. Young and Erena each took an arm and
hoisted Mei up in a vigorous pendulum swing, her delectable laughter filling the air, repetition after repetition: *Again,* guh guh, *again!*

The diner was crowded with the usual Saturday-morning mix of hungover youth who hadn't made it to bed yet and the elderly who didn't need much sleep anymore. Coffee and carbs, the common middle ground—everyone hungry and eyeing the hot platters balanced by the waitstaff, wondering when their food would be delivered to their booths next.

"Hey, hon. Let me grab you some menus and a coloring set for the sweetie," the waitress said as she clutched the laminated spiral-bound sets and a black-and-white sheet with a little pack of crayons. "Follow me to the back, and we'll get you seated."

Mei always wanted the same thing when she came here—scrambled eggs, sausage, fries, and toast. Young would get pancakes or waffles so Mei could also have a taste of something sweet. He'd inevitably finish her leftovers.

"Hi, hi! Can I get the bagel lox deluxe with extra onions and a side of sausage? And can I get fries with gravy instead of home fries? And obviously, can we get his chocolate chip pancakes with extra whipped cream—on the side, please? As much as you are allowed to give us without the boss getting mad, you know what I mean?"

"Absolutely, ma'am! Coffee will be right out, and I'll make sure to bring your little girl a juice in a plastic cup with a lid."

"Yes, please! My *daughter* would absolutely love the juice with a straw. She'd like apple juice—right, Mei? *Apple?* Yes, apple! And can you bring some half-and-half for my *husband?* He takes his coffee light and sweet, just how he likes his lovely wife! Right, darling?" Erena said without missing a beat—Young, compelled to smile and roll his eyes, playing along.

"Half-and-half would be great. Thank you."

* * *

"Mei, did you have a good time with Erena *jie jie?* Did you love it when we had story time, when we sang, and had yummy breakfast? I had so much fun with you, and I'll see you again soon, OK?" Erena hugged Mei. It wasn't evident who was more enamored with who.

"You've got two choices: we can call you a livery cab back to the city, or we can walk you to the bus stop."

"Call me a car? *Oi!* Do I look that posh? Take a walk with me to the bus stop. But first, I may have overindulged. The smoked fish and four cups of coffee are demanding last night's popcorn vacate the premises and make room for the new tenants."

"You can use the bathroom in the basement."

"Yes, I think that would be best. The good ol' 2–2. May need a snack for the road later."

Young took Mei upstairs to wash the syrup from her hands and face. "Stop, too rough, *guh*," Mei said as Young rubbed the warm towel over her cheeks, under her chin. "I'm clean already."

"Hello, my two *guai, guai. Bao bei*, are you upstairs?" Ma's voice rang out, stunning Young.

Mei flew out of the bathroom, down the stairs, and hopped up to try to unlatch the front door. Ma was over the doorstep with her suitcase, Bah locking up the car and following behind.

As he descended the stairs, in a confluence of perfect timing and/or the cosmos conspiring against Young, he could hear Erena as she surfaced from the basement: "I recommend that you do not attempt to go down there for at least a good hour. You are out of Glade, so I just fanned the door a bit—that probably made things worse. *Oh, hello. You must be Young's parents.* I guess you're back early?"

"*Ah!* And you are Young's friend—we heard you might help watch our Mei. Thank you!" Bah said, trying to conceal his *my-boy-done-good* grin.

Ma edged her way closer and gave the girl a quick once-over: "Young didn't tell us his friend was so pretty! And this is you without any makeup and wearing sweat clothes. Nice to meet you—"

"Hi, hi. I'm Erena."

"Such a pretty name. I never heard this name before. What is it? Where from?"

"My parents told me it's Greek, and it means—"

"Oh, *Greek*? You're not *Greek-Greek*! What's your last name? Surname?"

"Oh, I'm Erena Yasuda."

"*Ah, Japanese*—or at least part Japanese? Now that I see you, I can see you are—*a mix*?"

"Yes, I guess that's right. I'm part Japanese, Korean, and a lot of other stuff."

"That's why you have such pretty eyes and skin! Your hair is so dark, though. I thought it would be lighter. And you have some purple in there also! How fun! And what are you studying at school?"

Young shook off his stunned stupor and stepped in before his mother was able to inflict any more damage, stalling the hawk before it snatched up the kitten.

"Ma, Bah! You are back already! We weren't expecting you until tomorrow night! Mei and I were just about to walk Erena to the bus. She's heading back to school to study."

"Our weekend plans had to be rescheduled, but you can still enjoy and go *xuexi* with Erena. Am I saying that correct? *ERRRR-UH-NUUH*? So nice to meet you! Young—here, here, some money. Take Erena out to a nice dinner tonight. Thank her for spending time with Mei. We'll see you later, Young. *Whenever.* You go study, eat. Stay in the city if it gets too late, uh?" Bah stuffed a wad of cash into Young's hand. Ma glared at Bah, but melted softly once Mei hugged her around her waist.

"Mei, did you have a nice time with *jie jie*?" Ma asked as she scooped up her precious *xin gan bao*.

Mei wrapped her arms around her mother's neck. "We watched *Beauty and the Beast*, and *jie jie* is like Belle. She read stories and sang songs."

"And what else?"

"And we went to eat at the diner. The lady said she's like a mommy and I'm like the baby. Silly. She's too young for a mommy. Not old like you."

* * *

Young and Erena rode the bus and subway trains for the forty-five-minute commute back to the NYU campus for a responsible Saturday night in of studying and snacking.

Erena had a difficult time staying still, balancing highlighters on her upper lip, shooting crumpled papers into the wastebasket, aiming gum wrappers at Young's orifices. Young decided that some sort of intervention was necessary and hit PLAY on Erena's tape deck. He welcomed a distraction, anything to divert attention from being pelted by random objects.

"OK, serious question: How are Metallica and Iron Maiden and Queensrÿche and these other bands *that* much different from what I like? Why are you *allowed* to like this, when it's all basically the same shit?"

"First: impressed that you remembered the bands I told you about before! Points for you. These musicians are all pioneers and masters in their specific subgenres. Metallica: thrash metal at its peak and the gateway drug to their counterparts—Anthrax, Megadeth. Iron Maiden: new wave of British metal, known for their intricate fretwork and literary subject matter. Queensrÿche: their concept album *Operation: Mindcrime*, incredibly cinematic in its storytelling and a modern masterpiece. Can you name a band that you love that can combine elements of dystopian religious cult science fiction with harmonious twin guitar leads AND soaring, operatic vocals?"

Ride the Lightning began spinning as Erena cranked the volume dial. She threw a packet of Lay's chips over to Young.

"*OOOOH! I dig this!* But how is this not exactly the same as my bands again? You have to concede, it's got a generic rhythm—*boomandboomandboom*—and the same heavy guitars. And then it's all *RAAAHHH GRRRRRR. ZHUUSSSH ZHUUSSSH. DUNNNNN DAAAAHHHH DUUUUN.* I admit that this is badass. But is it really that *revolutionary?*" Erena made some half-mocking headbanger poses in time to the best of Lars, James, Cliff, and Kirk.

"In this particular lane of the overall genre, it's considered canon. Listen to that pure artistry! 'Creeping Death' is about God's wrath come upon those that would harm His people! It was inspired by *The Ten Commandments*—you know, Charlton Heston, Yul Brynner. Obviously from the Bible—"

"So, Metallica is another undercover Christian band? *Exodus, Testament, and now Metallica?* I'm feeling guilty that I've taken you away from fellowship time and your Sunday school duties!"

"Biblical and literary references are at the core of heavy metal and hard rock—and you'll find songs about subjects and themes from science fiction, fantasy, mythology. These expansive worlds are the baseline inspiration for this type of aggressive and thought-provoking music. Led Zeppelin and Tolkien! *Come on!*"

"I'm just making a funny. *Sheesh, calm down, Professor Yellow-Mellow-Fellow Drama.* This stuff is considered *the best*? But do I need to know the entire backstory, every fart that went into creating a stupid song? Why can't I just like it for what it is—massively awesome guitars, a catchy chorus that lives in my head? I don't have to trace the entire genealogy of each band member or know the exact number of pubes on their balls just to *like a thing*! I can simply enjoy this today, and I can change my fucking mind tomorrow! Momentary pleasures, passing fancy! It doesn't have to be that involved, babe. It doesn't have to define you—who you are, your very soul."

Young crossed the dorm room to dampen the sonic tide, turning the dial down. In a hushed, controlled tone: "I'm all for eclectic. I wholeheartedly support a comprehensive appreciation of modern music. But for me, it's about *taste*. It's how the best informs how you think and feel. All the art you experience—you filter the world through the lens of your being, through all your senses. It is who you are. It permeates deep and determines how you react and respond to the world. *What you consume, you don't just expel.* Some of that intake remains inside, incorporated. It's not all smoke and fumes. *Poof. Gone.*"

With a flick of Erena's wrist, the first arpeggios of "The Call of Ktulu" blasted out of the speakers at full volume.

"I respectfully disagree. I like American cheese most of the time. Most days, I don't want your creamy Brie, your funky stinky bleu cheese, or whatever else crawled out of some European crotch. Give me the unnatural orange/yellow slices wrapped in cellophane, and I'm a happy girl. But on another day when I've got a nice hot espresso, tempt me with some melty Gruyère on a crusty baguette, and you can smack my ass and call me Genevieve! But it all comes out the same! *Downtown to Browntown!* Temporary and ever-changing—*taste*! I don't let things affect me that much and get convoluted in my mind, internalized in my essence, and influence all of my being." Erena was clearly pushing her boyfriend's buttons at this point, proceeding to show off her best air-guitar windmills.

"OK, Forever Young—let's take some Aussie bands, for instance. AC/DC—you love them, no doubt. What about INXS?"

"Brilliant. *Listen Like Thieves* and *Kick*—back-to-back perfect albums."

"See, we agree on something! What about—Men at Work?"

"You mean of 'Who Can It Be Now?' and 'Down Under' fame? One-hit, two-hit wonders! Novelty act—great example of '80s mainstream pop rock."

"But what about 'Overkill'? (Obviously, the name of their song. Nothing to do with that heavy metal band, but *heh*.) It's a hit from their *second* album."

"I'm—I'm not familiar with that one."

"I challenge you to listen to that song and tell me they are just a 'novelty act.' You can't judge and assume on first impressions. We all evolve, we all change and grow. *ASS-U-ME*—and you're the asshole." Erena, with her chin jutted out and pointer finger poking, playfully accusatory.

"Fine. I'm open. I'm sure Jim has a used copy."

"And what about Mei's beloved *Beauty and the Beast* soundtrack? Do those songs exhibit 'mastery in their respective subgenres'?"

"That's entirely different."

"*Is it? Is it?* Are you going to be an asshole and tell Mei her favorite songs are just 'treacly showtunes'? *Come on—you love them, too!* You were correcting my lyrics the entire subway ride back! You don't have to justify, rationalize why you like something. No need to overthink—that would be *overkill.*" The wink was devastating.

The distortion kicked in and now Ktulu (*really, Cthulhu*) was lowing like a proper Elder God. Young shouted over the guttural rumble: "You're missing my point! I'm just trying to steer you in the direction of what I consider the top-tier paradigm! What future art will be judged against, the pop culture that will stand the test of time! You can continue to like your rap metal boy bands, for all I care."

"Is this all because you have a vendetta against my sweet treat 311? I was just nudging and prodding because I wanted a break from reading about the Federal Reserve! Winding up my favorite Young-in-the-box! But you just hate the fact that I absolutely love 3-FUCKIN'-E-LE-VEN!" Erena's eyes went wide as she paused her headbanging and pounced on the bed on her back, feet kicking in time to Metallica's riffs, cackling like a (*beauty of a*) witch witnessing the coming storm of the true and terrible Beast.

Young straddled his girlfriend, his weight gently resting on her belly. He looked deep into her eyes and continued, "YES! How can you say *they* are your favorite band? You can like them and their music—but *your favorite?* Of everything you've ever heard? If you like heavy, aggressive, masculine music with a driving groove, there's so much out there that is better! Of all the amazing music that has come out since the history of time—*311 is your favorite band? Favorite-favorite?*"

"They are my favorite band *right now.* That blue album is *THE BOMB.* It's metal AND reggae AND has a cool Cali / West Coast vibe. Maybe you just don't understand them? I have 'Down' on constant repeat when I hit the gym. It makes me feel good—*period.* I don't think too hard about it. I would rather listen to them over the Beatles, the Rolling Stones, David Bowie! (But not Fleetwood

Mac or Stevie Nicks. He's the best. *She, she!* I was making a funny!)
There's two cute guys in the band—and one of them has rad hair!
I'm allowed to like them. I'm allowed to *fucking love them!* I love
you—and you are some weird goth, nerd-meister, woodland creature! What does that say about my taste?" Erena squinted, scrunched
up her nose. Young stared at this brilliant proto-lawyer presenting
her case—her and her most adorable *lemonsourface*.

Young rose slowly and sat next to her, his back against the wall.

"You love me?"

"Yeah, I guess so—total dipshit that you are sometimes. We have
so much fun when you aren't being such a space cadet. You're a
good kisser, and it's a perfect fit when we snuggle. You let me climb
you like I'm a lackadaisical koala and you're the tangy, tasty eucalyp-
tus tree (*but neither of us has gone 'down under' yet*). I haven't felt this
way about anyone in a long time. Besides, we're apparently already
married and starting a family, according to Maureen at the Starshine
Diner." Erena slid up to sit beside Young, pressing close. She could
feel his heart pounding, almost in time to Hammett's fretboard
frenzy, Ulrich's double bass bashing.

She breathed playfully in Young's ear: "Still don't know anything
about what's hiding in your kookaburra bush. I know it works, but I
sure haven't seen it yet." She laughed as Young exhaled, exasperated.
"But I figure it will all pan out when the time is right. *Mazel tov*, my
shy guy." Erena got up to shut the window to diffuse the tension—
both in the air, and in Young's pants.

"I don't know what to say, it just seems so fast. I mean, you're my
girlfriend now—and I have strong feelings for you, Erena—"

"I just said 'I love you' and I made several clever asides to ease the
anxiety level. And I get—'strong feelings for you'? That's all?" Erena
thwacked Young playfully in the arm, a half-hearted karate chop—at
least he thought so.

"I don't know what to say."

(*888, get it straight, bangbangbang.*)

"Hello, Young Stun Gun? Anyone there? I mean—*sheesh*—leave a girl hanging."

"I—I—"

"Speechless! *I will take that!* I've rendered you absolutely inert with my effusiveness! It's OK. You don't have to say it back right now! I've got a lot of love in this tiny body! I've got a big mouth. No impulse control! No filter! You don't have to say anyth—"

Young pulled Erena close with ease and warmth. He kissed her tenderly, then with more strength, trying to convey what he was too scared to put into weak words.

Somewhere over Brooklyn, lightning touched ground and thunder boomed in the distance. Rain was on the way. They held each other and waited for the droplets to hit the pane. They kissed again in silence. They had done all of this before—but everything had changed now.

Young saw his reflection in the pane of glass—happy, excited, at ease. He turned to face Erena. His eyes locked with hers—he met her gaze and didn't avert his eyes.

Young's hand curled against Erena's back, the thumb and pinkie touching her spine— "hang loose," "the Chinese way." But he needed to be sure. He whispered quietly to himself, but Erena thought she could read his lips in the flash of light: *Number six? Number six.*

Fourth Love: "Live Through This"

1992–1994

Soundtrack highlights:
- "In Bloom"—Nirvana
- "Bastards of Young"—The Replacements
- "Until the End of the World"—U2

You have never heard of Stuyvesant or any of the other elite public high schools in NYC until the Choudharys have an emergency dinner with your parents and the Villanuevas. One night in May, at the close of seventh grade, their treat at an all-you-can-eat Indian buffet (one of the OG places on Roosevelt Avenue), Mr. Choudhary explains that one of his brightest residents went to Stuyvesant (and subsequently got into Columbia), and he has confirmed that it is the only public high school worth attending in NYC. (Hunter, Bronx Science, Brooklyn Tech, Townsend Harris, and a handful of others make up the specialized school list. But ask any Stuy alum, and they'll quickly dismiss these as second-tier.) "Harvard, MIT, Yale—the best top schools—they have Stuyvesant alumni at all of these! Such prestige!"

Ma's eyes widen with each bite of *tandoori* chicken. Mr. Villanueva and Bah are happily gorging themselves on *sag paneer*, be-mused at all this talk of academia. Paris throws bits of *popadum* into your mouth. Gina tries her best to ignore the two of you.

"Our children are talented and bright! Talented AND gifted! I love my son, but I am aware he's not the smartest and will need some help. He has two of the best friends—and best friends need to encourage each other." Mr. Choudhary goes on to explain that acceptance into the specialized high schools is determined by a single entrance exam, testing English language arts and math. The cold, hard score will sort you. No sponsorship, no legacy, no letters of recommendation begging for special consideration—it's all up to a No. 2 pencil and a cool head.

Mr. Choudhary has found an excellent test prep program and has already paid for three seats, three times a week. Your parents applaud and thank him profusely for this. He lifts his Heineken and toasts to your future.

Paris shoves a ball of *gulab jamun* into his mouth. He's grown resigned to the fact that you'll be spending afternoons taking practice exams. Mrs. Villanueva is near tears: she was planning to send Gina to test prep anyway, but it was too expensive. Gina hugs her mom and rubs her back. She looks at you and rolls her eyes, mouthing, *DRA-MA-TIC*. More school, more Paris and G time, less handball, less church activities, less unstructured messing around—*overall a good deal?*

In the end, the three of you barely squeak into your top choice—the only choice: Stuyvesant High School.

* * *

Up at 5:00 or 6:00 a.m. Back home by 6:00 or 7:00 p.m. Eat, homework, sleep—repeat. Ninety minutes each way, five times a week, from Queens all the way to lower Manhattan. This is your life now. High school is supposed to be some of the best years of your life. But you aren't sure what you'll remember after the human cocktail of testosterone, adrenaline, bile, and stomach acid has evaporated from the fleshy hormonal engine of your teenage body.

The changes in your corporeal and spiritual self have taken a toll. Your OCD tendencies remain undiagnosed and untreated. You are positive you are moderately obsessive and mildly compulsive. The more psychology texts you read, the more confident you are in your self-awareness, self-regulation. (You think you can manage alone—*of course you can*.) The stakes are higher in high school, and you grow more conscious of your system of numbers and patterns.

You have your routines and rules. You try to stick by these as much as possible to minimize negativity and maximize all positive outcomes. Your world revolves around the underlying goal of dialing in to the frequency that results in all 8s, with 7s and 9s a distant compromise. But it's getting harder and harder to maintain. The rituals are teetering on the rails. You have to compromise, cut corners, sacrifice symmetry for the sake of your sanity.

You consider *maybe* changing your name. Now might be the best time to ditch all the potential "Young" puns. An entire sea of fresh faces from all five boroughs. Do they have to call you by your given name? Couldn't you go by "Austin" or "Dane" or "Whitson"—names of the streets in your beloved Forest Hills? Or something like "Xavier" or "Zach," a close vector to your Y?

A handful from 215, a few kids from test prep, and some from 121 are now all at Stuy. But most of these classmates are unknown entities. You don't know if they are *actually* better than you or just *think* they are. But you don't have to be the "Wee Young One" anymore.

"Young, come on, man—it's cool! Own it! Besides, they'll be Korean kids who are named 'Young-Jee' or 'Young-Mi'—same Asian-y difference! You won't be the only one anymore! We are going to make up the *majority* for once! So many Choudharys, Patels, Shahs—all my peoples! 3,000 kids total—and 51 percent are Asian! We'll have to be careful we don't hook up with a distant cousin!"

* * *

Your family is thriving in the '90s. Su Su helps with Mei, especially since he's between jobs (immigration law advice or windshield repair, occasionally). Mei is whipsmart. She loves science and is a talented artist (drawings of insects and bunnies, especially). Bah is relaxed and happy with his rooftop tomatoes and research (fertilizers and water conservation, mostly).

Ma is a bona fide local celebrity, with a pedigree and a paycheck. She stars in some ads, appears on local cable, and becomes the spokesperson for Shanghai Johnny's mini chain (Brooklyn, Manhattan, and Flushing locations). The bilingual commercials are a big hit and air at all hours. Her English and Mandarin come across pleasant, clear, and professional. She's dainty, beautiful, and dressed in a gold-and-red *qipao*: Huan ying, huan ying! *Welcome to Shanghai Johnny's, where our* xiao long bao *are the best you've ever tried! Bite into the succulent dumplings, sip the soup! It's hot and tasty every time!*

Wendy still sends you letters and postcards—at least during the beginning of your first year of high school. It's apparent that your pen pal days are drawing to a close. Her letters get shorter and shorter, as do your replies. She mostly sends pictures of the latest places she's visited: spots in China (Guangzhou and Hunan); a trip to Japan (*kawaii* in a My Melody jumper); and Italy (by the Trevi Fountain, pistachio gelato in hand). The last photo is from Angkor Wat: she's wearing a bright-orange silk wrap dress, a wisp of makeup enhancing her wide-set eyes, her light pink lips. *She's becoming really pretty.*

You're amazed that she's permitted to travel that much, to be a tourist. "Silly baby, of course she can go all over the place! Xia family has money. They can do whatever they want! Same as if they lived in San Francisco or Chicago or Toronto." You're certain Ma doesn't realize the true oppression of the Communist Party. Her friend's family is probably under constant surveillance. Maybe they're diplomats? Maybe they have a special dispensation and are working with the government on international contracts? Xia Su Su works with "computers"—but what do they actually "compute"? *Maybe he really is a spy.* But you no longer have time to speculate on this international intrigue. Wendy can summer on the beaches of Bali all she wants. *Good for her and her milky skin.* They can afford the best sunscreen that Chinese renminbi can buy.

You write: "I wish you well, Wendy. Maybe our paths will converge when I cross the Atlantic one day, or if you visit us in New York. If and when, then you can finally see Meiguo for yourself."

You send her a picture of you in all black on the corner of 14th Street and Avenue A. You are earnest in your intentions and projected imagery. No irony here: *Real grit. Real New York. Still rockin' in the free world.*

* * *

Paris and Gina are never that distant for the duration of high school. You part and do your own things, inevitably finding time to reunite. Your bonds are everlasting, unshakable. You're best friends, but Stuyvesant offers the opportunity for new friends, from as far and as foreign as Staten Island or the Bronx.

You enjoy two years at what will become known as the "old building"—the original Stuyvesant High School in Stuyvesant Town. The school is old and musty, everything a shade of gray or brown or patinaed green. The creak in every hinge of every centennially used wooden door or window gives you goose bumps. If the school weren't so overcrowded, you'd be afraid to be alone in the stairwells.

You will always remember the padded elevated indoor track. You run thirty laps once during gym class—the zenith of your physical fitness. You will always remember the auditorium—the smooth coolness of the lacquered wood chair as you watch Gina gyrate to Salt-N-Pepa for soph-frosh SING! rehearsals.

You spend lunch periods in the scary park across the street (drug deals, sex deals, homeless people) with Paris and Gina and some new friends in tow. Everyone gets fried food at the corner bodega and smokes cigarettes behind the dumpster. The gaggle of loud kids in the noon hours perpetuates the daily scatter of the local color, but the plastic baggies, used condoms, and syringe detritus remain and still freak you out.

But things change junior year. You are moving to the "new building." An architectural, technological marvel: $350 million of concrete and steel. This hulking gem of a behemoth, a few blocks from the World Trade Center, is new and full of glorious purpose, with a shiny bespoke bridge striding across the West Side Highway, built to keep the best and brightest's tender, overactive brains intact and protected from the speeding cars below. The escalators inside stretch the expanse of two floors—go up or down two, then take the stairs one flight, as needed. Gigantic and modern, all overlooking the Hudson River. Battery Park is your new home.

* * *

You think nearly every other female you encounter—on-screen, in print, on the radio, and in person—is the epitome of loveliness. You are surrounded by a myriad of enticing (physical and spiritual) aspects of the female form.

Who and what you find desirable seems like a contradictory mess: a sexy, God-fearing, *brunetteredheadblonde*, wafer-thin with giant *nay-nays*. An equal parts chaste, suburban Amy Grant–ish and sultry, beach bunny Yasmine Bleeth–esque wonder woman. (*Wonder Woman is pretty hot, too.*)

Your dream girl is short and curvy, but also could be tall and lean. She is adorably bashful and yet the loudest voice in the room. A partner, a friend, a lover. She exists—and yet she does not. Another theoretical construct: a Schrödinger's (pussy) cat—the ultimate object of all your love and lust. You're still too scared to take action and "look in the box," the possibilities endless, unexplored, hypothetical.

You want to *kiss and make out and be naked and do it*. And yet you are absolutely terrified of what comes next. Most of the love scenes you've witnessed fade to black during the good parts—and when the sappy saxophone soundtrack cues the exhausted sighs and postcoital cigarettes, everything has already been said and done off camera. *So, what do you actually do with/to boobies (breasts), what are you supposed to do with/to a chach (vagina)?* God knows. (And God—and Pastor Chen—says to wait until after marriage anyway.)

Paris made the mistake of showing you porn that one time in sixth grade. He's learned his lesson and vows not to traumatize you again. He says the *Playboys* at the barbershop are boring, and you'll never learn anything that way—but it's more useful than what you'd learn from your biology textbook.

The daily struggle continues: the muted angel on your shoulder urging you to encourage your high school sisters to be holy in these confusing years versus the horny little devil on the opposing side, poking you in all your delicate, vulnerable spots, whispering the machinations of how to get into their pants instead.

* * *

You dream of John Hughes. In the dream, he is wearing Nike high-tops and a brown leather bomber jacket with "Flying Tigers" emblazoned on the back in red and orange. He's got on some badass aviator sunglasses and is sporting a wicked mullet. You notice all this and approach him from behind.

Oh, hello. I didn't see you standing there. I'm world-famous director, producer, and screenwriter John Hughes. You may know me from some of the most beloved movies about high school: The Breakfast Club, Sixteen Candles, Pretty in Pink, Ferris Bueller's Day Off, *and of course your personal favorite, you pervy nerd—*Weird Science!

I'm just here as a reminder that my movies take place in a world where the teenagers are only sometimes real teens but are mostly adults creeping into their thirties. Also, my fictional Illinois is based on good ol' fashioned Midwestern values (God, guns, and girls). *Mischief and mayhem have*

little real consequence there, except for maybe unreasonable detention and
sad stories of duct tape on butt cheeks! But teen pregnancy is always a true
danger, and kids do get beat up by bullies (both parental and peer), so it's
not all sunshine and puppy dogs!

Let's face it. Your high school experience is going to be much, much
different. Your school is comprised of mostly minorities: Asians, Jews,
Greeks, Latinos, Black people, et cetera. Shermer High School seems posi-
tively Aryan and WASPy compared to Stuyvesant! Long Duk Dong—why,
he'd absolutely disappear into the background in NYC! Oh, and ah, so sorry
about making him so over-the-top! His name is obviously not Japanese—but
"DONG-ER" is such a rad nickname! I'm surprised you haven't been called
the "WANG-ER" yet! Oh, you have? A lot? So, then, you're welcome!

Academic pressure is sort of a boring story arc, but that's really the
main throughline for the kids at your school. Bunch of nerds who take the
subway! No one's cruising around in convertibles here! Maybe some kids
will get knocked up, dip into recreational drug use. You might have the oc-
casional teacher/student sex scandal and the rare flash of violence—these
being the best chance of dramatic rising action.

Really, it's the pressure of getting into a good college for you and your
peers. B-O-R-ING! Sure, when you boil it down—the whole rich/poor and
have/have-not struggle—it's the same anywhere. The color of green unites
and divides as much as any shade of brown! But the Shermer vs. Stuyvesant
respective melting pots—well, our idea of exotic is more like a gooey cheese
fondue (very European, but one-note!) and nothing like your Szechuan hot
pot! Put it this way: John Cougar Mellencamp's Jack and Diane could have
been Shermer High grads; less so, Bon Jovi's more "ethnic" Tommy and
Gina; but Huang Wei and Li Yan would be ultrarare! A touch too spicy for
our suburban palate.

But what do I know? I'm just the architect of the most cherished filmic
teenage American storytelling of your generation! Oh, and sorry—I know
you are still conflicted about losing your virginity. I mean, it's not that big
a deal in the grand scheme of things. Lots of good Christian White boys
are doing the deed, and still sing in the choir on Sundays!

I acknowledge the double dose of general Chinese/Asian conservatism and Pastor Chen preaching about keeping it in your pants. But man, there are some cute girls at your school—with brains, too! Find someone to love (at least by senior prom)—and just do it already! Wrap your rascal and you'll be fine! And I don't mean with duct tape! Save that salute for when you are ready to use it, though! And I don't mean raising your fist in the air!

TIME TO WAKE UP! AND YOU'D BETTER COVER UP YOUR JEANS WITH YOUR JANSPORT—UNLESS YOU WANT THE WHOLE E TRAIN TO KNOW WHAT'S-A-HAPPENIN'-HOT-STUFF! CHAMBERS STREET NEXT!

* * *

You will kiss exactly three girls in high school. And touch exactly one breast.

The FIRST girl you kiss: Yelena Kristovich.

Yelena is a tall, thin brunette who speaks in a breathy whisper that makes you sweat. Mrs. Manheim assigns the two of you a scene from *Same Time, Next Year*. You play a middle-aged man and woman who meet up for an annual affair. You are both acting novices, but you rise to the occasion. You practice the kissing scene exactly once. (More out of fear and respect for Yelena's boyfriend, Ramon, one of the nicest and most muscular guys on the football team. He doesn't mind. You clearly aren't a threat.)

You expect the stage kiss to elicit expressions of shock and awe from your classmates, but no one seems to care. Yelena is just glad it's over and you didn't try to use tongue. You get a B+/A–, mainly because "your portrayal of a pathetic, lusty older gentleman was thoroughly convincing."

The SECOND girl you kiss: Allison Paik.

Allison is a proud "black-white-and-red-wearing" goth and introduces you to her curated bludgeoning industrial playlist while you dissect specimens together in Vertebrate Zoology. Bah pulls some strings with "Uncle Smitty" at the Museum of Natural History and procures access for you to observe and report on a rare preserved coelacanth specimen for your final project.

You end up making out in the Hall of Meteorites when she gets overexcited by the overwhelming beauty of "all the life and death across millennia" on display. She apologizes for getting carried away. She has a boyfriend who lives out of state and happens to be a proud "tie-dye, sandals-wearing" hippie. They met at sleepaway camp when they were kids and share a love of Tolkien. (It's not hard to guess who is on "Team Hobbit" and who is on "Team Mordor.") You get an A on your paper, mainly because Mrs. Belinsky thinks your report and photos "expressed the qualities of this peculiar beauty that few of us will ever get to see up close."

* * *

The THIRD girl you kiss: Gina Villanueva. *Your Gina.*

For a tense two weeks during freshman year, Paris debates asking Gina out—as in, "more than friends." Traversing this unspoken boundary—well, you admit the same thought had crossed your mind.

Paris has a solid rationale: "Dude, have you seen her natural upgrades? When we were kids she was cute and all, but now? *Damn,* I swear she's been chugging milk or some shit! Puberty is such a fickle bitch. I may not grow any taller, put on any muscle—and here Gina's developing into this brown-skinned pinup. Yeah, she's been like a sister to us—on the inside, emotionally (more like a stepsister or foster sister or second cousin). But now—*PHYS-IC-AL-LY*—I'm *all about it.* This tropical flower blooming before our eyes! Maybe I've been in love all this time and finally realizing it? Maybe I should lock that shit down before any of these fools figure it out?"

"She's guaranteed a bevy of new admirers. It's just going to get more intense. But she's always going to be the girl who made fun of your Teddy Ruxpin collection."

"Ahh, fuck that! You're right! I'll never forgive her. You know, she can have a real nasty streak. And she does have a mean bone in her body—and it's *not mine*. But *damn*, she is blossoming."

"She has always been a rare beauty—"

"And a *beast*! *A heartless, judgmental, bear-hating beast!* I mean, I love her—like you and I will always love her. Just not in that LOVE-love way. Maybe *spank bank* material? I'm just being honest! You thought it, too! Don't pretend to be so holy and innocent! I've been by when your mom made me wait for you to get 'cleaned up'—*pffft*—'sweaty from running around'? Those long showers? And if I'm being honest, in the movies in my mind, your mom has helped me make an *occasional withdrawal*, she's helped me to get *cleaned up*."

You punch Paris hard in the arm. Three sharp strikes.

* * *

Gina spent most of junior high (and now high school) crushing on Sean Grennan. Sean was the complete package: a jock (on the football and baseball teams) with the voice of an angel (musical theater). He was on the debate team (for fun) AND could rap the entire Tribe Called Quest album *The Low End Theory*, even the Phife Dawg Caribbean patois parts. With a good smattering of working-class Irish Catholic cops and newshounds in his fourth-generation veins, this kid was for sure headed to Harvard on a scholarship.

Gina never lost her cool and could flirt with the best of them. She would cock her hip (subtly shifting her weight to the perfect enticing angle) and accentuate the sensual curve of her dancer's behind—Sean, matching wits with a sideways grin, running his hand through thick strawberry-blond hair, eyeing her up and down. They would have hooked up long ago, if it weren't for Fiona.

Fiona was seemingly ordinary. Cute in a conventional way: small, short, polite, bland. Dark-black hair with a wisp of an Eastern European accent (Romanian, to be exact. *Kind of sexy, in a female Bela Lugosi sort of way?*). What mainly set her apart was her passion for *Star*

Trek. In any other high school it would be reason for derision, but in the hallowed halls of "nerd is Word" Stuy, it was street cred. She was Mr. Mattles's favorite mechanical drafting ingenue and could sketch the bridge of the USS *Enterprise* (Kirk's NCC-1701 and Picard's NCC-1701-D) nearly complete from memory.

No one really knew what Sean and Fiona had, but rumors circulated that she was incredible in bed. The gossip: Sean had lost his virginity to her. He was "assimilated into the Borg" and could not "disengage his impulse thrusters."

Gina was never friends with Fiona. She would make polite conversation about AP History, talk about the Red Cross fundraiser, and commiserate on how Mr. Boone would try to look down their shirts. Gina never particularly liked or respected Fiona, but she would never break girl code and make a move on Sean.

This led Gina to some half-hearted dates with David Li (*too hairy, can't get over the neck fur*) and a two-week stint with Jake Orlando (*such a mama's boy, hasn't met a mirror he didn't love*), and she got to second base with Raj Kapoor (*hot, but a terrible, slobbery kisser*). Then she fastened her chastity belt for the remainder of high school. At least a dozen fairly decent guys asked you and Paris to "put in a good word" for them. Gina's word in reply: *hellnofuckthat*.

Gina's focus now is on her studies and dance. She's dead set on a career in physical therapy: she'll ace her studies, finish Stuy near the top of the class. She aims for a full ride to some immaculate, green-rolling-hills New England collegiate wonderland. She'll then graduate summa cum laude and be a physical therapist to the stars. She'll dance in local productions and contribute, annually and equally, to Alvin Ailey and the New York City Ballet. This is not only a plan, it is a *decree*. Gina writes these goals on a checklist and names you and Paris as witnesses (*initial here and here*). She seals the envelope with a Pochacco sticker and tapes it inside her locker door, to be opened upon graduation.

* * *

A Stuy tradition: one of your lifetime highlights is participating in SING! (*Yes, with the exclamation point.*) The annual competition (*since the 1940s!*) among the more artistically inclined students in school, it's divided into three productions, with the first- and second-year students collaborating on theirs—curtains rising every March/April for the big show. (Low stakes—the seniors always win.)

You (sets, writing, directing), Paris ("acting"—mostly dishing out punny, salacious one-liners), and Gina (dance, of course) all contribute throughout the years. It's fun and an excuse to hang out, fool around, and flex your creative side, a break from the hard-core math and science curricula.

For Senior SING! the lead director, Sean Grennan (yes, *THAT* Sean), appreciates your deep knowledge of pop culture and has you on double duty. Besides, you're a fellow fourth or fifth period "Manheim-schooled" thespian—he admired your scene with Yelena, and how you portrayed "middle-aged loser" so realistically. You work with the team on the script and even help direct some scenes.

This year's production captures the zeitgeist of the intense, "real" music coming from Seattle. It's a send-up of all things grunge, featuring a four-piece band named "Jam-vana" trying to make it big in the scuzzy, nasty '90s. You help write many of the double entendres, mainly around fruit preserves. Paris gets the honor of some choice lines: "I put the A-S-S in BASS! I put the jelly and jiggle in the bottom end! I get down low and slow and my rhythm method is unmatched!"

Gina is head choreographer this final year, and she's frustrated by the lack of real danceability: there are no hip-hop beats, no hair-metal stripper sleaze. She's ready for this uninspired grunge phase to be over. But at least she has quality "Sean-time" as he hangs around and comments on the progress of her routines, or takes walks with her to iron out disputes with the drummer and review the dancers' wardrobe.

Sean clearly enjoys Gina's company, and Gina is over playing it cool. The easy way they lean against lockers and lock eyes, all their in-jokes, which Gina never explains to you ("The butt is not the behind! It's facing forward!")—it drives you mental. *So annoying and unbecoming.*

Nothing gets past Fiona, either. You catch her glaring at them, then slinking over to snatch Sean away, demanding that he check out her newly painted props and maybe engage in some backstage action.

The weeks go by quick. The final performance rocks the auditorium to the rafters. Chants of *SENIOR SING! SENIOR SING! SENIOR SING!* at earsplitting levels.

But, in a shocking turn: the seniors *lose.* "There is no guarantee that Senior SING! must win every year," one of the judges explains. Another alum: "Making light of the Seattle scene is in poor taste, so soon after Kurt Cobain taking his own life." But does that mean Junior SING! should take the prize? *Hellnofuckthat.*

There's yelling and screaming. Crying and stomping. It's utter chaos (pronounced: *KAY-oss*). Gina is backstage, slumped down against the dressing room door, her head thrown back in joyous rapture—she's just glad it's over, and it was a blast. She had a great time dancing and having playtime with friends. She's happy you saw her "do what she do"—and she got to see you and Paris in a (mostly) brand-new light, *her two doofballs—her Tweedledum and Tweedledee—* making the crowd laugh and cheer. Her two faves leaving the building, proud and forever weird.

* * *

Another Stuy tradition: at some point during junior or senior year there's the option to take Ballroom Dance to fulfill a physical education requirement (not to mention a handy skill to have in time for prom). No matter how underdeveloped and undercoordinated, your fellow geeks can learn to glide across the shiny wooden planks and stare deep into the mirrored expanses of their corporeal bodies for forty-five minutes at a time.

Gina was looking forward to this automatic ace, guaranteed that she would literally dance her way to a GPA-enhancing grade. The real question: whether you and/or Paris might be fortunate enough to be partnered with your own "Gina" Rogers. (You, *"Fred A-Starin'-at-Your-Feet"*?)

Lucky ducks, both. You end up sharing fourth period with Gina. Over the semester you will learn half a dozen or so classic dances— the waltz, the cha-cha, the Lindy, the tango—all set to music that your parents and grandparents would barely remember. At the end, a final performance worth most of your final grade.

Counting the steps, memorizing the patterns, and learning the angles of pivot, turn, and return—this is easy for you. What isn't: getting your body to listen to your brain. You think faster than you can catch the rhythm. Your gangly extremes can't compete with your ganglia. The neurons are firing, but your internal metronome is out of sync. You can think it—but you can't do it, *can't feel it.*

Paris, however, is doing well. His natural rhythm and eagerness to take a female in his arms without fear of rejection works wonders for his confidence. Gina gives him a jock-esque pat on the tush. *Go team, go.*

You step on Stephanie Gold, you trip Karima Jacobi, you bump butts with Cara Dhaverna. You wilt at the waltz, the cha-cha is cha-challenging, the tango has you twisted in your own Gordian knot.

"Dude, loosen up. Not like going-to-the-club loose, but get out of your head. I know your numbers thing is unstoppable, and you are supposed to count when you are dancing—but with your body, not just your brain. Stop computing so much. *Let go.* Let your body move—naturally, instinctually." Gina slips behind you to shake out your limbs until she's satisfied with the gelatinous consistency.

She whispers numbers behind you. Her hot breath in your ear, the metered counting—it makes you sweat, makes the hair on your arms bristle, makes your legs quiver in time to the whirling—and the *1-and-2-and-3-and-4* of it all.

"OK, now you lead."

* * *

Wanda Bernice agrees to pair with Paris for the final project. You are stunned. Gina shakes her head and mumbles *Lucky asshole* whenever Paris looks over to gloat. In Wanda's presence, he is a perfect gentleman: respectful, gracious, and kind. He hasn't poked her with an erection yet.

Paris is becoming a very good dancer. His hours of bopping his head along to hip-hop and improving his layup have instilled an inner rhythm that Wanda can count on for a solid grade. Gina is begrudgingly impressed: *Shit, he totally has that tango down.*

Your final cha-cha project will be set to "Tower of Strength," a classic performed by Gene McDaniels (*and written by the legendary BUuUuUurt BacharaaaAaaach—jazz hands*). This R&B staple has a mellow 120-ish BPM and clocks in at about 2:15, nice numbers you can get behind. It's just long enough for you to display all the moves you've learned. Gina will put together the simple choreography (*with added flair*). You simply need to be present and capable, and avoid turning an ankle or breaking a toe.

You are struggling. Gina is no longer shy about touching you inappropriately for the sole appropriate purpose of making sure you won't tank this cha-cha. Her hands are on your hips, your shoulders, your back, your chest. She grabs your ass to make *you move-to-the-left-and-TURN-two-arm-up-and-SWING-through-dammit-again-AND*—

You ask her if you should switch to a waltz—or maybe she should partner with someone else. "Seriously? I need this challenge, and you need a passing grade. I'm going to make you *excel* at this. We are going to be the definition of smooth, like Swayze and Baby."

You go on a *Dirty Dancing* tangent and tell Gina all about Patrick Swayze (*He should be getting more leading roles—what a triple threat!*) and Jennifer Grey (*Now there, there is some real talent in that bloodline! Joel Grey, such a triple threat!*). They have great chemistry. (*And they were in* Red Dawn *together!*) From murdering—and being murdered by—invading Russians to tackling abortion issues and steamy salsa in the Catskills—who knew?

"Tell me more—but keep moving."

You tell Gina that you are torn about the Mia Sara versus Jennifer Grey ranking on your list of alluring actresses. It would have been Mia by a mile, ethereal in *Legend* (*but come on, the only reason to watch that was for Tim Curry and the incredible makeup and effects work*), and you have a love/hate relationship with Jeanie Bueller (*annoying, but also kind of badass*).

"And don't forget to *step-two-cha-cha-cha-and-turn*—"

"So, on one hand you have *Legend* / *Ferris Bueller*, and on the other *Ferris Bueller* / *Dirty Dancing*. Weighing all factors, this is headed for an obvious tie. But Mia Sara has that *darkbrunettesexymystery*—which makes her seem a bit more mature—with potential for more dramatic, meaty roles. While Jennifer Grey has that bit of edge and wit and sharp comedic timing—and what a fantastic figure in *Dancing*—whereas in *Ferris*, she's in that one ugly, chunky outfit mostly. Well, guess the verdict isn't as clear when you consider that—"

"Good, sweet baby Jesus. Thank you, Lord, for watching over your child and blessing him." Gina is beaming with pride. She steps back and looks at your reflection. You see the two of you standing next to each other at your ending marks—perfectly timed and all symmetrical lines.

You look at your reflection in the mirror and meet your gaze. You smile as Gina turns to hug you tight.

"You did it, you lovable idiot savant. *No mistakes.* That was perfect."

* * *

You manage to get a perfect score for your final in Ballroom Dance, thanks to Gina's genius and covert puppeteering. Paris and Wanda have made a real connection in class and are going to prom together. Gina only really considers a Sean Grennan–level prom date. Unfortunately, that means only Sean will do. Fiona and Sean's "Federation Alliance" isn't going anywhere this late in the game: the couples' yearbook page has been collaged, paid for, and sent off to the press.

Gina is getting tired of saying "No, thank you" to her procession of suitors: the former classmates (Derek from Econ, Matt from Calc), the extracurric lotharios (Robert from SING!, Adario from bowling), and the random admirers who go for the ballsy last-ditch attempt (Wayne Cheaung—*mad props to you, dude*). Finally, Gina asks you to go to prom. You shrug. She punches you hard in the arm. Three sharp strikes.

It makes sense. Prom is a big deal in the grand scheme of future nostalgia planning and rearview mirror replays. No one else could bear all that weight of memory.

* * *

You meet at Villanueva Central with black tuxedos and shiny cummerbunds, flowers in hand. Gina's parents are relieved that she is going to prom with you—*just a friend, nothing to worry about*. They even insist on giving you some extra cash for ice cream afterward.

The Choudharys are bursting with pride that such a beautiful girl (*early acceptance to Amherst!*) would allow their son this ultimate honor. Paris wholeheartedly agrees—Wanda is way out of his league. Her flawless brown skin draped in a peach crepe gown—it's amazing he hasn't kissed her arm up and down, like Pepé Le Pew. Wanda is demure and shy—too much attention from the collective gaggle of parents is making her blush—which makes her even more appealing. How Paris's eyes aren't rolling back in pure ecstasy is a mystery for the ages.

Mrs. Villanueva pins the boutonnieres on you and Paris with expert precision and no stabs. Your lapels are adorned, and bow ties straightened.

Gina rushes down the stairs, a small bag of trash in her hand. She apologizes for making everyone wait. She ruins the slow-motion reveal: no one was ready with their cameras. "Don't make me come down the stairs again. Let's just take pictures in the hall and by the door, OK?"

Bah and Ma are making a fuss of how beautiful and grown-up Gina looks in her iridescent blue dress. Ma fixes her eye makeup for her, dabs some of her Trésor behind her ears, on each wrist, gives her a firm little kiss. Bah repeats the stories of how Gina would ask for his homemade dumplings when she was over after school, and how Paris always ate all the pork rinds.

Gina sticks out her arm, and you slip on the elastic band of flowers. "Nice. Very classy. Good job, bud. You look good."

"You're gorgeous, G. You surpass Molly Ringwald in her prime."

"*Oh, please.* That skinny ginger? No comparison." The wink is devastating.

* * *

The limo driver is mostly silent, but directs you to help yourselves to free soda and snacks. He rolls up the divider and cranks the air-conditioning. The traffic into the city is beyond a turtle's crawl, positively slugtastic at this point. Wanda is threatening to puke, but Paris strokes her thigh and rests his hand on a butt cheek, which has an amazing therapeutic effect.

Gina is digging around for a Canada Dry and cracks open the can for Wanda—7UPs and Pepsi for the rest of you. "Oooh, mixed nuts, some Linden's cookies, chips, and pretzels. But no booze, of course." She is annoyingly upbeat while the rest of you simmer and stew.

"Guys, we are going to miss the official photographer, and they'll be having chicken Kiev by the time we walk in the door. Might as well take advantage of the limo stash, or you are going to be starving. I see the cops and fire trucks up ahead, so we should be able to clear this and make it in time for dancing."

Wanda cries a little. Paris hands her a monogrammed (*PAC*)

white handkerchief. You snag some butter crunch cookies and share the pack.

Traffic clears, and with arms up through the moon roof, you blow past the flares and shattered shards of red plastic. You steady the girls until they are half outside, outstretched in the bright night of New York City.

* * *

The Waldorf Astoria has been hosting the Stuy prom for years now. It's everything you expected it would be: art deco and gilded opulence. You half expect to see some *Great Gatsby*–esque ghost leap out while you pee in the fancy urinals.

The signs point you toward the ballroom. Desserts are being wheeled out as Jane Rin rushes over to meet your group: "Fucking accident before the Midtown Tunnel, right? So many of the kids from Queens just got here. You guys missed dinner and the intro speeches! That sucks! Go to Table 18. At least you'll have some sweets."

After some small talk and a few unsatisfying spoonfuls of chocolate lava cake, the DJ mans the "wheels of steel" and the dance floor opens up. You can almost smell the hormones emanating from this coterie of hornballs in haute couture.

Lip-syncing and wiggling her right shoulder in time to Lauryn Hill singing about quiet, kind, sexy slaying—Gina is lovely, with her head back, her hair flowing, her full-bodied laughter. She arches and flexes, spins and holds still. She throws her arms around your neck and looks you in the eye. You see yourself reflected there—relaxed, happy, simply as *you*.

> In this moment and in the culmination of all the other moments just like this—for years and years before, and for years and years to come—she has your heart.

> (Your heart, your heart.)

"Hey, what's wrong? Aren't you having fun?" Gina in your ear, filling all your other senses. Warm and soft and sweet and—

"I'm just glad we decided to come together. This has been a night to remember."

"The right choice. The only choice, babyboy."

The DJ puts on "September" by Earth, Wind & Fire, and the crowd erupts. Not only is it a killer oldie-but-goodie party jam, but the BPM, the swing and sway, the attitude—it's everything Ballroom Dance prepared you for.

The dance floor instinctually parts. Pairs go off whirling together around the room. Joyous screams of *BAAAA-DEEE-YAA!*, flailing, jumping bodies, and fun for all, but you wonder if anyone else thinks about next September. In three or four months from now—*we won't be together*.

In September, that ninth month of the year—on the cusp of brown and red and crumple and crinkle—Gina will be settling in and enjoying the quintessential collegiate rolling hills of New England. Paris will be rushing some frat and decked out in Wolverines gear (*college sports, not X-Men*). And you'll be striding down St. Mark's alone in all black (*on the outside, on the inside*).

"Dude, come on. *Step-two-cha-cha-cha-and-turn*—" You're used to stern Gina yelling dance commands, but this is syrupy Gina with a misty look in her eyes now.

You use all your strength and hoist her up by the waist and spin. You spin and spin and spin. *You, spaghetti-armed Swayze, can only do so much.*

Gina hollers with glee, pumps her fist in the air, as your classmates encourage you. Paris sees you failing and runs over to help. Gina slides down. The three of you end up with arms around one another, sweaty foreheads meeting in the middle.

"We haven't huddled like this since touch football in eighth grade," Paris wheezes.

"Because you always went for my goody bits, you degenerate."

"You have a lot of goody bits, girl! And they have gained dividends in these subsequent years."

Gina punches Paris in the arm, three sharp strikes. Then kisses him hard on the cheek. The three of you hug and spin. Wanda ducks in under your arm and pulls Paris away for the slow dance.

"Somebody" by Depeche Mode plays. You pull Gina tight and she lets you take the wheel (*for once*). You drift together and you clasp her hand in yours, the other settles just above her hip. You start to sing quietly, and then the room booms loud together for the "may even be perverted!" lyric. Hoots and hollers—then you all collectively enjoy the silence.

You catch glimpses of couples making out left and right. Yelena and Ramon, tongues intertwined. David Li and Karima Jacobi, caressing sweetly. Sean and Fiona, anything but chaste. Gina gives you a *don't-you-dare* look, squints her eyes, and mumbles fake profanities at you. You laugh and blow raspberries on her cheeks, and she loves you for it. This was prom.

* * *

Every other teen movie ends at the prom: *the girl gets the guy, the guy gets the girl.* They speed off into the night in a convertible. There's kissing, there's hijinks.

You are mostly satisfied with your real-life prom experience—highway hiccups and all. (You think John Hughes would concur—but he'd likely add an additional zany subplot and want at least one bully to get his comeuppance.)

You aren't sure what to expect for the after prom and the *after-after prom*. Paris and Wanda are heading out to Jones Beach with her friends. Gina wants no part of that business because:

A. *Is it entirely legal to be on the beach after hours? I do not have time for these shenanigans and to have my scholarship pulled! There's going to be underage drinking!*

B. *I do not like sand in my personal places in a bathing suit, in the sunshine. Why would I go in a $200 gown, in the middle of the*

*night? Even if we get to change, where and when and how does
this costume swap happen?*

C. *I've seen enough of these assholes tonight, and some I do not care
to ever see again. I am more than happy to chill with my Young
Stallion dance protégé: ice cream, a scary movie, and a platonic,
no-stress sleepover.*

Paris escorts you both out of the limo and to the doorstep of
Villanueva Central. "Later, losers! I love you both! Have fun being
dorks and watching *Monster Squad* for the millionth time! I'm going
to catch the sun rise and shine on me in a whole new era!" he whispers, making a quick obscene index-finger-in-and-out-of-circle.

The limo door's ajar, exhaust sputtering. Wanda waves and
flashes a flask, pantomimes tucking it into her cleavage. Paris waves
back and gnashes his teeth. He barks and howls, rushes over, and
dives into Wanda's arms. You turn to Gina as they peel off, and she
whispers: "He's totally getting laid tonight. I can't believe it. Virgin
no more."

* * *

It's past 1:00 a.m., and everyone is asleep. You and Gina ease through
the rusty side door, head down to the basement. The same musty
den where you used to trade Pixy Stix (cherry) for Now and Laters
(banana), the scene of many a post–*Mario Kart* pillow fight (Gina
always Toad, never Princess), the loose wood panel where you hid
the butterfly knife that Paris thought he'd need for riding the train
(covered in notches, from every dropped practice flick and swivel).

"Ugh. Let me get these shoes off and change into jammies. Your
duffel is in the closet. You can use the basement bathroom to change.
I'll pop upstairs and be right back. Drinks are in the fridge. And if
you need to poop—I'm going to be a while, and there is plenty of
Glade in there." She sticks her tongue out at you and creeps away.

You slip on your Erasure WILD! tour T-shirt and gray sweatpants. You wash your face and look at your reflection in the oval mirror. Your eyes a bit puffy, but the same as usual. A little tired, but no worse for wear.

"Are you seriously pooping, Young?" Gina knocks and laughs. "I can come back!"

"G—come on. I'm just changing and freshening up."

"Oh. My. 'Freshening up!' Yes, madame!"

When you emerge, Gina surprises you. She's filming with her camcorder. "And here is our beautiful young miss, all ready for sleepybye! Look at that adorable fresh face and the signature, substantial mass of wavy jet-black hair! What a beauty, folks! *Spin, spin.*"

You humor Gina and do a tipsy turn, a half-hearted pirouette with your finger atop the center of your head. She chortles and snorts, the same way you've heard a thousand times.

"OK—this is the perfect chance for you to show me how to play that Cure song I love. The one about the truck and dying by your side—*hmmm hmmm pleasure is miiiiiinnne,*" Gina says with one eye shut, the other focusing on you through the lens.

You pick up Gina's battered acoustic, attach the capo, and strum. "First of all—for the audience out there—it's a song by the greatest band ever, THE SMITHS. This ethereal tune is called 'There Is a Light That Never Goes Out.' It is by *THE SMITHS, not THE CURE*—but I understand why you get this mixed up all the time. Both bands ascended in their popularity and significance in the '80s—THE CURE earlier and punkier than THE SMITHS. Both are revered for intense, atmospheric, god-tier guitar work. Both are stereotypically masters of the melancholy—in mood, tone, timbre, tempo, lyrics. Both share ties to the inimitable Siouxsie Sioux, songstress extraordinaire of 'Kiss Them for Me' and 'Cities in Dust.' So many other similarities—but again, just as many disparities.

"But—and here is where I suspect the confusion mainly lies—Robert Smith is the lead singer of THE CURE / basically *IS* THE CURE—the genius behind 'Just Like Heaven' and 'Boys Don't Cry.' Whereas Steven Patrick Morrissey *was* the lead singer of THE

SMITHS, vital vocalist of the aforementioned tune, as well as 'How Soon Is Now?' and 'Still Ill.' Morrissey is a solo act now, with poetic songs like 'Suedehead' and 'Everyday Is Like Sunday,' which our lovely Gina also adores. (Even if she originally thought it was sung by Rick Astley. *Rick Astley! Ugh!* How, how, can you possibly confuse the prowess, the perspicuity, the genius, of a true crooner like Morrissey—for *Rick Ass-less*?) Oh, and supposedly, they hate each other—Robert Smith and Morrissey, I mean. I'm not sure how they feel about Rick Astley. They're probably just ambivalent."

"Hmm-mm, yes of course, *fascinating*. Anything else you want to mention for your MTV *Alternative Nation* audition?"

You didn't realize she was still filming. *"Gina! Erase that please, please, please! C'mon!* I was just kidding around." Guitar set aside and leaning on the couch, defensive posture, and likely not getting what you want.

"Never! You were mugging for the camera! I will treasure this snippet forever! This is what I'll think about when I'm off at Wellesley alone and missing home. However far away, I will always remember and love this. You being really, really into something and full of these dorky facts and figures. *So, so cute.*"

"Don't make fun of me! Give it here, please, *please.*"

Gina plays keep-away and easily dodges you, playfully shifting the camcorder from hand to hand, around her back, now in front.

You grab her from behind, by the waist, and hold her tight. "Fine. Just don't show anyone else. Especially Paris."

"I swear. It's just for me." She sets the device down on the table and turns to hold your head in her hands.

You're not sure what she's reading on your face—no clue what your furrowed brow and tired eyes must look like to her. She puckers her lips, a smirking curl to the right. Is she pointing to the bottled water or the TV remote? Her eyebrows are raised, as if to say *Yes*, but you haven't asked her anything. Not playing shy or coy, no hidden language.

"Hang on, let me try something," Gina whispers.

She kisses you. She kisses you gently on the lips. She kisses you again, and you meet her tongue with yours. Her hand slides down your chest and stops on the ten-ton truck hammering in your left side.

"That was——" You pause.

(Your heart, your heart.)

"*TOTALLY WEIRD. OH MY YUCKNESS, YOUNG! EEEEEEW!!!* It was like kissing my, my—*cousin or something*! I am so sorry! *What was I thinking?* I kept telling you I was ready for a complete change in every aspect of my life, but I did not mean like this! I blame prom-xiety! Prom-goggles! Prom—uh—"

"*Prom-iscuous-ness?*"

You both laugh and hug and spin. *Dance partners, lab partners, co-op video game partners.* Partners, but maybe not in everything. She's completely right.

She's right. You love her, maybe always loved her, but this feels wrong. *Right?*

Gina hugs you tight, slow dancing in slippers, the linoleum shuffle soundtrack generated underneath your feet.

"Young, I love you." Gina pushes her hot cheek against yours.

"I know."

"Don't Han Solo me. I mean it. *I love you, forever.*"

"I know, G. I love you, too. But 'fall in love and get married' love?"

"Seriously? Are we going there? Yes? No? I don't know."

"So, let's say we have a summer thing before college—and we *don't* end up together, married with children. I'm not your 'Asian Al,' you are not my 'Pinay Peggy.' Imagine us in the future: still best of friends, having barbecues with our respective spouses and kids. With Uncle Paris, his second or third wife in tow, rubbing his round belly, snacking on ribs. Think about that backyard full of future children: mouthfuls of chicharron, running around with water balloons, spiking volleyballs. Can you bear the thought of them looking at Uncle Young—who teaches them the names of all the Green Lantern Corps, who takes them to the latest Disney movies, who sneaks them gummy treats—and he's the same guy who lost his virginity to their mom? Can you imagine that?"

"Wait. You're still a virgin?"

"*YES*. Aren't you?"

"Of course I am! And of course you are, too! I was just trying to break the tension! *So gross.*"

"Yes. *So gross.*"

"But then again."

"NO."

"*Oh my goddess!* I was just kidding-*lah*! OK-*lah*? So serious and stupid-*lah*!"

"To be honest, I always thought that you might end up with Paris. On the surface, you have more in common—your interests and all. And that Wanda thing is never going to last."

"No friggin' way! Me and Paris? *Uh-uh!* And Paris likes the berries DARK, or lily-ass white! Nothing close to my shade of caramel! He goes for the extremes! He's either into pale, pale blondes or redheads—or sexy Black girls. It may depend on his level of self-loathing, but I think he's still going to end up with a hot Indian girl. Remember Anjali from test prep? The one who went to Bronx Science? She was cute and wicked smart. Paris just ignored her. What a dumbass."

You barely noticed, but the two of you have moved across the room. You are sitting on the couch now, side by side, with Gina's legs slung in your lap. She reaches over to take your hand.

"So, the cliché: when we're 40 and still single, we'll get married? Or suicide pact? *Hmmm hmmm pleasure is miiiiiinnne?*" Gina, as she slaps your palm and turns your hand over. She plucks a hair and slaps again.

"Suicide pact, but death by chocolate: full on overdose of Reese's Peanut Butter Cups and packs of Twix. Two hearts stopped by too many dual chocolate servings, times two hundred. Maybe some Oreo milkshakes to wash it all down, but just two. More would be overkill."

"Done and done, babyboy. Cross my heart and hope to fly."

She takes your hand and puts it over her left breast. You don't move. You feel the sweat start to bead on your forehead. You feel her heart, under the thin T-shirt—the slow constant rhythm of this supple mechanism.

(Her heart, your heart.)

Gina pecks you on the lips. You pause. A quick punctuation on this conversation: *a comma, not a period.*

* * *

You fall asleep on the coach with MTV playing in the background. You don't remember hearing any songs you liked. And you think Gina may have left the camcorder running the whole time. That boxy square lying on its side, tape slowly running out, the clack and exhausted sigh as it comes to an end—all the while capturing a spot on that familiar wall, your voices, your laughter, static then silence, these late hours into the next morning.

Would she realize what was recorded on these reels? The two of you alone this night—what happened here—was it something to be treasured and rewatched, slipped neatly on a shelf, or erased and forgotten? Was this something to be remembered?

* * *

You look at your reflection in the mirror and meet your gaze. You avert your eyes—turn on the tap, scrub your face. This same basement bathroom where you filled squirt guns, dared each other to repeat "Bloody Mary," styled each other's hair.

You expect her to barge in: frenzied knocking at the door, excited to see you awake and tired, happy, blissfully mournful and wanting diner food. You think coffee will help tamp down these strange, unkempt feelings.

You blame this dizzying tempo—the pull of nostalgia defeated by the rush and push of change. The pace and your pulse quickening—the steps too fast, too sudden. The same partner, but this last dance growing unfamiliar. Reaching out to hold on, before you spin too far out past your marks. You aren't ready to let go.

But she's your friend, your found family. The trust and hope you have in her—and her in you—remain infallible, a privilege. This kind of love is unconditional. This kind of love is eternal.

That kind of love was what it was—but it was never meant to last (*at least, not like this*). But you'll remember—everything.

She was your fourth. She will always, always
be your fourth—and more. She's your Gina.

Su Su Special Delivery and Road Trip Revelations: Santa Cruz

JUNE 1994

On the breakfast table, an opened cardboard box: a tie-dyed teddy bear with a surfboard; a Santa Cruz Skateboards T-shirt with the iconic blue Screaming Hand; chardonnay and merlot from a winery in the Sonoma Valley; and finally, a photo with a letter paper-clipped to the back.

The photo:

Su Su is getting acquainted with the locals in Santa Cruz. Long hair slicked back with salt spray, skintight wetsuit glistening in the balmy breeze, pleasantly exhausted and leaning easy against the shiny length of surfboard planked upright in the sand. His hand is on the shoulder of a bikini-clad, tattooed babe with a pink mohawk, as if to say, *Her hair's not the only thing that's going to be stiff!*

The letter:

My dear Young,

The sun and surf in Santa Cruz are unbeatable! My new friend, Dawn, treated me very well and helped "wax my board."

I even made it out to Sonoma and Napa to have incredible wine with some friends. Success or strife—feast or famine? *My treat, my treat*—they were shocked at how much has changed!

I still couldn't bring myself to visit San Francisco. The memories there—I didn't need to revisit them. Old friends and girlfriends—*peng you* and *nu peng you*. Can men and women be friends? Sometimes things just happen, sometimes we get to pick and choose—but *prepare to lose!* Auntie Corrina (sweet and fun), Jeannie (still great friends), Alexis (uncomplicated), Yi Shen (worth it), Wu Jing (painful but necessary).

Ma and Bah—that was an easy decision for your father. He knew he would risk it—*all or nothing.* Once they became friends, he didn't need to look elsewhere. She didn't either. He got to her by being a role model for her *huan dan* little brother! Charmed the whole family! Your Gong Gong and Po Po adored him because he was good to everyone—including himself. But most importantly, they trusted him to do right by the ones he loved, protect them from anything. He was safe, sturdy, supportive. Above all, he was her best friend.

You see how they balance each other out now—*huo* and *shuai*, yin and yang, the fierce phoenix and her steadfast dragon.

He lets her enjoy the spotlight because that is what she needs. He can easily have the whole banquet hall in the palm of his hand also, but he wants his wife to have the glory—it reflects back on him even brighter that way.

I need to find that kind of love in my life—and so do you. But timing and the right partner—you'll have to take that risk, *at the right time.* You can't really love someone until you understand them as a friend, and they can't truly love you unless you are one to yourself.

Peace and grease!

Your ever-loving, one and only,

Su Su

P.S. Have you visited Uncle Tang recently? I know you don't want to see his cranky ass without a good reason—but take the hint and go soon!

CHAPTER FIVE

"Heaven Up Here"

MARCH 1996

Soundtrack highlights:
- "Love Song"—Tesla
- "Love Untold"—Paul Westerberg
- "Love My Way"—The Psychedelic Furs

Young was working the afternoon shift at the Undertow on a chilly Wednesday, with Erena along to keep him company. She mostly kept quiet: snacked, studied, stayed out of the way in the cut-out cubby corner of the stockroom. Young never took the busy weekend shifts anymore, but filled in on the odd weekday, when the more laconic patrons came in to peruse the latest releases or the bargain bin.

Erena would inevitably feel cooped-up and emerge to pace the floor, pushing forward from behind the curtain of the ever-changing specialty string lights (still snowmen—much better than sharp-beaked turkeys or angry-antlered reindeer). She would do a loop of the floor: absentmindedly riffle through the new music, fresh DVDs, rental-worn VHS tapes, and random merchandise like Astronaut Ice Cream (essentially, hardened nondairy creamer).

Never starting a conversation, but never one to deny the chance to chat—Erena was never more than a CD flip away from someone hitting on her, young, old, men, women, *everyone*.

"Can I get your number? Maybe we could meet up and talk about the latest Björk album?" a tall, blond bohemian with rugged stubble asked her, as he continued flippantly flipping through Bauhaus, Bad Religion, Beck, Blondie—

"Erena. Hey, Erena!" Young shouted, trying not to sound tense or panicked.

"Young, you're going to have to expect a girl like that to get some attention," Jim said as he handed Young a stack of Foo Fighters CDs to price. "Especially when she's not hiding in a hooded sweatshirt. You can't hold on too tight. Just relax—and watch."

"No, thanks," Erena was saying. "I just wanted to check out this cover art. She's super cute, but all that caterwauling—not my jam. And I'm a hundo percent taken! See that tall drink of seltzer water over there? The untamable mop of fur atop that pale head? The Samson to my Delilah (*hehheh*), that guy behind the cash register pretending to read that comic book—oh sorry, *graphic novel*? That's my significant other—*significant* being the operative word—because how in the living daylights did he snag such a babe, you're thinking? That's a *significant* surprise! Anyway, I'm still technically a teenager, and you look at least thirty-two. Maybe you should buy some discs, take them home, settle in with your headphones, and spank it to the photo inserts of Björk-y Björk? *Wait, wait!* I wasn't done! Hang on! You walked right past the Tori Amos section—she, I like! And the photos inside are super hot!"

Jim laughed as he witnessed this exchange, patted Young on the shoulders, and stacked the new shipment from Merge Records. "She's right. What does she see in you? She's a keeper, Young. And that guy never buys anything anyway. No big loss."

Erena scooted over to the till and high-fived Jim: "Jimbo! Big Jim! Sorry about that. You saw, I tried to sell that dude some CDs and he wasn't having it! Besides, you don't pay me enough for my charm offensive."

"I don't pay you anything, short stuff!" Jim joked, passing a box over for Erena to stack.

"*Aha! There you go!* You want to give me a shift or two?" Erena used her most dashing smile.

"I would gladly give you any of Young's hours if you want them, sweetheart."

"Nah! I was just kidding! Young needs the cash and the perks. I already spend enough time with one nerd, don't need to fill my entire life with them. *I've met my quota! I've met my quota!*" Erena with dramatic waving hands, looking skyward.

"Go, *shoo*," said Young. "I'll stack the boxes. Pack up your stuff, and we can get you a slice when I clock out. Jim, you'll have the pleasure of *our* company next week. If you don't mind my delightful partner taking up space."

"Jim loves me! Everyone loves me! I don't mind being your sales and marketing executive, but I draw the line at physical labor! Not going to give you the free show of me bending over and exposing my pulchritudinous peach. You two perverts!" Erena kissed both hard on the cheeks.

"Young, you are never going to do better than this little loudmouth! If you show up without her, you're fired!" Jim gave Erena a smooch, handed her a five-dollar bill. "Pizza's on me."

"Fuck, Jim! Very sweet of you, sir! Don't make it a habit, contributing to his delinquency! Gotta make the boy work hard for the money, to take out his honey! *Pssh psssh!*" Erena cracked an imaginary whip, as Young suppressed the urge to point out the paraphrased Donna Summer lyric that Erena inadvertently plucked out of the air—or through osmosis from the "D for DISCO" section.

* * *

Young's pager buzzed and shocked his hip. He looked at the display: the ten digits of his home number. He found a pay phone outside the lecture hall and called to find his father on the end of the line.

"Hi, *guai guai*. So convenient you have this beeper now! Nothing important, but Tang Bo Bo wanted you to call him. He said he was cleaning up Su Su's things. There is a box that he forgot to give you. Want to come home for dinner after? I made beef curry, and I'm trying the *pancit* Uncle Villanueva brought us last time."

"Thanks, Bah. I'll be home tomorrow, and I can pick up any leftovers. I can come see you and Uncle Tang in one trip then."

"Good plan. Tell Erena—how you say her name? *ERRRR-UH-NUUH?* Tell your *nu peng you* thank you for your beeper and for the cat necklace she got for Mei."

"I will, Bah."

"Ah, so she is your *girlfriend*, not just *friend-friend?*"

"Yes, Bah. She is." The smile on Young's face was evident in his voice across the phone line.

"So great! So pretty—and you say she is studying to be a lawyer?"

"She is the smartest girl I have ever met."

"Good, good. You studying together and not having too much fun, yeah? Doing well in school and then you go eat and—"

"Yes, Bah. We study together all the time, most of the time."

"*Xiao xin*, be careful, yeah? You understand?"

Young paused, wondering if his father meant what he thought he meant, or if it was a more general "be careful."

"OK, *guai guai*. See you tomorrow. You go call Tang Bo Bo now."

* * *

Uncle Tang had always been around, ever since Young could remember. He was always drinking beer, tossing back peanuts, pounding his father or Su Su hard on the back. The camaraderie expressed by older Chinese men always involved some sort of beverage or snack being handled wildly—spilling and pouring, munching and crunching, and roaring and roughhousing, all things Young wanted no part of.

The auto shop was a trek from the Main Street 7 train station, fifteen or twenty blocks off Kissena Boulevard. Young remembered the walk, could recognize the sign—mostly in Chinese characters, but TANG AUTO was in bright red across the awning. If he walked farther, he'd reach a steep hill with a clear view of Shea Stadium. Su Su used to love taking that detour to catch a glimpse of the Mets in action, hear an echo of the cheering crowd.

"Young. *Hao jiu bu jian*—haven't seen you in long time! You got taller, still too skinny." Uncle Tang placed a muscular arm around Young's shoulder and led him inside to a cold, rusty folding chair. "*Lai, he bei cha,*" he said, offering Young a Styrofoam cup of hot oolong tea.

"*Xie xie, Tang Bo Bo.* You have something for me from Su Su?"

"*AAAY!* What's the correct name for your uncle?"

"*Xiao jiu jiu.* My *xiao jiu jiu.*"

"I never understand why your family is so confusing with names. 'Su Su' is wrong—everyone knows that! But your family love you so much—let you and your *mei mei* call him the wrong thing all these years." Uncle Tang laughed and shook his head, pulled out a Reebok shoebox (Michael Chang, Size 10 1/2 Reebok Pumps)—the packing tape in layers, a small note visible under the yellowing stickiness: FOR YOUNG—WHEN HE STARTS COLLEGE.

"Sorry, Young. I forgot I kept this box for you. I was cleaning out the safe and found it. Your uncle even called me last year to remind me. Sorry, sorry. *Wo wang le.* Your *bo bo* is getting old. Can't remember! And you didn't come visit me—so partly your fault! *Ni de chuo, xiao di! Heh heh!*"

Young thanked Uncle Tang for the tea and stuffed the shoebox in his backpack. Uncle Tang let him turn the old brass key for old time's sake, the rusty chain rattling the garage door open.

A block away from the train entrance, Young's pager buzzed: "911*3123174," code to call Erena back, ASAP.

"Hi, loverboy! I know you were supposed to go home for dinner, but any chance you can come over to me instead? My RA reminded me it was my turn to supply late-night hall snacks and I entirely spaced! Could use your help lugging the num-nums back from Kmart: Little Debbies, soda, and some of that cheesy party mix. Can you meet me in an hour, pretty please?"

Young called his father to explain. Bah was disappointed that his latest trial run of beef curry was destined for the freezer, but proud that his son was being useful to someone else.

* * *

"You sure you don't want to come out and socialize? Dana and Ash will be there, and you love them! They consider you one of us already! Tanya might swing by in her PJs later. You can ogle those big ol' bitties in their natural environment."

"No, thanks. I've got to finish reading this chapter on enzymes and catalysis and other boring stuff."

"OK, fine. I won't be out too long. And you can figure out what to do with your brand-new—"

Erena walked over to her dresser and pulled out the bottom drawer. It was empty except for a pair of Young's T-shirts (both black: Tool and *Æon Flux*) and sweatpants (plain gray).

"*Ta-da!* If we are cohabitating, we can be *adults*. You need some territory of your own, a bit of real estate you can arrange and rearrange to your heart's desire. I left my lucky Wonder Woman panties in there. I'm marking the territory with my scent, asserting myself as the alpha! Just teasing. I thought the lingerie would be funny, and you'd get a surprise boner every now and then. But feel free to move in. And stop smiling like a creep-o! I know you love it. *Toodle-oo, kangaroo. See you in a while, crocodile.*"

Young put on his "Movie Moments" mixtape to drown out the sounds of the junk-food party outside the door. As a break from the finer intricacies of molecular reactions, he pulled out the drawer and transferred the items from his backpack: his toiletry bag, two pairs of boxer briefs, and a pair of black socks, keeping his Hawkman graphic novel with him for train rides. Then he decided to open the box his uncle had left for him.

On Erena's desk, an opened shoebox: a Monkey King clay figure that Young had dropped and broken when he was a kid. The head was knocked clean off, the hand clasping the iconic golden staff cracked—not invincible, as the myth promised. Now it was fixed and expertly superglued together, bubble wrapped, and rubber banded.

A ticket stub for Billy Idol and Faith No More at Jones Beach Theater. Su Su had chaperoned the three friends there. Paris and Gina agreed that Billy Idol and Su Su were the most kickass over-thirties they knew.

And a small plastic dome, bright-green flattop sealing the semi-transparent cup. It was the kind from the ShopRite machines, by the automatic doors—the ones that usually housed finger puppets, erasers, or stickers. A spare quarter, crank, dispense, lift the metal door for treasure or trash.

A photo:

Young (age ten or eleven) and Su Su with microphones, staring at a large blue screen with "Country roads, take me home" in stark white letters. Probably from the Christmas party that year Auntie Yi Shen knocked over all the sesame cookies.

A letter:

My dear Young—

I know you love surprises and secrets like this! *It is very Indiana Jones of me!* If you are reading this, then Uncle Tang did right and gave you this mystery box.

Consider this your graduation present—the sentimental stuff I had to leave behind. I wanted to make sure this ended up with you, Young Stud.

The ring in the plastic ball is the main reason I left this box in Uncle Tang's safe. (I hope he remembers the combination! If not, I'm wasting time writing to my nephew in the future! *See, sounds like a movie!*)

You never got the full story, Young M.C.A. You never met Auntie Wu Jing. I was going to ask her to marry me. She was my number "2" greatest love—so I used 25 as one of my lotto numbers, since her name sounds like *wu*, for "5"—so there you go and get "2–5," 25. (*I turned some of that bad mojo into good!*)

Remember that time when I came to visit, and you and your ma came with me to that jewelry store in Chinatown? We got you those Doraemon stickers and special *dan ta* from the bakery? I bought this ring that day—your ma helped me to pick it out.

When I flew back to San Francisco, I was ready to propose. I told her I had saved money and wanted to quit my suit-and-tie job for something more "me." I had a business plan and everything! But she broke up with me instead, broke my heart—didn't believe in my vision, didn't want the risk of marrying an "entrepreneur" (*she didn't use that word*). She wanted the stability of "Su Su, Esquire," and I couldn't bear another day dressed like that, grinding my life away. I didn't love her enough to sacrifice my youth. She didn't love me enough to watch me soar.

I'm glad I could spend time with you two these past years—happy to have helped our friends and family while I figured out my past, made use of the present. But now I need to find what I want to do with the future. I had some major luck along the way, but luck is what you make of it—and I'm ready to roll the dice! I'm ready to bet on *me*.

Money's not everything—do NOT forget that. Money can fix some things, help others go away. I'm leaving this as a "minor problem solver" for you. It's a cushion, if you ever need something to fall back on. The rock is yours. *YOURS.*

Peace and grease!

Your ever-loving, one and only,
Su Su

P.S. I hope I've sent you some postcards and pictures by the time you get this. Am I looking good in the future? How's my hair? Am I with a naughty hottie? More than one?

P.P.S. You need a safe place to stash the ring. Your ma looks through your stuff when she cleans your room. She found that *Playboy*, behind the record player. I said it was mine! You are welcome, Cream-of-Some-Young-Guy!

P.P.P.S. I'm probably not going to go back to SF. But I may wind up in California somewhere—after I've seen the rest of the world! When I get settled and you have time, I'll let you know where your rich uncle bought a mansion! It will be the one with the roaring tiger and rising dragon decorating the massive entryway!

* * *

Young traced the edge of the green plastic cap with his nails and squeezed with his other palm. A satisfying pop and release.

The ring was smaller than what Young had pictured. It had a single shiny diamond at the center, two small red gems beside it. It was beautiful and unexpected—exactly like something Su Su would have chosen. Young loved it.

* * *

It was nearing midnight, and Young had completed all his assignments. He had listened to "If You Leave" and "Don't You (Forget About Me)" at least twice now. He didn't want to venture out and risk the chitchat with the cool kids, the stoner crowd, the hipsters—anyone.

He was missing her company—missing the sound of her voice, the curves of her body. Her eyes—especially when her face was *this* close—her head crooked at an angle, a smile fighting to escape, patient and waiting for him to fill in the silence. He missed her little hand—the way her fingers would shift until they were satisfied and comfortable, intertwined with his. He missed her kisses—sometimes soft and warm, sometimes sharp and quick, sometimes slow and seductive. He missed how he felt when he was with her. He missed her—and only her. None before, none after.

He was in love and ready to say it—at least in some way. He didn't need to wait for a special occasion, other than the fact that they could be together again—and soon.

Young picked up the receiver and started dialing the numbers to Erena's pager.

* * *

"Hey! You missed out on a rager! Stuart crammed cheese snacks up his nose and launched them at Spencer. So gross how they shot out—*took flight*! The cheese and snot aftermath made it that much worse! What's the matter? Why so quiet? Why are you looking at me like that?"

"I paged you. Check your beeper."

"That's why I came back to the room. They're playing card games, if you want to take a break. I came back to check on you. What does '143' mean? I can't figure it out. 'I-A-E'? Is that Latin? Or am I supposed to read it backwards or something?"

"I thought you would know. Terry had this cheat sheet of pager codes that he showed me."

"Uh-uh. Didn't get to study all of those. Don't know this one, mate. Must have missed it."

* * *

Young still hadn't uttered the words to her. Were they a curse, or were they the incantation to finally free him from all this uncertainty?

143 was widely known as pager code for "I love you":

Ⅰ = I / 1 letter
Ч = L-O-V-E / 4 letters
Ⅎ = Y-O-U / 3 letters
(AND 1 + 4 + 3 = 8)

It was perfect.

* * *

"*Oh shit!* This is you saying it. *SAYING IT.* In the most special *beep-boop*, space-cadet, Young Obi-Wang way!"

He nodded slowly.

"Oh, wow. Baby, I'm so proud of you! *This is huge!* It means the world to me, but I knew this whole time. Not in so much what you say, but what you do. I was just waiting for you to find the right time, the right way." Erena smiling, laughing—in tears.

"I love you, Erena. I love you."

"I know, Princess Leia. I know. *1–4–3, beepboop.*"

Fifth Love: "Daydream Nation"

JUNE–AUGUST 1994

Soundtrack highlights:
- "Out There"—Dinosaur Jr.
- "The Wild Ones"—Suede
- "Something I Can Never Have"—Nine Inch Nails

You are finally done with high school and going to NYU in the fall—cap and gown and all that's passed, a happy memory. Your family is overjoyed that you've managed to obtain grants, scholarships, *and* financial aid. You suspect that Ma might be a little conflicted with your choice, given the Cornell, Brown, and Binghamton acceptances, but the near full ride to NYU certainly makes up for it.

You are firm: *NYU is the best choice.* NYC is the steadfast lover, and you have no reason to leave her for a new mistress. All these suburban kids reveling in the freedom of being in THE CITY, of becoming the cultural and intellectual elite, bred on a diet of neon and ennui—*you know better.* You spent four years hurtling underground every day to emerge bleary-eyed at Stuyvesant High School. These other kids probably smoked and shotgunned beers in some wooded parking lot, while you clocked the inspiration for every Scorsese-scented tableau. *You are better than them, at least you think you are.*

Just before graduation, your parents arrange for you to spend some time in China. They agree that before you dive into your studies and plot the course for the rest of your life (*in the medical profession*) you should see mainland China, at least Beijing and Shanghai. A graduation present for you: a quick jaunt through the land of your ancestors, which they subsequently abandoned for their slice of *tian tang* in Queens, New York.

Even better still, you will finally meet your pen pal in person. Truth be told, neither of your pens have been in motion these past few years. You can't remember the last exchange shared. You dig into your cigar box of old letters and find one from the summer of 1992. Wendy sent you a picture of her sitting on a picnic blanket, about to nibble on a giant *mantou*, the other hand clutching a Coke with Chinese letters (*bet no one peed in* that *can*), a sweet half smile—all peachy-cheeked and sun-shaded fair.

Half a world away, this girl that you barely remember writing half-hearted letters to about baseball players she'd never know (Dwight Gooden, Wally Backman), movies she'd have to watch on blurry reels and obscured by subtitles ("What do you call Superman in Chinese? Will you ever get to see *The Goonies*?"), and music that she was sure to be offended by ("Cinderella is a group of guys with guitars, in blouses and heavy makeup").

The plan: Wendy and Xia Ai Yi will come to New York for two weeks first. They will do some touristy things on their own and have you accompany Wendy for some "young person fun," letting Ma and Auntie luxuriate in their nostalgia. The Xia ladies would be staying in the city, at the Marriott near Koreatown (easier to get to the Broadway shows). After that, you'll fly to China later in the summer for your "Coming to China / Terms with Communism" tour. You wonder if you'll feel anything—if your soul will glow.

Ma is relieved that they don't want to stay at your house. She often calls your home a *gou wuo*—a dog pen. She never has time to clean up the way she wants to. She is always "out," socializing, never "in," entertaining.

Su Su is mildly distraught that he is going to miss Xia Ai Yi's visit. He's forever on his road trip, somewhere in California helping the odd friend with some odd jobs: pulling weeds, fixing up rusty old cars, trying to sell off sweet vintage Harleys. You tell him on the phone that you are finally going to meet Wendy. He tells you to be sure to *pai pai pigu*, just like he used to do to Xia Ai Yi when they were kids. Ma grabs the phone from you and yells at him to quit it, stop boasting about old games of grab-ass and his general bullshit—*hu shuo ba dao! Gou pi!* (literally "dog farts"—one of your favorite phrases in Mandarin—funnier in the *gou wuo*). But she ends up laughing and chatting with her brother, stretching the cord across the kitchen, her voice piping in through the receiver, half an octave higher than usual. You love his packages and mail, but it's not the same. You miss him.

Ma explains that the Xia family has come into even more money recently, selling the land-use rights for country fields that their ancestors held for generations. (You decide against asking too many questions. You'll just never understand the *ifs, ands, or buts* of what does or doesn't pass in "Communist" China.) That, plus Xia Su Su's job (*computer things*) means that Ai Yi and Wendy are free to have a "true international summer holiday"—this year, every year. Rich and replete with Chinese renminbi, they have more money to spend than ideas how to spend it. "Everything for your China trip, Xia Ai Yi arranged for you. She insisted she pay for it, can pull strings for 'VIP treatment.' Don't worry, they can afford a hotel room in Manhattan for a few nights," she huffs.

* * *

You ask your mother: "Why eat at Shanghai Johnny's if Wendy and Ai Yi can have the real thing any day, every day?" She reponds: "We always have visitors eat what they are comfortable with at first. Show them that *hua qiao* can make Chinese food here almost as good as back home! You can take them to eat American junk later. *Ni pei ta men pao* and Ma will give you some extra money for hamburger and pizza in the city, OK?"

The sun is just setting when the yellow cab pulls up to the curb. Ma starts knocking excitedly on the window. Auntie Xia bursts forth and is immediately fighting with Ma to pay the cabbie. You hand Mei over to Bah and try to intervene. With a terse, smiling nod, Ma telepathically communicates to you to go help Wendy out of the car.

You offer your upturned hand into the passenger door and feel the slight warmth on your palm. You hear the squeak of the vinyl seat shift as a long, pale leg emerges, and a small foot avoids a slick rainbow oil puddle. On the streets of Flushing, June 6, 1994, you meet Wendy Xia in the flesh for the first time.

* * *

Bah orders for the table. Ma and Ai Yi chat away, exchanging compliments and denials, as expected. Xia Ai Yi is well-dressed, all neat lines and tasteful jewelry. Her full face is pleasant and sweet. She doesn't look quite comfortable in her clothes, her mannerisms, and only speaks in an elevated whisper. Humble and gentle, she seems almost embarrassed by her wealth, her hand on her chest covering her necklace every time she leans in to hear Ma speak. She looks *plain, average*, in spite of her designer wares: a country girl still intimidated by her clever, gorgeous friend.

Wendy sits between you and your mother. You assumed she might be quiet and reticent like Xia Ai Yi, but she is beautiful, captivating, and extroverted. Her *Chinglish* is polished and exemplary, her Mandarin flawless, her British-inflected English posh but in a cheeky, Helen Mirren *Excalibur*-era way. Her smile is warm and friendly. She takes Ma's hands in her hands. She says how she's seen pictures of the two friends when they were her age, and how she wishes she will grow as beautiful as the years pass. Her eyes seem to sparkle. *No—her eyes sparkle infinitely.*

She gets up to say hello to Bah and gives Mei kiss after kiss. She produces a stuffed panda out of thin air, and Mei is enraptured. Bah is positively blushing and can't stop complimenting her height and beauty: *Hao gao, hao shou, hao piao liang!*

You've been left out of the "Xia Charisma Tour 1994" thus far, but Wendy finally turns her attention to you. She rounds the table and sits back down, the napkin gingerly folded across her lap. Her hand tucks long, lustrous black hair behind her right ear. You gulp hard as she looks at you—unflinching eye contact. As if on cue, her white cheeks flush strawberry sweet.

"Young *guh guh*—we properly, finally meet." The English elocution, the emphasis on the last lingering *t*, the flash of tongue between her teeth, is intoxicating and spellbinding.

* * *

On the drive home, Bah is effusive. He can't stop talking about *Wen Ding, Xiao Ding, Ding Ding, Wen Wen, Wendy—hao gao, hao shou, hao piao liang!*

You are lost in thought and desire. Wendy is stunning: tall, slender, still with the mochi-cute plump cheeks from those childhood pictures. With heels on, you think, she could look you dead in the eye—and then *you'd be lost.*

She's up to date on all the latest Western movies (seen *Jurassic Park* in London!); has great taste in music (New Order, live in Japan!), and is amazingly well read (loves Margaret Atwood). *She even said grace for the table before we ate. Lord, is this a sign? Do I need to pray on this?*

"*Guai*, show her some fun and take her around the city. She's going to decide where she wants to go to university soon. Maybe she will come here, NYU—and, you know, *ni men liang guh*, you two. Eh? Eh?" Bah elbows you hard. You can't help but smile as you remind him to keep his hands at 10 and 2. "She even admitted that she kept your photo taped on her mirror for years. *Waaaah! Shuai guh!*"

"She's going to Oxford, Xia Ming already said." You peek at Ma from the side-view mirror. Your mother sits quietly, staring out the window and holding Mei's hand. Your sweet, slobbery baby sister is asleep in her car seat, clutching the panda in her other arm. You think you can hear Ma singing in Chinese, but you can't say for sure.

* * *

Ai Yi and Wendy call your mother to report about what they have seen and done on their own: taken the Staten Island Ferry back and forth, gone up and down the Empire State Building, matinees of *Les Miz* and *Phantom*, steaks at the Palm, shopping along Fifth.

Xia Ai Yi wants to treat your mother to a spa treatment at Elizabeth Arden in Connecticut for the weekend.

"What about Wendy?"

"Wendy is more mature than you. *In-de-pen-dent*. Traveled the world already! She spent last summer in Italy, just her and three Chinese school friends, alone in Rome and Venice and Florence. You can take her to the movies and go *guang-guang* around Manhattan. See your 'hanging out' places for the kids—wherever you go with Paris and Gina. You want to invite them and introduce her to your *peng you*?" Ma shouts at you as she packs her rolling suitcase.

"Paris and Gina aren't home now. So just me and Wendy. I'll take her around the Village?"

"Whatever you want. You're a big boy, and she is a big girl."

* * *

You want to impress Wendy with *real* American New Yorker sites. You take her to Louie's Lobster Lodge in the East Village. The place is ironically decorated in Americana from the '50s and '60s—all "*Beach Blanket Bingo* and Gidget-y." Old yellow posters and nets on the walls, plastic fish, and tin signs for Moxie and other strange regional beverages that never made it to New York City. You sense that Wendy's polite giggle and occasional eye roll is in good fun at enjoying the kitsch.

She eats her lobster roll like a hot dog. She just chomps through the buttered bun, the sweet meat, the creamy mayo, the minced onion and celery. Eats it like a rich person who has this for a typical Saturday lunch. You savor each forkful, each briny morsel a lingering pleasure—prolonging the experience as long as you can, every red cent reflected in the red-flecked flesh. *Does she not know the value of the noble crustacean? Is* long xia *that easy to come by in Shanghai?*

"*Kuai dian, mah.* Hurry up and eat, Young *guh guh*! Let's go play!" Wendy tosses the fries in the trash and leads you out by the wrist. She lays down $50 on the table and doesn't wait for change.

* * *

You take her down through St. Mark's and buy her a bootleg Ramones button. She shrugs, but lets you attach it to her floppy denim hat anyway. You walk by the Rubik's Cube–looking sculpture by Cooper Union. On your way to the park, you stop for a papaya drink, but Wendy has other ideas.

"Can you get us some kind of *jiu*? Anything. It doesn't matter what." Wendy clutches your arm and looks up with full mischievous twinkle.

"Sure. I know a guy who works at this store that lets NYU students buy whatever. I can probably get us some beer or something." You smirk.

"No *pi jiu*, something stronger, please."

Half an hour later, the two of you are taking sips of Stoli Orange out of a brown paper bag and lounging around in a patch of hidden shade in Washington Square Park. Tribal drumming, shirtless punks, and stoned NYU summer school students encamp you and your fetching tourist. Wendy isn't shy about drinking in front of the locals. She swigs deep and bums a smoke from your secret pack of Marlboros.

"Mama and Ai Yi would not be happy to know we are doing this! But they used to *xi yen* and *he jiao* all the time when they were younger! They pretend that they did not, but I hear the stories of when they were schoolgirls," she reels off as she takes a drag. "Mama doesn't know what I do with my friends. I love her and want to make her happy, but it's so *wu liao! Ming bai, ma?*"

You nod slowly. You get it, sure—*so boring.* She's entitled to go wild, especially with a purse full of *yuan* to spend. But isn't China uber-restrictive? Isn't the *gong chan dang* keeping tabs on everything she does and wants to do? Thought police and all?

"*Kai wan xiao!* You only think that because you see things from America and ignorant Western films. That's *your* propaganda! We can do whatever we want! At least in a big city like Shanghai! And in 1997, in Hong Kong it will be—how would I say this so you would understand—*hen da de* PARTY! I don't think much is going to change when the British leave. Just more fun!"

She finishes the last of the booze and lies down across the bench. Her thick, glossy hair fills your lap, and she closes her eyes. "*Wo he tai quai le! Ni zhao gu wo, ma?* Too fast, oh, no. Take care of me, please, please."

The sun streams through the elm trees, and the shadows fall across her face in waves. The sweat beads on her forehead, and she unbuttons her cardigan. Her blue bra straps peek out around her shoulder, the pink tank top in bright contrast to her delicate porcelain skin. She lifts her arm and sways her hand in time with the muggy summer breeze, in time with whatever sweet Chinese pop melody she is humming now.

She closes her eyes. You can barely hear what she's saying: *somethingsomething* then *chong xiao* and *jian mian.* You think she says she's been waiting to meet you in person, ever since she was small. She says something else, but you can't manage this depth of Mandarin. Eyes still shut and smiling, she rises up on her elbows for a minute and shifts her head into your lap.

She looks up at you through long eyelashes and blinks slowly, the high-pitched tune still wavering from her, through her. Her eyes are dark and clear in the dusky sunlight. She's not the little girl on the other side of the world anymore. She's here, she's warm, and she's staring at you like she has a secret. She puts her hand into the black shag of your hair and pulls you down to her parted lips. She rises to meet you. The stuttering rhythm of the hops and skids of skateboards, forever intertwined with this memory of your first kiss.

* * *

You both sober up over iced coffees and bottled water. You tentatively hold hands for the long walk along Broadway, fingers awkwardly caressing and then parting, coming together and then away. Wendy can't contain her glee and hugs your torso, making you trip and laugh. Still high off emotions and adrenaline, the inebriation fading, you duck into McDonald's to freshen up before meeting your family in Koreatown. You agree to limit this newfound affection and the physical nature of your international friendship—for now.

When you arrive at the hotel, Ma and Xia Ai Yi are already in the lobby waiting for the hired car. You're surprised that your mother has a Nike duffel bag slung across her suitcase.

"Xia Ai Yi paid for another room for you here. *Ta bu fang xin*—doesn't want Wendy to stay here by herself for the weekend. She thinks NYC is *tai luan le*. After all the places she has traveled, New York is too much for her! Worse than London! *Aiya. Mei ban fa.* I packed you some clothes, and here's some extra money for the weekend. Have fun and be good, *guai-guai.*" Your mother kisses you tenderly on the cheek, much to your surprise. You think she's slipped into relaxation mode a little early.

Wendy dazzles again. She's pattering on with your mother and her mother, wishing them the best time to "rejuvenate their bodies and rekindle their sisterhood." She kisses them both goodbye.

You hear Xia Ai Yi ask Wendy, *"Ni men yo he jiu, ma?"* And you think that your life is over—that you've been caught underage drinking and are to blame for leading this unblemished creature astray.

"Yi dian dian, mama! Just a tiny bit! Just a taste!" That sparkle, that dazzle, that enthralling measure of innocent honeyed magic.

Ma glares at you and shakes her head. She grits her teeth, mouths something only you can see, but you can't quite understand. Ai Yi laughs and kisses her girl. The two of you wave goodbye as the sedan heads east into the night.

Wendy whispers: "Let's go upstairs."

* * *

Wendy and her mother are staying in Room 808 (you imagine they requested the exact room number and paid extra). "Twenty minutes. I'll knock," Wendy says and closes the door.

You fumble the keys to 807. You toss your bag in the corner, and then crank the shower on. You wash the sweat away and try to steady your pulse. You take a deep breath and sputter out the lukewarm water. Damp and naked, you are thankful that your mother packed well: toiletries, two full outfits, and clean underwear. You brush your teeth, drag a comb through.

You look at your reflection in the mirror and meet your gaze. You look fit in a black tank with matching boxer shorts. *Handsome, even.* But you avert your gaze, the anxious expression sapping your confidence.

You look out at the stalled traffic below on 6th Avenue and draw the curtains closed. You dim the lights, not sure what to do with yourself next. You hear a knock.

Through the peephole, you see Wendy in the white hotel robe, her hair in a neat bun on her head. She's wearing glasses. You breathe a little sign of relief—and disappointment. You expect that she'll have a deck of cards in hand, will want to play some *ding pai*, eat some shrimp chips, and watch basic cable before slumping down at this overnighter with her longtime buddy, *her pal.*

Wendy walks in without a word. She slips the DO NOT DISTURB card over the handle. She latches the lock and heads toward the bed.

"So, what do you want to do now?" Your voice is an ineffectual whisper, a choked gurgle.

You notice her ears stick out more than you thought—cute, but still more than expected—and *such sexy librarian frames*. Before you have a chance to comment, she takes off her glasses, folds them, and places them neatly on the bedside table. She glibly tosses the decorative pillows to the floor and unmakes the bed with a deft sweep of her arm. She lets her hair down with a shake. The white hotel robe drops. She's wearing a lacy blue slip—not appropriate for any sort of platonic sleepover.

You look at each other, soaking in these last moments before the world changes forever—before what comes next overtakes everything that came before.

* * *

She stands up, silent and sure. She places a hand on your chest, looks down the full length of your tense body, locks eyes with you, and says (*in English or in Chinese or both—you aren't sure anymore*): "Do you want me? Have you thought about the two of us like this before?"

"*All my life,*" you reply. You lie.

You try to channel a modicum of leading-man machismo, any testosterone you can muster in this moment. You still can't believe how Wendy—who you perpetually picture wearing a *"Keep smile! Don't forget best sun? Duck, every day!"* sweatshirt—is now half-naked before you and threatening to claim your "unsullied flower garden."

She runs a hand up your back, under your thin undershirt, pulls it over your head, and tosses it aside. The awkwardness of all your gooseflesh and full erection, now with nowhere to hide.

She strips off her silk top. She stands before you in matching powder-blue panties. The sheer contrast of her dark hair and her brown nipples against the unblemished canvas of her ivory skin makes you lose all rational thought. This is the first time you've been in the presence of naked breasts (in your adult life, in an overtly sexual nature). You notice a beauty mark in the shape of a bird on her rib cage. On her left knee, a scab, still healing.

My God, what am I going to do with all of this—THIS? Lord, help me.

Then her slick tongue is in your mouth, and her breathing is ragged and rapid. You are on top of the sheets, bodies moving against each other. The air-conditioning is on full blast, the white noise and cold air doing nothing to drown out the moans, stave off the sweat.

Her kisses are hard and forceful. She bites your lower lip. She grabs a handful of the thick mat of your hair and pushes you down the curved trail of her chest. You pause to take the dark grape of her areola into your mouth. She cups your head and pushes you into her armpit and makes you lick the tender fold between her arm and her clavicle. She turns her head into the pillow—a sharp cry.

There is no point in questioning if this is lust or love. Your bodies take over, and motion follows motion. Her legs are wrapped around your waist, and she pulls your body in tight. You feel the warmth of her sex rub against yours. You match her rhythm, the friction through thin fabric sending twin impulses of pleasure and pain.

Hot breath in your ear: she says something you can't comprehend. As you meet her mouth again, her hand slides under your waistband and grazes you *there*. Your heart beats uncontrollably as you search her eyes.

(Your heart, your heart.)

She laughs and rolls away. She shakes her head and gets up from bed: "Not tonight. *Not everything.*" She strips off her underwear and kicks them playfully toward you. Before you can register what's happened, the water is flowing and the steam is rising.

"*Come here. Come. Here.*" A clear call from that other room. She opens the curtain and water escapes, hitting your face, your chest. Your naked bodies together now under the cool spray. She kisses you and smiles through the droplets. You wipe the water from her face. She doesn't look anything like that girl in your photos anymore.

You start to speak, not sure which words or which language will emerge. She lifts a finger to your lips and then silences you with her tongue again. Her hand moves down, her fingers grip around you: a caress, a twist, a pull, and a gasp—and you've lost a bit of your virginity.

* * *

You spend the rest of the night in your hotel room—alone. You decide to head down to the street to smoke some cigarettes, decompress. Exhausted, you limit your curbside brooding to ten minutes and two cigs, the heat dissipating from the asphalt, the humid NYC air clinging to you.

You pause outside her door. Wendy must be quietly snoring, spread-eagled in the gigantic bed, satin eye mask on. She was right to be safe and not sleep in the same room, in case your mothers return from their spa weekend early, or the two of you manage to snooze late in each other's arms. Best to avoid scandal in this bilingual rom-com (*with international rights reserved—a Golden Harvest production!*).

You splash water on your face and swish the complimentary green mouthwash. You look at the reflection of your tired eyes, ridiculous grin, and shut off the lights. The amber glow of the digital clock reads 3:36 before you start drifting off.

You dream of melting ice cream that you can't eat fast enough. A kitten laps at the pooling mess on the ground. Mrs. Greene unspooling roll after roll of paper towels for you. Paris and Gina are there, and you think they are holding hands, or they might be pinching each other's elbows. Paris is pumping his fist in the air when he notices you. He sprouts angel's wings and is about to take off, leaving Gina grounded.

You hear a sharp rap at the door. You bolt upright. "*Guai*, time to go home."

You open the door. Ma looks fresh and beautiful. Her skin is flawless, just a whisper of red lipstick. Her hair is neat and up in a bun. She rubs your cheek and tells you to wash up and get your things.

"Back so soon? Did you have a good time with Xia Ai Yi at the spa?" you say as you towel off your face.

"Just OK. Ai Yi left you a *hong bao*. Wendy looked very happy, but so tired. Not so pretty without her makeup on. You take her to eat? Movie?"

"Walked around school. Had a good time. Should we take them for *yum cha* or American brunch?"

"*Aiya*—did Wendy not tell you? They already left in the taxi. They changed their flight to earlier, rushing out as soon as we got back. She told us not to wake you up. Ma was in the lobby having free coffee, to let you sleep until checkout time. You'll see them again in a few weeks. *Kuai dian mah!* Hurry up! Maybe we can catch late-afternoon Sunday service."

* * *

"Dude. That is the *hottest shit*! But I will give you credit that it's also very romantic, in a Japanese-love-hotel-on-the-down-low kind of way. I can't believe that dorky Sanrio girl looks like *THIS* now? And you got to do stuff, *actual STUFF*." Paris starts miming all kinds of sexual acts, half of which you can't even identify.

"It was *a lot*. I just went on autopilot. I'm still in shock."

"Of course you would be! You and your inexperienced ways! (I can let you know what worked for Wanda Bernice.) But if wily ol' Wendy was taking the lead and everything, she must have gotten *somethin' somethin'* before. She's not so innocent. Don't be fooled! Don't be naive, Young Grasshopper!"

"I mean—sure, she must have—"

"And you are headed to her territory next! She's got it all planned out! She wants to make it special for you! Back to the motherland, to finally become a man! You'll be overlooking the Great Wall or some pagoda shit! You are going to get down to the sexing and the blowing and the—" (More obscene hand gestures.)

"We've known each other since we were like seven. It's not like that."

"Over a decade for her to obsess on *shuai guh* sexcapades! Maybe she wants to exchange her services for a green card? All part of the plan, so she can marry you and move to the *U-S-A! U-S-A! F-U-C-K! Get you LAID!*" (Fist pumping and more hand gestures.)

"*Moron. Stop.*"

"I see your creepy smile! So friggin' excited for you, my brother! Make me proud, OK? I can tell you've been working out and doing some push-ups. Bulking up your scrawny ass and all."

"Just don't tell Gina."

"Are you kidding? Already told her you had a tryst with your baby-time pen pal! She's heard plenty! Don't worry—she doesn't think less of you. We both hope you make 'beautiful memories in the land of your ancestors.' But I'm calling it the 'Sexy Summer of Wet n' Wild Wendy!'"

* * *

Day One: Travel to Shanghai

You will spend a total of nearly twenty-four hours in transit to get to Shanghai. From there, Xi'an, and then you'll fly to Beijing for the second leg of your tour. A rare opportunity: *hen nan duh.*

You scribble your thoughts: *Flight: smoking section in the back is a blessing and a curse. Airline food is surprisingly good. Unlimited cup ramen if you ask for it.*

The cabin lights dim, and the snoring comes in from all directions, all tongues, all ages. You look out the window and clock the miles, the nebulous ocean, the distance from here to there. *International waters—anything can happen.* You sleep. You don't dream.

* * *

Outside customs, you spy a woman in her late twenties / early thirties. She is in a peach-colored suit, bright-green silk scarf around her neck, dark sunglasses perched atop her head, and clutching a sign that reads "YOUNG." Underneath it is your full name in Chinese characters. She introduces herself as Vicky, the tour director, and tries her best to only speak in English to you. "Welcome to China and beautiful Shanghai! American Born Chinese—ABC—we will show you so many nice things in your homeland!"

You climb into a black limousine and take in the clashing land-scape: timeworn buildings, busy roads packed with cars and bikes, soaring metal juggernauts, and glass guardians patrolling the water. Cranes and heavy machinery are everywhere you look. Everything is either going up or coming down, the ancient shoulder to shoulder with the future present.

Five-star hotel accommodations: *there's even a bidet!* The first time you've seen one in person (you try it—and *hate it, hate it, hate it*). The bed is firm but comfortable. You shower off the stink of re-circulated plane air and admire the amenities: free slippers, a comb, a shoeshine kit—quality knickknacks that you pack for Ma and Bah as souvenirs.

Hotels in China are called *fan dian*, the literal translation: *food store* or *restaurant*. The etymology isn't much of a mystery, since the food ends up being amazing. You order room service and ask for the special Chinese meal of the day, *not the Western one*. You get stir-fried veggies and rice cakes, slow-cooked chicken soup with a hint of that herby, medicinal flavor (reminds you of when Ma was pregnant with Mei), and the best spicy shredded pork dish of your life. You fall asleep with a full, piggy belly. You don't dream.

Day Two: Shanghai

You hear a hard rap at the door. You are surprised to find Vicky standing in front of you in a casual black dress.

"Good morning, *xiao di*! I can call you my *xiao di*? We have a full agenda. VIP tour! Just you and me! Consider me your *da jie* for this trip!"

You mumble *"Ni hao"* and shake off the remnants of sleep.

"But there is a change of plans. Our time in Shanghai is going to be very short. Xia family arrange for you to meet their daughter in Xi'an right away! Sorry, you will not get to see much here—just one day and night."

* * *

The mix of East and West is extreme: the omnipresent shine stretching skyward, the screaming iridescent buzz, the food stalls with steaming delicacies, the cacophony of traditional Chinese music with the *thumpbuddathumpDUM* of the latest Eurodance tracks. It's too much for you to process as current reality. It's *Blade Runner*, *Buck Rogers*, and *Bubblegum Crisis* barely a breath away.

The Bund is astounding—the meeting of the whole world at this port. If you blinked and turned, you might fool yourself into thinking these were buildings along Central Park West or, in the distance, London or Paris. You're amazed and thrown off balance. You look up and the vertigo hits you. *This is 1994*—you can't imagine what this will look like in 2004. *Are we a decade away from jetpacks?* The world expands and contracts at the same time—the ancient, the modern past, the hyper-tomorrow.

* * *

You wait in line for the Chinese opera, the *jingxi* performance. Next door, there is a small steam-enveloped food stall selling a dozen mini *xiao long bao* served in a small paper tray, like how you'd get an order of French fries at the beach snack shack. You hand over the equivalent of two US dollars and get a no-nonsense serving from the no-nonsense vendor. You don't even have time to splash on some sauce or ginger shreds. You wolf them down as Vicky presents the tickets for the show. You may just be ravenous, but these are the best soup dumplings you've ever had. The intense flavor of the morsels of meat and the unctuous broth—perfection. Shanghai Johnny's are not far off, but nowhere near the same. You will always remember this hasty meal and compare all others to this streetside delight, one you may never find again.

The theater space is small but elegant. The ceiling is low, and the room barely fits 150 people in the sweltering box. Vicky scoots you over to your spot and gives you a hand fan that smells of sandalwood. The performers take the stage, only elevated a few feet above the seated audience. Then comes the traditional cadence of drums, cymbals, and strings.

The players emerge in full regalia: red and blue silk robes, elaborate headdresses, and even some prop swords and fighting staffs for dramatic flair. Ma would hum or sing this kind of music when she was feeling homesick, but never for long. These overwrought, high-pitched vocals have never been your favorite. (*They sound like Bruce Lee warming up.*)

The exaggerated head tilts, turns, and tics; the finger poses and hand shapes; the flip and turn of wrists; the flourish of long sleeves; the rush and scuffle across the stage; the layers of thick makeup for emphasis upon *emphasis*—all things you've seen on videotapes that you never cared for, but live and in the flesh here, you are entranced.

The repetition of the melodies and the rhythm is hypnotic: the clapper, the gongs, the vibrating strings, the crash and bang, the sustained weaving high notes. Even if you can't understand the words, you try to follow the story: *Something about demons and dragons, maybe? There is a long-lost love and a betrayal—you are sure. A battle and the prince is triumphant! You think—or you hope.*

When the show ends, Vicky takes you through Nanjing Road. The pulsating lights and endless stretch of retail stores are as vast and vapid as anything you'd find in Times Square. Traditional snacks steeped in soy sauce and sweet brown sugar, just outside the Shanghai McDonald's.

You take in the cityscape from the promenade. You lean across the rail together and watch the water mirror the nebula of neon surrounding you. The real world here is burning and scrambling your senses, lights brighter than the fantasy on-screen and in your dreams. The Oriental Pearl Tower, with its distinct outline of spire and bulbs, threatens to launch into the stratosphere. The entire skyline is crackling with science-fiction energy, gravity scarcely holding these structures back from liftoff.

Vicky slides a chunk of grilled lamb from the bamboo skewer and offers you the rest. "Delicious! Eat while it is hot!" She puts an arm on your shoulder. "University soon, yes? Many fun years for you. What are you going to study?"

"Maybe psychology—maybe pre-med studies." You chew and shrug.

"I don't see that for you. Maybe literature? Maybe art? I can tell from your looks." She gives you a friendly pat-pat in the center of your back. "Come back to Shanghai after college. Even more *fazhan* then, like a real-life video game alien city. You know—*pewpewpew, bangbangbang,* very cool!"

Back at the hotel, your suitcase still zipped shut, never unpacked, ready for Xi'an. You sleep. You don't dream.

Days Three and Four: Xi'an

Vicky finds the limo outside the airport terminal. You are straight off to visit the famous Terracotta Warriors. You have three days in Xi'an, and only one for sightseeing, before Wendy has her way with you. (*An-ti-ci-pa-tion.*)

You walk along the edge of the excavation site to the first pit, toward the other tourists milling about the guardrails and reading the multilingual placards. The way the sun streams into this colossal hangar and highlights the stone and dust—you can't help but hum John Williams's Indiana Jones fanfare.

Often called the Eighth Wonder of the World and only discovered in the mid-1970s by local farmers digging for a well, these 8,000-plus life-size statues are the most extreme collection of action figures on the planet—neat rows of archers, swordsmen, horses, generals, all in orderly battle formation. You are in awe of the meticulous organization. If only you could activate some Pym Particles, you'd grow to Giant-Man proportions and pluck up these army men for some serious playtime.

You imagine the child emperor commissioning these silent sentinels into creation, determined to tame the afterlife with this funtime arcane nation, well before he had a chance to understand his own earthly realm; conquering flesh and blood in the here and now, the Middle Kingdom ground under heel, his gilded glory reaching as far as the horizon—and yet he knew he couldn't defeat the guarantee of decay. The greater the accomplishments, the more he had to lose: the neurotic and necrotic gnawing at his soul.

All that power, and still this immeasurable fear of frail humanity. How many thousands of artisans and laborers were serving at the emperor's pleasure under this decree of foolish distraction?

Did he really believe that these inanimate soldiers could storm the Gates of Heaven? Was his faith in the hereafter that unshakable? Did he simply ease his fears by arranging the chariots, the high command as play-pretend? Did sovereignty of this mimicry in clay make him feel in control of the uncontrollable? Did incense, incantations, stars, tea leaves, bones, *prayershopesdreamssystemssymmetry* play a part in all of this? Did this inordinate, overwhelming order quell all the coming, consuming chaos (pronounced: *KAY-oss*)? *Does this all sound too familiar?*

Or maybe this was the whole purpose? The everlasting foresight that centuries later, generations of royalty and peasants alike would continue to bear witness to the emperor's great work. That these solid shadows were mere tributes to the living legions, infinitely grander than these fearsome, frozen figures. Flesh and fire fade, but we perpetually reach for the eternal, the immortal, through the stories we create and leave behind.

Vicky surprises you with a souvenir: a green-and-yellow-fabric-covered box. Inside, a set of figurines lying in a bed of red silk, a chip of fake ivory to latch it closed.

This playset: the stoic swordsman, the steely general, the fumbling archer, the willful horse. *Who are you, in your empathy? Who do you serve? Why do you serve? Who has power over you now?*

Maybe you are the fickle king (*"Wang" is your namesake, after all*) still haplessly arranging and rearranging, again and again. *Action, inaction—are you waiting to move forward or waiting to be still? And what exactly are you waiting for?*

* * *

"Bell Tower and the Drum Tower are close by, but you will see similar places in Beijing. Just eat some unique food and then over to meet your pretty girl, *xiao gu niang*, eh?" Vicky explains and directs the limo to the Muslim quarter / street, Huimin Jie.

You sample the *liangpi* cold noodles and the sesame-encrusted *bing*. You are fascinated by the Chinese covering their heads with *taqiyah* and other religious or indigenous garb, by the bins overflowing with spices, by the shops with beautiful outfits hanging from the rafters—and by the simple fact that there are Muslim Chinese.

"You are Christian, correct? How is this any different? Muslim Chinese have been here for many dynasties! Same with the Jewish. Even more recently, a lot in Shanghai since World War II. You have all these in the US? China is much closer to Middle East here. Not all religious people are White or Brown or Black!" Vicky gives you a friendly nudge, in between slurps of chili-oil-covered goodness.

"But what about religious freedom in China—"

"A lot of the issues are long past. The Cultural Revolution and today—many things are different and changing, lessons learned now. Religion here—much is history, tradition, ethnicity, minority. Some is considered superstition, some is art, some is seen as ancient Chinese culture. No easy answers for anyone. Same in USA, yes? But we are here for tasty food, not for questions! Do you want to try the sour milk? Like the *yogo* you have back home?"

You arrive at the hotel and check in. The sheets are crisp and cool. You try to nap. You don't dream.

* * *

Vicky meets you in the lobby bar and buys you a beer. She walks a few blocks outside with you, surprises you by asking for a cigarette. You cough and sputter. *These Chinese cigarettes are harsh.*

"The nightclub is straight down the street, only four or five streets. You have all day tomorrow alone with Xia daughter—and then we three go to Beijing for your VIP tour! What happens in Xi'an can be your secret. Two young kids! See you day after tomorrow!" She stomps out her smoke and adjusts your collar for you. "We are good friends now? *Hao peng you?* Listen to your *da jie*, OK? Don't think too much. So serious face you have! Too *nian qin* to have *this*—" She rubs hard in the middle of your eyebrows. "Fun, only, *xiao di!* Young and carefree! Good time summer memories!"

* * *

Xi'an X Bar could have been a nightclub anywhere in the world— one that blasts music with nonsensical lyrics and booms a driving beat. The translucent dance floor is lit with squares that alternate colors. The strobing lights above, the low rumble of the bass, compounded with the jet lag, are giving you a migraine.

You see Wendy standing at a high table in the far corner. You've started to cross the room when the DJ announces a special performance: a man with spiky hair in a shiny sequined suit, surrounded by three *lah mei* on each side. He's singing into a microphone, the melody of a nationalistic anthem—*but this must be the dance remix?* The electronic synths, laser show, and thunderous rhythm has everyone clapping along. You manage to skulk under a crossbeam and wait for this late-night pep rally to end.

A quick scan of the room, and you notice the crowd is a mix of about 70% Chinese and 30% expats or tourists—*wai guo ren*. Lots of tight-fitting dresses and loud silk shirts. You are simply clad head-to-toe in black: black button-down, black jeans, black shoes.

Wendy, dressed in all white: a tiny tank top and cigarette-white pants. Her pink underwear is visible through her outfit. The piercing, rotating rays reveal the silhouette of her slender figure. She's wearing big hoop earrings, and her makeup makes her look older, more mature. She's with a group of four girls, all dressed similarly. They are laughing, clinking glasses; one of their boyfriends refills their drinks. Another boy kisses his girl's neck, and she playfully swats at him until he drags her away by the waist. You swallow hard and move in.

* * *

"Young *guh guh!*" Wendy squeals and throws her arms around your neck, kisses your face. You can smell the alcohol on her breath, but she is firmly in control. Her body's cool from the air-conditioning, but quickly warming as she presses close to you. She makes a quick introduction to her circle of girls. You can't hear any of their names. You nod, and they cover their mouths and laugh. *(Like Hello Kitty and friends.)* They shout and smile at you, smile and then point. You don't think you'd understand them, even if the music weren't drowning out each word. They give Wendy a squeeze and collectively push her toward you, into you. They all wave goodbye, and now it's the two of you, alone with the spiraling swirl above.

"Do you want to—dance?"

"No, no time. Here, finish my drink."

Vodka soda. You gulp it down.

"*Lai.* Come with me."

Oh, dear Jesus. Please help me. What fresh heaven or hell is coming next?

* * *

Wendy slings her purse over her shoulder and leads you down the corridor toward the back of the club. You rush through the tunnel, pass the fluorescent restroom cubicles, and come to a red door.

Wendy says hello to the bouncer, who opens a private entrance into an elevator bank.

When you enter, you notice there is only one button, which leads straight to the top floor. There, as you peer down the hallway, it's clear this is some VIP retreat, with a few discreet rooms on a massive floor, in a tower. It's dark except for some spare spotlights on glass-encased art and artifacts, everything in imperial gold and red and black.

Wendy stops at Room 1406, and the latch clicks open. It's a beautiful, modern hotel room, stark and all curved angles—a huge television, a white leather couch, and a king-size bed. The floor-to-ceiling windows overlook the otherwise quiet world of Xi'an outside, now being covered by motorized curtains.

Wendy steps away from the control panel and turns to you. She puts her hand in the bramble of your hair and pushes it away to get a clear look at your face.

"So delicate. *Handsome, really.* Always hiding under all this *tou fa*, aren't you." She smiles, those eyes dark and shimmering. "Are you scared?"

"*No, never.*" You lie.

"*You lie.* I can feel your heart beating so fast! My neighbor used to have a small dog, a shih tzu named Zhen Zhen. When I would pet him in my lap, his heart would beat like a drum. Your heart is faster."

Wendy pulls your shirt out of your jeans and starts unbuttoning. You inhale sharply—electricity up your spine. Wendy takes great delight in this reaction to her touch. She takes her time undressing you. She slows her pace—no rush anymore, now that the two of you are alone in a foreign city, a world away from everyone. She examines you in the dim room, those dark eyes still sparkling. She pauses—quiet, as she rests her forehead on your bare chest.

"Have you been with anyone else like this? Am I really your first girl? *Di yi ge?*"

"I've never been with anyone like this. I've been waiting. *Maybe I've been waiting for you all this time.*" You lie.

Wendy's mouth and tongue are tender and soft. You find your

hands on her hips, and she pulls her top over her head. Her pants, unbuckled and left in a pile of white on the carpet. The bright pink through your fingers as you cup her breasts and behind. Then the buckles and clasps are no longer a struggle. The two of you free and only flesh.

You are entwined in each other's limbs. Naked. You prepare yourself. You are about to make love for the first time.

You ask Wendy if she has protection.

"*Bu xu yao. Mei guan xi.*" She purrs at you that it's not necessary, it's OK.

You hesitate and want to stop, but she straddles you, and her hands are all over you: her mouth is on you, her hair cascades into your face, down your neck. Her breathing comes like a torrent, panting hot, followed by sharp inhalations. She moans in your ear, and you are *lost, lost, lost.*

The sensation is something you've never felt before. You shake and shudder, hold your breath, and grip the sheets tight. You may float away heavenward and never return. Your heart—a bloodred balloon about to burst.

She wants you again. This time she pulls you on top of her. Her legs spread with you between, clasped in her warmth. Hands on your back, guiding you until your motions are parallel with hers.

You sleep and wake, and make love again. You think this night of youthful lust can't continue, but you don't know when you might be together like this again. You have each other in every position you can imagine: every half-seen, half-read fantasy from every film, magazine, textbook illustration. You are blissfully exhausted.

Your eyes meet, and you can't look away. Her mouth open in pleasure and surprise. Her hands pushing your hair from your face, down your neck, and then resting on your clavicle. A nip, a bite. This is what you will see repeated, again and again—when you dream, when you cry, when you think of this night.

* * *

Wendy wakes you gently, her head on your chest. She's tracing a line down your belly. She kisses you and leads you into the shower. You laugh and fool around. Tired and euphoric, you dry off. Wendy offers you a sealed package of a new undershirt and boxer briefs.

"Funny! What? Are you selling these in the market outside?"

"No, my boyfriend always makes me keep these in my suitcase. Just in case he needs a fresh set. I have so many. He won't miss them."

"*Boyfriend?*"

(Your heart. Your heart.)

"I have a few. I have one in Shanghai, one in London. Maybe not 'boyfriend'—*lover* is a better word?"

"So, so—"

"Yes. You are my *American lover*, now. Don't be mad! Did you think I was going to be your only one? Exclusive? We are both going far away for adventure soon! Three, four years of school—and then the world!"

"But what happens now? When will I see you again? I didn't think that this would be—"

(Your heart. Your heart.)

"It's very easy. This was part of closing up the past. Do you understand? *Ming bai?* Putting away our childish things. I wanted to spend time with you, ever since I was small—*my wish*. My parents agreed to let me see you before I leave home. They paid for everything, made special arrangements for your trip—to play with me, to have some sweet time together."

"Wendy, I know we'll be far apart when we are at school, but we can always visit. You can come to New York, and I can return to China or, or—*I've always wanted to see London!* All of my favorite bands and favorite movies are from the UK! We can plan for later this year—and we'll keep writing letters to each other, like we always did. It could work—"

"I won't have time to play around later. I am their *nen gan de bao bei nu er*—one and only smart, precious daughter. I studied hard and was accepted into Oxford, the best school in the world. They gave me this time to do whatever I want, a summertime moment with you. Can't we have this nice memory?"

"But I thought *wo men liang ge*—the two of us. Our journey from when we were little—and now together! It's an amazing love story! We have all this history, and—*wo hen xi huan ni, wo ai ni*—"

"Zhongwen, bie jiang luh. Ni de ko ing, zen de shi ma-ma, hu-hu. Wo de erduo tong. English only, *please*! You do not know what love is! I do not know what *ai* means! We had sugary youthful wishes. This is the truth, Young *guh guh*."

"I'm sorry. I said too much. I just assumed that we would—"

(*Your heart. Your heart.*)

"*Ai-ya. Ni zen de shi hen ke ai.* You really are cute! You try to be so cool, but you are the boy who was always trying to impress me with silly things. I didn't want to say this—but you need to hear it, or you will always think something else. *This was just for fun. My childhood crush.* I wanted the dream of you from the past, but I grew up—and you stayed the same. America feeding your brain with these useless playthings. *Ke ai*—cute. Not *zhen ai*—real love."

You shake your head. No comforting words, no calming numbers—nothing but the sound of your labored breathing keeping pace with your rampant, raging, mournful heart.

(*Your heart. Your heart.*)

"You will remember me always and our time together. Our special summer secret, *your secret*. This is my way to say goodbye."

"*Goodbye?* Won't we see each other when you visit America again? And we still have a week in Beijing together!"

"I'm not going to Beijing with you. I have somewhere else to be. I asked Mama to leave a message with the tour guide tonight. And America? US? *Meiguo?* I don't need *Meiguo*, I don't want *Meiguo*! Do you think *Meiguo* needs you? *Or wants you?* I have Brussels, Rome, Madrid—the rest of the world to see, anywhere a plane, a train, or a boat can take me! History, art, and culture! Why even leave Shanghai—or Xi'an—or Hong Kong? Look at where we are! This is going to be the future! *Zhongguo is the future*! China is the future! This is that *Blade Runner* movie you love so much! *This is it, just outside!* Look at the lights, the water, the buildings, the highway. Tell me your tiny house in Queens is better than any of what is already here, what will be here tomorrow!"

"But what about us? Don't you want to come back to New York and see me again?"

"No *us*. We had our time. It felt wonderful, yes? When you leave, you can think about me. *Dream.* Maybe we will write or call, maybe not. I don't know the future, but I won't return to New York for a very long time. The world is too big to go back to America."

You pause. She walks over to the window. A sharp sliver of light slashes through the room.

"I may meet a future millionaire or CEO. I can have many lovers—everywhere and anywhere. This face, this body? Men can't resist a beautiful Chinese young woman—*piao liang de Zhongguo gu niang*. I have *power*. I'll decide who to marry and live wherever I want. If I choose not to marry, I'll make my own wealth! Times are changing, and I am prepared for the new century. I will work hard, and my future will be red and gold."

"*Money?* Is that all this is about?"

"Money is only as powerful as the opportunity—to have the best of the best, to provide whatever I need. Your family has a happy tiny life—a *xiao sheng huo*. You view the world on make-believe screens, but *I can live it for real*. You watch the subtitles go by, but I speak the languages to the most glamorous people in the most glamorous places, *comprenez-vous, wakarimasu ka?* You may feel you have plenty, but beyond Queens, New York, you are *chong.* You know this word? *Chong*—poor. When we started our letters and pictures, you were so cool—*shuai guh.* I wanted to be like you, but then I dreamed I could be *better* than you. Once Mother and Father had money, it was no longer a dream."

She turns and runs her hand through your hair. Her smooth hand on your pallid face—a kindness.

"America is not the world. Can you not see that, Young *guh guh?* When my family moved to the city, glorious Shanghai—I knew there was nothing I couldn't do. Chinese, American, or not Chinese, not American—it doesn't matter. When you have money—you can do everything, anything."

She starts speaking faster than you can understand. Her Mandarin cuts you to pieces, deft in her lifetime of knowing the nuances of this ancient tongue. Each half-understood phrase you complete in your mind with your feral imagination, your desperation to make sense of this prelude to your inevitable parting.

She says: *Somethingsomething in Chinese, somethingsomething cold, somethingsomething callous.*

What you think you understand is probably worse than the literal, but it murders you the same: *A poor yellow brother with no means has no power in the world. Not Chinese, not American. You are somewhere in between and neither side accepts you—invisible. Weakness in those two legs. You are standing on two continents and neither of them truly yours.*

And you feel the world slowly start to drift and pull away. The ocean beneath you, the dragging tide—waiting for you to slip and drown, the wide-open maw of the apathetic abyss below.

Somethingsomething in Chinese, somethingsomething cutting, somethingsomething final.

"But I will have what no one else can, that money cannot buy: your first experience, your virginity. *That is mine.* I will always have that. *We* will always have that. It is a gift for *us.* A lovely memory for you. Like what you imagine, from your favorite movies, yes? A special secret story for us?"

You have nothing now but silence to swallow down. Wendy hasn't said anything that wasn't the truth. This is her form of cold cruel mercy, a killing kindness.

The longing lust was evident. Since the moment your eyes met, your bodies were assured to collide. But was it wrong to want more than youthful hunger? Was it absurd to crave genuine emotion and connection and to pray for some divine denouement? Why was this ache for romance and love such an inane response to her touch? Was it weak to think this story could end in some blessed cliché?

Wendy turns her attention to gathering her things. She has somewhere else to be—without you.

"The room is paid for until tomorrow. You can stay here if you'd like. The tour director and Beijing will be waiting for you. I suggest you make the most of the trip. I'm not sure you will have the opportunity again—*hen nan duh.*"

She sits beside you on the couch and draws close to kiss you. A finale, a concluding moment that you deny her. You turn away to face the sunrise slicing through the slit in the curtain.

"*Zai jian.*"

"Goodbye" in Chinese literally translates to: "*See you again.*" It is something that you dare not hope for—something that may turn your foolish world, your foolish heart, into stone, into immovable clay.

Day Five: Xi'an to Beijing

"Your Xia Ai Yi called. Your *xiao gu niang* is heading to Mallorca with friends. I'm so sorry. Your tour is paid for, and it's not easy to change your flight back to New York. You've already traveled across the world, have five-star hotel rooms, excellent food, and a lovely VIP guide to show you around! *Hen nan duh*—it's special, rare. This is how you say the word? '*RAAAYY-RRRUH*'? Enjoy this once-in-a-lifetime experience on, how you say—'their dime.'

"I don't know what happened—but I know your *xin tong*, you have heartache in your eyes. I know you have your ma, *mei mei*, *peng you*, at home. But do you have a *da jie* to give you real advice on matters of the heart? This trip cost a fortune! Xia family already paid me. I have nothing more to gain, so I can speak plainly. Tell you what only a big sister should!

"We can talk later, or you can be silent. But for the next few days, I am in charge. You listen to your *da jie*. People come from all over the world and ask me what they should see and do. *I know what to do. Trust me.*

"One of my clients was spending a lot of money from her divorce, told me that a famous Western poet said: 'The best revenge is living well.' (We Chinese have similar sayings, but I think you can appreciate this one better.) Maybe think of this as one less vacation, fewer dresses, minus several pairs of shoes for your *xiao gu niang*. Traveling is good for healing, *xiao di*. Trust me. *Da jie* will not guide you wrong."

Vicky helps you through the airport. She places a cold hand on your hot forehead. You are grateful for this take-charge, practical (*bossy, mostly*), fun-loving older sister. "Short flight. Take some rest. We will be there soon."

You both wake to the skidding screech of asphalt as you touch down in Beijing. You soon arrive at another luxurious hotel. Check in and sleep. You don't dream.

Day Six: Tiananmen Square / Forbidden City

Vicky's decked out in her bright peach and chartreuse outfit, her official tour guide uniform. You are no longer her sole client. She's back leading a busload of *others*.

She barrels through her script with ease and confidence. "Look to left. You can see many of international companies starting new businesses in Beijing." For the sake of the *others*, you want to correct her pronunciation a half dozen times but hold your Western tongue. Her English is eons beyond your Chinese.

The tour bus is filled with two dozen visitors: some Japanese, some English, but the majority seem to be either Canadians or Americans. As the bus goes too fast over a bump, you hear a *crikey!* and a deep-throated laugh—an Aussie or two in the back.

Vicky shuts off the mic and sits next to you. The familiarity is comforting. She pulls out a white handkerchief and dabs under her eyes, above her upper lip.

You ask her if she was in Beijing in June 1989. She shushes you and looks around. "I was in Shandong that year. Wonderful summer! Do you know Tsingtao Beer? *Pi jiu*? It's from Shandong. Very famous! We can have some when we have lunch today." Vicky forces a smile, wipes the sweat from her brow, and eases herself down into the seat. You take the hint and drop the subject.

You close your eyes and try to focus on the rhythm of the road, the sound of small talk behind you, anything to keep your thoughts from drifting back, replaying the last pale vision of Wendy. You wince and swallow hard.

Vicky turns to you. With her oversize sunglasses, she looks like a fly, circling your pallid body. You see your distorted reflection—the sullen, sunken eyes staring back at you—your spirit threatening to leave this realm as she whispers to you calmly, with care.

"*Xiao di*, I know you are not feeling well, take some time to rest on the ride. But promise me you will try to see and appreciate. Even if you make much money as a famous writer in the future, when you visit again, it will not be the same! *You* will not be the same as when you first saw the beauty of your homeland. Right here, on this date, this *shuai guh* sitting beside me is ever changing!

"I will take pictures for you. Smile or no smile! Even if all your sadness, confusion, anger is part of these memories, when all is calm and well, you can look back later to reflect and learn. No need to do anything or say anything now. You can feel sad and hurt—or you can avoid thinking of her at all. You can simply be a guest here. No action needed more than walking around to see these sights, maybe write in your notebook."

Physically exhausted and emotionally bereft, you agree that it's best to just be led—*observe and report.*

The bus wheezes to a stop, and you disembark in the heart of Beijing. This is China—the one you expected. This expanse of concrete, leading up to the ancient city gates, recognizable from the books and movies you've seen. But up close now, you feel even more distant—foreign and *other.*

You are proudly wearing your favorite Siouxsie and the Banshees T-shirt, the black one with a hot pink star. You hope that your self-styled goth branding prevents you from being mistaken for a local. But it's your height (*and attitude*) that distinguishes you from the general throngs of minute Mainlanders. You stick out like a lanky, bloodless, outstretched middle finger.

You put on your sunglasses and Mets cap, tie your purple bandanna around your neck. You look like a confused ghoul of the Western world, trying to hide your zombified corpse of multiculturalism and recent heartbreak.

Vicky calls everyone over and extends her retractable baton, a reflective green flag tied to the tip. *Wave, wave.* You follow as she motions up toward the massive Chinese flag: the large banner with five glorious five-pointed gold stars. The burnished red in the blistering heat makes your eyeballs throb. Should you be feeling anything stir while looking at this flapping bold swatch of fabric? *Dread? Fear? Pride?*

You nod politely behind your dark lenses as Vicky points out details and asks you to pose in front of the People's Monument and Mao's Tomb, and then moves you through into the Forbidden City. You all head toward the underpass that connects the modern to the ancient. You suppress the urge to whistle the *Doctor Who* theme.

* * *

You imagine the emperor and the royal court: concubines waiting to be chosen (*all as gorgeous as Gong Li*), eunuchs bound in servitude (*ouch*), and all sorts of kung fu and swordplay. Everything you saw in *Raise the Red Lantern, Farewell My Concubine, The Last Emperor* happened here—all that Zhang Yimou, Chen Kaige, and Bernardo Bertolucci could get away with putting on film.

The statues, carvings, and paintings of dragons (which look like dragons) and lions (which look like demonic dogs), the ornate doorways, colossal courtyards, deep-red pillars, the thousands of rooms—they all begin to look alike. The excessive detail and magnitude of the acroteria, the brushwork of the calligraphy, and the craftsmanship of each painted tile—it all makes you feel small and insignificant. You can't tell your "Ming" from your "Ching," your "Celestial" from your "Heavenly." You feel like an ignorant, insignificant child. You try to count every golden orb on each gateway door to make you feel better. You give up once you hit the 500s.

You finish the tour at the Imperial Gardens. You sit outside, surrounded by miniature pagodas, timeworn trees, and rocks (which look like rocks). Your feet ache. Your Nikes are covered in a film of gray dust. You blow your nose and find the tissue filled black: the pollution in the air is the price of progress for the proletariat. But you are thankful for this distraction, for having the time and place to allow your grief to recede in this mystifying stretch of history.

Vicky herds you and your comrades (*heh, comrades*) back on the bus. You slump down in the seat and look out the window. She turns to you and whispers: "Today—worth a pair of high-heeled shoes." You smirk.

Vicky asks the driver to turn on some music. You drift off to "Wake Me Up Before You Go-Go." You think it's an odd selection, but Vicky explains that in 1985, Wham! (*yes, with the exclamation point*) was the first modern Western act to perform here in Beijing. You picture George Michael wagging his tush (his *xiao pi gu*) and leading throngs of your countrymen to clap along. You sleep. You don't dream.

Day Seven: Temple of Heaven (Tiantan)

Vicky leads you through the main entrance. She explains that the symbolism of square (Earth) and circle (Heaven) can be seen throughout this complex. You notice this everywhere, and obsess over sky and stone, dirt and air.

Completed in 1420, decades before Columbus sailed the ocean blue, the buildings are in equal parts brilliant cerulean and crimson. The main edifice is the Temple of Good Harvest. This immense wooden building was erected without a single nail (*good ol' Chinese ingenuity and stubbornness*). You appreciate the minutiae of the repeating patterns, vibrant colors, symbols, and shapes. Four main pillars inside represent the seasons; twelve pillars outside, the months and hours.

There is an echo wall outside the Imperial Vault of Heaven where sound travels along the curve of stone. The tourists test the novelty and *clapclapclap*. Children yell and giggle, jump with glee, as they shout secrets (and profanities). You would rather be profound. You shout: "TRUTH AND BEAUTY!!!" Inappropriately Victorian, but it *"expresses what is most important to your soul."* A tear comes to the corner of your eye. You yell it again.

The last thing Vicky points out is a specific spot in the courtyard. A mound: an ancient altar where the acoustics are designed to carry sound heavenward. She motions to the concentric circles of stones. The one in the middle: this is where the emperor was to stand and explain the business of the kingdom upward to the sky. *Observe and report.*

The details around this area—stones, steps, and railings—were built specifically in permutations and expressions of the sacred number 9: there are 9 stones in this ring, 18 in the next, and then 81.

Your head itches, and you feel a deep sense of satisfaction: here are the numbers and symmetry that you've carried with you all your life, here is the evidence that it was always in your blood—*primordial.* You are certain your ancestors worried away days and years, counting and changing their plans, unable to move forward unless the geometrical guidance proved propitious. Waiting for the shadows to fall at precise angles, waiting on the right times and the right seasons. Your forebears, deeply spiritual, thoroughly superstitious, seeking favor from Shangdi, the Lord Above and the Lord on Earth. Before the Communists, Confucius in all his confusion, the dire doubt of the Dao, the haziness of the Han. All of them so much like you, so different from you.

"Today? Worth a nice dress." Vicky exhales as she hands you a completed roll of film. "I think I might have a picture of you smiling. Maybe two!"

You skip dinner. You sleep. You don't dream.

Day Eight: Beihai Park

Beihai Park is astounding: at once lush, ancient, and kitschy modern. Vicky wastes no time with her metal switch—pointing toward the straight hike and quick boat ride to the middle of the lake, to visit the famed white tiered edifice. The sightseers follow her like gawky geese, pausing for quick snaps by the edge of the water.

The island in the middle of the park is home to the Tibetan lama tower. It offers the best view of the city. From up on high, near the gourdlike framework, you take in Beijing below: the incredibly ancient buttressed up against the insanely postmodern; the iconography of ethereal empires adjacent to the persistent proletariat; the complex roots of the past, propelling the future, skyscrapers casting shadows on pagodas.

Vicky gestures to a bronze turtle sculpture (*ugh, demonic*) and others: phoenix, dragon, and tiger. Turtle represents the North; Phoenix, the South; Tiger, the West; and Dragon, the East. Sometimes there is also another bonus dragon "somewhere in the middle, between." She waves her hand and says she can never keep it straight. You figure there must be a picture book that explains the mythology, or some sort of anime adaptation.

Vicky lets the group wander in this section and pulls you aside: "We Chinese people, one of the oldest cultures, have seen everything under the sun, moon, stars. North, South, East, West—these immortal beasts have seen all that *nan, nu* have experienced. There is nothing new. It is sand and dust, smoke and ash—to them. But a broken heart still feels like the world ending to a young one. You must simply move on when you can, *xiao di*. When a woman makes up her mind, nothing can change it. She gets nothing from your pain, except maybe pity. But you can use this pain one day for something better. You cannot let one person ruin you for all that there is to come."

You think on your corporeal existence, your wavering pulse, her haunting smile—a blip in time and place. Centuries before Washington Square Park was even an idea, this natural retreat in the heart of a living city welcomed lifetimes. The willow trees crinkle in the warm breeze, their cascade of light green calming. You breathe deep; the air enters your lungs, and you cough until your eyes water. Your tissue is all sooty snot again. Your red-rimmed eyes fill with tears.

* * *

Vicky gathers the group, urges everyone to take plenty of photos here: the famous Nine Dragon Wall in Beihai Park, almost a hundred feet of phenomenally detailed glazed tiles: blue, gold, bronze, and red dragons.

Built in the Qing dynasty (another monument older than the entirety of Meiguo), the dragon wall is filled with symbols, the grand calculus designed to be "superior" and "fortuitous" for the emperor.

Throughout the tiles, nine large dragons and nearly three hundred smaller ones. Odd numbers (especially 9 and 5) are expressed in repeated motifs in every eye, fang, scale, every roaring mouth, each golden orb, swirling cloud, coral branch. Vicky apologizes for not getting all the information correct, but all you hear is *dragons, dragons, dragons,* 9, 5, 9, 5, 9, 5.

Your head spins with excitement. The dopamine rolls through

you like a tide. You circle the entirety of the wall (*1–2–3*) three times, feasting on the exquisite patterns and permutations of repetition, all crafted with intent. Raised figures of mythical creatures in battle (*or at play*), across a barrier meant to ward off bad luck, in a park designed for long relaxing strolls. In front of you, in brick and stone, the clash and combination of physical and metaphysical; the practical and artistic; the symbological and illogical; the spiritual and coldly mathematical. Strict rules of order, upheld by magical system guidelines. You love this.

You click pictures from multiple angles. A woman with a toothy grin asks if you want a picture with the wall. You hand over your camera and shuffle over. She lines up her shot and asks you to smile: *xiao, xiao*. You're sure you are stiff and grimacing, but she seems content. Vicky looks over at you. She covers her mouth to laugh and nod in approval.

She directs everyone back to the bus. Outside, a small group of locals are lounging in the shade and singing spirited (*nationalistic*) songs. You lag behind and enjoy the final strains of: *somethingsomething Zhongguo (China), somethingsomething youngyuen (forever), somethingsomething cheerful.*

Vicky saves the copilot seat up front for you. "For everything today, I estimate the cost of one purse. Real leather!" You can't help but smile. You crumple next to her, exhausted. You sleep and don't dream.

Day Nine: The Great Wall

Today, you get to see a bona fide Wonder of the World—visible from space, older than the country of your birth—*older than the birth of your Savior!* This is what kept the Mongolian hordes from raping your ancestors. Why Bah boasts that you are "pure Han Chinese!"

The Mutianyu section is where you'll visit. Today you and Vicky are only joined by a small group from Caterpillar Construction. They go by the "CAT Crew," outfitted in matching gray polo shirts with the CAT logo in yellow stitched letters (which disappointingly has no feline, nor a squirmy insect).

The three men and one woman—Paul, Loretta, John, and "Felix," or maybe "Felipe"—mostly joke around and keep to themselves. You introduce yourself, and they try their best cornball one-liner on you: *What did the porn star order from the Chinese takeout? Cream-of-Some-Young-Guy!*

Vicky is blank and expressionless; she doesn't get it. The joke and innuendo is beyond her English. You've heard this one all your life. They hoot and holler: "Just joshin', kid, just joshin'!" You match their winks and finger guns with your own. *Bangbangbang.*

* * *

The view is spectacular and literally breathtaking: a combination of the altitude, lingering Beijing pollution (and cigarettes), the physical strain of the climb, and the persistent misery of your body, your memory. You lean against the wall (THE. WALL.) and appreciate the clearing blue sky. As the haziness gives way to sunlight, you slide down the face of the brick and sit. You pause.

Your ancestors were accustomed to their existence as mere dots along the edge of this landscape, minuscule details in the natural, eternal frame. Then, purposefully resolute, they began carving and stacking this mighty stone dragon into being. Tracing the backbone of earth with rock and mortar formed by their own hands, they announced their presence loudly in bas-relief—your forefathers, saying as much in these newly occupied spaces as in the empty expanses elsewhere.

Gray, brown, and green: seemingly unending. These steep and dramatic hills and vistas, the near vertical climb up these steps and ramps leading to countless dugouts and turrets: *Who shot an arrow here? Who bled and died here? How many centuries ago? How many times my greatgreatgreatgrandfather? How much immeasurably braver than me?*

You've been dreaming of visiting the *changcheng* ever since you saw *Big Bird in China* and David Copperfield magically walking through the Wall. You imagined that you would be instantly transported to ancient Zhongguo, and that you'd feel a calling in your soul, a rumbling in your chest, the hairs on your arm prickle as the sky crackled with energy. You admire the view, but if you are being honest: *sadconfuseditchy, sweatyhungrythirsty.*

You see scratched graffiti to the left and right of you. A Sven (*an actual Sven!*) was here in 1989. You see some Chinese characters that you can't read. A smiley face. A peace sign. More names, initials, dates. You are appalled by the audacity, but would love to add your own modern-day etching.

You duck under a shaded arch and feel for a coin in your pocket. You casually wander over to an unpopulated section, find a small jag of privacy, your own crenel. There are some faded letters here and there, but you find a clear swath of brick. You quickly scrape "88" (*more indelibly meaningful to you than the date*) and the character for your last name: "Wang"—*king*. You finish with a dash and your initials. Done. *Magic. Sealed sigil. Infinity upon infinity.* Part of history: "88—汪—YZW."

You are a giddy criminal for a few seconds, but swiftly regain your composure as you pass two young men in uniform. They are stern and silent, pensive. You try to emulate the same.

You see Vicky in the distance, pointing out something along the horizon to the CAT Crew. They all have matching papers in their hands. The woman in the group (Loretta) is fanning herself frantically.

You walk over to close the distance and pass a man sitting behind a small table. He has an elaborate beard: long, black, and very *sifu / Master of Kung Fu.* He points to the sign below: 50 YUAN FOR PHOTO AND CERTIFICATE. The offer: a Polaroid and a thin piece of vellum where you can fill in your name and date, CLIMBED GREAT WALL OF CHINA in bold letters and some additional red Chinese characters, to make it more "official."

You hand over the money, and the man rises with his camera. Completely silent, he guides you to a scenic spot and squares up your shoulders. He holds up his hand with the palm facing you, to indicate that you should stay put. He walks back a few meters and lowers himself into an incredible stretch: right leg in full extension, he slides close to the ground, in almost a perfect split, his hands guiding the camera in strong, firm focus. You name this stance "Fist of the Clear Eye." He takes the photo without warning.

Flapflapflap, and the picture develops. Your eyes are open, slight smile, a nice section of Wall behind you.

He points to the line: *Fill in your name and date*. He places the Polaroid underneath and seals it all inside a clear laminated sheet: the perfect record of your historical visit. *YOU WERE HERE. YOU DID THIS. YOU EXIST.* You say *xie xie*, and he gives you a silent, curt bow. You half expect him to vanish in a plume of smoke, but he just sits back down at the table, waiting to take his next portrait. You love this.

* * *

"On this side of the Wall over a billion—what the Westerners say?— 'other fish in the sea.' Maybe a nice *xiao gu niang* here in Beijing? Certainly there are many waiting for you back home, *shuai guh!*" Vicky says to you as she leads your party back down the hill. The air-conditioned bus and forthcoming dinner entice you to quickly scuttle down the steep and uneven terrain.

You know you are getting close to the lot when the hawkers begin to converge: *"COLD-A WAH-TAH! COLD-A BEE-AH! COLD-A WAH-TAH! COLD-A BEE-AH! FIVE YUAN / TEN YUAN!"*

There are tables, tarps, carts, stands with old men and women selling trinkets and snacks. You should probably purchase something "authentic" here: miniature versions of a section of Wall. You ask an old woman how much for two: "Thirty yuan! Good price!" Vicky swoops in and haggles the woman (all sun-weathered skin and bones) down to 20 yuan. You give her 30 anyway and walk away with your haul.

"*Aiya*. She got too much from you! Those souvenirs would be 15 to 20 yuan from anyone else. All cheap stuff to *pian wai guo ren*—trick the foreigners, you know?"

One of the CAT crew spots your interaction and rolls his eyes. He proceeds to buy out nearly all the water and beer from an old man in a dusty brown shirt. He hands over a bill, doesn't wait for change.

"Hey, campers! *It's Miller Time*—well, *Yanjing Time*! Kid, here's a few roadies for you. Chug that water first, though." Paul hands you a few drinks. You thank him with a nod as he heads to the back of the bus.

Vicky offers you a chilled towel. She opens the beer, and you happily slurp down the cool, bitter suds. Overseas, you might only be "underage" under God's eyes. But no one here really cared to check. *(And was there actually a legal drinking age in China? Ma always said it was "no sin for small sips," anyway.)* "Close your eyes. I'll wake you up for the surprise later."

Vicky pulls down the shade for you. You nap. You don't dream.

* * *

At first, you aren't sure what you are looking at: three large cement structures, tiered pools filled with greenish water cascading down each level. Motion and foam, a soothing steady stream: it's a man-made watershed flowing into a small lake. You notice a flicker of a sleek, dark form and then another—*fish*.

"This is reserved for *top-top-VI-VIPs* only!" Vicky distributes rudimentary poles: bamboo canes with a twenty-foot lead of transparent wire, a rusty hook. She gives you a handful of *mantou* morsels: bready bait to coax and capture whatever slips and slides beneath.

You can almost feel the collective shrug, but you all get to threading white balls onto the barbs and cast away. In no more than sixty seconds, one of the men (Felix/Felipe) is getting splashed by a good-size flexing trout. In quick succession, Loretta, John, and Paul are all yanking out their hard-earned catches.

You continue to dip and flick. You check your useless stick. Your bait, long gone. But sure enough, you finally catch one of your own. Only a matter of time until an unlucky bastard gives into its basest instincts, illusory freedom broken by the sudden snag of the tenuous filament of fate.

Vicky applauds and gathers you all for a late-afternoon photo: your respective catches and their wiggling tails, clutched tightly in hand, the sun's westward trajectory bathing you all in a gorgeous glow.

* * *

Vicky introduces you to the grounds crew who manage the machinery and some of the scientists who keep the water clean and the fish healthy. The small group from the facility beam proudly, bow, thank you for visiting.

Everyone assembles by the edge of the water, at the table where dinner will be served. What follows is one of the best meals that you will ever have in your life: the trout is flavorful and juicy with only a bit of salt, pepper, and oil; the shredded beef and pepper dish is spicy and tasty; but what surprises you the most are the roasted almonds. "From here, too." Vicky points to the trees close by.

You pop the crunchy bite into your mouth. The city mouse noshing on the nutty saltiness, the slight bitter note at the back. You close your eyes and inhale: the invigorating air; the sun, warm and inviting; the water, a pleasing muted roar. This was not the China you thought you would see, but it is the one you will remember. You love this.

"Hey, Mr. Chen. Come sit and eat with us! Have a beer! *Gan bei! Gan bei!*" Loretta yells at one of the scientists. He politely clinks glasses and quickly excuses himself. "Awww, come back! Have some nuts!"

"Don't get me wrong. This is amazing," Felix/Felipe says. "Some of the best fish I've ever eaten, but it's *safe*. I don't think they get us here, man. We want to try the *kind-of-weird shit*—not the *really-weird shit*, but at least the *kind-of-weird shit*! Don't give me the sweet and sour pork or the chicken and broccoli! I can get that at 88 Lucky Harvest back home!" Everyone cracks up, like he's making his open mic night debut at the Chuckle Barn.

"We Americans deserve some more credit!" John, testifying righteously. "They think we can only handle burgers and pizza. Shit, I've had some pickled pig trotters in my day! Stinky-ass cheese that would make you slap your mama something fierce! Give me a thousand-year-old egg, any day! *Am I right, or am I right?*"

"They may have us beat on innovation and general cookery—but, man, we Americans are the best at bullshit and boozin'! Right, kid?" Paul clinks his bottle with yours. "Cheers, bud! Look at this view! *Whooooo–ee!*"

You smile, almost blush. You're not sure how to feel. The Southern accent, the amiable twinkle-wink, the hard pat of congeniality on your back—*is this what you want? To be not "them" but "us," as in "US," All-American? USA! USA! A good ol' red-white-and-blue-and-yellow boy?*

You look over at Vicky in her suit and dark shades. She's sipping a beer and laugh-leaning into John-Loretta, egging the two of them on. With the sun dipping low, the pliant green boughs rustling, the crickets stirring soft, you feel guilty for feeling *good*, for the first time since Xi'an.

Before Vicky has a chance to say anything, you tell her: "Today was priceless, Vicky. I'll never forget it. Thank you."

She responds: "But the total value is about the same price as a day in Tokyo." She squeezes your shoulder. You laugh.

* * *

As the sun sets on your raucous comrades (*heh, comrades*), you excuse yourself from the table. Vicky looks over at you—a flash of concern, but you tell her that you are fine, you just needed to get up and stretch. You walk to the edge of the terrace. You hadn't noticed, but Vicky followed just behind. You offer your hand, and the two of you climb up a level and stare down at the glint of shiny scales. "See, your *da jie* promised you plenty of fish!"

You give her a half-hearted chortle as she takes your arm and continues: "Like water, you must follow the flow of the stream to where it will lead you in your journey. This water from the small lake travels all the way to the pools here and back out again. Maybe the other fish in the lake will be caught and live up here? Maybe these pools will become too full, and the fish will be released back into the lake there? The fish don't know what is ahead for them, they swim, they make eggs, they eat, they are eaten—they just follow the ripples and waves and are all too happy.

"*Da jie* knows you will find your place and the person meant to be with you. You will find your own stream, pond, ocean, one day. But lucky for you, you are no fish! You can make your own choice of where you want to swim, and who you want to swim with, *xiao di*! But go with the flow and see where life leads you for now. Sometimes you move with the current, other times you fight to head upstream instead. Timing and opportunity are the most important! You just need to be ready to take action!"

Surprising you with her spry steps, Vicky bounds back down to join the group, leaving you to the burble of water, calming in its tireless rhythm. Below, the fish jump and plunge, rise and dive, again and again, unaware that an unexplored world is just beyond their line of sight. You want to throw a handful of rocks to wake them up: *Try harder, try harder. You could swim free if you just try harder.*

That night, you toss and turn in your sleep. You don't dream.

Day Ten: Canceled Plans / Free Day

Vicky calls up to your room to check on you. A rough night: you didn't vomit, but your head still hurts. Your persistent cough is from the general air quality issues (and acrid cigarettes). It burns when you pee. Vicky thinks you may just be dehydrated and exhausted.

You would hate to miss out on the Summer Palace, but she assures you that it's more "old buildings by the water." *You will just have to visit again when you sell your first screenplay.* The real disappointment is that you will miss the Beijing Zoo. No real-life pandas for you. You think you may never get to see one, here or in America.

"Sleep more. When you wake up, walk around the neighborhood— *guang-guang.* Eat something, drink lots of water. *Xiao di, bao zhong!"* Vicky, urging you to take care.

You roll out of bed a few hours later. Your stomach rumbles, and you feel parched. You head outside, and the heat immediately makes you woozy.

A few blocks from the hotel, you spot a local restaurant with a small line out the door. You ask a portly man in the queue what's good here. He tells you: *shaobing, youtiao, doujiang,* the Chinese breakfast staples.

You get seated inside at a small table. A young waitress eases over and is already speaking too fast, in Beijing-accented Chinese. She laughs as you gesture with your hands to slow down. You try to order in elementary Mandarin. *"Bu cuo, bu cuo! Ma shang lai!"* You get the gist: *Not bad, not bad—food is coming up!*

The waitress returns with two full bowls, a plate with sesame-seeded flatbread, and a golden fried pastry rod. She explains slowly that they are famous for their homemade *doujiang* and *do hua.* You must try the spicy chili tofu, along with the sweet soy milk—on the house.

The food is fantastic, though not much different from what you've had growing up. Some weekends, Bah would come home from Flushing with a greasy paper bag of flaky sticks, their golden heads poking out, a bouquet of doughy deliciousness. You put the *youtiao* in the *shaobing*—the traditional carb-on-carb bundle that you never understood but grew to love—and crunch down heartily. You wash it down with spoonfuls of the cool, sugary soup. You are surprised that this makes you homesick.

The waitress returns with a small platter of sliced beef. She tells you that the owner wanted you to enjoy it—no charge.

Her smile reminds you of Gloria Huang from Stuy. You never had a *thing* for Gloria (*always nice, sweet, bright*), but the waitress has the same arched eyebrows, same height, same thin waist. It's the echo of palliative familiarity that makes you pause and take in this alluring *"Beijing Gloria"*—but it's the gasping, gaping void left by Wendy that compels you to grasp at any futile fantasy that someone else could be your lifeline back to breath.

You imagine how Beijing Gloria might be bold and pull a chair over—dusting off her apron for a break, asking you about life in New York. If she took down her ponytail, the inky black hair would fall in luscious waves, and she'd smell like jasmine. Beijing Gloria would explain that she is studying English literature at university, and desperately wants to practice her pronunciation, discuss Titus Andronicus *with you. Beijing Gloria thinks you are very handsome,* shuai guh. *She is compelled by your energy. Your intelligent eyes and patient demeanor signify that you might be the one— the one to save her from the constraints of a life in China.*

She would be free to start a family with you in America. She could read all the books she wanted to, any book she wanted to! *You could start a family of 3 or 4 fat, sweet, roly-poly babies—maybe 5 or 6—boys* AND *girls—because she could! She would cook amazing, authentic Chinese cuisine for you, give you nice haircuts, and sing lullabies to those babies every night, in Chinese and English. She would cherish going to church on Sunday mornings and spending the afternoons powerwalking laps around the mall. She would savor the buttery popcorn, dig her face deep into your shoulder, and cry at the cinema. She would ride the Staten Island Ferry back and forth, just to enjoy the view of the skyline, the silhouette of the Statue of Liberty. She could have a perfect tiny life, be content with a xiao sheng huo—a perfect story—with you.*

The waitress breaks you out of your reverie as she walks by and leaves a scrap of paper without a word. *Could she, would she—be passing you a message?* In Chinese or English: "I like you. Meet me in the alley behind the restaurant"?

You feel your face flush with embarrassment as you turn over the note. It's a bill for 30 yuan.

Her *xie, xie* is extra sweet. You stumble on the curb—dizzy, nauseous, your stomach overfull of the local delights, with a side of marinated shame and seasoned sheepishness.

It's getting hotter and hotter out. You wander and find a ramshackle store that sells odds and ends, the Chinese cousin to your favorite bodega back home. You squeeze inside and pick out a few postcards. You get two popsicles and *scrambleslobber* them down before they melt.

You find a shaded bench outside the hotel. You'll beat the mail back to New York, but they want *the postmark*, they want *the stamps*. You scribble a note to Ma and Bah; for Mei, one with a cartoon panda (shame, no real-life panda visit); one for Gina; and one to Paris. You start to write one to Su Su, but realize you have no idea where to send it.

You scarcely recognize your own handwriting at this point. You feel sick. The existential crisis and sensory overload of these days have burned you dry. The *hotcoldhot* of the unrelenting summer heat and the spotty air-conditioning has been an exhausting cycle of clamminess. You aren't sure what to write and what not to say (assuming all the mail gets reviewed by the government censors anyway). You keep it simple: *Had a great time, saw amazing things, ate great food.*

You mention nothing about Shanghai, Xi'an, or Wendy.

Clicking the pen closed, you retreat inside to rest. You'll be heading home late tonight.

China—thank you for showing me, teaching me, healing me—at least a little. Sweet dreams for you and for me.

Zai jian.

Day Eleven: Flight Back Home

Vicky meets you at the hotel restaurant for your last meal in China: succulent Peking duck with all the trimmings—cucumber, scallions, sweet and savory sauce, and fluffy *mantou*.

Now that the sun has sunk below the horizon and the air is more bearable, Vicky suggests a light stroll to aid your digestion, and to see the bustling Beijing night one last time.

"This entire trip—*tai shang huo*—your *huo qi*. Too hot—you understand? When you get home, you will cool down and feel better. More balance in your yin and yang." She wipes a smudge of sauce off the corner of your mouth.

You ask if Vicky wants more beyond her duties as a tour director, if she has other aspirations. "What do you want to do with the rest of your life, Vicky *jie jie?*"

"*Ay, ni xian zai tsai jiao wo jie jie?*" Vicky is elated that you finally break out and call her big sister, at the very end. "What do you mean? I'm very happy. I love to travel. I like to share our culture. I like to guide and direct people. This is my life."

"Do you have someone? A boyfriend?"

"*Oh, xiao di!* You are very handsome, but too young for me! Why you ask?"

"You've given me all this great advice, but I don't see a wedding ring. You must meet all these *wai guo ren*—all these foreigners. Someone must have asked you, you must have been invited—"

"Of course, of course. Maybe—*lah?* I don't have a boyfriend right now, but maybe again one day. Nice guy who likes to sing karaoke and have *pi jiu*. That's all I need! I am very happy to live in Zhongguo. China is rising fast! It's changing every year, things are getting better and better. Why would I want to leave, when I get to see China become stronger?"

You wince. This sanitized sentiment conjures Wendy and the faint echo of her last words to you.

Vicky takes you by the arm. It feels comfortable and reassuring—unconditional. She stops to pop a cigarette in your mouth and lights it and her own.

"We are good friends now? *Hao peng you?* Listen to your *da jie,* OK? Take care of yourself, *xiao di.* Guard your heart. There is much more outside *Meiguo* and all of its 'beauty' and beyond *Zhongguo.* The 'Middle Kingdom' might be at the center, *the heart*—but there is so much more of Mother Earth's body to see! *Ahhh, so young,* so many years ahead!"

"I know the Xia family has more money than they know what to do with. But thank you for humoring me and helping me feel better, *da jie.*"

"When I told you about 'revenge' before—that was wrong. Think about this time as a *reward* instead. Maybe a reward for not getting what you imagined you wanted? Maybe it's a reward for your pain? Find something good from this time. Turn this into something that helps you heal and grow. It may take ten days, it may take ten years, but you will heal. I don't know what happened with your *xiao gu niang,* but this feeling will pass. It will pass like smoke—*like this.*"

Vicky exhales, waves her arm, and tries not to cough. She stomps out the cigarette and gives you a quick hug.

"I know your family is originally from Zhejiang, Henan—then in Shanghai and Taipei—and then Meiguo. You only get a small taste of your history on this trip! Most important to know where you came from, so you know where you are going! If you visit again, let me know, OK? I would be very happy to see you! Here's my business card. I have an email now! How was my tour? How was my English?"

"Excellent, Vicky! You speak English better than I speak *Zhongwen, Putonghua.* Thank you so much for everything. Will you ever come visit New York? Have you ever been?"

"No, not New York. I don't need to see another crowded city! Maybe I will visit West Coast: Las Vegas, Seattle—maybe California. I like *Jiazhou*—Hollywood and sunshine and beach!"

Vicky rides with you to the airport, helps you check in and get ready to board.

"One last word of advice, last lesson from your big sister to her nice young man, new at love and hurt. *Xin* is 'heart,' but also *xin* means 'new.' *Xin teng* is to 'love dearly,' *xin tong*—one sound away—is 'heartache.' Young hearts—*new hearts*—have a lifetime to experience heartbreak, heart healing, heart scars. All the time to grow older and wiser. But you will be fine. You will find peace. Just take each day, each moment—one heartbeat at a time."

Before you head beyond where she cannot follow, she gives you another hug and a double cheek kiss. *"Zai jian, xiao di! Yi lu shun feng!* Good luck!"

She looks up at you, and you playfully tip her sunglasses down over her eyes—the way you'd most like to remember her. You see your tired appreciative reflection, and do your best to smile.

You wonder if you'll ever see Vicky again, somewhere in China or back on your home turf. You think you'd take her to Starshine Diner for their Red Storm burgers, get her an authentic water-boiled bagel, see *Tommy* on Broadway, take a ride up to the observation deck of the Empire State Building.

"OK, maybe New York, too," she shouts at you from the end of the terminal hallway. "I have friends and old customers *everywhere*. Chinatown is everywhere! Chinese people everywhere! Now I am friends with you, too! This is my reward! This is priceless!"

* * *

Another *20–21–22* hours imprisoned in this metal canister: the processed Chinese meals in compartmentalized trays and the smell of stale smoke make you retch. You ask for ginger ale and swallow two paracetamol. You suck on wintergreen mints until your "Soothing Sounds of Slumber" mixtape (Indigo Girls, the Sundays, Portishead) does its trick.

You sleep. You dream.

A silent, majestic white tiger leaps and soars across a violet starfield. As she dives and rises, hot red and gold flames blaze across the sky in her wake. Below, a drowsy grand turtle stretches his neck to look up. He can't bear the heat and pulls into his shell, head and limbs retracting inward. A happy brown rabbit and gray mouse sniff and prod at the shy turtle. Unrelenting and cheerful, they dance and sing, make a table of his shell as he pouts inside. They clink glasses and spit out the hulls of sunflower seeds and lean against him under a shaded patch of grass. The tiger ascends higher and higher, cresting above the clouds. She disappears into the atmosphere with a final deafening roar that reverberates and fades, ash falling behind like the dust of the past. The turtle tentatively emerges and invites the other animals to ride on its back. They plod along together, toward an oasis of verdant green across the plain. A day's trek or more: they shout and clap with each methodical step, in no hurry to see what is just over the next hill.

You gasp awake, tears streaming down your face. You feel the dense rock in your throat suffocating you; the pounding in your temples is unholy cacophony. You squeeze yourself into the tiny, stinking compartment and slide the lock closed. Trapped, contained, the gauzy yellow light makes you nauseous. You splash the stale water in your face and choke back the sobs. You don't look in the mirror, for fear of who you might see looking back.

* * *

You've been back at home two days before you feel like something is really wrong. The Tylenol, Pepto Bismol, Benadryl, and Neosporin aren't working. You think the stomach bug you caught in Beijing has returned for *double-dragon revenge*, but this feels worse. It still hurts when you pee (when you *can* pee). When the pus appears, you know it must be something bad. Something new, something *other*.

Paris would know what to do.

"Bro. Seriously. No jokes. I got you. My folks have friends at the clinic, and they are super discreet. We'll go first thing in the morning."

You are prescribed antibiotics. You can sense Paris start to freak out, but he hugs you instead. "Dude, badge of honor! I'm so sorry this happened to you on your first outing. It happens to the best of us. (Not me, though! Wanda Bernice was not messing around!) You did OK, man. You're OK."

It takes about *10–11–12* days for your body to heal, closer to whole. But that stone in the center of your chest, the solid lump you can't swallow down—that hard mass only starts to dissipate when you sneak cigarettes and take long late-night walks alone down Kissena Boulevard. You try biking for a bit, but get winded too easily. You chug water and do some push-ups—it helps, until it doesn't. You yell into your pillow, then go completely silent. You rock yourself to sleep, praying for forgiveness. You don't feel normal. You think you may never feel normal again.

* * *

"Don't tell Gina."

"I won't. Trust me. Not my story to tell."

"I'm not sure I want to tell her or anyone anything—*ever*. I feel so stupid. Do I need to get in touch with Wendy and let her know?"

"Oh, believe me—*she knows*. I'm sure she's screaming at—or being screamed at by—some dude right now. It honestly could have been much worse."

"I thought this was going to be an epic love story with my childhood sweetheart. It was incredible—it would have been incredible."

"This is where your encyclopedic knowledge of pop culture gets you a *big fat zero*. That trash only happens in books and movies: *FIC-TION-AL*. You had a summer fling! And come on—did you ever really 'love her'? Wasn't she just that dorky, FOB-y chick you used to waste Sanrio stationery on? She lucked out, won the puberty jackpot, and got hot—*big whoop*! You had a few nice weeks of hooking up and messing around. And you lost your V-card! Unfortunately, you had incredibly stupid unprotected sex and got an STD. I mean—what is this, the '70s? Didn't they used to talk about 'getting the clap' in those funky old films and shows you like? *What a trip, so not groovy, man!*" Paris tries to make you laugh. You don't.

Inconsolable and woeful, you light up and offer your Marlboro Light. "Are you stupid? Stop it with that shit. But hand it over. I'll have a smoke with you if you really want one."

Paris takes a drag and coughs. You sit on the stoop beside him and just let your cigarette burn to ash—the smoke, like incense rising.

* * *

You look at your reflection in the mirror and meet your gaze. You avert your eyes and swallow down another pill. You were barely starting to understand where you came from, your place in this world—but now you feel even more lost than before you left. Still sleepless and sullen, sore and sorry—sorry for assuming this was leading to some storybook promise, but denied (*and denying*) a last kiss to seal this chapter.

You count the letters that you must have exchanged across the span of your lifetime (*32*). You count the years (*12*) collected in photos (*20*). You count off the breaths that now come forced (*501*). You count every pitiful heartbeat (*your heart, your heart—644*). You count the days until you might make something of yourself (*1,642*). You count every lie that makes the next moment bearable (*10,000*). You count yourself back to sleep (*8, 8, 8—to infinity*). This immutability of numbers, the cold comfort in the uncertainty of being alone, drifting wherever the cruel current takes you.

The effigy, in faded photographs and yellowed letters, in cursed images and false tongues, up in smoke and now in cinders. All is silent ash—*falling, falling.*

She was your fifth. She will always be your fifth. But this memory is mauled and bitter, this love is dead and burnt.

Su Su Special Delivery and Road Trip Revelations: San Diego

JULY 1994

On the breakfast table, an opened cardboard box: a stuffed panda bear from the San Diego Zoo; a Comic-Con T-shirt with a bright toucan leaning against large orange letters; a bottle of expensive-looking tequila; and finally, a photo with a letter paper-clipped to the back.

The photo:

Su Su is getting acquainted with the locals in San Diego. Head back, eyes closed, bright-orange flower-patterned shirt unbuttoned to the navel, mouth wide open to receive a dangerously long pour of strong booze. Both his thumbs are up, giving a double shot of approval to the busty bartender with the open blouse, as if to say, *It's not just the liquor that is overflowing!*

The letter:

My dearest Young,

I've been thinking about you the whole time! Remember how you used to do the Pee-wee dance and shout "TEQUILA!" I have been dancing and shouting A LOT!

You would love it here! But the zoo—no pandas! Just a plush toy placeholder sitting in the new space! China and US still can't agree on the terms! Hopefully, one day they will—this political push and pull won't save the endangered species.

There is something called "Comic-Con" in July, with all the nerdy, kiddy things you love. One day, Su Su will take you. And after you turn the BIG 2–1, we can go to Mexico for *adult* fun!

San Diego / Tijuana: dollars and pesos. Su Su is a thankful drunken panda—plenty of leaves in both paws! I can literally have one foot in America and one foot in another country!

Do you feel the same way, Young-at-heart? Panda trapped between two worlds? Would you thrive if released to the wild unknown, or would you yearn for safe enclosure?

As you are getting older, look at where our family is from and where you should be going. Zhejiang and Henan, Taipei and Shanghai—that's where you can trace your roots, "your bamboo shoots." Lineage runs deep in your blood, but it should be a living history: learn from the past to be encouraged by our triumphs, to be wary of our mistakes, and to move beyond all of this—in *your* future.

I'm glad that Ma, Bah, and the Xia family are letting you and Wendy see some of China together. You'll go as tourists and get a taste. Both young adults! So much has changed—the years fly by.

The Xia family has money and status now, but it wasn't always like this for them. Money allows one to do many things, have privilege. But it's just a tool, Young. It can open doors, but they can slam back in your face. Never hang your hopes and dreams on something so fickle. (And to be clear: I mean *money, power, women*—in that order.)

It's how you wield that power that is the most important. And it's never 100% good or evil. *Capitalism / Socialism. Wall Street greed / hippie idealism! American Revolutionary War / Chinese Communist Revolution. American patriotism / Chinese nationalism.* Nothing is 100% positive or negative in either direction. Red and yellow—red, white, and blue—all shades of gray!

You are still young (not old) and finding yourself! Seize every opportunity! Go out into the world and experience it all! Have some *mou tai jiao*, and I'll have a shot of tequila for you! *Gan bei*, cheers, *salud!*

Peace and grease!

Your ever-loving, one and only,
Su Su

P.S. When you get back, maybe take some Chinese classes at NYU? Maybe some film classes? Figure out what you want to do, are meant to do. You will make us proud, whatever you decide. I know you grew up with the idea of "filial piety" and how we did everything for Yeh Yeh, Nai Nai, Gong Gong, and Po Po. But trust me, they would tell you the same. They would want you to be happy and healthy. They would want you to feel free.

CHAPTER SIX

"For Your Pleasure"

MARCH 8, 1996

Soundtrack highlights:
• "Do You Remember the First Time?"—Pulp
• "Relax"—Frankie Goes To Hollywood
• "I Want Your Sex"—George Michael

A re you awake?"

"Hmmm? I am now. Was dreaming about fried chicken and corn bread. Can we go find some today?"

"Sure, later. But how do you feel right now?"

"Tired. What time is it? Is something wrong?"

"It's 2:18. Couldn't sleep. I was thinking. I'm thinking, I'm ready."

"Ready for what? Late-night eats? Is there a chicken place open now?"

"No. *I'M READY.* You know."

"I don't know! I can't read your mind when I am fully conscious—no idea what you are mumbling about in the middle of the night! Speak your mind, or let me go back to my savory visions."

"I consent. I give my consent."

"Wait—you mean—"

"Yes. I'm ready to. *With you.*"

"Is this part and parcel of that whole '143' thing? Not a special occasion or special day or anything? It's Friday—uh, March 8th. Not the Ides of March, that's next week. That's bad anyway, right?"

"Nothing special. Early morning on a Friday, hours from dawn. Everyone sleeping. You and me in a room together."

"You want kisses and *more*? You only recently let me 'koala' you, and now this big leap forward?"

"Your 'koala' move is a full-contact sport! You grip me so tight around my torso."

"It's extreme snuggling, and you are built like a tree. I'm going to want to get my claws in and climb you. But *this*, I mean, *this*?"

"If you are ready and want to. I think I'm ready."

"Get up. Go over and pull open your drawer. Look under my stack of panties. Bring out what you find."

Young pulls forth a plastic bag, filled with different types of condoms: lubricated, nonlubricated, ribbed (*for her pleasure*), flavored, extra-large, colored, glow-in-the-dark, one with Japanese characters, one with Russian letters.

"What were you planning to do—*and with whom*?"

"Options, options! In hopes it would be for you! I live in a residence hall at a major university in New York City. Wasn't hard to get this variety bundle—and for free. Barter system! It was kind of fun! Trading with dorm mates and laughing at the ridiculous ones! Banana flavored? Like *that* is ever going to happen! All that swapping and comparing—it's like the Magic: The Splattering game you were showing me at the comic store."

"Magic: *The Gathering*—and not my area of expertise. The play mechanics and collectability aspect—it's too anxiety-inducing. That's why I never managed to get into Dungeons & Dragons when I was old enough to understand the collector's market. Keeping things 'mint in box'—I shudder at all the action figures and memorabilia that I opened—"

"*Shhh.* Hush. Are you nervous? Is that what's going on? Second thoughts?"

"Not at all. I feel completely comfortable. Normal and relaxed. We were just having a regular conversation."

"I'm going to put on some music."

"Oh, no. Let me choose, *please.* Wait—this, this actually isn't bad. What is it?"

"*Right?* Jim gave me this chill-out ambient electronic mix. Great background tunes. Nice and mellow, *sensual.*"

"I bet he assumes we're already engaging in all sorts of activities. You didn't specifically ask him for mood music for us?"

"For studying. *Relax.*"

"Oh, that makes sense."

"Nervous? Excited? Horny?"

"Um, yes."

"Want to stop talking?"

"Yes."

* * *

Young worries that this was a mistake. Maybe they should wait for an auspicious day (*the anniversary of their first date*) or someplace special (*splurge on a bed-and-breakfast along the Hudson line*)? But Young is proud of being impulsive—that he is leading with his heart, his brain, his body, his—

Erena kisses Young, moving her hand up his chest, pulling his Batman T-shirt up over his head, then off with her own plain navy V-neck. She stops and looks away, crossing her arms across her naked breasts.

"What's wrong? I've seen them before. *I've felt them before.*"

"I don't know. It's different. I'm feeling—*shy?*"

"This is so unlike you, Erena."

"No shit! I'm—I'm excited. I love you—and this feels so right.

Like *stupidright*. And the timing—it's not too fast. I'm just a little overwhelmed. I—I—"

"At a loss for words. Wow. We can wait—"

"*Hellnofuckthat*. Let's just—come here."

Young sits on the edge of the bed. Erena walks over, her naked figure before him. She wraps her arms around his head, holds his face to her chest, the bristles of his hair giving way to her supple skin. Listening to her heartbeat, Young looks up and kisses her, smiles, and lets her in under the covers.

They shuffle and scoot their underwear off, laughing as they pull clothes through the comforter and toss them across the room. Fully nude together, for the first time, they embrace and kiss, giggling and biting, blowing raspberries on each other's skin. The electricity between them sparks fire across their bodies.

"OK, OK. Once we do this, there's no going back. Your bony ass is mine."

"It already is. I'm ready. Are you ready?"

"Yeah, yeah. Keep going. We'll take it slow. It's no big deal. Just *sexy-sex*. Doing it. Plain vanilla. Missionary position. Here we go."

Erena mocks pinching her nose, holding her breath, and dives down below, throwing the duvet over Young's head. Underneath the ripple of fabric the light from the desk lamp diffuses through, casting their figures in iridescent blue. Erena's smile—her clear eyes, crinkly at the corners, calming down from laughter. Now beautiful and serene, eyelids closing, lips moving toward his—they shift and move together.

Young unwraps and fumbles under the sheet, but it's safe. He feels safe, she feels safe.

Erena mouths a brief *Ow.* Young pauses until she nods, and they move together again slowly, in time to the barely audible lingering cascade and splash of cymbals, the skip-stuttering beat. As the chords crescendo—the repeated melody reverberates, echoes, and fades.

* * *

"Wow. That was *a thing. We did a thing.*"

"We did. Do we high-five now?"

"YES. WE. FUCKING. HIGH. FIVE!"

"I love you, Erena."

"143, baby. *1–4–3. Beepboop.*"

* * *

Erena and Young shower together in the residence hall facilities. Not uncommon to find couples sneaking about in the nude, but for Young and Erena it's a major milestone—albeit, one done under the pretense that 5:00 a.m. on a Friday morning is much too early to bump into anyone else, other than maybe a motivated jogger.

"I've *seen everything, felt everything*, even got to scrub some hitherto unknown parts clean! I approve of this new level of intimacy, Taiwan-tush!"

"My birthmark."

"I love it. It's the perfect island shape—drifting toward the Youngiana Trench! *The Great Divide!* Your parents must think you are an angelic, blessed baby. A sign that you would never forget their culture—even on the distant shores of America!" Erena mockingly clasps her hands in prayer, dramatically wiping away a fake tear—then pinches Young on the butt, in the same arc of motion.

"That's where my parents met and fell in love, spent most of their lives before moving here. I joke that I was 'Designed in Taiwan, manufactured in the USA.' But I've learned the distinction: we are Chinese, not Taiwanese—a huge world of difference. There's all sorts of political ramifications and nuances—"

"Want to continue your political diatribe? I can absolutely pivot and meet you in that headspace—or you can help me dry off my naked loveliness? Have a nice postcoital 'koala' cuddle?"

"*That*. Please."

Young and Erena change into clean sleep clothes, big spoon and little spoon vying for position, never quite satisfied until their bodies cool off and they can settle still.

"Stop fighting me! Let me get the wall so I can press my ass against it. I'm still hot from the shower! It's still my bed, my room, my rules!"

"OK, OK. All yours."

"*Ho-ho*. Still want to play, I see! You have a thing for when I yell and I'm bossy? That's me most of the time! So, should I expect this kind of reaction from you from now on?"

"Stop it. Let's go back to sleep, so we won't be so tired for date night. I want to see that new Coen brothers movie."

"Date night, too! Dinner and a movie—some foreplay and even more adult situations to cap off the evening. It could get torrid and steamy, Young Lover! There's stuff I want to try, if you are into it. *Ho-ho!* I see that you are! *Gosh, too easy!* My 'Skinemax' marketing tease and innuendo, and *BAM*, you're ready to salute again!"

"Seriously, stop it. Let's cuddle and pass out for a bit."

"All right, all right. I had my fun. I could use the snooze. I'm so glad we're at this point now. *Lovers. Love.* It's so grown-up and nice. Mostly wholesome."

"Mmmm."

"I would have thought you'd be more intense, losing your virginity and all. Thought you would be praying to God for forgiveness. *Breaking your vow of chastity! Premarital sex! The line! Crossed!*"

Young stays silent. Tired, mind racing, calculating all the things he should or shouldn't say in this moment. Erena, her hand on his shoulder, props up her chin, trying to see if whatever isn't being transmitted through his eyes is coming across his lips.

"You don't have to say anything, right now. It's a lot to process. I understand. If it makes you feel any better about it, I am—actually, well, I *was*—a virgin, too. Our first time was together. Wasn't that perfect?"

More silence from Young. Still testing options: the dire threats of string theory, butterfly effect, chaos (pronounced: *KAY-oss*) in general. *Dear Lord, please help me in my moment of weakness and save me from my—*

"I'm being serious. I talk a big fucking game, but you know me now. I'm 90 percent mouth! The jokes and patter are my weapons! Sometimes I have to take a defensive posture—and you know what they say about defense and offense. I've had to deal with creep-o types ever since I hit puberty—all my years of martial arts were really put to good use. It's not like I was waiting to do it, but I wasn't rushing to either. I came to New York to experiment and experience, so there was always the high, high probability of finally doing the deed here. I just happened to meet you. And I couldn't have asked for a better experience! To be honest, I was willing to go to third base with you from the get-go. (*Haha, remember that?* Your annoying emails that wore me down after you skedaddled? *Classic.*) But knocking one out of the park now, *that*—that was a surprise swing! *Oh, wait—sports analogy!* You get that one, right? 'Home run,' fully ingrained in the cultural lexicon, infused in all of pop culture! *Sports! Yay, team!* I'm just filling the uncomfortable silence now. I said you didn't need to say anything, but give a girl a break! What's going on in that head of yours?"

Young finally: "I—I never said I was a virgin. My first experience didn't turn out how I expected. I've been cautious ever since. It hasn't been easy. I don't like talking about it. *We've* never really talked about it."

"No, I know—you've done *stuff.* I've done *stuff.* We've done stuff together! I'm not talking about the hand-and-mouth-Christian-teen-fooling-around business. I mean, the proverbial 'home run,' completing the circuit of the whole fucking sports analogy! *Out of the stadium!* GO, HOME TEAM!"

"Erena, I've—I've had sex before. I thought you had, too. The way you talk and how you've always been so forward with me—"

Erena pops out from under the covers like a wombat, up and pacing around the room, the emerging lawyer cross-examining: "Fair. I never confirmed that I *was or wasn't* a virgin. But this explains so, so much. *FUCK! ASS-U-ME!* It probably even worked to your advantage! You, being all hesitant and denying me carnal pleasures—that actually made me more inclined to keep you in my orbit. *Holy shit!* You Machiavellian Romeo! Did you make me *want to have sex with you, by denying you wanted to have sex with me this whole time?* You fucking genius son of a—"

Erena picks up her pillow and thwacks Young repeatedly. She relents when his outstretched hand trembles in the air, trying to snatch his next breath.

"My fault for assuming—*FUCK! ASS-U-ME!* Your fault for not offering. At first, it was fun to think that I had this much power over you. That you weren't begging to go further than I wanted. I was in control of this shy boy! Then the more time we spent together—it went beyond the physical, an experience I wanted to finally have. It was something special, with someone special, that I was impatiently waiting to happen. I got lost in the romance and cliché of it. Am I the asshole for assuming you were a scaredy-cat-virgin-baby? Am I the asshole for not laying out my entire hookup history? *Fuck no!* Are you the asshole for not revealing your sordid past of sleeping around, and all your *tomfuckery*?"

"It was just one girl—and she broke my heart." Young out of bed, an arm across his bare chest.

"Sure, sure. Fine. We're past that now. I don't need to know. *WAIT*—wait. Did you do it with Gina? *Oh, shit.*"

"No, it wasn't Gina."

"But you've done stuff with her before? Or at least the two of you tried. *I know, I can tell.* But it's not like that now?" Erena, holding his gaze.

"She's my best friend. She's family." Young exhales. A breath, a pause.

"*Oh, thank fuck!* So, this other heretofore nameless seductress (who shall remain nameless) is out of the picture? *Nuh-nuh—shhh*—just answer the simple question. Don't offer more information than is requested. I didn't ask for details."

"Done. Gone. Gone forever."

"*Good riddance.* So, am I the asshole for being horny?"

"Can we stop talking about assholes?"

"Yes—that may be too advanced for us novices. Maybe in time, Wang, in time." The wink is devastating.

She leaps on top of the slack-jawed, stunned boy, tackling him, hugging him, covering him with healing kisses up and down his body: "KOALA COMBAT CREW! KOALA COMBAT CREW!" Full-throated laughter, shrieks of joy.

Out of breath and on her back, next to Young: "It's you and me. *New page. New chapter. New book.* All good, right here and right now—between *us*. Let's keep doing what works—and now we can do *other things*. I was on the pill already, and we've got to sample all these weird condoms at some point. I'm supposed to be gathering feedback and advising my dorm mates! And one other thing we haven't tried: I suspect you might be a 'cunning linguist,' given your propensity for verbal gymnastics."

"You're one to talk!"

"*Aha! Literally!* Takes one to know one! We've got similar *jobs* to fulfill, don't *blow* your chance at making good on this opportunity! See what I did there? Do you need me to review what I said in a full *oral* report?"

"You are going to be the death of me."

"*The little death.* Multiple times, in a variety of methods and mechanisms—orchestrated by this mastermind!"

"Clever, clever."

"*So* getting laid."

"We so are."

Erena rolls over, pops out of the kangaroo-pouch warmth of the shared sheet—and grabs a notepad and pen. She scrawls:

Friday, fried chicken!
Fargo, *new movie to see!*
Fucking—date night, yay!

Young ponders for a minute, before he puts pen to page and replies with:

Sweet weekend meeting—
Mac and cheese, cinema screen
Making love all night.

"Same deal. I'm getting some chicken, either way. Six of one, half a dozen of the other."

"Yes, absolutely—number six, number six."

Fourth Love (Redux):
"Let Your Dim Light Shine"

AUGUST 1995

Soundtrack highlights:
- "Rebirth of the Cool"—The Afghan Whigs
- "Shrine"—The Dambuilders
- "Seether"—Veruca Salt

The prospect of a full first year of intense new academic pressure is nothing compared to the solitude you burrow into when you return to New York from China. You feel the knot in your throat threaten to creep and snake its way down and through the center stem of your body, devouring the last vestiges of any male sexual pride you might have been nurturing. Utterly powerless and spiritually bereft, you wonder if this is how Rilke might have felt (*for a moment*), and if this is how Morrissey feels (*always*).

You devote your energy to intellectual and cultural pursuits and manage to reshape your blob-self back into humanoid form as an NYU freshman. You are absorbed in your usual escapism: film, TV, music, literature. You are compelled to consume, or otherwise be consumed. You feel safe in the fictional otherness of these things you love and remain wary of intractable, real contact. Time ticks by, and you continue to count the seconds until you start feeling whole again. *Observe and report, view and evade.*

* * *

Gina had an amazingly fulfilling first semester at Wellesley—notched a 3.76 GPA, was named the most promising recruit on the Wellesley College Dancers, found the best chocolate silk pie at Alden Merrell—and she was finally with Sean. *The* Sean. Sean Grennan. From SING! From Mrs. Manheim's class. *That* Sean.

Sean was at Harvard. His acceptance was based entirely on merit, brains, and balls. He was a first-generation overachiever, and not a drop of Grennan blood in the legacy ledger. Fiona was across the country at Stanford, her acceptance based entirely on piss and vinegar, pure test-taking mastery, and undeniable confidence in herself. She was still very much into *Star Trek: The Next Generation* (and *Deep Space Nine*). They were incubating future greatness: a career in politics, technology, medicine, law. There was something significant, if not intergalactic, in store for those two.

But the sheer continental distance between them proved too much. The speculation that their relationship was mostly based on sex had been confirmed. They parted, claiming that the flyover states between them were too much distance to sustain their more perfect union.

Sean was distraught and reeling from separation anxiety when Gina invited him to Wellesley's famous Tower Court Mixer on campus. "You could tell he wasn't sleeping or eating right. He put on the Freshman Fifteen—in like fifteen days!" she tells you on your first catch-up call that September as new college students.

"He came to campus on the 'Fuck Truck' like all the other Cambridge boys, but he wasn't into the scene that night. We ended up taking a walk away from the noise, and it was *so romantic*. He opened up and was vulnerable—not like how he was back in high school, all 'chest puffed up.' He said he was unsure about what he wanted to major in, how he worried about his dad cheating on his stepmom, how he wanted to travel to Africa over the summer. He didn't really talk about Fiona—which was a good sign, right? It's like he's already resigned to the fact that it's over. We snuck some peach schnapps and talked for hours until he had to hop back on the bus. It was so cute! He gave me a shy little kiss on the lips, and then I told him he could take me out next weekend! *(Oh, there was no fucking way he was staying over.)* We *connected* that night—and we are going to dinner and a movie at the Brattle on Saturday!"

"Wow, Gina. That's a scene lifted straight out of a teen rom-com if I ever heard one."

"Fuck you! I'm serious! It was *amazing.* I'm going to remember that night for the rest of my life."

"I will be sure to include this anecdote when I give the toast at your forthcoming nuptials."

"Double fuck you."

* * *

Gina tells you about her magical months in Massachusetts, shuttling between Wellesley and Cambridge: studying in grand reading rooms with her pasty new Irish boyfriend, who was highlighting textbooks right beside her; romantic walks along the Charles; ramen date nights in Porter Square. You want to live vicariously in this new-found enthusiasm with a new partner, this new track and groove in her voice, the ups in inflection far outweighing any dips. *We splurged on a B&B and spent the weekend at Martha's Vineyard! Like a real couple!*

Over the holidays and before the start of the second semester, you only get to see Gina for dinner one night. You and Paris needle her for being so MIA and spending most of her break with the Grennans.

"There's only so much time between classes and studying, but we try to have fun when school isn't so intense." She's beaming and twirling her hair. You sort of *hate it.* She's never been this happy, this *type* of happy. "Oh—and *the sex.* So much of it."

You try to support and bask in this particular cycle of joy, for her sake—in a purely conceptual, mental capacity. Gina's new spark and flutter is too delicate for you to criticize. You hope it lasts.

* * *

The rest of the semester passes in flashes of memory. You try not to categorize things pre– and post–"Summer of Wendy," but the chasm is too large to ignore. You recall a few things: getting an awesome part-time job; going to lectures and furiously scribbling notes you can't decipher; finally finishing *Moby-Dick*; crying when you hear "Time After Time" come on in Kmart.

You don't cross paths with Gina again that freshman year, even after May. Gina spends most of the summer of 1995 in DC at dance workshops. You wrap up a full calendar year nursing a broken heart, all the way from Xi'an.

* * *

It's August when you feel like you can breathe again. Every humid New York summer inhale is another moment marked further in time, another blip farther from China. The way you have been changed and humbled—you cannot feel anything much deeper yet.

Gina calls with news: "Juliana Hatfield and Superchunk are playing by the CambridgeSide Galleria Friday. Shudder to Think, Fluffy, and Velocity Girl are opening the block party thing on Lansdowne on Saturday, with Morphine headlining. You want to stay at Wellesley for a few days?"

She graciously makes arrangements for your visit. Indie rock and a change of scenery will exorcise the aching ghosts of past summer, help you revive and return for a fresh fall.

You stare out the window of the Peter Pan bus, startling yourself as you catch your own reflection in the glass, looking back. You sleep as the bus rumbles along the 95 to South Station. *4hours7minutes1stop-to-pee-and-smoke.* You don't dream.

Gina meets you at the depot Thursday night. She hugs you tighter than expected. Her eyes are bloodshot and pink. She's sniffling, and coughs to cover up the crack in her voice.

You push her away gently: "Hey, hey. It's been a while! What's going on?" You laugh off the unusual display of affection and follow Gina through the transit terminal, the smell of Honey Dew Donuts trailing in your wake.

Once you've settled in on the commuter rail out of the city, Gina leans her head back on the purple seat and sighs. "We broke up. He's transferring to Stanford to be with Fiona." She shushes you before you have a chance to ask any questions. "*Nhhh.* Don't want to talk about it. Still raw."

You don't ask, but you know. Sean was her first, her first *everything*—and now it's over.

"Oh, Gina. That really sucks. This is such bad timing. Are you sure it's OK if I'm here for the weekend?"

"And have you miss out on your concert fix? *Hellnofuckthat.* I hear they are going to be playing on a boat, floating outside the mall! You aren't going to be getting that back home. No bobbing bands on the East River or anything."

"I don't need to see them play on a boat."

"Oh, you so do, babyboy. Don't worry about me. We'll have time to catch up over the weekend. But I've got all this dance prep for welcome week, so I can't jump around with you and all the bleached/dyed kids. I'm just going to be lame if I tag along to these rock shows. It's more your thing, anyway. But we'll absolutely hang on campus—I give you my word." She squeezes your hand and leans on you. The lights from the oncoming train streak across her face. She looks thin, the slightest kiss of darkness below her eyes, but as lovely as you always remembered.

* * *

"Here's the boy's—*ahem*—men's bathroom. It's a one-r, so you'll have your privacy. It's not even a thing. For a women's college, there are always a bunch of dudes around. Sean practically lived here half the week."

Gina unlocks her dorm room. The waft of recently extinguished vanilla candle makes your head spin.

"Vanessa is out this weekend. Do NOT touch her bed, do NOT touch her chair. She will know. You can have my bed tonight. I'm going to be out late at practice. But let's go eat first, then we can take a walk around campus before it gets too dark."

Gina eats her salad and soup in silence. You take bites of grilled chicken. You babble on about why Shudder to Think is so revolutionary—*the crazy time signatures and muscular guitar buzz, juxtaposed with their androgynous style and swagger*. Gina manages to nod and shrug at the same time.

The pristine green hills and the sneeze-inducing botanicals of the Wellesley campus are antithetical to the piss-and-concrete-marijuana-falafel-soul of NYU. You can't imagine settling in somewhere other than NYC—you'd never feel at home. But Gina is comfortable here. Belonging anywhere has always been easy for her, with her ready smile, her natural affability. It's something you've always admired but could never adopt for yourself. Sticking to your self-imposed outsider ideology has become exhausting.

She walks a few steps slightly ahead of you, pointing out Claflin Hall here, the library there, and Severance Hill, where everyone goes traying in the winter. She waves to a Diana, shouts *hey* to a Kerry. She doesn't introduce you. You don't mind.

"Clean sheets are on the bed. Don't worry about locking the door. I'll be over at Rena's or Tasha's. If I miss you in the morning, here's all the info you need to get to the Galleria. Give yourself plenty of travel time to stake a good spot by the water. Oh, the food court has that bourbon chicken you like. Leave a message on the machine when you are ready to return, and I'll meet you at the depot." Gina goes through the motions of the "care and feeding of Young."

You hold your tongue and resist the urge to comment. You give her a half-hearted *pat-pat*, JanSport squished in between you. She gives you a little wave with the back of her hand and rounds the corner. She doesn't look back.

* * *

Juliana Hatfield rampages through a short set, her sea legs firm and sure on the little dinghy outside the mall. *Such a weird place for a gig, but it's free and the weather's nice.* She closes (*a little on the nose*) with "Feelin' Massachusetts," and you clap loudly. You give her a few *woooo*s of appreciation and make your way to the front for Superchunk.

To your left, you catch a glimpse of a slender Asian girl in a yellow sundress and Doc Martens. Your heart spikes and sinks, fooled into imagining it's Wendy: *Wendy, deciding she was wrong about everything. Wendy, tracking you down to Massachusetts to embrace you and whisper* "Wo yongyuan ai ni." But Wendy is thousands of miles away, living a lustful life without you, not giving you a second thought.

But *2–3–4*, and you are lost in "Precision Auto," followed by "For Tension." You jump along in unison with the crowd for "Hyper Enough." By the time Mac, Laura, Jim, and Jon are blasting out "Slack Motherfucker," you are enveloped in a manic rapture and *shoutsinging "You motherfuucccckkkkerrrrr! You MOTHERRRRfuu- cccckkkkerrrrr!"* You can't hide the buzz you feel. You high-five some guy with a Dinosaur Jr. baseball cap. You feel silly and blissful. You don't care. You feel *good*. You love this.

By the time you get back to Wellesley, the euphoric swell has worn off. You crick your neck and try to pop your ears. The slight ringing is your only souvenir of afternoon aquatic audio adventures. Gina greets you at the bus stop with a weak smile and a paper sack: "For our after-dinner party for two."

Over salads, you tell Gina how the sound was terrible, but worth it. She plucks a sunflower seed from the corner of your mouth and flicks it at you. She laughs, and the sound reminds you of home.

Gina takes your arm for a sunset stroll. You kick a stone hard enough to plunk it in the water. The sun dips slowly. You tell Gina you are worried about mosquitoes. You think you see the outline of a face in every gnarled, knotted tree. She pinches you in gnatty nips and you yelp. "Keep walking and enjoy the fresh air, city mouse," she says.

"My RA told me the legend: if a young suitor accompanies a Wellesley gal for three loops around the lake, he has to propose, or the lady of the lake will pull his eternal soul down into the depths and drown him."

"Jeez, G! Why are you telling me this creepy story now? It's getting dark! THREE times? Good thing we're only on loop two."

"I made up that last bit. It's three times, and if he doesn't propose, the woman can kick his ass into the water. The sisters here would support that! Profeminist action! Sean almost completed two, but your weak ass only did one and a half. Three full loops, *he's the fella you marry.*"

The nocturnal symphony cues up, the low hum of cellophane wings. Gina clears some leaves from a bench and takes the paper sack from you. "To keep the bugs and monsters from getting you," she says, and lights a stumpy glass candle. "And some liquid courage for us both, my brave babyboy." She takes a swig of something spicy and brown. You embrace the expanse of nature here with your friend, 250 miles from home. The familiar cold comfort of concrete can wait.

She puts her head on your shoulder, her thick brown curls a nest of loveliness: "To my *punyeta* and your *chou gu niang*—wherever they may be. And to us heartbroken losers! *Tagay! Gan bei!*" You drink and let it burn. The water ripples, a roiling reflection of the last edges of sunset, the impressionistic smudge of a pair by candlelight.

"Are you ready to talk about it, then?"

"*Are you?* All I know is you finally met your pen pal from China, she was really hot, you hooked up and 'did hand stuff.' And then you went to see her in China, and something shitty went down. That's all Paris told me. I was tied up in my own world. I'm sorry."

"That's plenty. I'm not even sure what's left to say."

"Same club. Let's just sit here, then. OK, babyboy?"

"I get 'babyboy,' just because I called Mrs. Kwan 'mom' once?"

"It's fine if you're in kindergarten, but seventh grade? You'll never live that down!"

"What was it? '100 Grand, Glamorous, Original Gangster'— G-G-G-*Gina!*"

"I still stand by that talent show intro! Paris did good by me, but 'French Curry'? We'll never find a good nickname for him, huh, babyboy?"

"We'll come up with something, G. One of these days."

She squeezes your arm and tries to find a comfortable crook in the nape of your neck. You both take sips and let the slow hum rise, let the chirps echo in the dark, and let the glowing green orbs keep away all the things you want to forget.

* * *

"Come up here, don't be a wuss. You can have the wall side. Just face it, and you don't even have to look at me," Gina slurs, pulling you up from the sleeping bag and onto the bed.

The blue polyester catches your ankle on the way up. You fall beside her. Your vision is blurred, but you see the mattress, the leg of the bed frame, and Gina's outstretched arm.

She shoves you against the painted brick, turns away from you: "Go sleep, Young. Night." Her breathing slows. The steady rhythm of her back rising and falling against yours. You sleep ass-to-ass, bumping butts.

It's past 3:00 a.m. when you stumble in from using the bathroom. You slide into bed, and you've started drifting off again when you feel Gina press close to you.

Your back's against the brick now. Her back's nestled into you, the big spoon. A moan escapes as she slips her hand up your neck to the side of your face. She turns toward you and pulls you in close for a kiss, her lips pointing in your direction, eyebrows raised—*yes, yes*. Her hips rock slightly, her warmth against your emerging hardness.

"Gina, stop."

"Young, it's OK. I want to. *It's us*. It's OK."

"Gina, *we can't*," you plead, but her lips are so soft, the curves of her body so perfect. You can't help but touch and explore, tangled in this tenuous tango.

"We've always been together through everything. Don't you want to?" Her breathing grows heavy. You've never heard this quality in her voice. It scares and excites you.

"We shouldn't. *It's not right*. We went through this already. It's—"

"I'll be gentle. Your first time, and it will be with me. *I want to*. Don't you want to?"

"Gina, no. Stop."

You get up and turn on the lights. You can't catch your breath—the mess and disorder of your hair and clothes, Gina's red-rimmed eyes, the sudden sober tension, the unease of being alone together and so far away from when and where you were kids.

Now tears are flowing down Gina's face. You pull her close. She's apologizing over and over again. You hold on tight. Her tears soak through your Depeche Mode T-shirt, the red rose now a wet maroon. She shivers against you. You don't let go. You count: *1-and-2-and-3-and-4-and-8-and-8-and-8.*

When she's calm again, when you are both sober, she takes your face in her hands and kisses you sweetly on the cheek. "You'll understand when you are used to having a warm body next to you, *a partner*. The absence—missing that extension of yourself, then feeling utterly alone—it's too much to handle sometimes. I'm sorry for being an asshole before."

You want to offer the cavernous depths of your reflections on the past few months, but the hurt still reverberates too loudly to form coherent words. Your thoughts: *I know, I know, I know.* You'll share your sorrow over Wendy with her, but not now. You grab her some tissues and let her continue.

"If it was any other boring-ass White boy, I wouldn't be like this! *But it was Sean.* The one who helped me with my Madison essay, who would buy me banana Now and Laters, the boy with all those freckles on his back. I'm not sure what to do on my own now. I feel like I lost a piece of myself. He was the one that I always wanted, who I had for such a short while. My first, *my first.* Which makes this hurt so much more."

"But you and me, it's—"

"It was stupid, *stupid.* But sometimes, don't you think it would just be so easy for us to be together? Just comfortable and no drama?"

"Gina, neither one of us is looking for 'comfortable and no drama.' You've always thought of me as a frigid grandmother. You don't want to settle for me. For all—THIS." You gesture to your concave chest, your bony butt.

Gina laughs and gives you a look. The wink is devastating.

"With Wendy, it was . . . *I can empathize with you more than you think I can.* We can talk about her later. But you can't let one person ruin you, let one person lay claim over your thoughts, your heart, your eternal spirit. It's not even a zero-sum game. It's worse."

Gina laughs uncontrollably and slams her pillow in your face. "Wow. I was wrong about the 'no drama'! Do you hear the words coming out of your mouth? Shouldn't you be saving that for your screenplay? Or are you going to write some Smiths-esque lyrics?"

You tackle Gina playfully, but she uses your weight against you. She pins you down on the rug, straddles you, looks down, clear-eyed and thoughtful. You think she may say something or kiss you again. Her lips, eyebrows, unmoving. She rolls off without a word, walks over to the light switch, and then slips under the covers in Vanessa's bed.

"Morrissey and THE SMITHS. *Not THE CURE, not Robert Smith.*" She says and pulls the comforter up to her nose.

"You got it, G."

"I love you, Young. Thanks for being my best friend. My family."

"I love you, too. *Period.* No Han Solo."

You think, *Oh, she snores now.* You don't wake up until noon. You don't dream.

* * *

"The 'new era' begins now. We are both going to be receptive to new things, new people, new experiences! Need to get you out of that sullen, uncomfortable comfort zone! I'm starting with a fresh new look. *How's this?* Is this punk? Is this goth? Do I look hot?" Gina twists her waist, modeling a torn black T-shirt and tight black jeans, dark eyeliner and even darker lips.

"Very. I'm getting sexy-extra-in-the-background-of-a-Troma-film vibes."

"No idea what that means, but works for me—at least for to-night! We'll make it in time for 'Stutter to Stink' and 'Veloci-raptor' if we leave now."

"It's Shudder to Think and Velocity Girl."

"*I know, Tweedledum-dum-Young-One!* Aren't you so glad I'm coming with you now?" That same smug look you've seen a million times: the corner of her lips at that lovable cocky angle, the dimple you want to pluck, the arm you want to bite.

* * *

Gina clearly does not know any of these songs. She jumps along to "Red House" as Craig Wedren hits the high notes and raises his guitar overhead. She's beaming and goofy, lost in the collective ache of this sea of young bodies. You scan the sweaty faces of Boston's finest youth—maybe someone out there for her.

You imagine her at MIT in an oversize sweatshirt, books spilling out of her backpack. She's got her arms folded and lays her head down on the table, just to rest for a moment. A nice boy sits beside her and gently shakes her awake. He points to an open lounge chair and suggests that she'd be more comfortable there. Gina's a little embarrassed, but thankful. She says she can sleep after her exam, just needs to finish reading up on metatarsals. He offers to buy her coffee. The rest is history.

You're not sure how to feel. *Gina, my Gina. I can't deny that she was my fourth. But if we tried something now, would that mean she was really my sixth? Should I give this a chance? Should we? How do I count her if what I feel is immeasurable?*

If not for the ghost of past summer—you might have. A night of passion with someone you love? *Why would that be wrong?* It wouldn't be a reflex of lusting after her body. Your love for her transcends blood and bone. *But—but—*

(Your heart, your heart.)

There may always be some confusion. No need to remind her that neither of you "like" each other "like that." Her Bauhaus (the art) versus your Bauhaus (the band); her salsa / samba versus your Star Wars / Star Trek; her radiant sunshine and rap versus your moody moonlight and metal.

Visceral and effervescent Gina, always in motion. Joy and healing, her inspiration. Her body—a vessel barely containing all that prime potential. You, sullen and sedentary, driven by compulsion and fear: the twin motors propelling your limbs herky-jerky toward oblivion.

You will always share a wealth of memories, the childhood and adolescence that bind you tight and warm. But you fear your passions and pursuits may lead you far away from each other. Tonight you are still close, but it's not like how you held hands to cross the street to the corner bodega. It's nothing like sharing popcorn at

Cineplex Odeon. It's not how you guarded her purse as she rummaged through the sales racks. *You've changed. You're growing.*

You watch Gina as she shuts her eyes and moves to the music. Across her face, you see an inkling of hesitation or a painful memory, but then she is through it, enthralled in the beat again—following her own choreography, alone. You can imagine her saying her goodbyes in her heart *(her heart)* and moving on—healing herself, one step at a time. You love this. You love her.

You are envious, proud—and confused. Wanting for yourself what you wish for her, wanting so many unspoken things. You pause.

In time to the squealing Gibson Les Paul guitars: you pray for God to protect, to love, and to guide this sweaty, bouncing, brilliant woman until the next time you return, revisit, are restored—*forever and ever. Amen, amen.*

* * *

You look at your reflection in the bus window and meet your gaze. You avert your eyes as you reach in your pocket to switch the tape in your Walkman. You pop in a copy of the R&B / hip-hop dance mix that Gina was practicing to all weekend. A change of pace—something new, but still familiar.

> *She was your fourth. She will always, always be your fourth—and more. She's your Gina.*

Su Su Special Delivery and Road Trip Revelations: Rio de Janeiro

AUGUST 1994

On the breakfast table, an opened cardboard box: a stuffed jaguar; a bright-green-and-yellow soccer jersey with BRASIL on the front and ROMÁRIO and the number 11 on the back; a bottle of cachaça; and finally, a photo with a letter paper-clipped to the back.

The photo:

Su Su is getting acquainted with the locals in Rio de Janeiro. Sunburned and shirtless, white pants too tight for comfort, a length of gold chain around his neck, midnight-black sunglasses reflecting the sands of Copacabana Beach, a caipirinha in one hand, the other covering his mouth in mock shock. His neck is craned comically toward a brunette bombshell with the tiniest bikini, as if to say, *Check out this* pão de queijo!

The letter:

"Olá! Tudo bem?" I am learning Portuguese now! Your silly Su Su was so confident in the Spanish he picked up in Mexico—thought it would help here, but it's completely different!

I am loving Brazil! (I know you love that weird movie with the same name—but it's nothing like that here!) Went to the World Cup in Pasadena—decided to continue the celebration! Were the Brazilian victory parties more fun outside the Rose Bowl or more exciting in the streets of Rio? *(And where would they be playing Duran Duran the loudest?)*

Where should I be? Where should I go? I can have a good time anywhere, everywhere—so it doesn't really matter! I'm glad I can have these experiences—back and forth, here and there. It's all *excelente*!

Pick a direction, make a decision—and *go*. As long as I am not standing still! You know what they say about sharks—they would die if they stopped moving! The same goes for any dragon, tiger, superspy, space warrior, world champion athlete—always in pursuit, always on a quest—moving toward a *goooooooaaal!*

My Young Sun, you and Mei are my pride and joy—whatever you do, wherever you are. I hope you are making the most of your youth. Don't be afraid to try new things, to make mistakes. It's OK to contradict yourself, go a different route—or retrace your steps and try again. There aren't any video game restarts or playground redos in real life, but never give up on getting things right. Until the day you die, you can change and adjust. You don't fail. You get another opportunity to improve, to be better. *You persevere.*

I have yet to meet my perfect "Girl from Ipanema" (ask your Ma about that song—or maybe not), so I'll travel through South America some more—climb Machu Picchu, compare my big head to the ones on Easter Island, feel the water at Iguazu Falls, meet the cowboys on the Pampas, and come back here in time for Carnaval! And since my Spanish and Portuguese will be *muy bien / muito bom*—maybe over to Spain and Europe next!

If you don't hear from me for a while, know that I am doing well, having fun. I'll try to write when I can. There's so much of the world left to see! Australia? Antarctica next? The Middle East? Maybe Africa? *Where are the best-looking women? What if they are all back home in Queens? Ha, ha!* I'll let you know!

Peace and grease!

Your ever-loving, one and only,
Su Su

P.S. *I love you, I love you, I love you.* Good luck, Young Gun! *Bangbangbang!*

Sixth Love: "The End of the Innocence"

APRIL–MAY 1996 / (NOVEMBER 1995–????)

Soundtrack highlights:
- "What You Need"—INXS
- "When You Were Mine"—Prince
- "Bravado"—Rush

Your girlfriend has a bad habit of overeating, overexercising, and overcompensating for being overconfident. For the second time this morning, you are holding her hair back as she vomits into the trash pail. Her lucky cat necklace becomes an eye-poking pendulum with each forward toss and retch.

Erena's "boot and rally" strategy of editing her term papers, reviewing for final exams, studying/socializing with classmates, spending quality time with you (meals, sex, goofing off), and getting the optimal amount of cardio every day has worn down her pipes and pistons. Maximum effort, minimal caution: *Either help me—or get out of the way!*

You think you are doing well—no worse for wear, nothing you can't manage. When your right eye starts to twitch, you chalk it up to lack of sleep (*or those Mountain Dews*). You see no harm in being cleanlier than usual when you need to wash your hands again and again, after touching *your notebook, pen, chair, door handle, the tabletop with the brown stain, your wallet, your keys*—

When it is late, and too quiet, you find filler for the paucity of noise: you repeat the Oreo cookie jingle (*Who's that kid with the OREO cookie!*) or the Big Mac one (*Two all-beef patties, special sauce, lettuce, cheese!*). But you find it harder and harder to stop the repetition.

When you start hyperventilating when you come across an unhealthy, unkind number sequence (*4:44—terrifying*)—you confess to yourself and God that things may have gotten worse.

Normally, you don't feel like you are going to have a heart attack. You take deep breaths—no wheezing or obstructed pathways. You rotate your shoulders, neck on a swivel, back-cracking twists—loose and limber. But something isn't right. That same bestial gnawing at the base of your being—the itch that can't be scratched—it's undulating under the skin along your spine, tracing your organs. The only thing that makes it disappear is time and distraction.

But you feel like all of your routines, rituals, rigamarole, systems, symmetry, synapses have become erratic and evolving, unpredictable and unnerving.

* * *

The secret of your pager is out. You've had to keep extra batteries and a roll of quarters with you, at all times. For your challenging academic calendar (study groups); for the need for pocket money (hours at the Undertow); for the relief of connecting with friends and family (Mei leaving a voice message) or the anxiety of not hearing from them (Gina not responding for days); and for the desire (*pure desire*) to meet with Erena whenever possible.

The beeper will come in handy over the summer when Paris and Gina are back in town—perhaps you can even get them to invest in their own devices. Ma and Bah may need to reach you when Mei has her summer playdates.

"I'm thrilled that my gift is making such a return on investment—but I'm not a completely selfless saint! I want to make sure my pages are getting through and not being mistaken for anyone else's. They don't have to take precedence, but I want you to know it's me and have you respond in kind."

You'll have to start tagging each other's messages: a signature to formalize each communiqué. It's old-fashioned AND completely modern. You love this.

A few points of clarification, to best ameliorate any confusion. And it has to be agreed upon by all intended users, for most situations, otherwise the context clues could crash into chaos (pronounced: *KAY-oss*).

So, for general use:

A = 8—for the pure *sound* of the letter A ("ay") and number 8 ("ayt").

B = 8—for the pure *visual* mapping of the letter B and number 8.

Now 4 is tough, potentially: A, F, H, or Y (or 4 = *for*, in the most Prince "I Would Die 4 U" type of way). Too much confusion around the digit. It is to be avoided, only used when absolutely necessary.

411 means a general "What, huh, tell me more." This requires a follow-up with a call or voice message to provide more information.

911*411 means "Important / Call me right now."

Tagged with *99 or *6: the electronic wax seals of your best friends.

* * *

Paris is 981215 or sometimes just 99 (PP). He's been sending you 7175*981215 (TITS) and 80085*99 (BOOBS). Sometimes he ends with *187—the police code for murder, which he learned from Dr. Dre and Snoop Dogg's bumpin' gangsta rap.

"Dude, I'm so ready to come home for the summer. I can't believe I miss stinky Flushing and your dumb ass. I've been dying for some real Chinese food. Can your folks take us for dim sum? We've got that banquet for your Ma in a few weeks, but I'm not sure I can wait that long!"

Gina is 61178 or sometimes 633 or just *6. You mostly get a nice 177155*400*6 (MISS YOU) and call her back when you can. She sounds tired. She's been really into the club scene lately: Club Europe Asian Night (*Tuesdays—why Tuesdays?*) in downtown Boston. She met a nice guy from Singapore: "Good-looking and loaded—his parents bought him a Porsche for local use! He's letting one of his Tufts friends borrow it over the summer. Can't dance for shit, but he's handsome and shy in that typical I'm-an-overseas-international-Asian-boy-*lah* way. Still undecided if I keep in touch after May."

Ma and Bah simply page you with your home phone number to call. Sometimes just to check on you and hear your voice. "I'm trying to make *pho* with a recipe from Dr. Nguyen, but it takes too long to make the broth. Pho Bang just as good. We can go next time you are home. Hold on, Ma wants to say hello."

"*Guai*, remember, once the school year ends in May, we will have our big function at Shanghai Johnny's. Everyone will come for the fundraiser, and it will be perfect for the sauce product launch special promotion! The new sauces will be on sale at supermarkets along the East Coast—not just Chinese markets, not just Asian supermarkets! In the regular American stores like the ShopRite! Your mommy is going to be the cover girl—the *ming xing*—so it's a very big deal!

We'll all celebrate at the big banquet. Paris, Gina, and all the aunties and uncles are invited. You can invite your *nu peng you*, too. Your *xiao ri ben gu niang*."

"She's not only Japanese—and she's definitely not a prissy miss either, Ma."

"*Gu niang—aiya*, that word is not so simple. 'Young lady'—that is my only meaning. Not enough Chinese school for you! She is invited to come along. Your *mei mei* always asks about her, all the time. So pretty. Too pretty for you!"

Mei hollers in the receiver for you to bring Erena *jie jie* for a visit and take her to the park, since it's starting to get warm: "You can come, too, *guh*."

* * *

You get an unexpected page: 07734 (HELLO), followed by *51151, and realize that it's Su Su.

When you go home to bring Mei some of your recent Happy Meal toy hits (Kermit in a boat, Fozzy in a wig, and a Bambi toy in a mini VHS case), Ma tells you that Su Su called: "*Ni de hun dan xiao jiu jiu*—your rotten Su Su—having lots of fun all over the world! He finished traveling in Sydney and Melbourne—sent you a picture and short note."

Su Su in front of the Sydney Opera House: dressed to the 7–8–9s in a white tuxedo, black bow tie, glossy black shoes, a white cashmere scarf fluttering in the wind. His hair is drawn tight in a neat ponytail; dark sunglasses hide his eyes, in sharp contrast to his bright toothy smile (*brand-new veneers*). A glass of champagne, tipped at a jaunty angle, is pointed at the camera—*just so*. Standing beside him in a skintight black dress and heels, clutching his arm, a gorgeous redhead with luxurious auburn hair, her steely blue eyes unprotected. The vibrant Australian sun reflects off the water. She's squinting—which makes her even sexier.

On the back of the photo:

Forget the opera, mate—check out my flaming hot date! Deborah might be Nicole Kidman's cousin, twice removed! Maybe we go visit Tom Cruise and get a role in his next movie! I can be the Chinese triad bad guy! I look the part in this tux!

    Peace and Grease! (Or "NO PEACE—I'LL SMEAR YOU LIKE GREASE—AGENT TOM!" BWAHAHAHA!)

                        Your Sexy Shuai Guh Su Su

* * *

Some pager messages are obviously from Erena—or meant to be for Erena. The numbers eventually take natural shape and added meaning, recognizable as part of a rotating routine:

121117 = RUN: Erena at the NYU track or in the park

80857 = BOBST: studying at the library

711*387 = meet at 7-Eleven for snacks

14*57*6*8113 = an example of a street and avenue meet-up spot (i.e., 14th Street and 6th Avenue)

As more contacts use the pager system in your ecosphere, to make doubly sure there is no confusion (Erena wants credit for a well-timed 80085, over the long-distance 80085 from *99)—the signoff code is required.

At first, logically:

3123178 = ERENA

4011176 = YOUNG

As time passes, it becomes evident that the extra digits aren't necessary (and that 4 and 6 are just *unpleasant*). A shorthand for the signature, the simpler and sweeter:

8883 = BABE

or

8889 = BABY

Ultimately, just 888.
Get it straight.
Bang, bang, bang.

888

This was it. The most magical of numbers: the triple 8. The triple A, top grade, best of the best. Infinity upon infinity upon infinity. It was 888 *love.*

A message—only from me to you. Even for the most mundane reasons—it will carry whatever magic I can imbue, whatever blessing from these finger taps on number keys. My thoughts travel across these electronic blips and pings, across these trusty wires, from invisible rays beaming down from the skies—full of my best intentions—in hopes that you are blessed when you find me reaching out to you.

143*888*143

* * *

911*4012174*5325*888 = 911*HORNY*SEX*888

Without the 888, you would have assumed it was a joke from Paris. The page comes stamped with 888—hence, a legitimate message from your girlfriend. Whether or not she is trying to elicit relations with you is yet to be determined.

"Yes, my love? I see that you rang."

"And where are you right now, my lust machine? Why are you not on your way to my *boudoir*?"

"Calling to confirm if this was for serious, or if it was for *play-play*."

"I've got your *play-play* right *here-here*! Come over and pick up some heroes: turkey, bacon, lettuce, tomato, honey mustard, and mayo. And a bag of chips—big bag, not snack size. Cheese flavor. You pick. And a two-liter of Sunkist. And if they have any Hostess, just grab a bunch. And a chocolate milk, too."

"Are we planning a picnic or a romantic rendezvous?"

"Both. *Always both.* My appetites are insatiable. Hello? Are you still there? Did the blood all rush to your boner? *Hello?*"

"Hold up. Fishing out my wallet to see if I have enough cash on me."

"Dude, I got you. Just get whatever you can afford. I was at the bank earlier today and I've got a few hundos. *Your sugahmama wants what she wants.* If you swing by that shop with the international aisle, see if they have any Tim Tams? There's going to be a big tip in it for you, if you bring your big—"

"Got it. Give me twenty minutes."

* * *

The *can-you-imagine-how-good-this-will-feel-when* countdown has begun. By or before May 17th, all of your papers and exams will be complete.

You'll have to declare a major by June. First semester of junior year will need to be semisolid and mapped out, and you'll have to plan for a summer in New York mostly without Erena. She'll linger a few days after the academic year comes to a close, while the residence halls are still open—but she'll need to head back to California soon after.

You realize that Erena's friends and family may not know about you at all. *Has anyone out West heard what this past year for her—with you—has been like?* You may only exist solely for Erena, while she's been living in this NYC snow globe—this urban dome, not to be shaken until she's out and on the opposite side of the continent. You may be her Schrödinger's cat of theoretical college boyfriends.

Erena has been reluctant to discuss her life back home. You didn't want to pry early on, but now it's a new regime under the banner of 143. She should be ready to open the gates to the kingdom, offer her origin story, share her character profile, her—

"So, I'm thinking that you could come out to Cali at the end of May, early June? I've met your folks and friends—figure you'd want to do the same? No use practicing the Japanese you learned from anime—my dad can't even order sushi. Mention *toro*, and he expects you to wave a red flag at a bull. My mom might know a touch more Korean and German. She does know her *bulgogi* from her *bitte* and her *kraut* from her *kamsahamnida*.

"And my cousins—not sure where they are (they may be overseas for all I know—fuckin' Min Jee—probably in New Zealand eating kiwis—*fruit, not birds*!). And then my friends—seriously, Melissa hasn't called me since she went to Cancún. And fuckin' Janey's in Portland—too busy living the high life. I'll get the whole drama dump over the summer from everyone. If you can't tell, lots of free spirits in my biosphere.

"I'll give you the entire who's-who-and-what's-what after finals. Skeletons finally released from their closets! *You'll know where the bodies are buried!* Once you are on my home turf, I will release the hounds of truth, the hounds of love. (*Heh*, Kate Bush reference—*made you horny.*) The truth is stranger than fiction—but nowhere near that dramatic. Well, maybe for *New Yawkers* like you it might be odd. But for the hippie-dippie Cali crew, it's no big deal. Hey! Did you hear what I said? What's with the creep-o stare? Why are you smiling like that? Is that your poop face? *Ugh, stop."*

Bicoastal romance—it could work! If you venture out to visit California, this improves your chances of staying together. Ingratiating yourself to her kin and ken—a productive use of your free time in the sunshine! The summer has never been kind to you, especially in recent years. But now the odds may be in your favor—and you've always wanted to visit LA! You love this.

* * *

Pulp Fiction is your favorite movie. At the beginning of freshman year, you went by yourself the week it opened. Just for you—*alone*. No small talk, no answering questions about the plot—solo enjoyment of all the shock and awe, visceral violence, inappropriately appealing whip-smart dialogue (much like your beloved *Clerks*, but also completely different). It was pure, selfish cinematic manna. Neck arched painful from the merciless front-row angle, the sold-out crowd roaring thunderously at Vincent's and Jules's gunplay, everyone gasping and stone silent as Butch escapes from the dungeon, samurai sword slashing his way to salvation. You savored every moment.

Salma Hayek is the epitome of loveliness. You and Erena devour *Desperado*. You were thoroughly impressed with *El Mariachi*—Robert Rodriguez's debut was a true masterpiece, created on a shoestring budget. The previews promised shoot-'em-up action, searing drama, and a steamy romance (*bonus: Steve Buscemi is in it. Double bonus: he's not involved in the love story*). It was perfect for date night.

Salma Hayek immediately captures Erena's attention and yours. Her confidence and screen presence are undeniable. She holds her own against the magnetic machismo of Antonio Banderas. Her accent (foreign, but so familiar), her composure (unafraid and powerful), her body (*perfect*). You are embarrassed when Erena asks, "Are you thinking about her again? When you are *with me*? I don't blame you. Sometimes I think of her, too. *Damn it."*

Salma Hayek also reminds you of someone. Erena, in part (more curvaceous than she cares to flaunt). You are afraid to admit who else. But her complexion, smooth skin, rich brown *cabello*—they crowd your fantasies, more than you can control.

* * *

You dream of Kevin Smith and Quentin Tarantino. In the dream, they are smoking cigarettes (tobacco and "wacky tobacky") and munching on noodles from takeout containers. You recognize them from the iconic backwards-turned dirty white baseball cap, jean shorts, knee-length jacket—and the dark shades, skinny tie, dark suit. At first they fumble with thin plastic forks, then they draw forth elaborate gilded chopsticks from the breast pockets of their respective trench coat and black velvet blazer.

QT: *Oh, hello—we didn't see you there. We paid the other guy already. Oops, my fuckin' bad! You aren't from Wang Hop—you're a completely different kind of Wang! I'm Quentin Tarantino—writer, director, producer, actor, former employee of the month at Video Archives, Manhattan Beach, California.*

KS: *And I'm Kevin Smith (no relation to Robert Smith or THE Smiths—I know how that gets confusing)—writer, director, producer, actor, former shitbag for hire at the Quick Stop, Leonardo, New Jersey. Hey man, why don't you join us for a spell? You seem like a cool cat! We were having a smoke, chowing down, and shooting the shit. We were discussing our mutual love of pop culture, all things which you happen to enjoy, too!*

QT: *Fuckin' A, right! OK, OK—so I was explaining the ties to Yojimbo and obviously classic wu xia films and how our bud Rob (I can call him Rob, but he hates that) added some choice Sam Raimi dolly shots, '80s action callback shit, a dash of Tajín seasoning—and voilà! Rob has his own bona fide fuckin' blockbuster masterpiece! If it makes more bank than Reservoir Dogs, I'll gladly tip my hat—but I'll be kinda pissed.*

KS: *I concur, but that ingredient list is too simplistic. I think Rodriguez deserves more credit. The sum of the parts is greater than the whole—a fresh new vision.*

QT: *Says the man who cribbed from Linklater, Cassavetes, Woody Allen, and—*

KS: *Fuckin' Tarantino.*

QT: *Just kidding, my New Jersey Sammo Hung! And I say that with the utmost respect.*

KS: *Damn straight! I won't always be fat! I won't always play a silent stoner! (I may just be a stoner. Period.)*

QT: *Sure, sure—OK, OK. So look, Young—you've got the brain trust here. And we've been gnawing away at your subconscious. As what? Inspiration? Aspiration? Role models deserving of jealousy? We're two fanboys who found our voices toiling away at video stores and corner convenience shops. Not too far removed from what you do at the Undertow.*

KS: *Righteous spot.*

QT: *Consider this a sign then. (Or you are about to have an aneurysm because of finals!) Listen here, buck-o: you are headed into junior year of college! Time to pull yourself up by your bootstraps, OK? Be the best there is at whatever you want to be—OK, bub? A psychiatrist, filmmaker, writer, or cashier—*

KS: *I prefer the term "clerk."*

QT: *Fuckin' clerk (a little on the nose, Kevin)! You need to embrace all of your shit, your personal carry-on baggage (in a glowing briefcase or a hollowed-out guitar case). Take what's useful—*

KS: *—and let go of the rest of the shit weighing you down, man. Jettison the check-in! You've got the ability—nay, the right!—to charge forth and take action. Don't wait for some bolt of lightning that may never come! The signs and wonders, the "ancient Chinese wisdom"—that's all up for interpretation, for debate. Be confident in your own youthful exuberance and convictions, breathe in that rarified air, and surrender to the unpredictable!*

QT: *Like order chicken lo mein instead of a "Royale with Cheese"—right, Rob?*

Robert Rodriguez: It's "Robert."

QT: Sure, sure. What Kevin is saying: it's the mid-'90s, it's almost the fuckin' new millennium! The world is getting bigger and getting smaller at the same time! World Wide Web global monoculture, here we go! There is no right formula for success anymore! You can just do that shit yourself now! Carve your own path. Be your own sifu. See the world in Shawscope: shadows elongated as the sun sets, those triumphant trumpets blaring loud—freeze-frame on you, emerging proud—and kicking some ass! The saga continues well beyond the credits. You're ready to write—and star—in your own story! Observe and report—on something new, something you.

RR: And things don't have to follow the same trajectory. The symmetry and parallels from your past, you can let that craft your future without being beholden to anything that's come before. Honor the blueprint, but you can color outside those lines. There wouldn't be Desperado without El Mariachi. The trace DNA is there, but it's new, full of possibility, a bigger budget vision. There's volition in the violence, intention in the intensity.

KS: Speaking of intense violence (and leaving a trail of DNA everywhere), would the maestro care to say a few words?

Brian De Palma: Gentlemen, gentlemen! Hello, Young. I'm Brian De Palma—the brains behind Carrie, Phantom of the Paradise, Dressed to Kill, Blow Out—

RR: ¡Qué magnífico! ¡El maestro, por supuesto!

BDP: Scarface, Body Double, The Untouchables—

QT: THE! MAN!

BDP: Casualties of War, The Bonfire of the Vanities, Carlito's Way, Mission: Impossible—starring Tom Cruise—opening in a few weeks. You better get your tickets now.

KS: Fuck me sideways! I'm not worthy!

BDP: And of course, the inspiration for "indepalmamyhands76"—

RR: Young, I highly recommend you listen to every word carefully. Verdad.

BDP: What these young guns are saying (and yes, you can be a "Young Gun," too) is true. You've been blessed with a bloodline rich in history and culture. Holy mackerel! *Just spending a week in China pitched your perspective in an entirely new direction! And this unctuous richness of living in the thrilling '80s and '90s! This new amalgamated, borderless world is indelibly a part of your personhood now. Enhanced by your experience, incubated in your imagination—you can offer your own distinctive voice to the collective American narrative. All of us beg, borrow, and steal from our forebears, but we add our own flavor, new spices to the mix.*

KS: *We all found our unique skewed viewpoints, vivacious voices in our chosen form of media (and lifestyle). We draw from our origin stories, from whence we came—whether it be working-class Jersey or badass San Antonio. This influence (and our nerd-ery) brings to light our pride (and shame) in all its glorious imperfection. Now what about you? What are you going to do with the one and only Young Wang–ness you've got? Mr. Hailing-from-Queens-NY-via-Taipei-Shanghai-Tasty-Combo-Number-88? What's your story to tell?*

QT: *Listen to Silent Bill!*

KS: *It's "Bob." The character's name is "Silent BOB."*

QT: *I'm just fucking with you, Smitty! Come on! OK? OK. True romance has got to start somewhere. Nothing gets chicks like passion and creativity. That smoking hot babe you've been parading on your arm isn't in this for the looks! Neither is my gorgeous dame! And "Tubb-o Bob-o" and "Double-R-Ranch-Hand" aren't exactly "Prettyboy Pitt" / "Leonardo DiCapri-WHOA" / "Bill Smith, the Fresh Prince of Hello-There."*

KS: *Um, have you seen Robert?* Dude.

RR: *I believe the term you are looking for is shuai guh.*

QT: *Fuck! Not going to argue with that. OK, OK! Parting thoughts? Last words of wisdom for "Cream-of-Some-Young-Guy"?*

RR: *Salma Hayek is a star! You have my full blessing for that overwhelming crush you have.* Doesn't she remind you of—

QT: *Agreed. I got quality time with her on* From Dusk till Dawn. *She does have a striking similarity to—*

KS: *You were good in that flick. Too bad Clooney owns my boner.*

QT: *That he does, that he does. Hey, Young—are you certain you are straight? It's OK to have a man-crush every now and then—*

KS: *I'm going to have to work with Salma one of these days (I swear, she's got that same vibe as someone). Mallrats should open some doors for me. Young, you liked that flick, right? Sorry, I don't speak Chinese. Not sure what ma-ma hu-hu means, but it's not sounding like an endorsement! Claire Forlani and Shannen Doherty don't float your boat? But Stan Lee—you fuckin' came in your sweatpants when you saw him! And that scene when I did my Fatman cosplay with the grappling gun—you spooged a little, right?*

QT: *You're right about that, Kev! Look at the reaction you're getting from "Jackie Chan Jr." here!*

KS: *We should be calling this one "Sammo HUNG"!*

RR: *"Bruce (Boner) Lee"? "Toshiro Mifun-nyfeelinginmypants"?*

BDP: *Fellas, the classiest, obvious pun here is: "Akira K-ome-ah-so-hard-ah."*

ALL: *TIME TO WAKE UP, CABALLERO! ERENA'S FEELING FRISKY AND SHE'S GOT HER HANDS DOWN YOUR SHORTS! NO SILENT BOB—JUST A SCREAMING KNOB! SHE WANTS YOUR KATANA, BUTCH! BUT BETTER GO PEE FIRST—BEFORE SHE SAYS HELLO TO YOUR LITTLE FRIEND!*

* * *

The flashing 911*888 makes you panic. You spill quarters all over the pavement as you run to a pay phone and call Erena's room.

"Hey, what's wrong? I got to a phone as fast as I could!"

"Poop issues. We overdid it with the K-Town BBQ meat feast. Can you get me some of those pills and the pink stuff?"

"Sure. Need anything else while I'm out and about?"

"Some bland-o stuff helps: crackers, bread, bagels, ginger ale. Maybe some digestive biscuits if the international aisle has any?"

"I will procure all of it. Anything else?"

"We can talk about it later. Nothing important. Would like to hug you and have you rub my belly."

"Absolutely—'koala curative course,' coming right up."

* * *

Erena's room is stacked with half-packed boxes, and much of the walls are bare. One sheet of printer paper is stuck above Erena's desk. You recognize your handwriting on the back, in large pink highlighter marker: "*GANBATTE!!! JIAYOU!!!*" In the corner of the page, a doodle of yourself driving Speed Racer's Mach Five: a stick figure with a *scribblecloud* of hair, holding up two fingers—a peace sign / a V for Victory.

Erena always thinks the nerdiest of you—especially when you try to adopt these half-learned, half-understood idioms into your daily lives: the general pan-Asian-ness of it all (even if the Korean "FIGHTING!" has yet to make the rotation); the rationale and history (pop culture or otherwise); the pronunciation (so close, but never perfectly genuine); the intentional humor (*GANBATTE!!! / JIAYOU!!!*—when overstuffed and pushing to finish the last slice of pepperoni); the unintentional, earnest use (*GANBATTE!!! / JIAYOU!!!*—at the top of your lungs as she completes another lap around the park). What Erena appreciates most is that you say (*shout*) it with the purest desires, utmost determination, and honest belief.

Erena lies in bed, ass pressed against the concrete, resting along the cold wall, back perpendicular and legs parallel.

"Does that position help? Do you feel any better?"

"Nah. I couldn't get comfortable and ended up trying this out."

"Let me feel your head. Not warm. All good."

"Tired. A lot going on. I can't believe we are two exams and a term paper away from being done with this year! It was superfast and superslow at the same time! You, me, NYC—our weekend in Connecticut. (*I love how your dad pronounces all the Cs—ConneCtiCuT!*

Is that racist?) I still think about that fisherman's platter. Oh, and when we took Mei to see *James and the Giant Peach!* She HATED it. She was so scared and bolted out the seat! You made me wait in the lobby with her and a bag of gummies while you sat in the dark by yourself. *Oh, and she loves me!* She kisses me so, so many times! Those juicy slobbery little lips! And that time we hung out with Clara and Alexei—you got all huffy and spilled hot soup down your leg when they said that they couldn't tell the difference between—"

"Stormtroopers and Scout Troopers. *All a function of the job! Helmets and armor are completely different!* What's with the stroll down memory lane?"

"You know, another year done and closing it out. *Sign my year-book, KIT.* That kind of nonsense. Same shit all those teen movies you love make such a big deal about—the good, awesome fun times. Packing up my stuff in boxes made the gears spin. Got to thinking about this year, next year. Usually, you're the one who gets stuck in your head—it's my turn. We should really talk about—"

"Can it wait? I can't even see beyond next week right now. How about I help you clean up and get organized? We can do 4–5 categories: 1) what gets shipped, 2) what gets packed for storage, 3) what gets donated, 4) what gets trashed—*and uh, uh*—5) what I should take. Speaking of which, I'll have to clear out my drawer, and we'll have to say goodbye to 'Helen's Haven' soon."

"She is actually doing really well. She may be back next semester, or she may transfer somewhere closer to home."

"Good for Helen! Can you hand me my duffel? I'll sort out my drawer stuff while we're at it."

"*No. Don't. Not yet. It's too soon.*"

"The drawer is busting at the seams! And you've been more than generous with the shelf space. I'm still going to be crashing here, but lugging my knickknacks back to Queens will take more than one trip: that Cyclops action figure, this Joy Division shirt, those Sandman graphic novels (which you never did read)—they can come with me. Three pairs of sweatpants? Just need one."

"Hey, what's in this? You usually make me suffer through show-and-tell of all the 'awesome collectibles' you score."

She shakes the half globe. The rattle of the ring against the plastic curve causes your heart to leap into your throat. The pop of the cap makes your upper lip sweat, the hairs on your neck stand up like barbs.

"Did I ruin the surprise? Is this for me? *Whoa, really nice!* It's much better than the gumballs and temporary tattoos I get outside the Vons!"

"It's not a toy. It's—real."

"Cubic zirconium? Is this from that lady with that table we passed in Union Square?"

"No. *Real*—as in an engagement ring."

"Wait, Young. What are you saying?"

You explain: Su Su's fortune and misfortunes, how he left the ring for you, how your mother likes to snoop. You explain the belief in "seven great loves" (name-dropping Denise Scolerio, Natalie Chang, and Jennifer Coscarelli). You finally tell her about Wendy—how you wanted that story of childhood love realized, how you were devastated and felt so small, so powerless, so lost and closed off—until this year, until you met her. Erena is your unexpected number six—but also your 888, your *bangbangbang*, *your babe*, your *baby*, your love, your !43*888. Your *888 love*. It doesn't all make sense, and you are afraid of—

"*Breathe, boy, breathe!* You're burying the fucking lede here! I'm going to take a wild guess, powers of deduction: insert Gina as number four (*too hot not to be*), and Wendy is five—the one who popped your cherry. Making me number six. Which means I am dangerously close to the end-all, be-all! Is this like how cats have nine lives? Or 'three strikes and you're out'—not in the literal baseball-yay-sports way, but the metaphorical use? Or like how in the Bible you have to forgive someone 'seventy times seven times'? I've never heard of this 'seven great loves' tomfuckery business. And you say Su Su said it was some old Asian thing? But I'm number six. 'Number six.' *I'll take it.*" Erena, with a Cheshire cat grin of self-satisfaction, poking you in the ribs repeatedly, pawing at her superstitious sexy *shuai guh.*

"Don't make fun of me. I spilled my guts to you just now."

"Spilled is right! Need I remind you that I'm really, really attracted to the mysterious side of you—*aloof and alluring?* Isn't that what you love most about me? How you have to sometimes peel back my onion layers? I love the verbose glitchy braniac you usually are, but the reticent, ponderous thinker—*ooh, that's sexy.* And I thoroughly encourage—"

"I want you to have it. At least, hold on to it for a while. It's *not*— and *it is*—and I'm asking you to *consider.*"

"So . . . just for *play-play?*"

"Hang on to it for me. At least until we get through the school year and everything stressing me out right now. I can't risk having it at home and Ma taking it away."

"I'll treat it like a prize! My reward for us doing *it* a hundred times. *Eeew*—wait, that makes me sound whorish."

"Erena, please. Will you accept it? For now?"

"It's a beautiful ring—unique. It's not mine, but it's *on loan, escrow, collateral.* Seriously, I'll be careful with it. I'll keep it safe."

Erena puts the ring on her left hand, raises it to the light—the straightening of her fingers, a little flex. She flutters her eyelashes, clutches her hands to her chest, and chases you around the room: "*Oh, honey! YES, YES, a thousand times YES!*"

Her voice drops an octave into a monstrous, cartoon growl: "*BEFORE WE GET MARRIED, I HAVE TO REVEAL THE SECRET OF MY CURSE. ON THE EVE OF EVERY MENSES I WILL NEED TO CONSUME THREE BABIES. PLEDGE THIS TO ME AND I SHALL GIVE YOU FORTUNE BEYOND BELIEF, YOUNG SWEET MORTAL!*"

You howl in delight as she "koala-clutches" you onto the bed.

"How about this—so it's not so engage-y." Erena unhooks the chain around her neck and slips the ring through. The red gems in the setting, matching the red in the cat's ears and collar—a red string of fate, connecting you two.

The satisfying slide and clink of the diamond in the center, meeting the outstretched paw—the two totems make contact in a fortuitous high-five. You love this.

Erena hands the golden strands to you. She sweeps her hair to the side, exposing her neck. You delicately latch the clasp. She turns back and looks at you. The wink is devastating. You love this.

Erena straightens out the chain across her chest: "I was going to highlight how it dips into my cleavage, but I don't have time to deal with yet ANOTHER boner. Nicky Neko will stand guard. These precious jewels might even be a 'super luck power-up'—so I'm guaranteed to do incredibly well on these last papers and exams! Win-win for everyone!" Full of powerful potential—this Schrödinger's cat encircled by love and luck—hovering above the heart of your most precious one.

You love this. All of this. You love her. All of her.

* * *

You unashamedly drum your pencils hard against the cover of your Psych Stats textbook, keeping in time with the Afghan Whigs' "Gentlemen." The strut and swaggering groove give you confidence that you will obliterate the Scantron grid, the open-ended fill-ins, the blank paper canvas awaiting your fevered scrawl.

Erena is out for a run, to clear her mind and to breathlessly practice her final presentations. You promise to bring her food (turkey club hero), drink (Gatorade—red or blue flavor only), and kisses (Hershey and "Wang brand")—as soon as you finish this *poodoo* of a self-assessment.

Your pager does a jiggle dance on the tabletop. You are pleased that this is nearly syncopated with Greg Dulli's impassioned yowl coming through your headphones.

You assume it's Erena checking in on the status of her forthcoming snack (food—*and you*), or maybe she has second thoughts about wanting a pack of Chocodiles.

121*911*411*61178

It's Gina. She needs to speak "one-to-one," and right away. You call.

"Hey, babyboy. Just—just needed to hear your voice. Maybe whine a little. Not having the best week here in idyllic Wellesley, land of smart bitches with flat asses and fat trust funds. Whatcha doing? Where are you? Home or—"

"I'm in Erena's room, finishing up a practice exam. I have to meet Erena out by the track soon. She must be starving—and it looks like it might rain. So I'm on snack and umbrella duty."

"Young Hun, why didn't you stick with the Boy Scouts? You'd be like god-tier Eagle Scout level with your 'attentiveness to detail'— and I'm putting that in a nice way. But really, you are the best."

"You can diss me and/or butter me up anytime, but I need to get a move on. Everything OK? What do you need?"

"Young. *You, you*—OK, fine. As if studying for finals weren't hard enough, I turned my ankle—hurts like a motherfucker. And stupid Shannon Lim got selected over me for the committee lead. I heard my Auntie Tellie back in Manila has colon cancer. And I'm generally feeling homesick and lonely and—"

"1) Finals—you always rock. You are the best test taker I know. You just get nervous right before! 2) Ice/heat and elevate. 3) That committee is temporary, for a one-off event—right? The real position you want won't be decided until the fall. You've got all summer to rally for that—*and uh, uh*—4) And I'm so sorry about your auntie— hopefully they caught it early, and—"

"*Dude.* Just shut up and *listen.* I don't need advice or want you trying to fix things! I wanted to verbalize to a living nonjudgmental person and not be talking to a wall. A few grunting 'uh-huhs' might be nice—or 'I hear you' would be perfect. I know I am a badass babe, OK? That doesn't change. Needed to vent to get back in my groove, that's all."

"*I hear you*, Gina. I'm sorry. Continue."

"Thank you. And I'm sorry for snapping, but sometimes you need it. *Social conventions*—read the signs! It's for your benefit—and for Erena, especially. I still don't know what kind of witchcraft you stumbled upon to help you score that—"

"*Uh-huh.* I'm listening."

"Fast learner. Good. So—"

"Yeah."

"So—so—the worst thing. I found this stack of index cards tucked in my shelf—blue rubber band around it, wedged in between two textbooks. Handwritten flashcards with all these mnemonic devices, color-coded charts, dates of important events—they were Sean's. He must have left them in my room last year. I thought I had tossed or packed away everything that reminded me of him. Finding this stupid stack of notes brought it all back. And I was already having such a shitty week—"

Gina's voice rises and cracks. You hear the choking sob through the line. You close your eyes and say a quick prayer: *For strength, for healing. Amen, amen.*

"Seeing his pristine handwriting, remembering how we'd sit across from each other for hours—being close and doing our own thing but comfortably silent together, you know? And then on the back of this one card—in that unmistakable human font of his—I see: 'GV + SG = 4EVER'—and I just fucking lose it. He wrote that, Young. Sean wrote that! *And it's not true and it never will be!* He's back out there with Fiona, planning some amazing future—*without me.* It was never going to be me, was it? Was he thinking about her the whole time when we, *when we—*"

You let Gina cry and wait for her to continue.

"I'm mad at myself for letting this get to me. I'm mad at him for—*I'm mad.* I'm sad about—a lot of things. But I'm feeling this and letting it happen. *And I'm letting it go.* Hand and heart—unclenching. *Inhale, exhale. Going, going.*"

"Good. I'm here. I'm listening."

"Oh, Young. *Gosh*—I can tell you are really listening. I hear your heavy breathing over the line! *Too intense!* It's not meant to be *that* kind of call!" Gina laughs and blows her nose. You are relieved.

"Gina, you are the strongest person I know. I'm here whenever you need to talk. Page me, and I'll get to a phone when I can."

"*I know, I know.* So glad that you are reachable. You'll have to thank Erena again for the beeper. I even went on the internet and printed out a cheat sheet of pager codes and stuff."

"Oh, that's great! We have one tacked up on the wall downstairs at the Undertow! I committed most of the codes to memory. Erena's getting good with it, too. And you know all about numbers as letters—"

"I'm learning. No doubt you've got it all down pat. It was good hearing your voice. I can tell you're tired. But you light up when you talk about your charming, curvy shortstack."

"She's—*amazing.* She's out there burning laps and rehearsing her end-of-term speeches—a full brain and body workout."

"Oh, God. You two are *totally doing it.* I can hear it in your voice. I can practically see the creepy smile spreading across your face—*and the legs spreading in bed! Eeew.* But I can't hate on the *playa!* Wow—congrats."

"*Gina.*"

"OK, OK. I'll leave it to Paris to roast and/or toast you. I'm happy for you! And I'll bounce back soon. I feel better already! *I promise.* Thanks for the talk—and in a blink, I'll see you at your parents' shindig—as soon as we get out of this finals hellhole and we're all back in Queens. Back home. And sane. *Oh—hey, Grace! Jen! Yeah, I'll go down to Munger with you.* Gotta run, Young. Thanks for the ear, babyboy. Be good."

She hangs up before you get to say goodbye. You pause. You put down the receiver before the echo of the dial tone reminds you how far away Gina is right now—and how close she'll always feel.

* * *

The clouds have cleared, and it's a perfect spring evening. Erena is waving at you, both arms rotating in slow-helicopter chops—she's signaling to you, loosening up her shoulders. You think: *Her smile is the reflected glory of creation.* You bask in it. Backlit by the dipping sun, she's simply lovely.

"Turkey sub for the sexy, glistening genius? Yes, over here! Thank you, thank you! *Such a cute delivery boy, too!* Want my sweaty kisses as your well-deserved tip? Yes, yes?"

Erena trots over with arms wide. You welcome her salty, steamy, slick embrace. The paper bag crumples between you.

"My guy, my love—did you forget the juice?"

You search your backpack: a towel, umbrella, light hoodie, notebook, chocolates, lighter, smokes, your pager, but no beverage.

"I overdid it with the loops. Can I park it over yonder and start munching? Do you mind popping by the hot dog cart for a drink? I'll hang on to your stuff. *Oh, you thoughtful boy—the towel!* How are you not an official Boy Scout again?"

The hot dog cart doesn't have red Gatorade. You decide to make the effort and trot to the nearest bodega to secure the exact requested item. With your quest complete, you expect a handsome reward in the form of some endorphin-releasing affection.

What you find instead is Erena with eyes red-rimmed, wiping a smear of mayonnaise off her two-toned T-shirt, stomping across the field to meet you in the middle. She snatches the drink from your hand. She swaps it for your pager.

You look at the orange display and are puzzled by what you are seeing. Erena chugs the entire bottle while keeping her blazing stare aimed at you like the Eye of Sauron. The red liquid spills from her mouth down her three-toned T-shirt. She wipes herself down with the towel once more. She throws it—and the bottle—at your face. You don't even try to dodge or duck.

"*WHAT. THE. FUCK. IS. THIS?*"

"What? ١٤3*888."

"*I KNOW! WHO. THE. FUCK. IS. SENDING. THIS?* Your pager just lit up two minutes ago! I've got a mouth full of turkey and bacon, *sweating my balls off*, parched and waiting for some fucking juice—and *I'm nowhere near a fucking phone*! So it definitely wasn't fucking me sending you love notes!"

You think it might have been some system error. Maybe an old alert from Erena was re-sent or delayed—but that's unlikely. Occam's razor cuts sharp. You realize—

"*It must have been Gina.* We were talking before. She was having a hard time this week. Needed someone to listen. We hung up without really saying goodbye."

"Young, that's all fine and good. But this says 143*888. Did you tell her about it? I thought this was *our thing*—our special way of saying—"

Erena starts to cry ugly tears: the snot bubbling, the sweat soaking through her four-toned T-shirt.

"It—it—must have been a coincidence. Gina was just saying how she was learning pager code."

"143 equals 'I love you.' Friends, family can also page you this, for sure. I get that. But 888? 888? Young, you said that was *for me—for us. Special.* 888. Young, were you just saying this shit to me? Did you not mean it?"

You are at a loss for words. You haven't told anyone how Erena was your 888, how 888 became the beloved shorthand for your blessed, divine union. *Why—or how—did Gina . . . how could she decipher the code, plunder the syntax, usurp the secret?*

"888 equals BBB equals BABYBOY. That must be it. *It's just a coincidence! It just happened that way! A mistake.* There's too much room for interpretation. There's no hard-and-fast rules—it's all up in the air. I'll tell her to stick to 61178 or 633 or just *6 in the future. So there's no confusion or misinterpretation."

Erena has her hands on her knees, her head down. She looks tired, defeated. Now upright, she stretches and elongates her back—lithe and limber. She's lovely—and furious.

"Young."

"Yes. I'm listening. *Uh-huh.*"

"You—out of everyone I know on this living, vibrant planet—would be suspicious of anything that seems like *coincidence.* I want you to pause and be honest with me—with yourself. *Do you love Gina?*"

"I—I mean, of course. I love her. I love Gina. I love you. I love Ma, I love Mei—"

"No, you dumb, dumb, *baka, pabo, san-bah,* 'stupid' in every other language I know! You know what I mean. *Are you in love with her?*"

"No. *NO.* I don't love her in that way. I'm sure. *Sure.*"

"I will not be a part of some fucked-up, clichéd love triangle bull-shit, Young. This isn't Nora Ephron or whatever book-to-film shit! *It's my life.* And Gina—that body of hers? My tight curves are not going to be able to compete with that plump, toned goddess. And with the way I like to eat, my metabolic engine may collapse at any time, and this all goes to shit! Can she cook, too? I can barely make hard-boiled eggs! *I bet she can fucking do anything!* And she goes to FUCK-ING WELLESLEY! I couldn't even get into that school! I didn't even bother trying! I'm fucking smart as shit, I know—but, but—she's going to be rich one day! I may go on to do pro bono work! Bleeding-heart liberal attorney, struggling to make ends meet? Am I OK with that? *I don't know.* I don't know anything! You and Gina—there's too much history there that I won't get in between. *I don't think I could win that case!* The evidence would be stacked against me! FUCK! No offense, but forget you for a second—I don't know if I want to *be her* or if I want to *be with her.* Or—ugh—*she's so fucking cool.* Have you ever seen the way your face looks when you talk about Gina? You soften, you smile. You look concerned. You care. *You love her.*"

"She's my best friend. She's family. Of course I love her! I can't imagine what I look like *when I talk about YOU! When I think about YOU, Erena!* Apparently I have no control over this face! I must be grinning like the creepiest creep-o all the time! And my heart must be pounding through my Joy Division T-shirt for a reason! There's no competition here. I don't feel this way about anyone other than you. My love for you—my heart—"

"Whatever this is, between you and me—however long it lasts, how deep it gets—it's not nothing. I can talk my big game and all my motormouth bullshit—but I've felt something real, to my core. And either you are an incredible liar, a sociopath, or you have a re-markable ability to compartmentalize. I believe that *you believe* that you love me. But for this time in our lives—*right now*—I need to be *it*. No one else. Just the fucking singular-sensation Erena.

"I let you see my hand. You were *my first*. You'll always have that. I'm always going to remember. That can't be changed—and I wouldn't want it to be changed. *But I don't want to be lied to*. I don't want to be the someone who gets you over someone else—whoever that is. It can't be all lip service. It may sound selfish and devastating—*but I want the power here—and I can't lose*. Maybe it's just 'Crazytown Finals-ville' that has me so emotional. I'm tired and crampy. I'm hungry and thirsty. I think I have to poop, and I defi-nitely need to pee. I feel stupid, and I feel ugly. And—and *I want to be special*. You told me I was special. You made me feel special. *Am I special? Am I?*"

Erena shoves you hard—both palms flat. You topple over back-wards onto the thin layer of grass and look up at her. (You think Quentin Tarantino would argue for this well-deserved moment of violence—and he would be sure to follow it with some witty repar-tee, some humor to offset your absurd public tumble. *"Motherfuckin' this, motherfuckin' that, you motherfucker,"* about to spew forth from Erena's mouth at any minute.)

You expect her to laugh and offer you a hand. You expect her to say it was all *"just for play-play, asshole."* But she's looking down at you with an expression you've never seen on her face before—*hurt, disdain, confusion, exhaustion?* The salty sting of her tears and sweat falls on your face, down your cheeks, onto your lips.

Erena walks slowly away from you. She kicks the Gatorade bot-tle out of her path. She scoops up the towel and tosses it around her neck, wipes her eyes with it.

You won't let this happen. You won't nod and listen. You are not going to uh-huh *this. You aren't going to just observe. You are going to do something.*

"Erena! ERENA!"

"GO AWAY! Leave me alone! I need—"

"No, please—let me talk. *Please. Please.*"

"Asshole. Make it quick."

"OK, OK. You know how I have my systems and how I put things in order? Let me try to describe how I see and feel this, how I arrange this in my world—how I'm wired to think and feel about different kinds of love."

You breathe deep. You report on something new, something *you.*

"1) I love Gina. *Period.* Gina's love is purple, steady, dark. It smells like sandalwood and barbecue pork. It's chocolate silk pie. It's the sound of a deck of cards being shuffled. It's Reebok sneakers and half-chewed banana taffy spat into a trash pail. It's *Revenge of the Nerds* and *Major League.* It's Gene McDaniels and Velocity Girl. It's familiar, and it's always there."

"What the fuck—you dick! That sounds incredible! Way to make someone feel inadequate! What are you getting at?" Erena dips her head and quickens her pace across the field. You follow and get back to explaining.

"2) My love for Wendy was fluffy pink, and then red—shiny and flickering. It was white musk mixed with the way clothes smell after being in the sun too long. It was undercooked seafood—warm, not hot, not cold, like sashimi. It was somewhere in between—and *off.* It's orange juice made from frozen concentrate. It's ketchup and American cheese on pizza instead of tomato sauce and mozzarella. It's the sound of high heels on slick marble. It's *Chungking Express* and *Blade Runner.* It used to be Cyndi Lauper's greatest hits—but now, it's a Skinny Puppy 12-inch extended remix. And it's gone. *It's burned to ash.* It's dead."

Erena pauses. She scrunches up her face and kicks dirt your way. The smirk on her face is promising.

"3) My love for you, for this unique being named 'Erena,' is harder to describe. *It's ROYGBIV! Give me all the colors!* Put in some neons and metallics, too! It's the smell of suntan lotion, baby powder, and Cherry Coke. It's the freshly refilled crab leg tray at the Silver Harvest buffet, it's the prime rib carving station! It's the sound of hard rain and thunder finally stopping—and birds landing on the windowsill after the storm. It's *Pulp Fiction* and *Beauty and the Beast*. It's the Crash Test Dummies and 311. It's calm, shimmering water and the roiling, rolling foam of waves. It's hot, lustful—but it's also cool, pure. *Sink or swim. Burn or freeze. Float or fall—fight or flee.* It's infuriating, frightening, enlightening, exhilarating, and inevitable. *It's all of it—all at once.* The way you make me feel—the rest of the world collapses—and it feels like everything. Your love is everything. To infinity. 888. *Bangbangbang.*"

A beat. A moment passes. A pause—*a comma, not a period.*

Erena slows her pace. She doesn't look at you. She mutters under her breath: *"Motherfucking cunt."*

"Yes. I will respond to that name now."

"I'm sorry I pushed you so hard. Your bony ass went down too easily. I didn't even use any real throw or martial arts technique. *Pfft,* like your weak-ass yellow belt could even defend against me. Plain old playground push, and *splat.* No core strength whatsoever. Must have hurt."

"Yes. And my pride—*ouch.* Both. Double pain."

"And you swear, right now. While you are with me—and with me alone: *it's just me.* I don't care about the past or the future or whatever—that shit is for another time and place. My concern is the here and now. What we've got when we are together. It's just me filling the love-shaped hole in your soul. *I'm boxing out. I'm tucked in that burrow. I reside in that bush. I claim that hill. I occupy that tree.*"

"Your 'koala encampment' is secure, mate. I promise. Cross my heart and hope to fly."

You hold three fingers up, then switch to two fingers. The Boy Scout in you wants to be honorable, wants to be brave, wants to breathe again—in mutual, comfortable silence. *No lies here. Prepared for the truth. Signal, signal. Freeze, pause. Inhale. Peace signs / Vs for Victory. Everything is OK. (Your heart, your heart.) Lord, forgive me. She'll forgive me. Love is patient. Love is kind. She will—*

"So, are we having make-up sex before or after I shower?"

* * *

When you make love—*after Erena showers*—she runs her hands through the warm briar patch of your hair, the way she always likes—that you like. But this time she grasps and pulls a little too vigorously. Something new for you—but not wholly unexpected, nor undeserved, nor unwelcome.

* * *

You look at your reflection in the mirror of her eyes. You meet your gaze in hers. You avert your eyes—embarrassed at the overwhelming rush of feeling, feeling everything alive and free. *You love this. You love her.*

You don't need to say any more. You let her breath and laughter drown out all the static and noise outside, all the fear and hesitation within. *You love this. You love her.*

> *She is your sixth. She will always be your sixth. But she could be so much more. She could be your divine 888 love.*

CHAPTER SEVEN

"Nothing's Shocking"

APRIL 1996

Soundtrack highlights:
- "Head On"—The Jesus and Mary Chain
- "She's Lost Control"—Joy Division
- "Everything Zen"—Bush

You are relieved that the school year is finally over: thousands of words typed, printed, and submitted; hours gnawing on fingernails and pens; exams all done. You celebrate with food (*injera* and *key wat*) and love (snuggling and snogging).

But Erena seems quiet and distant. Truth be told, you aren't talkative or energetic either. You chalk it up to the crests and valleys of adrenaline and caffeine, the all-nighters and day-sleeping that has been throwing your wiring out of whack.

Erena packs and naps, goes out on runs. You shuttle back and forth between Queens and campus, helping Ma and Bah prepare for their big event.

The annual benefit for the cleanup of Flushing Bay is always a big deal: *flora, fauna, water, community*—the confluence of all things the Wang household truly cares about.

Bah and Ma are both equally involved: Bah coordinates with his colleagues at the Botanical Garden, Queens College, and the Environmental Protection Agency; Ma is the ideal emcee and works with the local sponsors and bureaucrats on their promotions and messaging. The "sauce spokesmodel" job is the new element that has Ma tapping into her new high-wire, third-rail intensity.

Ma spent a small fortune on a custom-made *qipao* (and a matching mini version for Mei), and sharp bespoke suits for you and Bah. Ma and Bah were strict with "broth and veggies only" dinners until the packages from Hong Kong arrived, four months later. A perfect fit, except that Bah's pants are a touch too long (*I must be shrinking in my age!*)—and yours are too tight around the belly (Erena's consumption influence).

Ma's beauty regimen: hair by Auntie Corrina, nails by Auntie Liang, makeup by herself (lessons from the Clinique and Lancôme counters). She made Bah get a haircut a week prior. *She knows to let you manage your own hair now.*

Her 4 x 6 index cards were prepared well in advance: her neat English words look typeset, her Chinese characters in clean calligraphy. She made Bah provide a list of his non-Chinese friends attending—phonetic notes next to each difficult-to-pronounce last name: *Wall-DUH-mun* (Waldman); *AHH-day-BAY-oh* (Adebayo); *OFF-zzEE* (Offsey); *MAN-kuh-WHIT-zzz* (Mankowitz); *MAHR-tin-NELL-EE* (Martinelli).

This year, Shanghai Johnny's will be hosting an all-you-can-eat *xiao long bao* gorge-a-thon. Bah has four tables booked for his coworkers and colleagues. The Choudharys and the Villanuevas cover another two tables between them. The rest of the restaurant will be comprised of local government luminaries, members of the Chinese business coalition, Pastor Chen and church members, miscellaneous friends—and of course a smattering of press to cover the event.

Your prime directive for the evening: shake hands, smile, and assume the role of catch-all errand boy. *Help when needed, stay out of the way when not, make sure things go smoothly.* Gina and Paris are always good soldiers, and will get slipped red envelopes from Ma for their help.

"Very good that *ERRRR-UH-NUUH* is still in New York," Bah says and reviews the seating plan. "She can help keep an eye on Mei."

"Do you think Ma will mind? Is it a big deal to bring my girlfriend to Ma's event? Are your Flushing friends going to gossip?"

"They will gossip anyway! They think you and Gina already together—for years! Don't worry about it! Ma will be occupied with everything else, and I have to watch over my guests. Your *nu peng you* will have a good time with you and your friends, eat some good food, learn about the environment from smart scientists. She will see our community in Flushing. Make sure she wears a nice outfit, but *not too pretty!* Spotlight on Ma that night!"

"OK, but please talk to Ma first. You know how she can get. No surprises."

"*Aiya*, there's *always surprises.* But let's be extra safe."

* * *

"Do I look OK? Is this respectable? Will my presence tonight honor you and your parents? Black purse matches, yeah? It feels tight. I was stress-eating, and I always get bloated around my period. *Fuck, my tits!* When did they get so huge! When you come to California, I'll have to show you pics of me in grade school. Puberty hit me so hard! *Fucking boobs! OW!* It's too tight, right?"

You stretch and cajole the slack in your collar, unbutton your jacket, wipe your brow with a black bandanna. You feel hot and attribute it to the warm May afternoon, but it's mostly how beguiling Erena looks in her sleek aquamarine dress. A classic Chinese style: high-necked, sleeveless, slit up the side; the plum blossom print matching the blue and green flecks in her eyes, dark mascara enhancing their almond-shaped beauty, her glossy red lips an attractive nuisance you'll have to avoid all night.

"You look amazing. Absolutely gorgeous. This *qipao*—you got it off the rack from that place in Chinatown? The one next to the ice cream shop?"

"Yeah—total steal! 60 bucks, but she gave it to me for 40. I figured it would be perfect for tonight. Added bonus—some cosplay fun! You can be the kung fu master and rescue me from the rival *dojo*."

"I think it's *wushu wuguan* for kung fu. *Dojo* is for karate. *Dojang* for taekwondo."

"Ugh. You can forget rescuing me—'Master Mood Killer'! I'll knee you in the nuts instead! *HIYA!* Learn to play along sometimes! Here, let me fix your tie. So handsome—and yet these brains—"

"Isn't it too warm for that scarf thing?"

"My fashionable pashmina? You never know the AC situation on the train or at the restaurant. I may need to cover up the 'twins'—or the 'gams and hams'—might be a pervert predicament, looking high or low. It will be my 'Modesty Muumuu.' The things us ladies have to go through when we get dolled up! Now you know why I wear my hoodies and camo gear all the time: 'Operation Undercover Hotness.' *Orders from high command: full-frontal assault maneuvers for tonight!*"

* * *

Your favorite part about the subway: when the 7 train takes you above-ground as you careen out of Manhattan and emerge in Queens. Erena leans her head on your shoulder, her arm through the comfy crook of your elbow. The train rocks, sways along the rickety track. You speed by the abandoned warehouses, the graffiti-covered brick apartments, and all the Chinese, Korean, Spanish, and Arabic signs along Queens Boulevard. In every gradient of skin tone and varia-tion of native tongue, the crowds shuffle in and squeeze their tired bodies across the polished benches. *Elmhurst, Junction Boulevard, Co-rona Plaza, Shea Stadium, Main Street. Home.*

* * *

This is the Shanghai Johnny's that you remember: the large tanks full of fresh seafood, the tall stacks of bamboo steamers, the sharp scent of ginger and vinegar, the clatter of spoons against the melamine bowls.

The entire rear section of the restaurant is cordoned off for the affair. The pink, green, gold, and red decor (with phoenix and dragon figures) has a new added feature to complement the existing aesthetic: lining the entranceway are life-size cardboard cutouts of Ma holding up "Shanghai Johnny's Dumpling Dipping Sauce" and "Shanghai Johnny's Garlic Sesame Marinade"—*COMING SOON TO A STORE NEAR YOU!*

The Villanuevas and Choudharys are milling about the tables, centering the placards and distributing postcards to each place setting. Gina hits Paris upside the head with a loud cardboard *THWACK* just as you turn to greet them.

"What did he do this time?" You plant a kiss on Gina's cheek.

"Tweedledee keeps speaking in a fake British accent. He's practicing for his study abroad program in London next year. Sounds like a moron, and not the posh kind either."

"She's just a wee bit jealous, mate. Can't get over the fact 'at she's stuck in ol' Beantown, while I gets away from the Colonies! Whaddaya fink about alla that?" Paris replies in a truly awful rendition of Michael Caine cockney.

"*G'day mate! Crikey!* How's my Aussie? Not sure why that pops up! Sounds kinda wack, huh? You must be Paris! So, we finally meet! I'm Erena. I'll totally give you a nice hug and we can talk about your study abroad plans, but only once you quit that stupid accent. *I stopped, you stop, too.*" Erena says without missing a beat. Gina mouths: *THANK. YOU.*—and gooses Erena in the caboose.

"Dude. *Dude.* Everything you said she would be—and more! *Enchanté, madame,*" Paris says with a flourish, reaching for Erena's hand.

"*Uh-uh.* That goes double for French!" Erena with Gina, both suppressing a laugh.

"Ouch. *Touché!* I mean—sorry! Nice to meet you, Erena. Both these jokers told me a lot about you. Better watch out for this one! I think she has a hard-core crush on you."

"He's not wrong! You ever break up with babyboy here, you give me a call, hot stuff. Let me look at you—*twirl, twirl.*"

Erena complies, but makes Gina do the same: "I cannot pull off that bright yellow. I am full of confidence, but simply do not have the booty to command a dress like that. Lovely work here— compliments to the chef!"

You watch these two women chat and catch up like sisters. Genuine and without envy—you feel their love for you is different in tone, but the same in overwhelming quantity. You are relieved and happy. You pause. You love this.

Mei runs over, adorable in her red-and-gold *qipao*. Ma, an absolute vision in hers, follows behind and greets you.

"*Guai.* You are a little late, but not bad. Help Bah with his professor and EPA friends. Erena, you look very beautiful in your *qipao.* Thank you for coming and attending our special event. Mei is very excited to see you—right, *mei mei?* You stay with *jie jie* while Ma gets ready for the show?"

Mei climbs onto a chair to get closer to eye level to Erena, hugging her: "*Jie jie.* You are the *most* beautiful. Third place is Gina. Second place is Mommy. *You win.*"

Erena looks at you and Ma sheepishly. She kisses Mei, scoops her up by the armpits, and brings her over to the "kids' table," where you'll be sitting with Paris and Gina.

"*Ta zhen de shi hen piao liang*—extremely pretty," Ma whispers to you, squeezing your shoulder. "I had no idea when we saw her before in baggy clothes, sweatshirt, sneakers. *Qipao* fits her well— looks much better than any kimono."

"And she's going to have close to a 4.0 GPA this year. She aced all her papers and exams," you say defiantly, proudly.

"Pretty and smart! Very good for her! *Ni ne?* What about you? Good? Happy?"

"Much better grades than last year. And I'm very happy. Just tired."

"Good. Now go have some *cha* with Tang Bo Bo. Make sure he doesn't get drunk and embarrass us. And say hello to all the other *ai yi* and *su su* that arrive. It's going to be a busy night."

* * *

The order of festivities:

1st: Bah and Ma greet all the attendees from the raised platform—formally, and in both English and Chinese. You feel that this is overly ostentatious, but it's tradition to honor the sponsors, presenters, and guests: by group, by table, by name, by title. It takes nearly thirty minutes. Pastor Chen yawns.

2nd: Your parents are overly patriotic. Everyone stands as a recording of "God Bless America" plays (*if the Mets do it, I want to do it, too!*). The repeat visitors miss Su Su's annual rendition, his dramatic warble and the dewy look in his eyes.

3rd: The booze is poured, and cold appetizers are served—seasoned tofu and mushrooms, chili beef, pickled cucumbers, pickled carrots and radishes, peanuts—followed by the soup of the day (hot and sour). Paris and Gina sip their red wine out in the open. They are sophisticated proto-adults now. You try to get Mei to eat. She only follows suit when Erena samples everything and even picks at your plate.

4th: Presentations—in English and Chinese. Bah's botanist, ecologist, and scientist friends click through their slideshows and present some dire findings about Flushing Bay. Given the ever-present murky, sludgy green hue, you're not surprised at the levels of pollution. You think maybe only half the room understands, or even pays attention—most are here for the dumplings and sideshow.

5th: The talent show, while the main dishes are served. Food:

pork and crab meat and regular pork *xiao long bao*, Shanghai stir-fried rice cakes, bean curd sheets with minced greens, pea shoots and garlic, whole steamed sea bass, braised pork shoulder. (Erena elbows you: *Everything here is scrumptious. We have to come back when I'm not strapped into a fucking girdle torture device. I feel like an over-stuffed Chinese sausage in here! But give me more of those crab meat ones, please. The best! The best!*)

Entertainment: song, dance, and "other." Auntie Tse and Shirley Tse doing their best Linda Ronstadt "When Will I Be Loved" karaoke (Paris isn't a fan: *I miss your uncle—no one is ever going to top his "How Deep Is Your Love" supreme Bee Gees falsetto! What a pimp.*); followed by the Taiwan Tiger House Dancers jamming along to some Cantonese techno (Gina: *Not bad for fifth graders, but it could have been tighter. The one on the right with the ponytail's got real poten-tial!*); and the Shum twins breaking some boards (in karate *gi*, not in kung fu *tangzhuang*). Erena points out the uniforms and makes an *eh-eh?-what's-up-with-this* gesture, palms up, hand sweeping. You shake your head in agreement.

6th: Ma's moment to shine. The waiters set up a large TV on the stage, and her commercial spot rolls: Ma is in a kitchen (*not yours*), water boiling and steam rising from the stovetop behind her. She serves dinner to the camera's point of view: a large plate of plump dumplings, piled high and glistening. She pours Shanghai Johnny's dipping sauce into a red bowl and sets it beside the platter of *jiaozi*: "*Dumplings are delicious—with a dip in Shanghai Johnny's special sauces! Look for the bottle at your favorite supermarket!*"

Much like the restaurant, the elusive "Johnny" does not make an appearance, nor is he further referenced. Ma is the star: the patron saint of this hearty home's hearth, demure goddess of this dumpling domicile. Your beautiful mother could sell the sauce all by herself.

The room erupts into applause, and champagne glasses are raised. Paris puts fingers in his mouth, whistles loudly. Bah surprisingly joins in, even louder. Ma blushes and smiles, waves everyone down so she can explain that there will be gift bags supplied by

Shanghai Johnny's, filled with sauce bottles and other goodies (the ubiquitous Ferrero Rocher and Almond Roca). *Don't leave without your present! There are coupons inside, too! Share with your friends! A portion of the proceeds will help our "Fresh Flushing Bay Fund"!*

7th: Closing time and farewells. Once the dessert arrives— orange slices and sweet mango taro tapioca soup—it doesn't take long for the gathering to disperse. The handshakes and pats on the back, the garbled *Chinglish* congratulations ("*Fei chang hao de* fundraiser this year!"), the rumple of departing gift bags—thus is marked the close of the successful evening.

The restaurant is still serving other patrons. It's only 9:45. But everyone is exhausted, and you are anxious to shuttle Erena safely back to Manhattan, since you'll need to remain in Queens for the cleanup.

"Young, babe—I'm overfull and hot." Erena unbuttons at the neck and fans with an old menu. "I'm letting the beastly paunch out. I'll hang here with Mei. Sorry if I'm lame and can't help you with postparty packing. I wouldn't be much help if I bent over, split my dress, and exposed my ass to everyone." Mei sidles over to the seat beside her and snuggles in, eyelids drooping, head nodding.

Ma and Bah continue to chat with their friends, prolonging the parting in the most Chinese way: reviewing the splendor of the night and discussing immediate plans to eat again. Paris and Gina help you pack up the leftover centerpieces for the community hall that weren't snatched up by the crowd. Uncle Tang shares a pot of lukewarm tea with Auntie Corrina. The Villanuevas and Choudharys kick off their shoes and finish the last drizzles of wine. Erena strokes Mei's hair and sings along with her as she starts to drift off to sleep, her little hand reaching for a squishy earlobe. You love this.

* * *

What happens next happens fast and slow. Time is suspended from here on. You'll replay this in your head again later. And again. And again.

* * *

"*Jie jie*, can your cat necklace come out to play with my kitty cat?" Mei reaches for Erena's necklace, now exposed on her throat. A gentle tug—and disaster.

* * *

You hear the silent inhale, a breath. It takes seconds for it to happen. The sounds are deafening, the impact is atomic: the chain breaking; the cat pendant plinking and spinning on linoleum; the ring bouncing and rolling across an oily rug, then stopping as it hits the side of a size 6 red shoe.

* * *

Ma picks up the ring. She holds it up in the unforgiving fluorescent light, a wave of puzzlement across her face—brows furrowed, trying to seize a shifting memory. Then the sudden recollection of where she has seen this thing before: those two red gems unmistakable and undeniable, the mocking eyes of imperfection past, marring this pristine night. The ghost of her still-living *wangbadan* scoundrel of a brother, making a surprise appearance. On her big night—abandoning and yet still haunting her, after all.

Ma looks at your ashen face and then over at Mei. Her baby girl is beginning to cry now. Erena holds tight to your sister, dabbing her tears with a clean napkin, telling her, *Everything is OK, the necklace can be fixed, it's not a big deal*, which makes Mei cry even more.

The stragglers *are* making a big deal, trying to comfort Mei (Lin Ai Yi and Cheung Su Su—*especially those two*). The talking down to her in elementary Mandarin and the unwanted cooing and shushing drive Mei into Erena's arms even more. She's hugging tightly, sobbing profusely.

Ma stomps over to you with that singular squint in her eye, the clenched jaw, her thin nostrils contracting. You see the words formulate and ready to steam forth from the furnace of her mouth.

* * *

And then it happens. Time has no meaning from here on. You'll replay this in your head again later. And again. And again.

* * *

Erena breaks away from Mei and lunges at a large empty soup bowl (hot and sour). She ousts the contents of the night's feast. She spews forth and shudders—something you have seen many times before (*all that hair-holding, sweat-wiping expression of your love*)—but never like this.

The disconnect remains: her in that graceful silk dress, then her echoing bellows into the porcelain tureen. Mei crying uncontrollably and still trying to rub and comfort Erena. The full weight of Ma's small frame in each of her pounding, approaching footsteps.

You step into the center, trying to diffuse, trying to deflect.

"*Ta huai yun le ma?* Your *ri ben gu niang* is pregnant? How could you? *How could you?*"

You hold both palms up, trying to process it all. (*Triple 8, get it straight, 888 and 888. Bangbangbang.*)

"What are you talking about, Ma? Are you crazy?"

"*Ta tu le!* She's vomiting! And she has your uncle's ring! You gave it to her? She's embarrassed herself, embarrassed you! *Embarrassed everyone!* You think your ma doesn't know what is going on? Our fault, we were so busy—didn't think you and your *ri ben gu niang* would do this! Be so careless!"

"You don't understand, Ma! That's not it at all! And her name is ERENA—pronounced '*ERRRR-UH-NUUH*.' Can't you even say her name right? '*Ri ben gu niang, ri ben gu niang*'! ARE YOU RACIST? *WHAT THE FUCK?*"

* * *

You hear the slap before you feel it. Fast as lightning, loud as thunder.

* * *

Your face stinging and warm, damp with sweat and the vestiges of mutinous tears. You've never said anything like this—at least not out loud—to anyone in your family. Especially not your mother.

Bah peels Ma off you. The flurry of her ongoing slaps, like a bird fighting against the thin bars of its cage. He helps her to quiet down, pulls her away from the third-rail shock. He looks over at you and mouths: *IT'S OK, IT'S OK.* You want to believe him.

The remaining guests have mostly fled into the night, taking their conspiratorial whispers with them. Uncle Tang is long gone, not waiting to be fingered as an accomplice. Pastor Chen will have to hear about this fiasco on Sunday. Mrs. Villanueva and Mrs. Choudhary sit your mom down and have her gulp some cool chrysanthemum tea. They blame the excitement, the heat, the champagne—*chuckle and fan, chuckle and fan.* She thanks them politely, but her eyes are still locked on you, burning a hole through your forehead.

Erena is crying—tears and snot and quivering lips. You've never seen her like this. That beautiful face, crimson in pain and embarrassment, silently looking at you from across the room—the true distance, unreachable. You feel powerless in this chaos (pronounced: *KAY-oss*). *You hate this.*

Gina nudges Paris to lead Erena away to the bathroom beyond the partition, and Gina takes Mei into her lap. Lets the tiny tears turn the shoulder of her dress a deep shade of mustard.

Bah calmly pulls you aside and asks you to explain. You tell him about Su Su and Tang Bo Bo, the box, your drawer, the quirks of Erena's distinct human machinery, entrusting her with your heart—and the ring—for safekeeping.

He laughs and hugs you close, a sharp pat on the square of your back. He will talk it through with Ma, will take care of everything. He places the ring and the remnants of Erena's necklace in your hand and urges you to look after your love.

You check on Mei. She's already passed out in Gina's arms and splayed out on a bench of chairs. Gina mouths: *GO.* You dash out into the hall.

You spy Paris just past the double doors outside on the sidewalk, staring down the street.

"Paris, Paris! Where is she?"

"I'm so sorry, dude. She made me flag down a cab for her. She's heading back into the city alone. Check your voice messages. She paged you. She just needs some time." Paris hands you a couple of quarters.

You race to the end of the street, trying to catch a glimpse of the yellow taxi. You circle the block and have no luck finding the cab. The only consolation—an empty phone booth. You slip a quarter through the slot and punch in all the digits, making sure not to make any mistakes. Erena's recorded voice on the other end:

"I'm sorry, Young. I'm all right. I'm a little embarrassed and my throat is sore—but OK. Dress is unscathed—surprisingly. I'm serious though. Do NOT come out to the city tonight. You need to talk to your mother and set things right. I've never heard you like that. It was scary. I don't think I've even heard you say FUCK. And I promise I'm not pregnant! We were super careful—and I started my period yesterday. I just need a little space. Please, don't be a dick and race out here. Seriously, I won't let you upstairs. I need some quiet to think. It's been a lot lately. OK? Voice mail is running out of time. I'm out of time. I lo—"

You plunk in your remaining coin. You decide against leaving a voice message. Your throat is parched and dry, words unstrung and dying in a miasma of meaninglessness. You key this instead:

911*888*143*911*888*143

* * *

Mr. Choudhary comes out to gather you and Paris: "Come, Young. Everyone has left. We'll give you a ride back home, son."

You thank the Choudharys for everything. Paris gives you a gentle knock on the shoulder: "Everything OK, bro? Talk to your mom. You got this. I'll swing by in the morning with Gina, and we can hit Starshine."

* * *

The house is dark except for the porch light. You creep upstairs to check on Mei first. She's sweetly snoring, slobber covering her tiny forearm. You want to clean up, swallow your pride, prepare to talk to your mother. You take off your jacket and untuck your shirt. You flip on the switch and see a note on the mirror. One word: ROOF.

The narrow staircase to the attic is through a door in your parents' bedroom. You ascend and reach the brittle glass door that leads outside. Weight limit still untested (*though it was enough for Su Su, Auntie Yi Shen, a boom box, and a cooler full of icy Tsingtaos*), the "roof" can only allow for a few of Bah's potted plants, a small side table, a couple of chairs. You love to come up here and hang over the side rail, Queens in her full glory below.

An encouraging sign: you hear Bah and Ma laughing. The smell of smoke surprises you. Your heart jumps, thinking there might be an unattended flame downstairs, but the skunky smell is undeniable—the pure essence of Washington Square Park on a Saturday afternoon.

"Ma, Bah—what are you doing?"

"*Ah, guai. Ni hui lai le. Lai, lai.* Come here."

"Bah—are you *smoking weed*? Is that marijuana?"

"A little *da ma*. One of my friends from the Botanical Garden brought it tonight. It's been a long time! Your Ma and I and Su Su used to have some when we were younger."

"*Even Ma?* Ma, are you smoking, too?"

"No, no! Bah has 'special chocolate' for me. I can't *xi yan*, like you stinky men. I know you smoke, too! You think your Ma can't smell the cigarettes on your clothes! *Muo ming qi miao!* You three boys! Bad influence!"

"OK, OK! *Guai*, come sit and spend some time with Ma. I explained, but she wants to hear it from you. Bah going to shower and sleep." Bah kisses you on the forehead, ducks in, and heads down.

Ma hands you a Styrofoam cup, fills it with hot tea from the metal thermos. You sit next to her, blowing over the steaming beverage as she shivers, the only sounds either of you make.

Ma breaks the tension by putting her hand on your leg, stopping your huffing and puffing: *"Mai le me tang.* It's not that hot."

You take a big gulp, and your mother starts to speak:

"Guai, ni da le. You're getting older now. There are things that you can start to understand, start to change. Almost an adult, but still a child in many things. I want you to experience so much, but I also want to protect you.

"My only son, my *da xin gan bao.* You and baby mean everything to me. I only want what is best for you, but you are also *hen te bie*—do you understand? You are *very special.* Ma wants to let you be yourself, do things your own way, grow up and be strong and smart. But I worry that you make decisions for the wrong reasons. You get lost in your numbers, your signs. *Where is your faith? Your belief?* You need to use your head: *nao jin,* and your heart: *xin*—yes? Make the right choices, for the right reasons."

You dip your head, your lip quivering at the gentle timbre of your mother's voice—something that pulls at your earliest memories and impulses. You hear her words and feel the frustration and anger, fighting against the logic and love.

"I love Erena, and I want to be with her. She's not the perfect Chinese Christian girl that you wanted for me. You know who I mean—but I never told you how she really was—"

"Aiya—why do you think I don't talk with Xia Ai Yi much anymore? That *chou xiao hai* Wendy. I could always see through her acting. Your ma is a better actress than she ever will be! *Fake, not*

real—and not for you. Let her do her own thing! And pray for your poor *ai yi* that she doesn't have a heart attack worrying. Spoiled, but so smart and pretty. She could do great things, but doesn't have the maturity yet. Neither do you. Neither does your Erena.

"What I was so worried about—so shocked by—was seeing her with the ring your *xiao jiu jiu* bought. I remember how things did not work out for him. His young love—not ready. Both of them not in the same place. (They say 'same page' in English?) Back then, he was older than you are now, had a good job, head full of ideas and dreams—and all that failed. Seeing that ring reminded me of everything my *di di*—my *hun dan* little brother—went through. You heard him drunk and crying at night. Your strong, tough Su Su was heartbroken for so long. I didn't want him—don't want you—to make the same mistakes."

"But we are different. You and Bah met in college and had me in your mid-twenties—and then—"

"*Let me finish.* Ma and Bah are from a different time and place— not like modern-day, New York City times. You are still so young, so unsettled. *What do you want to do with your life?* How can you make commitments to someone else, when you aren't even sure about yourself, your own path?"

"I'm doing well in school. I'm doing much better now—"

"*Let your Ma talk!* I'm not done! I am glad she is not pregnant. *Very glad!* When she vomited, and with the ring—that was my first thought. *Xia shi wo le*—scared me to death! And your reaction, what you said to me. What was I to think?"

"*I'm sorry, I'm sorry.* I didn't mean to. I overreacted. And you know I don't say things like that."

"Yes, yes. I know, I know. The f-word—that's not what I meant. *Aiya!* Your Ma says worse things in Chinese to your poor Bah all the time! But you used this word: 'racist.' Your Ma is many things, but she is not 'racist.' We have lived in the US all your life—more than your life! Twenty-two years and more. We have friends in all shapes, sizes, colors—gay, not-gay. There are some things in *dong fang xiang fa*—Eastern, Asian way of thinking—that are not meant to be anything 'racist,' but we can't express correctly in English to you ABC kids, kids who grew up here. Sometimes we can't say the correct thing, or you make assumption (this is the right word?) and you connect things in English that we don't mean in Chinese. You understand? Our head thinks one thing, but can't quite express through our words? *Frutation?* No, not that. *Frustration*—this is the word."

"When you keep calling Erena '*ri ben gu niang*'—"

"Is she not '*a Japanese young lady*'? Is that not correct?"

"Yes, sort of. But the way you say it. It's like—"

"*OK, maybe a little. I make fun a little.* But you ask any Chinese or Korean or Filipino—or even Jewish—there will always be something against Japanese. I didn't mean that about her tonight, but I did make fun—*a little.* Your Ma apologizes to you and your *nu peng you,* OK? I'll call her Erena. *ERRRR-UH-NUUH,* OK? It's not just her—any *nu peng you,* your ma would think is not good enough, not the right fit for you. You understand? My number one, Young Man! My good boy, my *nen gan de bao bei, xin gan bao.*"

"*Fine. OK.*"

Ma holds you close and kisses you like a newborn—gently, tenderly, love and mirth in her eyes. You admit it. You love this.

"Ma is sorry. Ma is sorry she hit you—*didn't hurt anyway, but sorry.* Everyone enjoyed our event! More excitement at the end! We can laugh at the extra bonus show to close the night! I know you have a lot of pressure at school now and figuring out what you want to do for the future. We always thought you loved reading, watching film, TV—*maybe you wanted to be a doctor or lawyer?* You loved to learn, good with words! *Or maybe a writer?* You love music! *Maybe something there?* But not an accountant—the numbers would drive you crazy. Hurt your brain too much. I know you like to worry, like things to be in order, just like your Ma. I sometimes wish you were more relaxed like Bah, even act wild like your *hun dan* Su Su. *(But sometimes, only sometimes.)* We just want you to find your own way. *Ni da le,* you are growing up. We came to the US to let our children do anything.

To let you make that choice for yourself. You have so much to do, *guai*—so much in front of you. If it feels like too much, you can talk to me and Bah. We are always here for you."

She holds you close, kisses you again. You love this. You love her.

"And one day, you can talk to your Su Su in person again. He makes big plans, but he always misses me too much—misses you and Mei more. *Ai!* He called us before from LA, I gave him your pager number. Go look on the kitchen table."

* * *

On the breakfast table, an opened cardboard box: a puffy stuffed brown otter; a goofy-looking dolphin with giant blue eyes; a baseball cap with a zippy yellow arrow and "IN-N-OUT" in big block letters; two bottles of wine; and finally, a red envelope, a photograph paper-clipped to the back.

Su Su, flashing a bright white smile. Sleeveless, in denim from head to toe, his arm slung around the waist of a young, thin, pretty Asian woman. She's wearing a simple white tank top and jeans. Both of them with jet-black shiny hair glistening in the California rays, their arms outstretched and pointing to the iconic HOLLYWOOD sign behind them, as if to say, *See this sign! It's a SIGN!*

On the back of the photo:

My Young One! Check out this cute babe! I was hiking in the hills when I chatted her up. Turns out she's from Jackson Heights, Chinese, and went to Stuyvesant—Class of '86! (Too old for you, but just right for me! Hehheh!) *I told her how you did SING! She did, too, and loved it! She's an actress! She was in 90120 in the Beverly Hills, THE EXES FILES, and Emergency Room. And soon to be in a new movie with Tom Cruise! Look out for Lucy Liu! She's going to be a big star! I'll page you / call you soon! Time to visit Cali! Peace and hair grease! —Su Su*

Other than Tim Robbins (amazing in *Jacob's Ladder*, *The Player*, and your beloved *Shawshank Redemption*) and the Beastie Boys (Ad-Rock famously sporting a Stuy T-shirt in the "Fight for Your Right" video), Lucy Liu was name-dropped most often by Stuy alums. Not only was she building up her résumé in Hollywood, she was the shining example of a smart Asian American kid who was succeeding in *the arts*. The roll call at the Ivy Leagues and Fortune 500 companies was filled with Stuy survivors, but it was magical to see one of your own doing something on-screen. She could *play* a doctor, a lawyer—anything she wanted.

Inside the red envelope, a check made out to you for $2,888. In the memo area: *"For a lucky break! Come out to Cali this summer!"*

* * *

You tuck these items into your jacket pocket and check your pager—nothing from Erena. You pick up the receiver and dial her dorm room number, but hang up. The words you have now aren't going to be the right ones.

You page: 10*4*888, as in *10–4 = OK* or *Are you OK?*

You receive: 3177817.

E-M-A-N? Is Erena making a joke? When you realize it's *EMAIL*, you are already halfway up the stairs, powering on your computer, impatiently waiting for the rattle and whirring to connect you to the World Wide Web and to her.

* * *

SUBJECT: Tonight
DATE: 5/20/96 1:12:55 Eastern Standard Time
FROM: fartprincess1
TO: indepalmamyhands76

Hi babe,

I didn't feel like talking, but wanted to let you know that everything is really OK. *Really.* (I know how your brain works.)

I hope you had a chance to patch things up with your mom. I know she isn't my biggest fan, but she was incredible tonight. Please let her know that I thought she was amazing—and I'm sorry I didn't get a chance to tell her in person.

And I'll make it up to Mei. Make sure she's not too shaken up, OK? She did nothing wrong—and I'm so, so sad I made her cry.

Well, the *cat's* out of the bag. The necklace idea was a good one while it lasted. The ring is back with you. You should find a better place to stash it. Maybe with your *Playboy*s. I know you still have those somewhere.

I want you to have a nice weekend with Paris and Gina in Queens—OK? I'll finish packing up, and you guys can take me to the airport on Monday. You can stay over with me Sunday night?

Page me back so I know you read this and that we are good.

Sleep tight, my sweet boy
My mouth, all rotten fish taste
Kiss me back, fucker

See you soon.

1–4–3—beep-boop.

Peace out,
—E

* * *

Your first instinct is to fire off a well-constructed, heartfelt, triple-proofread response. *You want to let her know how elegant she looked in that dress tonight, how much you love her for trying so hard, how you should just come over tonight and take her in your arms.*

But you power off the computer and free up the phone line. What you feel for her is more than you can say. You decide to leave that burden to the numbers:

You page: 143*888*4*311312—The "4 EVER" in the most Prince-like perfect way.

Her reply: 143*888*170*88124. The "NO BARF" makes you laugh, knowing she must be feeling better.

Once more, you convey your truth: 143*888*143*888*8381174, sending your love to your "BEAUTY."

She leaves you with: 6000*171647*705312 = GOOD NIGHT LOSER

You love this. You love her.

* * *

You dream of three Asian men. In the dream, all three are in dark sunglasses and black turtlenecks. Two have on bright-red silk jackets, the other a white tuxedo. They pull you toward a round table, the lazy Susan spinning slowly, with bamboo steamer baskets stacked up in fragrant towers.

One pulls out a chair; another deftly flips a pair of chopsticks, which land perfectly in your hand; the last pours you a cup of hot jasmine tea. He lays it on the clear plexiglass and spins the platter until it is square in front of you.

Wayne Wang: Oh, ni hao! You've had a rough night and have to wake up early to meet with your friends! Have a few dumplings first. Meet

Ang Lee—The Wedding Banquet, Eat Drink Man Woman, Sense
and Sensibility *(and NYU alum—go Bobcats, or whatever!). John
Woo*—Hard Boiled, The Killer, Hard Target. *And me, I'm Wayne
Wang (No relation? Maybe? Nah!)*—Chan Is Missing, The Joy
Luck Club, Smoke, *and* Blue in the Face.

Ang Lee: *Your dream of dim sum will have to do. No won ton for you
though! Remember backwards it's "not now"! John—can you get your
doves out of here? Someone is bound to think these are meant to get
roasted for the* siu mei / shao la *special.*

John Woo: Ngoh mm jee dao!

WW: *Do I need to translate from Cantonese? Young can barely manage
grade-school Mandarin!*

JW: No, no—*all fine!* Shoo, birds, shoo!

WW: *Nothing like a reminder from some Chinese male role models you can
look up to—ones who are proactive, well-spoken, act with dignity and
decorum—maybe are even erudite (pronounced ERR-yoo-DYTE, not
ERR-yoo-dee-tay).*

AL: *Hey, no need to be so snobby! You've lost your temper in public before!
You've taken an extended road trip with no real itinerary! And I'm
sure you've had your share of* da ma *in San Francisco! How your
family behaves! Not very typical Chinese, but still—*

JW: *LOUD! I like LOUD!*

WW: *I know your ma could never relate to* The Joy Luck Club: muo
ming qi miao, kai wan xiao, gou pi *stuff. You still saw her dab
tears in the theater though, even if the stories were nothing like her
life, your grandmothers' lives—and certainly not like yours. You've
been blessed with a relatively happy existence. In the grand scheme
of things, you've managed to avoid true sadness.* Not your story to
tell—thank God. *But still, it was good to see people who looked like
you up on the Cineplex Odeon screen at the White people American
theater, the "regular theater"—right?*

AL: *Sympathy and empathy. You feel so deeply! A trait that is admirable in
someone so young, Young. Maybe it's all that depressing British music
you listen to?*

JW: *Deng Li Jun—remember her? Go listen to her instead! Sweet and melodious. Maybe avoid the stress and darkness of that noise you love for a little while. SO DARK, MAN.*

WW: *Aiya! Let's get to the point, my friends.*

AL: *China, US, California, New York, Taipei, Hong Kong—even nineteenth-century England—in our movies, we can tell the stories of Chinese people from all over. As real-life Chinese storytellers, behind and beyond the camera, our vocation and personal journeys say as much. As global film directors, we've even been able to portray the narrative of non-Chinese, non-Asian lives—no Zhongguo ren in Jane Austen stories! (Can you imagine Sammo Hung beside Kate Winslet? Brigitte Lin and Hugh Grant?) But in everything we do, we are always representing our Asian culture: our way of thinking, our abilities, and "sensibilities" (sorry, I could not resist).*

By sharing our specific humanity, we speak to the universal and find common ground. "A stoic, enigmatic, repressed outsider with a dry, ironic wit"—am I talking about Elinor Dashwood? Jane Austen? Myself? You? All of us? (You would be correct to say a hundred percent it's Morrissey.)

It's a new world for those who are underrepresented, who still struggle to be heard, who need to be part of the conversation.

JW: 1997—*Hong Kong Handover—hen da de party! (Oh, maybe* shouldn't remind you that she will be there.) *And the state of Taiwan, ROC, and the PRC—aiya! But the year 2000 is approaching! We are entering the unpredictable future. Nothing is—"IMPOSSIBLE"!*

WW: *Yes, John—we know you want to work with Tom Cruise next. Better take it up with De Palma! So, how are you feeling, Young? Are you ready now? On the cusp of all this sea change?*

JW: *Young, are you ready to make a decision? Do you know where you are going?*

AL: *My movie—*The Wedding Banquet—*part of it was filmed close to Main Street, blocks from Shanghai Johnny's! But it only barely resembles your parent's festivities last night, even though there were lots of uncovered truths leading to a disaster at the end! The faces there: a* *rainbow of colors; gay, not-gay; Christian, not-Christian. Your family has such an amazing life, surrounded by amazing people—right here in NYC! You carry these stories with you, in whatever you do. You can show the world that we Chinese—you ABC, we Asian and Asian American people—are so much the same as anyone, and yet so wonderfully different. Aren't you excited for the possibilities?*

JW: *And your uncle! Such a perfect blend of East and West! He could stand in for Chow Yun Fat any time! Kick Van Damme in the* dan-dans! *Maybe shoot at Tom Cruise next—bangbangbang—"goodbye, Agent Tom!"*

WW: *He can fill in for Harvey Keitel any day! He's the exact American analogue for your Su Su: same gruff demeanor, but kind eyes—unpredictable, incalculable, masculine but sensitive. (I bet Tarantino agrees.)*

AL: *All combinations and contradictions—like the sister in* Eat Drink Man Woman. *Just because the horny Christians get married, it doesn't mean that solves their problems! Don't look at them as an example, but maybe in general, from the perspective of what Pastor Chen says, how "your life should be a living testimony."*

JW: *Not only about your faith, but in all that you represent. What makes you "Young Wang": divine, secular—faithful, faithless—shuai guh and shy guy. You are fearfully and wonderfully made. You contain multitudes. (Cue the doves, for dramatic effect. Fly, fly! Fai dee lah!)*

WW: *You march under a banner of these emblems:* of the son, the brother, the friend, the lover. Chinese, American, Asian American, Christian believer, gothmetalgeekpunk—*and so much more. All components that others may or may not see—it's part of your character, and you are still finding your balance.* You just need to decide what you want to tell, and how and when and who to tell it to. *You are your own soldier, own warrior—but which em*peror do you choose to serve?

JW: *Speak up, don't dwell in silence. Embrace all the ambiguity, the not-knowing-for-sure. Thrive in passion and creativity. This is your life* to live—ni de ming. *This is your story to tell.* ACTION. SPEED. ROLLING.

AL: *Truth and beauty.* TRUTH AND BEAUTY. *You've been waiting for signs and wonders and guidance your whole life. Your time is now. What do you want to tell the world?* Gai ni, xiao di.

WW: It's your turn, little brother.

ALL: *TIME TO WAKE UP! JIAYOU!!! RISE AND (STAR)SHINE! GINA AND PARIS ARE WAITING! IT WILL FEEL BETTER WITH SOME HARD-BOILED EGGS IN YOUR BELLY! LUCKY BOY, THINGS WILL ALL MAKE SENSE! YOU'LL HUG AND KISS YOUR "RI BEN GU NIANG" SOON ENOUGH! GANBATTE!!!*

* * *

"Pancakes are mine. Eggs and bacon for '2 Live Crew' over here. Eggs and sausage for 'goth scarecrow' there. Thank you!" Gina, punching down a little over Saturday brunch at the Starshine.

"So, Monday I'll drive in and fetch you two from NYU. Everything else OK, bro? Did you talk to her?"

"We paged, and she sent me an email. She sounded fine. She just needed time to process last night, the year, everything. It's been a lot."

"I'm impressed how well you are taking this. You've matured! Proud of you! Now give me some of your fries and you can have a hotcake." Gina grabs at your plate.

"Or it could be the *secondhand pot smoke*—" You smirk.

"Yo! CONFIRMED? You finally have proof? I knew your dad was getting in on that chronic! Always so mellow and even-keeled! Totally explains it! You should just get a side of bacon and fries next time, G! *Hands off!*"

"Just *A* PIECE, Paris! *Give it!* THANK YOU! What's your plan for California? Have things changed?"

"Same. I'll meet her in a week and a half. Two weeks in Cali together, before she heads out on her girls' trip to Colorado. Then I may not see her again until she's back on campus in August."

"Good! She's monopolized your wingman time! I'm getting you all to myself when you're back! I've got three weeks before London. Got to maximize my NYC swagger, parlay that into undeniable street cred when I hit the UCL campus. Those British birds won't be able to resist! *Born and raised in Queens, the birthplace of hip-hop. Yeah, straight from Hollis. It's where I learned the game, ya know what I'm sayin'?* And then vice versa: when I get back, my British accent will be impeccable! I'll be all suave and posh! Foolproof fucking plan!"

"This again! I swear, if this idiot comes back all *pip-pip-cheerio*—" Gina, stabbing at Paris with her fork.

"I believe '187' is the correct code you are looking for."

"*MURDER!* Absolutely! I will page you to swing by, and we will end his sorry life!" Gina, now threatening with a butter knife.

"What are you bozos going to do without me then?"

"We will survive. Young and I will move into a duplex, raise our respective families side by side. The cautionary tale of 'Uncle Paris the Pathetic Pervert' will scare our children into living a righteous life."

"I think he meant 'What are we going to do for the *rest of the summer*' without him."

"Oh, right. I was imagining a future where I got away with justifiable homicide. We'll take Mei to Playland and hit the beach with our fams. Then Young's coming up to Wellesley to help me move into my new suite. We'll go to Cape Cod with some of my summer session friends. Sound good?"

"10–4, G."

* * *

When you get back on campus, little has changed, but there is a different charge in the air. The streets feel just as congested, the air still smells like trash, smoke, and urine—but it's not the same. *Maybe it's you?*

Erena is standing on the corner of 12th and 6th Avenue. She paged you to meet there for your last NYC sushi dinner of the year together. You feel that unkind stone settle into the center of your body, the weight nestled at the bottom of your throat. You trace the infinite shapes of 8s on your thighs (*get it straight*). You find calm in the repeated symmetry, your sigil of strength and peace.

She spots you coming up to the street from the subway. She takes off running at you full speed. She's yelling something you can't make out, but her joy is apparent. Pedestrians squeeze tight into store entranceways to let her speed by. You hear: "MY DUDE! MY GUY!" repeatedly until she crashes full body-slam into you, her arms wrapped tight around your body, clutching koala firm. You are relieved. You love this. You love her.

"Did they discuss 'codependency' in your classes? I'm not sure what it is, but I may have it. Is this a symptom? When I'm so super stoked to see you and want your clammy, lanky bod all over me? It's been so lame and boring. Everyone's left campus. It's bursar *this*, registrar *that*, 'deposit depression'—is what it is! How are you? Everything OK with Mei and Papa Wang and Mama Model? What did you eat at Starshine without me? Did you declare your major yet? Psych, right? The best thing about being a psychology major is all the 'PSYCH!' jokes! Promise me you signed up for some film classes at least?"

"I missed you, too, Erena."

You explain that things are copacetic with your parents and tell her about Su Su's generous vacation fund.

"Our plan still works then: we'll crash at Min Jee's in Little Tokyo while she's out of town. We'll do the touristy, geeky stuff, meet up with your Su Su whenever he pages you the details. The rest is max time with your girl, before I head off to Denver with Mel and Janey."

"You'll have a car? You'll be able to drive around?"

"*Yes, city mouse.* I will be your chauffeur. Wow! I can't believe that the next time I see you, it will be on my home turf! Your pale visage in the sweet sunshine! Do you even tan? Are you going to get roasted like a tasty lobster?"

"SPF 100. I'll be fine. I'll even wear some colorful outfits."

* * *

You normally don't like to cross through Washington Square Park this late, but the days are stretching longer and the last slivers of sunlight prove too seductive to deny.

You walk under the arch, toward the round fountain feature—the drums and skateboards, the competing boom boxes blaring, the acoustic guitars and earnest vocals—a jumbled remix of this year's summer jam.

You mark the curative balm of time: nearly two years ago you were here, on a night like this. You remember being drunk on cheap booze, the humidity sapping your strength and senses, that first kiss—*on that bench, just over there.* The incandescent excitement of someone holding the frail hopes of your heart, then falling into the excruciating pain of catastrophe. You've let time cover over these scars of memory. Now you're revisiting these haunted locations with someone brave, inexhaustible—someone new. She guides you through these gates of fractured failings. *See? Nothing to be afraid of here—not anymore.*

Erena hops onto the track of concentric circles. Arm outstretched and holding your hand, she spins and dodges around the people sitting along the edge of the water. Giggling and vibrant, lovely in this spreading sunset, from the highest ring of concrete, toward the famed arch, she hoots: "I LOVE YOU NEW YORK! THANKS FOR A GREAT YEAR!" You look up at her. Backlit against the orange and red dusk, this exquisite being reaching down to you—you rise.

Side by side now, an arm around each other's waists, the other hand cupped to your mouths, you yell into the evening sky: *"THANK YOU, NYU! GANBATTE!!! JIAYOU!!!"* (You think John Woo would appreciate this virile scene—but he'd naturally have his fluttering doves instead of dirty New York pigeons scatter overhead from your exuberant, youthful shouts. Maybe have you wear sunglasses at night, pop a toothpick in the side of your mouth. Pan up and then freeze-frame on the—)

A flashlight in your eyes: "If you're done with your show of appreciation—which was very cute—you can come down now. Don't even think about getting into that water. It's full of piss and who knows what else." The campus security woman helps you both down. The radiating embarrassment on your faces, mingled with the superficial triumph of your wholesome act of rebellion, allows you two renegades to escape into the night, scot-free.

* * *

Erena's room is empty now except for her pillows, sheets, two suit-cases, and a backpack. The mattress, desk, bed frame, and phone are university rentals, to be returned and / or inspected for cleaning tomorrow—or they may linger in the vacant room, waiting for some other NYU Bobcat's use next year.

You've barely kicked off your shoes before Erena's mouth is on yours. She strips your clothes off, leads you to her bed. You make love again—and once more, for the last time in this room.

You stare up at the now-familiar ceiling, the weather-worn projection screen for all your hopes and dreams. You find the water stain pattern in the shape of a winking corgi. The other one, an old woman with a bouquet of flowers. *Farewell, pareidolia. Goodbye, leaky ceiling that witnessed our carnal fumblings. Rot and rust, love and lust.*

You look over at Erena: "Are you crying?"

"*Fuck you, I'm not crying!* Don't flatter yourself! The room is dusty from all the packing and shit. By the way, you can have the pleasure of tossing the bedding or taking it home and explaining the stains to your mom when she does the laundry."

"No more jokes. You can talk to me. I'm—I'm really happy. And I love being with you. *Tonight, every night.* Another great memory."

"Let's just hold hands and I can 'koala' you a bit, OK? Quiet reflection time? Think about all we've seen and done. Everything since I walked into the Undertow and graced you with my presence. *Shhh*—Young. Just—*quiet*."

"OK. I can do that."

"Thank you. Nice and chill. Our last night here together."

"I love you, Erena."

"I know. I know, princess. I love you, too."

CHAPTER EIGHT

"Forever Now"

MAY–JUNE 1996

Soundtrack highlights:
- "Please, Please, Please, Let Me Get What I Want" —
  The Smiths
- "Spiralling" — Erasure
- "Here's Where the Story Ends" — The Sundays
- (BONUS TRACK: "Down" — 311)

You pack light for your trip to California, saving room in your luggage for the souvenirs and collectibles you are sure to gather along the way. All you need: a few changes of clothing, your camera, a Walkman, a journal, a backpack. Erena's lucky cat—and the ring—on a chain around your neck for safekeeping.

The time spent in the land of glitz and glamour is memorialized in the things you carry, eat, and remember:

1. A *masu* cup. A small wooden box that once held some secret sake you drank from the *izakaya* around the corner from Min Jee's apartment.
2. Classic Mickey ears and a Space Mountain T-shirt that Erena insisted on buying for you

3. Classic Minnie ears and a Belle dress that Erena insisted on buying for Mei

4. Classic Minnie ears and a turkey leg (and a churro) that you insisted on buying for Erena

5. La Brea Tar Pits: A plastic woolly mammoth and saber-tooth tiger

6. Getty Museum: Postcards (Matisse, Van Gogh)

7. LACMA: More postcards (Picasso, Lichtenstein) and a Hokusai T-shirt of *The Great Wave off Kanagawa*

8. Pink's: Bacon chili cheese dogs (*and indigestion*)

9. Golden Apple Comics: A signed *X-Men* #1 (1991) by Jim Lee

10. Grauman's Chinese Theatre: Pictures with the foot- and handprints of George Lucas, Steven Spielberg, C-3PO, and R2-D2

11. Walk of Fame: Some snaps along Hollywood Boulevard. The clearest ones are of Sharon Stone's new star (*Erena throwing up peace signs. Then a V for Victory—with her tongue poking through her fingers*).

12. Griffith Observatory: Several attempts to get a good photo of the two of you with the Hollywood sign visible in the background—and a snow globe. And also—Erena being super suspicious, shooing you outside while she buys something.

* * *

"Babe, you seriously want Carl's Jr. over In-N-Out? You are aware that people travel to my fine state just to enjoy the 'Double Double' or 'Animal Style'? Are you embarrassed because the secret menu—and everything else, really—sounds pervy? I assure you, there is no such thing as 'Doggy Style'—no matter what Paris told you. I'm not going to be panting and moaning at the drive-through or anything! So, you *really* want Carl's instead? It's just Hardee's in surfer shorts."

You receive two pages as Erena pulls into the parking lot with your burgers. The first reads 43770*511511; the second one indicates you have voice mail.

You grab a fistful of quarters from the unused ashtray in the car and find the nearest pay phone to check your voice message:

"Young One! Your folks said you'd still be in the LA area when I'd be motoring by! I'm visiting friends in Ontario (Cali not Canada, duh!) to check out a piece of farmland that we might invest in! I'll be there at noon this Saturday. It's called the LA PAZ FARMS. LA PAZ FARMS, in Ontario! Saturday afternoon! Come find me! Love you!"

You can't stop beaming. It's the "love you" at the close that really did it. You run back to the car and start fisting fries into your gullet until your mouth is parched and you are forced to chug your 7UP. In between mouthfuls of bacon cheeseburger, Erena starts hooting and hollering. She cranks up the Guns N' Roses, happy that you are happy.

There was always a slim chance that you'd get to see your uncle here, in the land of perpetual sunlight. You are thrilled that Erena will get to witness the man, the myth, the legend—your beloved "Bastard of the High Roads," your *wang ba dan* of an uncle, your one and only Su Su—in the flesh.

"Ontario is about an hour from home. We can swing by, see your Su Su first, then dinner with my parents. You'll meet the 'mutants that birthed this miracle.' They say you are either a *reflection of* or a *reaction to* your parents—I'm firmly in between. You'll spend some time with good ol' Paul and Ji-Yeon, and you'll see—*you'll see.*"

* * *

It's just after 1:00 p.m. on Saturday. Erena pulls through the gates and onto the dusty path leading to the farm. Parked on the side of the road is a shiny new Harley-Davidson with monkey bar handles—exactly the kind Su Su always wanted. A man in a large straw hat tells Erena to ease in to the right: "Are you Young and his girl? Your uncle is over by the pond, waiting on his friends. They're running late. You can park here and head over."

Erena barely turns the ignition off, and you are already out the door. She fumbles with her sunglasses, purse, bottles of water. She waves you off—*go, go first.*

You want to barrel forward in a full-on sprint, but settle into a relaxed trot. Su Su has no such restraint. He bolts over and picks you up like you are a five-year-old.

"*Ni pang le!* You got some meat on your bones again! Healthy, taller, broader—a bit of a tan from being in Cali? *Wow. Wow.*" Su Su hugs you, kisses you, makes you spin around.

"You look great, too!" you say. "Your hair is *so long*! I can't believe you can braid it now! *So tan.* You look tough with the leather vest and the new bike! Without that same goofy grin, I'd be terrified and have to cross the street!"

"Have to channel my inner tiger while I'm traveling! You never know what kind of people you will run into. Beer is the great equalizer. You buy someone a tall glass, and that total asshole becomes your new best pal! (*Like Tang Bo Bo! Hehheh!*) Speaking of friends— your *nu peng you* over there, yeah? Looks like she ran into my friends and they're walking over together. *Yo, Paul! Jeannie!*"

* * *

It takes you a moment to register what is happening. The haze of the sun is making everything shimmer and ripple in your field of vision. Erena comes into focus first, walking toward you with a couple beside her. In the man, you see the duplicated outline of sharp Tinker Bell nose, the same light-brown hair, now walking closer in parallel, mirroring Erena's easy gait. In the woman, the matching figure, hiding the curves under an oversize sweater; identical poise, shoulders rolling in that particular easy way—and now, close enough to see—copies of those sparkling hazel eyes.

"Holy shit! *Uncle Andy?* That you? I haven't seen you since I was like 7 or 8!" Erena inexplicably hollers at Su Su.

"*Peace girl? What the heck?*" Su Su is guffawing, taking Erena's face in his big strong hands. He's bear-hugging her, then the couple, kissing them all in a joyous circle of reunion.

You stand, on the outskirts of this exceptional dream, waiting for someone to show you your mark: *stand here, check the slate, and ACTION.* Expecting Martin Scorsese to explain why your neurons are firing like this (*must have been the calamari from last night*). Anticipating the manifestation of John Carpenter (*and James Cameron—the expert on timeline anomalies*) to review this strange part of the screenplay being played out before you (*you are not buying these special effects, this stunt casting*).

"What's going on? Erena? *What's happening?*" You can barely eke out a winded whisper.

"This must be Young. I'm Ji-Yeon, and this is Paul. We are Peace's parents. This explains why Peace said she was coming out to Ontario! I didn't expect us all to be at the farm, though! Andy—your uncle—happens to be an old friend of ours. We've known him for decades! What a remarkable coincidence!"

"You're leaving out the best part, Jeannie! We used to *date!*" Su Su, with a shit-eating grin, resting his chin on her shoulder.

"Oh, *please.* We went out *ONCE*, and I couldn't handle your overwhelming BS—even though you were very handsome and extremely charming. And I wouldn't have met Paul if you hadn't introduced me. You did ask for my old roommate's number at the same time."

"*Ho, ho!* Yes, I remember Delia! We had great fun back then!"

"It was 'Dahlia,' and she's single," Paul interjects and pulls Su Su away, patting him on his firm behind. "She doesn't live that far from here."

"*Wait—WAIT—WAIT! Someone explain! Erena?*" You try your best to get someone to pay attention—*anyone.* Hands to the side of your head, the temples throbbing fast and loud, like brass gongs.

"Oh, '*Erena.*' Erena, our baby girl. Peace wanted to start going by her legal name when she went to college! It's beautiful and sophisticated, but everyone back home calls her 'Peace.' *Our Peace wanted a change of pace!* Wanted to do the whole 'finding herself at college' thing. We are so proud of our brilliant beauty, whatever name she goes by!" Paul, taking Erena by the hand. Erena whining "*Daaaad*," paired with a shy shoulder shrug.

"Your uncle Andy actually helped us name her. 'Erena' meaning 'peace' in Greek. He's always had a thing for the Mediterranean. Paul and I spent our honeymoon in Mykonos, where Erena was 'made.' So, a perfect name. We're glad she's finally come around to it. *Yeobo*, have we embarrassed her enough?" Ji-Yeon, taking Erena around the neck for a nuzzle, Erena whining "*Ummaaaaa*," paired with an exasperated stretch and huff.

"The genesis of 'peace and grease,' Su Su—your signature saying, your motto—it's—"

"Oh, I can see how you would think that! 'Peace,' 'grease'—it's been so long, meant so many good things to me. *Yeah, sure, why not!* The universe stitching things together!"

"Names have power and carry divine and eternal significance. '*Erena Ji-Yoon Renee Valentina Yasuda*'—a name that reflects our complex heritage and shared ideals. 'Yasuda' means something like 'peaceful field' in Japanese. So she's our 'double peace' daughter." Paul, now flashing two Vs for Victory, the obvious double peace signs.

"Dad—*ugh*! So, so stereotypically Japanese! Put your hands down! Young, remember what I said: 'reflection and reaction'—*down the middle, down the middle.*" Erena snickers as she eases over to calm you with her touch.

"Mr. and Mrs. Yasuda, Su Su—can you excuse us? I'm just—my head is spinning. I need some water and shade—and some time to talk to Erena."

"Please, Young. It's 'Paul' and 'Ji-Yeon,' or just 'Jeannie'—we're literally a bunch of old hippies! The 'Mr. and Mrs.' thing—*SO SQUARE, MAN*! Go chat, kids! What an auspicious introduction to La Paz

Farms! We knew it was a sign when we heard it—named after the capital of Bolivia, but it also translates to 'Peace Farms' in *español*! God is smiling down, blessing us with His knowing, cheeky wink! I've been telling you, all wonderful things! Andy, let's go for a loop around the property—show you where we are thinking of setting up the church."

"*Church?*"

"Come over here, my sweet boyfriend. I think you need a reset. I'll explain before you blow a gasket."

* * *

"Before you start spooging all over yourself, it's not that hard to connect the dots, OK? Let's look at the evidence calmly. I chose to go to NYU because my cousin Min Jee—who you unfortunately won't meet—loved her time in NYC. She's the analogue in my life, as Su Su is to yours: a full passport, same kinds of tall tales in the ledger. (*Goodness, gracious—we need to keep the two of them apart! The universe might implode if they ever got together.*) And I was a baby the last time I saw your uncle—'Uncle Andy' to me. Didn't even register that he spent so much time in NYC! He's always just been my parents' college friend who popped in every so often! And, c'mon—he looks totally different all the time! Always experimenting with his hair-style, facial hair, the way he dresses—doesn't look anything like his pictures at your place! He's unrecognizable with this new 'Warlord Biker' look!"

"Fine, fine—what about your parents?"

"You mean *Pastor* Paul and *Elder* Ji-Yeon? Like they said—*literal hippies* back in the day. They were all up in organic food and healthy consumable products and made their living that way. (Have you had kombucha yet?) And on a whim, they invested early on in Apple (computers), because 'Apple'—same name as the Beatles record la-bel. So there, you have that. They got hard-core into Christianity when I was a baby. All those flower-child ideals of 'becoming one with the cosmos' or 'being a drop of water returning to the ocean' were antithetical to their core beliefs of 'being precious individuals with unique souls' and 'you matter, you aren't just matter.' Dad enrolled in seminary and got ordained. *Umma* got back in touch with her Korean congregation roots and her pre–Age of Aquarius self. Now they would love to retire early, devote their lives to social justice and churchy stuff."

"Wow—*reflection/reaction.*"

"Why do you think I eat the way I do? Missed out on so much yummy junk when I was growing up! And how I know about the Bible and was asking about that confusing Christian metal crap? I've had my share of Sunday school."

"You told me your parents were in the 'importing/exporting business,' and that they had a 'heart for charity work.'"

"Yeah, so? *Not wrong.* They import and export food-related stuff. They run a faith-based nonprofit. You never pushed for exact details. What's the diff?"

"I'm just stunned. There's so much I didn't know."

"*Assumed.* 'ASS-U-ME'—like a third grader. 'Ask me no questions and I'll tell you no lies.' You prioritized the '*woo-ing,*' and maybe the '*woo-ee*'s' backstory wasn't so important once you got access to the goody bits. *I feel cheap.*"

"Erena—stop. I never meant—"

"Come on! Do you not know a funny when you hear one? *I do humor. Gah*—loosen up, already! You need to be more like your dad—like *my* dad!"

"Wow—my parents. *Your* parents—"

"What can I say? They are well-off, super socially liberal, and born-again Presbyterians."

"OH! *Presbyterians!* Incredible! My mom—oh, my mom—"

"*Hey, hey—totally legit!* What is it now?"

"Just—just humor me, OK? Thinking out loud here. Play along? Circles or squares?"

"Circles—*duh.* Who likes fucking squares, man?"

"What's your favorite integer? And why?"

"It's 8—because it's a cute fat guy. If he lies down, he transforms into infinity. And, *duh,* made of circles! And ever since you, 8 has taken on a new sheen. We've talked about all of this before. Are we playing killing-time games until my folks and your uncle are back?"

"And your birthday?"

"July 28th, 1977. You know, 7–28–77—not news. I gave you a list of potential gifts I'd like already—"

"Ice cream shop at the end of the world with limitless flavor combinations—what do you order?"

"Mocha almond fudge with Oreos, cookie dough, and chocolate sprinkles, peanut butter sauce on top, whipped cream. Gimme all the variations and options! (Anything but rum raisin or bubble gum.) My answer has not changed since our first date. If I recall correctly, we started making out right after we discussed desserts. Sundaes always make me horn—"

"And your dad is an *actual* pastor. He went to an accredited seminary school? He's not starting a cult or anything?"

"Is Presbyterian considered a cult? *HAHAHAHA!* Seriously, he's got a degree / certificate thing hanging in his office. *Legit, legit.*"

"And your mom—she dated Su Su when they were young. And your dad was friends with both of them."

"Yes. *YES.*"

"Don't you see how improbable—*how amazing*—this all sounds?"

"The whole 'Uncle Andy' thing is pretty freaky, if you look at it from a distance. But take it apart, and the evidence stacks up. Everything else: details and quirks that you are extrapolating, reaching for! *Coincidence!* Things you are picking and choosing to focus on for added significance! I don't feel any universal vibrations. God isn't revealing His master plan to me! It's not part of my super-secret origin story, or whatever you are getting at. *It's cool.* It's kind of awesome. I'll give you that."

"Don't you see how this story is unfolding? *It's too perfect!* You and me—this red string of fate connecting us, these nods from God at all these points in our lives, the universe conspiring to—"

"Babe, I'm sorry to interject and interrupt this discharge from your stream of consciousness, but we are done with *play-play*. You smell barbecue? My stomach takes precedence over your thought vomitorium. Smoked brisket trumps this silliness. Ribs over rants, burgers over babble. Let's go eat."

* * *

Dinner plans have evolved into an impromptu celebratory feast. Paul and Ji-Yeon are moving forward to invest in the farm and ranch: establish a community center, a church, a residential complex, a small organic food business. The goal is also to create a space for racial reconciliation and understanding. They will be building on the varied, rich culture and history of California—especially Japanese, Chinese, Korean, Mexican, African American, Native American. A practical way to bring together people of various backgrounds with equitable jobs, shared resources, and facilities. Growing, producing, and selling sustainable, healthy food products will provide funds to maintain the ecosystem. The dream: start small here, and then bring this paradigm worldwide to share with others.

"And that's where Peace, our future kick-ass international lawyer, comes in!" Paul says proudly, champagne glass in hand. "Our five-year plan: become a 501(c)(3) stateside as proof of concept, then push for others to replicate overseas. We need the support of folks who have a heart for ministering to the bodies and souls of immigrants and minority communities—like your uncle, our first official sponsor. Erena is going to be supplying some excellent legal counsel in the coming years."

"Basically, this is going to be a *hippie commune*." You, stating the seemingly obvious.

"Well, if you put it that way—yes, same general idea! The cynics would call it hokey and idealistic, but we believe that peace and love transcend everything. The Golden Rule of 'do unto others,' loving your neighbor, basic human kindness as universal. And we think our kimchi and kombucha are pretty tasty, anyway." Ji-Yeon fills your plate with more corn bread.

After you've all eaten, you take your constitutional and tour the plot of land. Acres and acres to renew, repurpose: the new church will go up here; fertile fields of rotating crops, there; this building will become the refurbished living and meeting space.

Relaxed and carefree, Erena walks arm in arm with her mother. Both so petite, the same strong posture—the silhouette you can spot a mile way. "Erena, *oori ddal*, my sweet daughter." Their heads rest together in loving whispers—then apart, voices now raised, incredulous, lips curled. They don't argue, but have strong conflicting opinions, and neither compromises easily. Paul, chattering at inhuman speed, walks backwards, cracks jokes, points out *the goat poop, the chicken coop, the basketball hoop*. He's inexhaustibly charming. You see where Erena gets it. You love this. You love her.

* * *

Su Su places a rough hand on your shoulder and slows your pace. He shouts to the Yasudas that you'll take a detour back and head to the pond for a "secret *shuai guh* symposium—mandatory attendance for two."

He leads you over to an idyllic spot: a bench, some shade—a clearing of gray pebbles, abundant and irresistible. You both snatch handfuls and start chucking them into the water.

"Awesome, right? This place, my friends, Peace girl, you—all of us *at this same spot*. It's beautiful. And we both made it out to California! I realize I have more good memories out here than bad. Now we get to share one together." Su Su, skipping a stone across the surface of the water.

"Incredible and unbelievable! You, *here*! Her parents! This whole year, this trip—it's all been pointing to *her*. So much has confirmed how Erena and I are meant to be together. Sign after sign, it adds up perfectly."

"*Guai*, I'm glad you feel so strongly, but don't get too caught up in—"

"I'm not. I promise. I have been doing so much better. I have Erena to thank for most of that. I'm sure Ma and Bah told you about Wendy." You, a high lob—*splash, glub.*

"I know—at least what your folks told me. I can guess some of the rest. You think your parents didn't notice, but they were really worried about you, didn't know how to help you heal. They left you alone to figure it out. I'm sorry I wasn't there, but I'm not so great in that area myself." Su Su, raining down a cluster.

"Erena's different. *She's the one.*"

Su Su moves his callused palm over your collarbone to still your hand. You've been absentmindedly running your fingers back and forth along the chain around your neck, a red semicircle traced on your clavicle by blunt fingernails.

"Young Buns, your Ma didn't go into all the details, but she said your girlfriend had the ring I gave you. '*Xiao ri ben gu niang!*' And it turns out that she's *Peace—whoah*! The whole story is hilarious! Look, you just need a safe place for it. Or you can sell it. Or—"

"*She's my number six.* I counted, and I'm sure that's correct. Yes, I'm afraid that number seven is out there. But she transcends all of that! She's something much more—*my 888 love.* I can't deny all the signs that affirm that this is right. I'm going to give the ring to Erena—*for real this time. Su Su? Su Su?*"

Your uncle is silent. He walks toward the short grass, gathers a cluster of pebbles, some larger flat rocks, picks up a few sticks, and lays them down on the granite bench.

"See that log sticking up in the middle of the water there? Let's see if we can hit it." Su Su, with that conspicuous glint in his eyes—90% guardian angel, 10% wicked influence.

You feel like a kid again. Your uncle launches rubble toward the horizon, flings stones across the mirrored surface, shot-puts spheres skyward. You try to match him, throw for throw.

"This one is for Wu Jing!" Su Su heaves a round, speckled rock. It falls short of knocking the log but splashes it with a satisfactory *plonk.* You think you see a shadow of a fish dart past.

Su Su pauses and sits down. He beckons you over to the empty space, a pile of hard projectiles in between you two. He reaches for the necklace, pulls it out through your shirt—the ring looped around the cat's triumphant paw—both up and out, free now, swaying slow in the warm breeze.

"Peace. *Hen tiao pi*—what a mischievous toddler! Always a sly smile, like this lucky cat! Gorgeous and sharp, the spitting image of her mother. It would be incredible if our families could join together one day—but it's not the right time for you now, not right for her."

"Sure, we would have to figure out the logistics as we finish school. We could make it a long engagement, we could—"

"Young, *guai.* You are still kids, with the whole world before you! Yes, it's astonishing that you found each other! But be practical, too, with clear vision and foresight! Why rush things? Enjoy the day as it comes! Ask yourself: *Is this really what you want? What she wants? For the right reasons, at the right time?* You need to first figure out who you want to be, what you will do! The last thing you should be thinking of is having such a serious relationship."

"It's fate! Can't you see that? How we met and fell in love! How all of THIS, and *THIS, and THIS*—how THIS ties together! Su Su! You are living proof of the theory—God, the universe, this divine road map, the numbers and patterns, sublime rhyme and reason—"

"Oh, Young-Don't-Be-Dumb! The numbers, *always the numbers*—all *mo ming qi miao* stuff! You can't live your life so, so—"

"But the *lottery!* The *letter!* You said so yourself! It worked! *It works!"*

"The lottery, the letter. I was so excited, emotional, caught up in the moment, with so much to say, and not knowing how to say it. I was

itching to hit the road and fly already—make up for all those lost years. But I didn't want to leave without a proper goodbye, an explanation. But you turned out OK? Yeah? You've grown, matured—like I knew you would.

"If it was luck, coincidence, magic—who knows, *who knows*? *It happened, it happens!* Out in the world these years, I've seen and learned so much. I was hoping my notes from the road would make up for me not being around to talk to you—to teach you—in person. I *am* very fortunate—and I thank God, my lucky stars, Gong Gong and Po Po watching over me—all of them! But I can't let superstitions and unfounded things control my life."

"*But I see it all around me.* Totally lines up perfectly. I couldn't make it up, even if I wanted to."

"Young—since you were little, you had trouble with everything. You constantly asked: *why, why, why.* So serious, taking all to heart— losing sleep, worrying, not eating, eating too much, not able to move, not able to stand still—it made you who you are.

"We would tell you stories: why we Chinese people did certain things, believed certain things. Some of it was culture and tradition—some was utter bullshit superstition, passed down from *forever.* When you were occupied, busy, it would pass—but then you would soon get stuck again. Had to push you to let things go, nudge you into making decisions—big and small. The numbers, patterns, organizing things in certain ways—it calmed you down, distracted you, *a nice shortcut.* We didn't encourage it, but we didn't stop you either. We just wanted you to move forward."

"I know all this. *I know.* But it helps me make choices. I don't trust myself—if I'm making the right decisions, following the right path."

"Ah, *guai*—I blame myself for all the *hu shuo ba dao, gou pi* garbage I told you. I wanted to make myself feel better, as much as I wanted you to. A true *tian cai*, my little genius—maybe you saw things no one else saw? But the simple truth is: *I played the lottery with numbers that sounded good*—with an inkling of meaning I attached to them. I was very lucky *once*. That's it. *Blind luck*. Maybe you need to consider it all the same way."

"*Fine. Fine.* That makes sense. And logically, I know your whole 'seven loves' theory is silly. I agree. But what if there is some truth to it? That there's a code to the cosmos—and *sometimes* we can see it or stumble on it? What if it's my belief that makes it true?"

"But are you listening to and relying on the wrong things? I've had my seventh great love—*how many times over?* There's always a hot babe around the corner, another gorgeous gal to fall in love with! There's a right place, moment, and reason—but is the 'magical number 7' going to be the one to finally tame this daring dragon, this terrifying tiger, this fiery phoenix? *6–7–8, a million—it takes however many it takes!* What I told you were bedtime stories when I was feeling sad and brokenhearted. A fairy tale I was telling you, telling myself—that I half made up, from some half-remembered Chinese folktale I must have misheard. Or maybe I confused it with the seven *types* of love—*eros, agape, philia*—all those Greek terms I learned in philosophy class or church."

"You and Greece, *again!*"

"*Aiya!* One mistake, one misunderstanding, and it goes on and on—distorts into something else completely!"

"I understand what you are trying to say. But I'm too scared on my own—not smart enough or strong enough, not sure. *I need direction, I need directions, I need to be directed.*"

"*You are strong enough!* Maybe you don't realize it with all the noise and voices in your head! Waiting for other people, other things to tell you what to do! But the loudest one on the top of the hill leading the charge, and the quietest one whispering the most sense in confidence—that's been your own voice all along. Maybe you just didn't recognize yourself guiding you, directing you, to what you *already know, already feel* is right.

"You have *agency, volition, free will, choice*—this is a blessing and curse. You aren't dead and motionless, ineffectual. *You have power and control.* Here, let me show you. What's the most important, potent number you believe in?"

Su Su clears a patch of dirt with his hefty black boot. Hands you a stick—ready to give you a lesson.

"*Triple 8, get it straight. 888. Ba, ba, ba. Bang, bang, bang.* Infinite luck."

"888. OK, multiply by 5."

"Oh, my—*4,440.*"

"The number 4, in Chinese—*si.* Death, right? And so many of them in a row! *Terrible! Aiya! Run, run!*"

"I never thought of that. That's—"

"Let's keep going! What's the worst, most cursed number? Ultimate bad luck?"

You are too scared to say it, not to mention etching it in dirt like an invocation, some stygian pagan ritual: "6_6" is all you manage to scrawl into the ground.

"My good boy! Can't even write it all out! No problem. Divide that evil number by 2, and you get—"

"*333.* The number 3—the sacred number of the Trinity. I think it's a—a good number. I'm not 100 percent sure. It makes sense it would be good, right? I don't know."

"That's my point, Young One. *You don't know. You aren't sure.* It's comforting to think that God, the universe, has a divine plan. But would you ever *really know?* The way set before you—*every possible turn, every door?* Not in this lifetime! *All you have for certain is you.* Hope and faith are what you shape from it. Hope and faith without action are useless—are dead.

"These numbers and patterns don't hold any answers. You can *manipulate them* if you want to, need to! You don't have to give it *all* up. If this 'magic' helps push you ahead—*use it.* Bad throw? *You roll again.* Make your own luck! Bet on yourself! What do the Westerners call it? 'Self-fulfilling prophecy'? Live like there is no real magic, other than what you create!

"When you are stuck and scared, silent and still—if there's too much of the whole picture for you to handle—close one eye and focus, *like your favorite film directors*! When you want to take aim: shut one eye, see it clearly, then fire away! Basketball, Bruce Willis movies, antidote vaccine, *pewpewpew, bangbangbang*—all true heroes *have to take the shot*, Young Gun. You *have to take action*. And you can always separate from the numbers, disengage from the patterns, and do it your *damn fucking self*!

"Change and transform—*like Bumblebee*! Harness your own energy—*like the Monkey King*! Use your own force field—*like Ultraman*! The strongest kung fu—*shuai guh, Sammo Hung*! You have the superpower—*Wolverine, X-Men*! You have POWER—*you are the He-Man now*! Young, don't ever think you can't do anything unless someone, something, else tells you it's right. Until your last breath—*you decide*. You own the triumphs and mistakes. You grow. *You persevere. You are not powerless!* In here, and here—AND HERE."

Su Su digs a finger into your temple, then your chest—and with the back of his hand, taps you in the balls.

You flinch, and he laughs, follows with a sharp smack on the back. He produces a palmful of pebbles when he turns over his hand. *It's magic.* You love this.

"Like these rocks—full of potential. OR—they can sit still here forever and not do a damn thing. *Lai*—come pick a stone. *Just pick!* Look at it quick. OK. Now—TOSS IT! THROW IT! *Don't think!*"

You seize the smooth white rock and launch it. A twinge in your shoulder, as it soars above in a respectable arc.

"That was for Wendy Xia! See ya!" Su Su hollers. You look at him in sudden, wild horror. You snap your head back in time to witness the stone make contact against the floating length of wood. *Thwack, kerplunk*—satisfactory sinking.

"Waaaah! Doesn't that feel good? *You did that!* Not bad for a kid who can't throw a spiral—one who liked baseball *cards*, not baseball! *Color, weight, shape, throw—and let go.* Simple! No counting, no calculation, no hesitation. Some people don't think enough—you think too much!

"When you need to force the decision, don't ask for guidance or permission—you can always apologize later! But often—time is the enemy, and circumstance is not your friend. Wait for the right conditions and moment. Be fluid and go with the flow of the current. You may have to change direction and consider things from a different perspective, a different point of view—to find 'the balance in your Force.' Then: 'No try, only do'—like Luke, like Yoda—like you are Obi-WANG. But in the end, it needs to be by your own hand—from your own heart, mind, will—not some mumbo-jumbo-gumbo, hu shuo ba dao, muo ming qi miao, gou pi!

"You will do amazing things! I will always believe in you and cheer you on. 'Jiayou'—you know this expression? Remember when you were small, I taught you? It means 'pedal to the metal'! When you fill up the gas tank—you jia you, you add oil."

"And oil—oil is grease."

"My tian cai, my little genius, always thinking! I know you want some validation that you are traveling in the right direction, and you'll get it when you truly need it. But first, take a hard look at yourself in the side mirror—and you'll find all the confirmation you need. Once in a while, you can use a jump start from someone, but you gotta steer your own motherfuckin' motorbike! When you add oil, put the pedal to the metal—you gotta move! Go, go go! Let's go! Peace and grease!"

* * *

Erena's parents nudge their one and only beloved daughter toward you. She's waving a fistful of cash.

"Papa Paul thinks you can win his girl a teddy bear at the pier! Let's go Whac-A-Mole and see what we can get! Thanks for the feeding, folks! Uncle Andy, it's been a wild trip! Don't be a stranger! Muah, muah!"

Paul and Ji-Yeon hug and kiss you warmly. They are effusive in their praise, genuine in their affection. Erena hugs Su Su, rubs his belly in a hearty goodbye. She sprints toward the car, letting you have a last moment alone with your uncle.

"You two have a lot to discuss. Take my advice—or don't. Like I said: *what you wish, when you wish—it's yours*. Who am I to judge? I'll be here when you need me. I'm off to Texas in the morning, but you have a pager now, and I have an electronic mail: 'dragonbikerdude1'— I am an 'American on the Line'! (And let Pastor Chen know I didn't forget about him either! Check is in the mail! Tell him I quoted James, Chapter 2 to you—*sort of*! He would be impressed!) I love you and I'm proud of you, Young. We'll always find each other— somewhere down the road." Su Su lifts you off your feet in a massive bear hug, gives you multiple kisses, and flips on his dark sunglasses.

He pops the double Vs for Victory and mouths: *"Peace and grease, baby! Peace and grease!"* Then he raises his right hand—the index finger, the pointer finger, the thumb raised. You know what this means. *It's "I love you"—the "Su Su way."*

Su Su straddles his bike, revs the motor—a wild storm of dust. The tailpipe sputters, bangs, roars—loud as lions, then softer, a slow purring rumble in the distance.

* * *

"What a cool son of a bitch. Motherfuckin' Uncle Andy!" Erena behind the wheel, peeling out of the farm gates. "I always had a *babycrush* on him—and you share DNA! (*And I've shared DNA with you—if you know what I mean!*) So, I guess I win, right?"

"Something was bugging me all afternoon. I finally realized—it's because you were the censored, G-rated version, the 'Baby Peace Girl' edition of Erena. Not a four-letter word was heard."

"Of course! I'm going to speak freely and fully in front of the delicate flower Ji-Yeon? My pop can't help the occasional 'shit'—but he'd be appalled by my deft handling of the intricacies of profanity! I keep it 'all-ages' when I'm around them. Restraint, decorum—I'm not above it. *I'm not an animal!*"

"'Peace.' Since I've known you, anything but."

"*Reflection, reaction, refraction, rebellion*—you get the full package, baby!"

* * *

You squeeze her thigh as she accelerates onto the freeway. Her fake yelp makes you laugh.

"*Creep-o alert! ALERT!* How did you sneak up on me, *freakazoid!*" Erena cranks the knob on the stereo and howls along to Robert Plant's battle cry from "Immigrant Song."

"Young, I want to do the *full-on cheese*! Cotton candy, roller coaster, Ferris wheel, carnival games—walk on the beach! All the corny stuff I haven't done since I was a kid! Our All-American date night experience! You'll love it! Perfect for your last night in LA!"

* * *

You arrive at the Santa Monica Pier and roll through much of Erena's checklist: you win a small pink teddy bear (*barely huggable*) by draining a blind luck basketball; wipe powdered sugar away from Erena's sweet face (*can't resist the funnel cakes*); and make out on the Ferris wheel (*just like in the movies*).

You go barefoot along the beach: glorious gradient of colors in the horizon, briny foam at your heels—the crowds barely thinning, couples trying to dodge kids, the thumping hip-hop beats of the neon rides fading the farther you travel across the shoreline.

"*FUCKING GORGEOUS, Cali! You still got it, baby!* Look at that view! Come along, *New Yawker*! Smell that Pacific Ocean air! You think Coney Island is better than this?"

"*AAAAAYY!* I'd take Coney Island over this any day!"

"You can have your grimy syringes and Nathan's snouts-and-assholes hot dogs! Admit it, you've loved this trip. *West Coast is the Best Coast? East Coast is the Least Coast?*"

"Never! But it's been a fantastic vacation. With you."

You grab Erena's hand and memorize her face—how the sky contrasts with her hair—the light-brown roots, the blond highlights, the last fading jet-black memories. You blink and capture the new dawning freckles across the bridge of her nose; the golden smooth-ness of her tanned shoulders; her hazel eyes, the colored flecks (*like sea glass*); the wry smirk and curl of those lips—lips that hold the secrets of your universe (*bigbangbangbang*).

"With you—it's been incredible. This whole year, everything we've done together, how we've grown. Erena, I love—"

"*Wait. Hold on.* I guess this is as good a place as any to do this."

* * *

Erena takes the lead: her shoes and anemic stuffed bear in one arm; purse flapping wildly, smacking against her butt; her other hand in yours, pulling you through the lick of waves, the sand and saltwater around your ankles, up to your calves.

"Before you say or do anything—I have something for you. Something for us." She directs you to stand beside the remnants of a sandcastle dissolving in the tide.

Erena drops the bear in the damp sand, opens her purse, and takes out two small velvet satchels. Inside are matching compass necklaces—gold and glass. She holds one up in the radiant sunset, hands it to you to inspect. The arrow spinning, wobbling—then settling straight along the vector of Cali to New York. The cross of N, S, E, W (*Turtle, Phoenix, Dragon, Tiger*)—the power of all possibil-ities, in all directions.

"Not the most original, but when I saw these at Griffith, I thought they would be nice. *Wait. I'm not done.* I know you are wearing my necklace. Hand it over."

The proverbial truth in this moment: *the cat's out of the bag— again.* No choice but to obey. You unclasp.

You pause. Erena takes the length of chain, the cat charm, the ring. She turns her back to you. You aren't sure what she's doing— until she makes you crouch down to slip the metal loop around your neck.

"One for each of us. No matter where we are, we'll know where the other is. We'll know how to find each other, even if we are apart. And one day, maybe we'll be back together in the same place."

(Your heart. Your heart.)

You are surprised by her words. The gift is sweet and unexpected—something to commemorate your trip together. *But these words?* They don't seem to match the right sentiment.

You assume something is getting lost in translation. You assume you didn't hear her correctly in the crashing swell. You assume she's being uncharacteristically, overly sensitive. You assume—

Maybe you've assumed too much. *If after all this time, everything has been pointing me to her, guiding me to her—why won't this damn beastly compass point in her direction? Is it broken? Is it broken? IS IT BROKEN? Am I broken?*

(Your heart. Your heart.)

You reach up to touch your neck. The new round object and the ring click and clack in cold contact. You look at Erena. Her cat pendant and compass, a pair now, rest against her skin. She's rubbing the smooth paw between her fingers. She's crying.

"I'm sorry, Young. I couldn't bring myself to tell you back in New York. It was always in the plan, a dream—but I didn't know if my grades would be good enough or how the credits or timing would work out. When I was accepted into the program, I almost changed my mind. But I can't. I want to do this so badly. I'm going to Australia for study abroad next year."

The mix of emotions flashes across your face: you want to cheer and congratulate her on this accomplishment—*an incredible addition to her future résumé, the natural course for an international relations prelaw major, essential real-world experience to reach her global goals.* It all made sense, but— But? *BUT*—

We can still make this work! We wouldn't have our pagers anymore, but there's email and Instant Messaging! They must have something like AUSSIE ON LINE! Phone calls might be tough, but we'd work around the time difference and budget for the bills. I miss getting actual mail—it would be nice to have a pen pal, get postcards and parcels again! And we could still have a really long engagement! I've met her parents, she's met my parents! She loves Su Su, Mei—she can't possibly give all that up! We'll find a way! It's going to be great!

But—but—your mind can't straddle the looming, unfeasible distance. The tears come flooding hot at the thought of what comes next.

(Your heart. Your heart.)

"Erena, Erena—"

"Young, we have to break up. *I'm choosing to do this.* I am breaking up with you."

"*No, no.* We can find a way! We can still be together! People do long-distance relationships all the time! It's only a year! It's not unheard of, it's not—"

"Young—what were you planning to do with the ring? Why did you bring it all the way to California?"

* * *

All around you: the distant laughter and lapping water, the buzz of electricity and hot lights, the sand—still warm under your feet. The sun, edging farther away, dipping lower. You let the air surround you. Let your breath, her breath, expand and contract.

"Just—just humor me, OK? Thinking out loud here. Play along? Favorite song, favorite band?"

She sniffles, moves toward the waves, returns with a half smile.

"OK, OK. 'Down,' by 311. But maybe not so much anymore. I'm getting into that Kate Bush album you gave me."

"And your favorite movie of all time?"

"Still *The Thing*. Fuckin' Kurt Russell is so hot. I'm still waiting for my sequel. That movie is killer. It makes me laugh and scream."

"And you love to laugh and scream."

"Yes. Any time. All the time."

"What's your favorite thing to scream—other than 'GANBATTE'—it's—"

"It's 'JIAYOU.' You know this."

"And 'JIAYOU' means 'add oil.' And you are 'Peace,' and your name is from Greece, and I've heard 'peace and grease' all my life from my Su Su, who happens to be 'Uncle Andy' to you—and, and, and—888. 1–4–3. 888. 143. 888, *get it straight. Ba, ba, ba. Infinity upon infinity. Bangbang*—"

"Young, please. I need to do this."

"We're meant to be together, Erena. The numbers—*everything*—prove it. You are—you are my *destiny*."

Erena walks away, her bare feet scuttling through the damp shifting ground. She turns around, a determined look:

"If we were really meant to be together in the movie of our lives—if I was supposed to end up with you, and you were my 'forever guy' and I was your 'forever girl'—you would have gotten the line right: 'You are my *density*.'

"And I would have immediately known it was from *Back to the Future*—and we would laugh and laugh, frolic in the water. And you would say in the most cutely annoying way: 'The magic speed in that movie is 88 miles per hour! *Too perfect!*' We would kiss, I would change my plans—and we would live happily ever after. *It's 'density,'* George. 'Density.' The wrong word in the right line, every time. *Everyone knows this. You know this. You've always known.*

"So subconsciously, maybe you think that there's a chance that we won't end up together. That I'm not 'the one'—at least not *one-hundred-'fucking-A-right'-percent*. That's why you just sabotaged your own perfect cinematic climax. *One take, one shot. No redos.*"

"Are you trying to 'lawyer' me now?"

"Hey, if the evidence fits—"

"It doesn't matter. Erena, I told you before that you were my number six—but you've gone beyond that! You're the one who transcends all the bullshit and fear. You're my *888 love*."

"Do you really believe that? I'm '*your 888*'? I'm your '*number six*'? What about your 'number seven,' then? So, there's someone else out there who comes after me? Or what if you miscalculated, and I'm only 'number four'—or worse yet, I'm 'number *thirteen*'? What if *I'm scary number '4' or '13'*? What then?"

"It's not as simple as just the numbers—it's every undeniable thing after another! *Why do I feel like I am getting blasted with both barrels on all of this?* You and Su Su—both of you! 'Uncle Andy,' or whatever you call him!"

"We need to shoot you down before you float away—basing your life choices on these weightless beliefs! You need to hear it from all angles, *from everyone*! And *damn fucking right* about 'Uncle Andy'! Who knows what that 'Battleworn Badass Biker' is calling himself now—but he's on *his journey* and figuring *his shit* out all on *his own*! The way he ought to!

"He's not even supposed to be 'Su Su'—you made the choice to call him that! *You named him*—that was your doing, your insistent stubbornness! There was no predetermined path, mystical motivation—in fact, you deliberately went against the grain there! *You put that magic on him!* Blessing or curse? Or simply just a loving nickname with a long-ass explanation? All signs point to 'Su Su' being wrong, but it still *fits*. You made it fit. *Just like 'density' is wrong, but it's ultimately right*."

"You're just pushing me away because you're scared."

"I'm not scared, Young—that much you should know by now. I am being *practical and logical*. I'm leaving for Sydney for a year. Maybe more! August to August! *365 or more days! 3–6–5—can you count how many that is?* Can you imagine how much can change? How *we* can change? All the things we saw and did in these last—*oh my fuckin'*—only 6 to 7 months? I'm going to be living *16 hours, SIXTEEN, '1–6,' that's 10 plus 6 HOURS*, ahead of you—in the *fucking future!* And we're only a few years from the millennium! *The year 2000! Anything could happen!*"

"Don't you even want to *try*? Don't you love me?"

"*I'm not even sure I know what love is!* I still feel like a baby, and maybe that's the only kind of love I understand. What is grown-up love supposed to feel like? *I may love sexy, curvy ladies! I may love big, buff dudes!* I don't know! *I don't know yet!* You are a boy who I met and really, really like. Love. *Love.* But I'm new at this—all of this—I'm—*dammit!*"

"Erena, what we have—*isn't that love?* These emotions and sensations, our experiences and intentions, the hope we have for each other—doesn't that feel timeless and true? Lifting someone up to become greater than they were alone? That's what I want for you—always."

"Of course, I love you—*you fucking idiot!* I love you more than I ever thought I could! You're right, I won't deny it. My first—first love, first *lover.* But you were the *first*—there's supposed to be more to come. *What if I get seven great loves, too?* What if all the numbers and signs and symmetry have been leading *me* to someone, something great in Australia? What do you think about that?"

You are silent. You had not considered her perspective, her point of view—*her.* She continues strong, but the quiver in her voice still gives you hope against hope.

"You were so good for me, supported me, and helped me to get closer to my dreams and my goals—and I did the same for you. Loving every unique thing about you. I'd hate myself if I tampered with your inner workings—denied all your quirks that made me fall for your stupid face.

"But Young, we don't have a cheat code for the galactic video game machine that leads to the perfect end scene. We can't conjure up a magic spell from a compulsion. The numbers and signs and coincidences—they're just things that make you go 'Mmmm'—like that Crash Test Dummies song. It's simply weird shit that happens to people sometimes. You go, '*Huh, would you look at that,*' you fuckin' shrug—and *you move on.* You can choose to avoid. You can choose to ignore. *It's still a choice.*

"Young—you're staying in New York and finally taking some real fuckin' film classes. Figure out what you want to do, who you want to be. I'm going to go box a kangaroo, wrestle a crocodile, cuddle *ACTUAL* koalas! The new people and places we might encounter along the way, the new yummy things to eat? I'm a *global citizen,* remember? Who would we be to deny these great adventures?

"I need to have full freedom to fly and not be tethered. I need to do this. And you need to do this. *I choose this.* I want you to uncover something good for you, for the best person you can be—for the right reasons. I love you, I love us—but I have to let you go. *You have to let me go.*"

(*Your heart. Your heart.*)

"Erena, I still see the universe telling us we belong. I want us to be together, and you are telling me no. You are the love of my life. *Not just 'number six.'*" The words catch dry and harsh in your throat.

"I know you think so. That this is meant to be. I have some say in this equation—and I disagree."

The look in Erena's eyes—the scales of deliberation teetering in the balance. You've seen her pause in thought like this hundreds of times before. You can trace the furrow of her brow, the crinkle of her eyelids, her tongue flicking to lick her lower lip—just before she floors you with some bright jewel of eloquence. *You love this. You love her.*

"Let's say you're wrong: all the numbers, patterns, and magic mirror moments that you've tallied these last months are meaningless. No input from the Big Man above. The cosmos is silent. Nothing is out there. Endless void and cold universe for eternity. The numbers and signs you've seen all your life, they came from you. *Just you.* You are the one who gave them meaning and significance—not the other way around. All of what you experience, you've filtered through the lens of your being. It permeates deep and determines how you react and respond to the world. *What you consume—you don't just expel.* What you take in gets incorporated into who you are—what you do. *It's who you are, because you chose it to be who you are.* It's never been about taste, *it's about choice.* Taste is temporary, it changes. *We change with every choice we make.*

"So, we simply met and had the best time. We fell in love. We were sweet together. *Is that so bad?*

"OK? But how about the inverse, contrapositive, heads-up side? Let's say *you're right*: that there *is* an underlying powerful conduit, and we are predestined to be together. That I am your '*true 888 love, made only for you.*' That we are singular soulmates in this world and the next. That the red string of fate connecting us is indestructible—drawn together, no matter the circumstance. But we—you and I—are mere mortals, players on a stage, and there are no true oracles that know the future.

"So, we have to let the film of our lives roll—as it *motherfuckin' rolls.*

"But I am still the protagonist of my own story. I just don't want to end up the surprise villain in your third act. And you do not get to be subjugated to the sidelines as a walk-on extra—a discarded sketch of a character that gets scrapped in the edit. *I won't let that happen.* I won't let whatever this plotline is get its claws and fangs into you. I can't be the reason you are holding back from all the things you could be—and I won't let you do that to me either. *I won't let one person ruin you, and no one is going to ruin me.*

"You are going to do great things, Young. *You get to be the hero. And so do I.* I'm taking ownership and control of my life. I've made up my mind and I am directing the action. *My 'destiny'—and my 'density.'* Either way, I'll make that call when I get there.

"Will you have faith in me, faith in yourself? Faith in *you and me?* Together or alone?"

You walk into the cool water, not sure if her words sting because of the truth they bear, or because hope hasn't fully succumbed.

You snatch up the soggy carnival prize, a handful of sand slipping through your grasp, scattered by the breeze. You dust off the clinging grains and grit. Its cold button eyes reflect a distorted image of you. You avert your gaze, blink back the hot tears. For a moment, you want to rear back your arm and launch it into the ocean, making an offering to a pagan sea god to salvage this night. The temporary temptation fades, and you cradle the trinket in your arm instead—saving the only other witness to your pain and pity.

(Your heart. Your heart.)

"The ring. I wanted to give it to you on this trip—for real this time. Maybe it would have been tonight."

"*I know, baby. I know.* But Nicky Neko is coming with me. He's spent a lot of time absorbing those gem superpowers. I'll have him close to my heart, wherever I go."

The pendant—that inscrutable smile, that perpetually raised paw—beckoning visitors to stay a while, promising joyous bounty. But now, waving goodbye and empty-handed, this Schrödinger's cat of luck and loss.

"And you—hang on to that ring of yours. You'll give it to an amazing girl someday, one day."

The ring—a precious treasure, meant to unite. But failing in its purpose again, joining none—a closed loop, impenetrable.

"Maybe—maybe she will be me one day. Let's see what happens. But not now. I'm sorry. Not now."

Erena takes your hand in hers, her entire body shivering and heaving, her tears matching your own. You embrace and clutch each other, only barely on this side of ruinous hurt.

(Your heart. Her heart.)

"*I'm 'Peace.' I'm 'fartprincess1.' I'm your 'number six,' 'your 888.' I'm 'Erena.'* I'm all of these. But I need to find out what I want to be named, what I want to be called.

"And you need to find yourself—without the numbers and signs, without waiting on thunder and lightning. You need to do this *for yourself, by yourself.* You can be 'Young Done-with-This-World' or 'Young-Fun-in-the-Sun.' You decide that from here on out—*my* 'Number-One-Young.' My 'first.' My 'first love.' First—always."

"That's why you are going to be such a badass lawyer. You've battered me into submission with your irrefutable argument. You present logic in the face of the illogical."

"My sensible, smart boy. You've got a bright future ahead! And you don't have to be a doctor, a psychiatrist, if you don't want to! You can make movies or—or—*be the soundtrack supervisor!* Your parents would support this! You can cast your mom in one of your films! *Total star!* And what if this year in film class, you finally meet that *hotgothanimegirl* of your dreams? What if she's your number seven? Your one true love, your '88888888 love.' What if she makes me look like *bantha poodoo?*"

"Erena Ji-Yoon Renee Valentina Yasuda—unprompted and unassisted—you just made the most obscure nerdy Star Wars reference."

"*I know.* Who said I never learned anything from you? Making sure you don't forget me, you scruffy-looking nerf herder." The wink is devasting.

"*Never, number six. Never.*"

* * *

"I'm so glad you could change your flight! I can catch up with Mel and Janey in Colorado Springs later. And you'll still have plenty of *play-play* time with Paris and Gina back in Queens. So, we'll hit Santa Barbara and drive up to Monterey and then on to San Francisco. Oh—we can avoid the Route 66 stuff if the number freaks you out. PCH Highway 1—the best! Here we come!"

Erena is the epitome of loveliness, gorgeous and badass: her hair atop her head in a loose bun, aviator sunglasses on, in a ripped-up

Dodgers T-shirt covering her yellow bikini top, classic Daisy Duke shorts, and Goofy flip-flops (*as in silly looking, but also the Disney dog-man*).

"Good gosh, you need to put on my spares or you'll burn your retinas out." Erena urges you to open the glove compartment and don her other mirrored pair.

You want to kiss her again. You give her another loving nip on the nape of her neck, which she finds annoying when she's driving: *Too distracting, you can wait for a pit stop, Romeo!*

She surprises you by popping your "New Wave(s) for Cali Trip" mixtape into the cassette deck. "I want the upbeat dance-y A side only—*hellnofuckthat* to the mopey B side. Then we can check out the 'Hippie Dippie Love Songs Mix' that Helen sent me. You have to educate yourself on some basic Dead, right? 'China Cat Sunflower' at least—it's kinda perfect, ya know?"

New Order's "Love Vigilantes" blasts out from the Toyota speakers: the mournful harmonica; Peter Hook's melodic bass line; Bernard Sumner singing of love and death (*and maybe ghosts*) during wartime. The underlying sadness is not lost on either of you, but the beat makes you roll down the windows and pump your fists. You let your hands surf through the unseen curls of wind, following where the current leads. You can't see it, but *you feel it*.

* * *

Erena's search for fried fish nuggets wrapped in corn tortillas has led you to a nondescript shack on a mostly unoccupied patch by the ocean. Picturesque rolling tide, powdery sand, and rocky cliffs—*not bad for a Monday afternoon.*

"What did I tell you? Squeeze of lime, some slaw—can't beat it! Let's go for a stroll—we're in no rush. Barely anyone around, so we can *play-play.*"

"No one around besides us and the taco masters. No one to impress. No pretense. Just you and me and the Pacific Ocean, under God."

"*Ooof.* You've got to work on that casual banter. Still too formal and stiff, creep-o! OK, so let's play your questions game as we kick around the shore. Uh—your favorite movie of all time?"

"For pure storytelling, technical prowess, and artful direction: *Citizen Kane.* For something more modern: *2001: A Space Odyssey.* For more contemporary: *Cinema Paradiso.*"

"Ugh, fuckin' pretense! *PRE-TEN-TIOUS!* What's the real fuckin' answer? Not impressing anyone here, remember?"

"Fine. *Return of the Jedi.* Princess Leia in her gold bikini, badass Scout Troopers, and Imperial Guards. I love the Ewoks. I don't care what people say—they're cute. My only real gripe is Boba Fett's undignified demise. Otherwise, it's perfect."

"*The HONESTY!* I'm so impressed with your honesty! OK, favorite band and song. Go."

"Def Leppard. 'Photograph' or 'Animal.' Not the 'coolest' or the most 'critically-high-minded-Christgau-approved' selections, but I completely wore those tapes out. After my third or fourth cassette of *Pyromania* (and second of *Hysteria*) I wised up and dubbed copies of the originals on cheap Maxells to listen to ad nauseum on my Walkman."

"Mullet city music and stripper-pole symphonies! *These* are your favorites! Full of surprises today! Oooh, you are one classy head-bangin' motherfucker!"

"Serving up the blunt honesty. *I'm making a choice.* What have I got to lose at this point? I'm going to be single and alone soon—might as well start from scratch and reevaluate."

"Sad sack. Stop it. Let's enjoy this time and have some fun, OK? I know something that will make you happy! That Yaz song you had on your mix—it might be one of my favorite songs now. I mean it. As in: *favorite of all time.* It sounds classic and fresh and cheerful and morose at the same time. Reminds me of a certain someone I know."

"*Paris?*"

"*AAAAAAYY!* Terrible attempt! *I do the humor!* Seriously, I love it. And I love you."

"Erena, you need to stop saying these things."

"*No way!* We don't have to be in a boyfriend-girlfriend relationship to share our feelings. Genuine affection doesn't *just end* because time and circumstance aren't on our side. Enough with the absolutes! Try being a little—*noncommittal.* It's a simple case of '*not now, but not never.*'"

You pause. Erena pecks you on the lips. A quick punctuation on this conversation: *a comma, not a period.*

* * *

Erena takes your hand as you amble over the sand dunes, digging your feet in where the heat is bearable, the sifting ground making it hard to stand. Sunglasses balanced on your heads—slashes of sunlight hit the lenses—flickering bright, refracting incalculable flashes in every direction. Seabirds coast along the shore. Surfers plunge and reappear in the distance. The clouds above: wisps, hovering still.

You stare into those clear amber eyes—that infinite green-and-blue-speckled field you float in when you dream, in every direction that the compass may spin. You see your reflection. You meet your own gaze in hers.

You turn your head and avert your eyes, for fear that she may see the tears forming in them. You pull her close in an embrace, her hand upon the back of your head, her scent filling your senses. Your respective necklaces, just barely making contact on your chests. Schrödinger's cat of patient, encircled silence—lying in wait, in the quiet potential of the unknown.

You feel like this is the end of something, the beginning of something else—it can exist as both, for now.

You love this. You'll always love her.

As you mark another moment in the movie of your life, you shut your eyes.

And you thank them for guiding you, you thank him for teaching you, you thank her for loving you.

You repeat to yourself:

1. *Love is patient.*
2. *Love is kind.*
3. *Love rejoices with the truth.*
4. *Love always protects.*
5. *Love always trusts.*
6. *Love always hopes.*
7. *Love always perseveres.*
8. *Love never fails.*

* * *

* * *

JOHN HUGHES: You're still here? It's over. GO HOME!

* * *

STEVEN SPIELBERG: *John, are you doing a bit from—*

JOHN HUGHES: *Seemed appropriate.*

GEORGE LUCAS: *Wait, is it really over? There's so much more to tell! I mean, I have reams of ideas for what comes after* Return of the Jedi! *And so much more to say about the Clone Wars era!*

ROB REINER: *Yes, George. We know all about it.*

DAVID LYNCH: *He's got a point. Did we witness any real pathos? Did the universe answer from the darkest depths and savage that fragile human heart?*

TIM BURTON: *Yes, more darkness. I'd like that.*

KEVIN SMITH: *Whoa, guys. Let's give Young a break! He's been through a lot. It hasn't been a "normal day at the Quick Stop" for this kid.*

QUENTIN TARANTINO: *Any regular day can turn completely ass-over-tits-fucked-up in a second! Drama in the minutiae and quotidian! It's what life is all about.*

ROBERT RODRIGUEZ: *It doesn't have to be all life-or-death consequences, it may just feel that way to the young man. Heartbreak can have the same impact as a thousand bullets.*

JOHN WOO: *Bangbangbang! Actual bullets piercing the flesh or metaphorical ones through the soul! Many of the heroes in Chinese and Asian cinema die at the end of the story.*

BRIAN DE PALMA: *If we are speaking in the traditional, most basic Western canon sense: the hero goes on a journey, learns a great lesson, and they are forever changed. They often get a bit of a happily-ever-after, however long that may last.*

ANG LEE: *High drama notwithstanding, this story is uniquely both Eastern and Western, Asian and American.*

WAYNE WANG: *With any fiction, even at the end—there's always much more to be told, more left to be imagined.*

GEORGE LUCAS: *I love the idea that the characters live on long after the credits roll. So, do we get to do the alternate endings? Multiple paths of possibility? A special extended bit of—*

PETER JACKSON: *Just chiming in—FROM THE FUTURE. I say everyone deserves an ending. If not a final, happy one, at least the potential for one—but let's give them a bit of choice in this adventure we call "life."*

JOHN HUGHES: *And life moves pretty fast! LIGHTS. ACTION. CUE THE MUSIC!*

Epilogue

Soundtrack highlights:
- "Don't You (Forget About Me)" — Simple Minds
- "Pretty in Pink" — The Psychedelic Furs
- "If You Leave" — OMD

FINALE CREDITS MONTAGE — VERSION 1.0
MUSIC CUE: "Going to California" — Led Zeppelin

You and Erena:

You graduate from NYU and move to Los Angeles for film school at USC. Erena returns from Australia and is enrolled at Boalt Hall (Berkeley Law, for the layman). You spend time taking in the beauty of the PCH on frequent road trips. You meet halfway in Monterey for your favorite fish tacos (this becomes known as "our thing").

You take a job as a production assistant and pay your *fuckin' dues.* Disney has an opening at one of their R&D startups, and you find gainful and rewarding employment in the audio department: sound effects and soundtrack. Erena has become enamored with intellectual property law, due in no small part to the music and movies you've exposed her to all these years. (She tries to add "Esquire" whenever she's introduced, whenever possible.) She decides to move (*always been a SoCal gal anyway*) so she can make time for pro bono work for La Paz Farms, and the two of you can give it a shot together, somewhere under the bright lights of Hollywood.

You fall deeper in love than when you were kids. You find a cozy apartment together and plan for a real wedding. You say you'll tie the knot when you've both made your first million—or at least are able to upgrade Erena's Toyota.

"*Holy shit, dude.* We are going to be rolling in fuckin' bank! Did you see my offer?"

"Steady paycheck aside, look at who you are going to rep! Plus all these talent agencies! Could they keep you on retainer?"

"Confidential. Can't say, can't share. *Stop peeking! None of your tomfuckery!*"

"The functions and parties! The opportunities to network and connect!"

"OOOH, foie gras and the finest *toro* for me. You can work the room if you want, my pervy plus-one."

"All you can eat. I'll need to get a new suit."

"And now we get to go to Disneyland? Any time we want—and maybe look behind the curtain?"

"Special perk of working for the 'House of Mouse.'"

"My panties are so wet for Splash Mountain. I'm gonna *scream*!"

"I would not expect anything less from you."

Erena proposes to you the next week. You love this. You love her.

* * *

Ma, Bah, and Mei travel often to see you. Su Su is spending most of his time on the West Coast. He finally met his match in a cute card dealer at Caesars Palace who took him for three grand the year before, a former tour guide who spent some time in California and is now loving the karaoke scene on the Vegas Strip. Her name is Vicky. You gave her his number. He finally cut off his ponytail, but got a bicep tattoo, a dragon wrapped around a tiger—they may or may not be engaged in coitus. You aren't sure. You don't ask. He flexes his arm, and Mei laughs at the creatures "wrestling."

Xia Ai Yi sends an annual Chinese New Year's greeting card. Ma politely sends one in return. You hear that Wendy is living in Singapore, working at the Sony satellite office there. You never hear from her again.

Paris and Gina visit, but it's not the same. Your new friends from work and Erena's lawyer friends (*the ones who aren't coked up in the bathroom*) fill your social calendar.

You keep in touch with Gina. She calls often and tells you about the "fuckin' ginormous freshmen" at St. John's. She assures you that Erena is the one for you: "Congrats, babyboy! Keep her happy because you'll never do better." You think you sense a twinge of sadness, but that never lasts long. "Tell that hot bitch she better bring you back home to Queens for Christmas."

Living with Erena, you have an easy shorthand: you anticipate each other's needs (mocha almond fudge ice cream and peanut butter sauce are always stocked), give each other space (Wednesday is late-night jogs / anime catch-up night), and have years of memories to reference (*"Remember when you were a fuckin' crybaby—like* waaah, waahh—9ǐǐ*888*ǐ43, 9ǐǐ*888*ǐ43?"*). Your sex life is amazing.

You buy her a brand-new ring with the money you earned from working on a recent theatrical blockbuster. She wears it on her ring finger. She never takes it off.

FINALE CREDITS MONTAGE—VERSION 2.0
MUSIC CUE: "New York State of Mind"—Billy Joel

You and Gina:

You graduate and stay in New York. You decide that you want it all: you get into NYU med school and pursue becoming a licensed psychiatrist. You spend your spare time downtown, helping out SVA and NYU film students on their projects. You don't need much sleep.

Gina moves back home and lands an amazing job as a sports trainer for St. John's Red Storm (basketball, for the layman). She commutes from home, which her parents love—and she hates. She often asks to crash at your new apartment on 2nd Avenue, to get away from Flushing—maybe hit the bars or a club on the weekend. She drags you out for drinks and to keep her company on the dance floor, buys you lamb-over-rice from the late-night halal carts (this becomes known as "our thing").

Both single, neither with much motivation to make the effort to meet others, you make a sober decision (over Saturday breakfast tacos and coffee) to "give it a shot." Gina chickens out and heads back home before anything happens. You are relieved, but hurt at the same time.

You spend the rest of that Saturday reviewing some unedited raw footage that needs some music. You search for a song with the right emotional tone for the scene: either Echo & the Bunnymen's "Lips Like Sugar" or "Under the Milky Way" by the Church. Gina rings the doorbell, and you let her up. She must be here for something she left.

The door opens. She smells heavenly (*Trésor*). She's in full makeup, looking glamorous. You say: "I can't go out tonight. I've got to help my friend with this. I haven't slept."

Gina takes off your Batman baseball cap and scruffs up your hair. She looks you straight in the eyes and kisses you deeply. She's crying.

"Why did it take us this long to really try this?"

"Because we're too close—scared of what would happen if it didn't work out. And you had Sean, and I had Wendy—and then Erena."

"It's just us now."

"I don't want to be the safe choice—comfortable and no drama. You could have anyone, be with anyone—"

"You and your craziness! You are nowhere near 'safe'! And I *WANT* comfortable and no drama. I don't have time for any other shit! I love you and will always love you. You've always been my perfect partner, you know that. You make me feel safe, seen. There's nothing wrong with 'safe.'"

Gina moves in the next week. You love this. You love her.

* * *

Ma, Bah, and Mei travel often to see you. Su Su is spending most of his time in the East Village. He finally met his match in a cute ticket booth worker at Belmont who helped him place his winning bet worth three grand last year. Her name is Min Jee, a former professional vagabond who recently settled back in the city she loves. Erena gave her his number. He finally cut off his ponytail, but got a calf tattoo, a dragon wrapped around a giant turtle—they may or may not be engaged in coitus. You aren't sure. You don't ask. He flexes his leg, and Mei laughs at the creatures "wrestling."

Xia Ai Yi sends the annual Chinese New Year's greeting card. Ma sends one in return—maybe *a little late*. You hear that Wendy is living in Malaysia, working at the Toshiba satellite office there. She's married to an investment banker, and they have a baby girl. You never hear from her again.

Paris visits often, and it's mostly the same: he's gained twenty pounds of pure muscle and brings a new girlfriend over every time you meet for poker and pork rinds. Your best friend, his "new friend(s)," and your families (a Villanueva in the living room, a Choudhary in the kitchen, a Wang in the bathroom) fill your social calendar.

You keep in touch with Erena. She calls occasionally and tells you about the "fuckin' ginormous spiders and snakes and shit" in Australia. She loved it out there in Sydney, and now she's living in Perth. "I'm not sure I want to come back to NY or Cali anytime soon. Seeing Min Jee and Uncle Andy together would give me the creeps. At least the universe didn't implode, but it just means we might be second cousins, twice removed, or some shit." She assures you that Gina is the one for you: "Congrats, Young Stud. Keep that sweet ass satisfied, because you'll never do better. I'm half a world away, off-limits, and not stoked to untangle our twisted family tree situation." You think you sense a twinge of sadness, but that doesn't last long. "Tell that hot bitch from Queens she better take good care of you, *tenderoni.*"

Living together with Gina, you have an easy shorthand: you antic-ipate each other's needs (*ube* buns, always stocked), give each other space (Wednesday is girls' night / anime catch-up night), and have decades of memories to reference (*"Yo, you've got to Wayne Cheaung"* / *"Wang Chung that shit and just do it!"*). And your sex life is amazing.

You give her a ring that Mrs. Villanueva insists you have. She explains that it was passed down from her mother, and her mother before her. Gina wears it with pride. She never takes it off.

FINALE CREDITS MONTAGE—VERSION 3.0
MUSIC CUE: "Tomorrow"—Morrissey

You:

You graduate and look for a full-time job in NYC. In your "spare" time, you help SVA and NYU film school students with their proj-ects. You work at the Undertow until you are hired at a clinic that specializes in music therapy and mental health support.

Your self-diagnosed OCD (obsessive compulsive disorder, for the layman) gets worse. You've been repeating actions in multi-ples of 8: lock turns, pen clicks, light switches. You refuse to see a professional, even though you are surrounded by professionals. You can manage your systems, superstitions, and urges: *self-contain, self-soothe, self-adjust, self-fulfill, self-destruct by myself—if I want.* You've gotten through life like this thus far, and you are *fine with it, dammit.*

You live at home to save money and to help with Mei. She is the best part of your day, every day. When you feel the heaviness of depression fill your lungs, you hold her tight and nuzzle her cheeks, blow raspberries until she squirms away smiling. Then you can breathe again. Her laughter is your salvation. Her love saves you.

You stare at the ceiling and listen to the sounds of life: the flittering of wings on your windowsill; the hiss of the school bus at the stop sign on the corner; Bah clattering terracotta planters in the kitchen; the click and shuffle of Ma's new shoes on the tile; Mei singing along to *The Little Mermaid*—wanting to be part of the world.

You are content with the *not-knowing*. You can soak in the sanctity of being here, calm in Queens, for a while. You are fine with not having any agenda and not chasing after much of anything. You just observe. You—*pause*.

* * *

Ma, Bah, and Mei welcome Su Su—who is spending most of his time back in Flushing. He finally met his match and reunited with Auntie Corrina. She sold her business (*no more perms*) and they bought a nice house in Rego Park for three hundred grand. They are planning to finally get married. Su Su is the happiest you have ever seen him: short hair, clean shaven, with a penchant for wearing tight T-shirts that show off his muscles. He even invested in the line of graphic tees and helped design the logo for the Flaming Phoenix and Roaring Dragon Co.—the two beasts on the label may or may not be engaged in coitus. You aren't sure. You don't ask. He flexes his abs, and Mei laughs at the creatures "wrestling."

Xia Ai Yi calls from Shanghai once or twice a year. Ma's chats with her are short. There isn't much to say anymore. She doesn't need to prattle on about long-gone times, long-gone ties. Her life is rich and full in the here and now.

You hear that Wendy is living in Hong Kong and thinking of moving back to London. She sends you a postcard: *I'm sorry and I miss you. I hope you are well.* You flip it over a dozen times: *that unmistakable handwriting, the fireworks over Kowloon Bay, Wendy's bubbly letters, those red and gold bursts*—back and forth and over again.

You don't reply. (*At least not right away.*)

Paris and Gina visit whenever they are in town, but it's not the same. Paris moves to the Windy City for a hedge fund job that he assures you *isn't too shady*. He's rooming with a few UMich pals and begs you to come check out the "chickety chicks in Chic-ago." Gina remains in Massachusetts. She's at Boston College for grad school and looking forward to a lucrative career in biotech or running a dance studio for middle-class White girls in the burbs—whichever comes first.

They both try to set you up on a few dates, but nothing sticks. You connect with a nice Jewish girl from Syosset—a friend of a friend who ultimately becomes "just a friend" (*even though that one night was mind-blowingly incredible*). You date a sexy Korean girl for a month, but end it when she spouts racist polemic after too much soju. You go on a blind date with an alluring all-American brunette, but while waiting on line for chocolate ice cream, she makes martial arts poses and whoops like Bruce Lee. You try again and fail. *You persevere*, but you hate this.

You keep in touch with Erena. She calls occasionally and tells you about the "fuckin' fuckers fuckin' around" at Fordham Law (*only a bus ride and two subway transfers away*). She assures you that you'll meet, once she gets a breather from 1L study group sessions: "It will be like old times, but better." You think you sense a twinge of sadness—it lingers on in the lonely echo of the dial tone. "Take care of yourself. We'll talk soon."

Living with so much uncertainty now, there is no easy shorthand. You aren't sure what you need or where you are headed. You feel like a splinter floating in space and time. Two decades is a blip—and yet it's the entirety of your known universe. Even if the scars run deep and the dull aches repeat—you are learning from the past, from the memories shared with those you treasure. Because of the joy, in spite of the pain—*you're healing*. You're becoming more than you were before. *You are taking action*. Your life is amazing.

You still see symmetry and glory everywhere: by design or by accident—it no longer matters. You learn to appreciate and love things simply as they are. You learn to love yourself.

You are young—*so young*. Repeat: *You. Are. Young.* Your name, which you never liked, hated even, is inscribed all around you.

In the physical, practical world: a reminder on every ID card, receipt, application form, piece of junk mail, name tag sticker on an old Transformer, carved graffiti brick on Beijing stone.

In the spiritual sense, imbued in you: in Chinese, *Young* invokes the ocean, and like the ocean, you contain multitudes; in English, *Young* conjures the eternal promise of potential and possibility.

Young—it has a nice ring to it. *Magical, sacred, boundless—free.* You are learning to be proud of it. You can never take it off.

BONUS AFTER-CREDITS SCENE

You look at your reflection in the full-length mirror and meet your gaze. You avert your eyes—sunglasses may be necessary to hide the champagne hangover from last night. Your classic black tux is fitted, white shirt pressed, and crisp bow tie charmingly askew. You turn in profile and make sure your pants are creased properly. You comb back your thick, wavy black hair. There, perfect—shuai guh.

A captivating, slender figure in bright red crosses the room before you. She's unsteady on her heels, but soon finds her balance. Her back is bare, her skin immaculate and pristine—only the lightest touches of makeup. She's breathtaking, a beauty. You help hook the clasp on her necklace; the lucky cat pendant, its paw raised triumphantly, falls and rests on her delicate collarbone. She straightens your tie. One last look to fix her earrings, as you kiss her playfully on the neck.

"Ready for the premiere?" Winona Ryder asks as she takes your arm—and you head out into the cool Manhattan night.

CODA

The glint of sun reflects off Erena's mirrored lenses and snaps you out of your reverie. "Stay in the shade over there, under that palm. I'm ready for a jog along the beach. Won't be gone long, won't go far."

Your fingers slide across hers. Moment by moment, the small whorls in each lose their tenuous hold. Your hands apart now, your arm still outstretched in her direction, you let it fall to your side.

Her ponytail keeps rhythm with every footfall away from you. You want to take off and sprint after her, but you settle back and watch instead.

You commit to memory the outline of her figure, each angle of bend and push and thrust. You regret not capturing these images on actual film.

You watch as she rushes forward, like so many times before— but now, a continent away from the concrete and asphalt of the city where you fell in love, where you will always call home.

You are compelled to cheer from the sidelines, that familiar cadence of *"GANBATTE!!! JIAYOU!!!* YOU CAN DO IT!!!"—and bask in the reward of that half-hand salute: her raised index, pointer, thumb. (*Bang. Bang. Bang.*)

You stare out at the Pacific ahead of her. The soft roaring reverberation of the breakers and the sound of children playing in the distance give way to the electronic beat and sway of Yaz's "Only You." Alison Moyet's androgynous haunting vocals fill you with yearning for the one who is pulling farther and further away. But you watch her go. You don't follow.

In the surf and sand of this dreamscape, with the ground beneath you unsteady; your namesake, *ocean*, immense and infinite; the sun blazing in the sky overhead—while you still have this time together, when you are still as close as blessed breath—you take off running, compass spinning, chasing down your own path.

And once more you repeat—for yourself, by yourself:

Love is patient.
Love is kind.
Love is not a burden.
Love is divine.

Acknowledgments

MUSIC CUE: "Thank You"—Led Zeppelin
Thanks! Acknowledgments! From me to you and yours!
Zack Wagman: My incredible, patient editor. Thank you for challenging me, helping me see things differently, and making me a better writer. *Faye Bender*: The most amazing agent. You changed my life. Thank you for believing, whispering, nudging. You have magical powers. NW/BB! Everything crossed! *Will Watkins*: for the hustle, for finding the universal in the specific. *Roger Levenson*: for making the "real" numbers make sense.

The remarkable team effort of Flatiron Books/Macmillan, The Book Group, CAA, and more: Jenny Meyer, Maxine Charles, Morgan Mitchell, Miranda Ottewell, Malati Chavali, Nancy Trypuc, Marlena Bittner, Megan Lynch, Bob Miller, Katherine Turro, Claire McLaughlin, Drew Kilman, Maria Snelling, Bria Strothers, Henry Sene Yee, Katy Robitzski, Eunice Wong, and all the other "bubble gum chewers and ass-kickers."

For my coworkers, friends, and found family in the publishing industry who offered immense advice in this process of navigating the "other side of the fence"—and for those who have been instrumental in teaching me the "day job" through the years, to do what we do, for the writers and books that we love and respect. Special *xie*

xie: Christian Trimmer, Tara Parsons, Meredith Vilarello, Johanna Castillo, Dana Trocker, Ariele Fredman Stewart, Sean Manning, Nicole Vines Verlin, the S&S Special Markets team, Gary Urda, Jon Karp, Liz Perl, Jenn Lipman, Sophia Gutierrez, Vanessa Ioannidi, Caroline Aaron, Jason Wittmer, Taylor Stein, Daniela Plunkett, Sydney Wright, Taline Najarian, Lauren Castner, Jim Conlin, Susan Kovar, Mike Vaccaro, Gary June, Brian Saliba, Susan Nittmann, LeeAnne Fisher, Heather Curtin, Jackie Hodgman, Sumya Ojakli, Michael Selleck, Jon Anderson, Anne Zafian, Michelle Leo, Ana Perez, Christine Naulty, Irene Kheradi, Nan Graham, Ed Schlesinger, Kaiya Muniz, Lesley Collins, Stu Smith, Sabrina Pyun, Vicky Wong, Theresa Pang, Paul Chong, Colin Shields, Michael Perlman, Keith Parent, Chris Cosgrove, Wendy Sheanin, Jeannie Ng, Kim Gray, Seema Mahanian, Dana Murphy, Rosanne McManus, Alison Morris, Brian Buerkle, Catriella Freedman, Anne Quirion, David Calcano, Jeremy Atkins, Kelley Allen, Alex Segura, James Lucas Jones, Nick Lowe, Nick McWhorter, Monique Sevy, Shy Boyd, Amy Huey, Matt Parkinson, Dirk Wood, Mandi Hart, Mark Rodgers, Jim McCann, David Bogart, Rob Bricken, Filip Sablik, Margot Wood, Morgan Perry, Mike Braff, Melanie Iglesias, Risa Kessler, Chuck Abate, C. J. Lyons, Elizabeth Celata, Jess Richardson, Matt Keller, Michele Wells, Morgan Spurlock, Alba Tull, Lauren Miller Rogen, and Seth Rogen.

A special thank-you to Michelle Offsey for participating in the M+E Book Club (membership of two) and for her early reactions and encouragement. My classmates and friends from: P.S. 131, Ryan Junior High School, Bronx High School of Science, Tufts University (and all the Boston area schools I used to frequent), University College London, NYU CWP, and my beloved Stuyvesant—all brilliant and more wonderful than fiction. My fellow seekers from: NYLLC, CT, NCPC. Extra thanks to our support/inspire squad and their families: Doris, Eunice, Gary, Shelby, Jack, Sowon, Kaori, Elaine, Sarah, Dan, Ann, Joyce, Karen, Josh, Val, Despina, Shannon, Claire, Amy, Christine, James, Grace, Enny, Carmen, Diana, Jen, Cindy, Gloria, Teresa, Sara, Romana, Ann, Andy, Michelle, Eve, Ada, Jaymie, Sean,

Pedro, Sylvia, Nadine, Emily, Cyd, Cat, Viv, Melissa, Chris, Peter, Kathy, Allison, Seth, Adam, Cecilia, Susan, Melani, Jessica, Danielle, Julie, Marisa, Halona, Jeana, Glennis, Yvette, Nancy, Sabrina, Steve, Ed, Brad, Susanna, Angela, Cedrick, Ventura, Nina, Jes Tones—and tons more (whom I am forgetting and will owe a beer. And Rabbi Malamy! Pastor Bryan!). And these cherished teachers: Elaine Bougdanos, Judith Kocela, Julie Sheinman, Peter Richards, Sharon Olds, E. L. Doctorow, Deborah Digges, Donald Hall, Galway Kinnell, Phil Levine.

My family and friends who have gone first: my grandparents, great-grandparents, aunties, uncles—I miss you and I know you would be proud of me: *young yuan, ai*. And especially for RW, AK, PE, RL, Da Bo, Xiao Mi Su, Vivian, Er Bo—gone too soon. You are in my thoughts and my memories—somewhere in these pages, something for you, about you.

My wonderful, atypical family of all shades and shapes. Too many to name, too much love and inspiration. Thank you to the Chang side, Jeng side, Levin side—my aunts, uncles, cousins, lovable little ones, my gratitude: Duh, Da Jo Ma, Lu, Amos, Tsai, Oph, Jenn, Ollie, Nina, Eric, Noah, Erynn, Hannah, Ren, Xiao Jo Ma, Chi, Niu, Hong, Uncle Alan, Alex, Da Bo Mu, Felicia, Brent, John-Ryan, Marley, Serena, Shang, Abby, Katherine, Er Bo Mu, Jack, Rachael, Isaac, Miles, Tabitha, Angela, Derrick, Dylan, Everett, Gu Gu, Gu Fu, Susan, Rob, Malcolm, Evie, Jenny, Morten, Theis, Sander, Nellie, Sen Sen, Mitchell, Phoenix, Preston, Joseph, Nathan, Nolan, Jocelyn, Terry, Anyo Su, Alyssa, Italy—and Harper. Extended thanks to these clans: Hsu, Cai, Wen, Gong, Chen, Tsuei, Kang, Offsey, Zusman, Davis, Edelman, Gac, Balinsky, Litman, Ringer, Fong, Avergas, Pien, Poe, Dee, Chang, Yeh, Miao, Lee, Chu, Dai, Yen, the NYP/WC team, and Bah's friends from the EPA! Doctors DP, SW, MF, EY, JY, JYK, TS, BB, GR!

Ma and Bah: *reflection/reaction*—but so different from Ma and Bah Wang! Thank you for being loud, opinionated, bold leaders. You raised our family to always be brave, to take action. My heart, my loves: Eric, Charlotte, Jeremy, and Benny. And Justin: if Mei could